EVA CHASE

RITES OF POSSESSION - BOOK 3

Secrets of Graves and Gold

Book 3 in the Rites of Possession series



First Digital Edition, 2024



Cover design: Fenix Cover Designs

Map design: Fictive Designs

Page Edge Designs: Painted Wings Publishing

Chapter Illustrations: Bojan Serafimovski

Ebook ISBN: 978-1-998752-72-0

Paperback ISBN: 978-1-998752-74-4

Hardcover ISBN: 978-1-998752-73-7

SILANA
BRY
STARSIL RIVER
THE PINCH
ZULINA
VELDUNY
ICAR
COUNTRY BORDERS
PROVINCES
COUNTIES
ROYAL RESIDENCES
FORTS

EEN
PIMA
NIKODI
EPPUN PROVINCE
COLIZ
TEMPLE OF TRANQUIL SKIES
SELCE
TUPNO
COTEA
SEAFELL CHANNEL
IBLIN
REGICA
FLORIAN
ABERNI PROVINCE
THE HAVEN
MIPONE
MAJOR PAWLEM'S FORT
SUNBLOWN SEA

# One

*Ivy*

I'm not sure I fully believe that the palace is under attack until I see the gate.

Or rather, what's left of the gate.

With a lurch of my heart, I jar to a stop in the cobblestone lane between the royal college and the king's primary residence. My hand clenches around the knife I've drawn.

The heavy wooden doors in the high stone wall normally loom nearly twice my admittedly unimpressive height. Now, they look as if they've been blasted off their hinges.

Dark streaks lash across the fallen slabs, blackening both the wood and the bands of steel that reinforce it. Even the stones that frame the doorway look scorched.

My ghostly passenger's arch voice resonates through my head with an air of shock. *Did someone decide to roast the doorway?*

The three men who raced over from the college with me have halted around me at the same moment. Alek flicks an unsteady hand down his front—forehead, heart, gut, and back up to his sternum—in the gesture of the divinities.

The scholar's voice comes out faint. "What in the realms...?"

A bang and a flurry of shouts reverberate from beyond the walls. Stavros launches his massive frame forward with impressive speed, his sword in his hand and the combat prosthetic he hastily donned flashing on his other wrist. "I have to protect the royal family."

Out of the four of us, the former general is the only one who has any direct mandate to defend our rulers. It's hard to say how much good a thief-playing-noble, a scholar, and a courtesan can do in this apparent disaster.

But the rest of us hustle after him just as we rushed the whole way from the college.

We're the only four people in the kingdom who have any real idea what exactly is going on here. Well, other than the villains who orchestrated this attack, and I'd be overjoyed to stop them before they cause any more mayhem.

We dash through the courtyard to the main palace building, past fallen guards who are burnt or bloody or both. Casimir's gorgeous face blanches beneath the tawny waves of his hair.

The courtesan is trained to see beauty in all things, but I doubt he can find anything to admire in this scene.

"He was right," he says in a low, strained voice that holds none of his usual calm. "How many captured daimon could the scourge sorcerers have gathered?"

I don't need to wonder who Casimir means by 'he.' Less than ten minutes ago, a guard who'd badgered me a few times around the campus turned up at Stavros's quarters to plead for my help. Why he picked me in particular, I didn't have time to find out.

We thought we'd defeated the psychopathic sorcerers and their cultish Order of the Wild last night. I watched the man we believed to be their leader die in a bonfire; a squadron of soldiers rounded up a couple dozen followers.

But the guard, Rheave, claimed that the conspirators have accomplished more with their magic than we realized. He said *he* is a daimon, one of the spirit creatures that flit through our world, trapped in a body made of clay that scourge sorcery brought to life.

And he told us that there are many more like him, all of whom were called to the palace by some still-living figure of authority within the Order—who instructed them to murder every member of the royal family.

As we sprint up the palace steps to the even grander door that's cracked right down the middle with more of those slashes of black, Casimir's question echoes through my head.

Have the scourge sorcerers built an entire army of captured daimon?

Inside the front hall, more guards sprawl across the marble floors. Blood soaks the lavish rugs and splatters the fine paintings hung on the walls. Cries ring out from up ahead.

My mouth tightens. "There must be a lot of the clay beings. But who the fuck is directing the daimon now?"

*A very good question,* Julita mutters faintly.

There's no way Ster. Torstem, the law professor we believed was leading the conspiracy, could have survived his burning alive. I saw him crumple in the flames. Stavros said the soldiers found the remains of his body.

Unless the scourge sorcerers have managed to twist their sick magic to defy death itself.

The thought makes me want to vomit, but I race on after Stavros toward the sounds of the fighting.

Through the haze of panicked adrenaline, I notice bodies that aren't in the sapphire blue uniforms of the palace guards and royal soldiers. A few wear fine formal shirts and trousers that would befit the palace's domestic staff, and I spot a couple of court nobles who were wandering the entry rooms unluckily early this morning.

Amid them are bodies that barely look like bodies at all: reddish-brown figures of fired clay, sculpted into human form.

Some have remained whole other than a blade jabbed through a chest. Others lie in broken but still identifiable pieces.

Alek has taken them in too. His bright brown eyes widen in the holes of his leather mask.

"Gods help us all," he mumbles.

Stavros slams past a door with a heave of his shoulder, and the four of us barge into another opulent palace hall.

This one is filled with total chaos. Several guards are swinging their swords to defend a cluster of nobles who are cringing at the far end of the vast room. The soldiers' expressions show as much confusion as they do protective furor.

Because the attackers they're fending off don't look like villains at all. A few of them sport the exact same rich blue uniforms as the defenders—guards like Rheave who were constructed for the scourge sorcerers' purposes? And the others…

From their simple clothing, most of the figures in the onslaught look like ordinary middle-ward citizens. A couple of grubbier ones might have come all the way from Florian's fringes.

Are they actual people caught up in the conspiracy, or more clay-captured daimon bound by the sorcerers' magic?

Stavros doesn't appear to think it important to stick around and find out. It's King Konram and his family he's most concerned about protecting, not the lesser nobles.

He hurtles toward a side door, waving for us to follow him.

As we dash after him, one of the attackers gives chase. A woman in a woolen dress that I'd expect on a shopkeeper or a craftswoman lunges at us with the dagger she's raised.

My years of street-honed instincts kick in. As she slashes at Alek, I spin around and stab out with my knife.

I'd prefer to simply disable her. I don't have much stomach for killing, not when any death I deal out reminds me of my very first and most regretted kill.

But the woman simply lurches away from my blow to her shoulder, heedless of the blood coursing through the bodice of her dress, and snatches Alek's slim wrist. There's determination and then there's being ludicrously single-minded, and she's clearly crossed that line.

The scholar wrenches backward with a hasty kick that doesn't quite land. Julita yelps in my head.

The woman rams her dagger toward Alek's neck, and every nerve in my body screams in denial.

I will not watch one of the men I love slump in a pool of blood. None of his brilliance or tenderness can save him from a blade.

But I can.

My magic flares in my chest. I'm moving before it has a chance to rattle my insides for freedom.

I plunge my knife into the woman's throat the instant before she can land her blow.

I only have a second for a jolt of guilt to shoot through me before her form hardens to clay. She thumps onto the floor and fractures across her torso and legs.

Julita's presence shivers. *Nicely done, Ivy.*

Alek sputters a ragged breath and swipes his messy black hair back from the top of his mask. "Thank you."

I snatch up the dagger the woman dropped—the only part of her that was real—and press its hilt into his hand with a tight clasp of my fingers. The warmth of his bronze-brown skin brings a lump into my throat.

He's all right. He's still all right—and I want him to stay that way.

I squeeze his hand. "If anyone else comes at you, just jab them as well as you can."

I should have given him one of my knives earlier. We had no idea what we'd be facing here—just how true Rheave's mad story would turn out to be.

Alek nods with a grateful if pained smile. The worry shining in his eyes is for me as much as himself.

Despite my horror at the riot around us, the knowledge that we're facing it together steadies me. I'm no longer on my own.

Side by side, we run the rest of the way to the door Stavros has already pushed through. Casimir ushers us onward, touching my arm in a brief but reassuring caress.

Stavros lopes onward, barely sounding winded. His military training has clearly held up well. "There are doubly fortified rooms in the basement that the royal family can descend to in an emergency—and a secret escape passage if the situation gets dire. With luck, they've already removed themselves—"

He cuts himself off with a hiss of breath as we come upon two more dead guards slumped outside a stairwell.

Stavros bends, the fall of his dark red hair across his tan forehead an unnervingly similar hue to the congealing splatters of blood. He hauls one of the murdered soldiers out of the way and heaves open the door.

Shouts and the clang of metal carry from below the stairs.

"Curse them all," the former general growls, leaping down the steps.

My stomach clenches at the sound of fighting ahead. A thin voice shrieks—is that one of the royal children?

Princess Klaudia and Prince Jacos are only sixteen and fourteen. I can't imagine they've ever seen violence on this level before, let alone directed at them and their parents.

My magic squirms inside my chest, tugging at my ribs for me to let it out.

It could hurl the villains back to wherever they came from. It could smash through them all.

But as always, I have no idea what else it might destroy to balance out the power I release. All magic requires sacrifice.

Until I know exactly what we're dealing with, we're all safer sticking with tools we can hold.

I slip my free hand between the folds of my riding gown's skirt and retrieve another knife from the hidden sheath there. As we barrel onward, I tap Casimir's arm to offer the weapon.

The courtesan glances down and shakes his head with a glint

of his deep blue eyes. "I fight better with my hands. Holding something will throw me off."

I've seen him dissuade a judgmental nobleman with a wrench of the fellow's wrist, so I know he has some defensive skills. I doubt he's ever found himself in the middle of a full-out battle, though. "If you change your mind…"

He manages to shoot me a fond smile. "I know who I can count on for extra blades."

At the bottom of the stairs, a short hall leads to a doorway half-filled with collapsed stone. Stavros curses and scrambles over the rubble, the rest of us following in his wake. The rough edges scrape at my palm.

The sprawling room behind is a picture of carnage. One of the inner walls has partly crumbled; the lanterns flicker wildly.

I nearly trip over a body half-buried by the doorway. More corpses lie scattered across the stone floor.

The wavering light gleams off a golden crown. King Konram is wearing his where he's braced next to his wife to shield a few smaller figures I assume include their children.

Six guards continue fighting valiantly in front of them, but one of them is swaying and another's sleeve is drenched in blood.

At least twice as many opponents have closed in on them, half of them in guard's uniforms, the others in plainer clothes like I saw upstairs. Most of them are wielding swords and daggers.

But in the first moment after I leap into the room, one man swipes out with his bare hand.

A crackling light escapes his fingers and smacks into one of the guards, searing blackened lines across his face. As the soldier staggers backward, a pool of ice forms in my gut.

The daimon have their own supernatural powers. Now we know how they barbequed the gate.

Another man snatches up a huge chunk of broken rock and hurls it at the royal guards. It slams into one woman's head, and she falls to her knees.

Stavros roars and throws himself forward with his sword whipping through the air. He cuts down two attacking men, who smash into clay shards on the floor before any of the others can react.

The largest of our opponents whirls. As Stavros moves to swing his sword, the equally immense man charges right into the former general like a battering ram. They slam through a side door and careen into the shadows of the room beyond.

Another attacker races to fight with Stavros, and two more spin toward the rest of us new arrivals. A burly man slashes his sword at me.

I duck and whirl around to kick at his legs. He stumbles backward but only for a second before he's lurching toward me again.

The other attacker has hurled herself at Casimir and Alek. Alek swipes inexpertly with his confiscated dagger before Casimir lands a blow to her head with both strength and his usual grace. The impact sends her reeling sideways into the wall.

The instant she hits the stone blocks, more energy sizzles from her hands. The wall cracks and bucks.

A deluge of stone batters the two men. I have to roll to the side to escape the slice of my attacker's sword, and when I glance again, both the scholar and the courtesan are pinned to their waists beneath the rubble.

Stavros gives a vicious cry and heaves one of his opponents back out of the side room. But that man takes the same tactic the woman did and slams his hands against the side of the doorway.

The stones crumple inward, cutting off Stavros from the room the rest of us are in.

Grit prickles in my throat. I cough and dodge, landing a blow with my knife to my attacker's thigh. As he staggers sideways, I kick his legs right out from under him.

He thumps to the floor but doesn't drop his sword. And as

he tenses to lunge at me again, my gaze slips past him to the royal family.

More clay litters the floor now, but so do more bodies of the real guards. The last of them is just collapsing with a blade through his gut.

The five clay-captured daimon still standing near the king launch themselves at the unguarded royal family.

*No!* Julita cries as my pulse stutters.

I hurl my knife at one of the attackers, but the others don't even look as their companion topples over.

Both King Konram and Queen Ishild have drawn blades of their own, but I can see those won't be enough. They're an instant from being overwhelmed.

Nothing would be enough.

"Ivy!" Alek rasps out from where he's shoving at the rubble on his legs. "Quick—you have to."

My stomach sinks at the same moment as my magic thrums through my bones.

Right. *I* would be enough.

There isn't time to think, isn't time to plead with the lesser god who's guided me in the past to help me control the backlash. One of the attackers stabs his sword toward Konram's heart just as the king parries a different blow from another—and with a choked sound, I fling my power at the swordsman.

The magical force wrenches the man to the side and snaps his neck. He collapses into a jumble of clay.

I heave my arms upward and will the stones from the walls to rise. My power surges through my limbs, vibrating to the core of my bones.

As I shove the stones back into place, a booming sound from above suggests my magic has torn down other walls somewhere else in the palace. I can't find the capacity to care just yet.

The woman who destroyed one of those walls stares at me with a flicker of light behind her eyes. "Riven!" she cries.

Stavros hurtles out of the newly restored side room and

crashes straight into another of the attackers sword-first. Alek and Casimir scramble to their feet.

The courtesan grabs at the swordsman in front of me, who was just making a lunge of his own. He yanks the man's arm around sharply enough for bone to crack just as I snatch another knife from the sheaths at my thighs.

As I push forward to slit the swordsman's throat, Queen Ishild plunges her short sword into the nearest figure's gut. King Konram stabs another in the chest—just as the man jerks his hand toward the ceiling.

The stone surface cracks. I let out a yelp of warning.

A surge of my own magic rattles up through my ribs.

The broken chunk freezes just inches from cracking Konram's skull. Then it slams back up to re-meld with the ceiling.

My skin twitches with the effort, sweat beading on the back of my neck.

Stavros cuts through the last of the attackers, and suddenly everything is still except the rasp of our labored breaths.

I wobble, and Casimir grasps my arm to steady me. I let myself lean just slightly toward him, relief washing over me at his calming presence.

We fended off the attack. King Konram and his family are alive and relatively uninjured.

My magic settles into a restless churning within my chest, uneasy but satisfied that it's pitched in as much as was necessary.

Julita's voice travels through my thoughts. *Well, I'd rather not ever do* that *again.*

I might have chuckled, but right then I notice the king staring at me.

Konram's gaze flicks upward to the mended ceiling and then back to my face. His expression has tensed even more than it was during the battle.

A chill pools in my gut.

His head jerks toward Stavros. "You heard what that one traitor said. You saw what she did."

Stavros's forehead furrows. "Your Highness… Ivy saved your life."

The king stares at him for a moment before a sickly pallor creeps over his face. "You already knew. You brought one of *them* into my palace, straight to my family…"

Stavros's entire massive frame goes rigid, as does his voice. "She saved your *life*," he repeats, as if he thinks possibly Konram missed that point the first time.

The king adjusts his grip on his sword, though he doesn't dare raise it toward me. At least, not yet. "She might have been behind this whole attack. My own guards turning on me—"

"The scourge sorcerers were behind it," Alek snaps. "Look at those guards now. We told you the conspirators were conjuring creatures out of clay that looked alive, and probably people too."

Julita gives a soft huff. *He can't seriously think we went through all the madness of the past few weeks just to turn on him now. I'd hope the man who governs all Silana has more sense than that.*

I can't summon much hope of my own. King Konram has been one of the biggest advocates for slaughtering all riven sorcerers. He parades every captured riven before his people so they can watch the sorcerers hang and know the country is that much safer.

I swallow against the sudden dryness in my throat. "Your Highness, I mean you and your family no harm. Now that the threat is dealt with, I'll leave."

Konram flinches as if my words were a threat themselves. He glances at Stavros again. "You know what needs to be done."

"Wait!"

I know that voice, but my pulse still skips in surprise when a familiar light brown face framed by sleek black hair appears from the corner the king and queen were guarding.

Petra must have been visiting with the royal family when the attack started. I didn't realize she associated with them that closely. From what Julita said, she's only a distant niece of the queen's.

But I had started to wonder if King Konram asked her to spy on me at the college. Maybe this is confirmation of my suspicions.

"F— Your Highness," she says with a brief fumbling of her words. "I don't think Ivy— We should at least hear them—"

"The laws are clear," the king interrupts, holding out his arm to push her back. "Stavros, if you'll continue to harbor a riven sorcerer, I have to consider you a traitor to the Crown as well."

The former general's jaw ticks, but that's the only sign he's affected by the words of the man he swore to serve to the death. "Please, Your Highness, if you understood—"

King Konram's knuckles whiten where he's clutching his sword. "The only thing to understand is that I've been betrayed from all sides." He raises his voice. "Guards! *Guards!*"

I don't know how many are left from the fighting to answer his summons, but footsteps pound against the ceiling overhead.

Stavros lunges forward to grab my arm. "We're getting out of here." He cuts his gaze toward the king. "Because *this* is how I can best serve you."

Konram takes a stiff step forward. "How dare you—"

Stavros doesn't give him time to finish his caustic words. He yanks me toward the doorway, and all at once I'm running again.

Alek and Casimir dash after us. We've barely made it to the stairwell before the king's voice reverberates through the air again, and I realize he's got some blessed item that's amplifying it through the palace. "Guards, don't let Ster. Stavros and his companions leave the palace! Cut them down if you must."

"Shit." Stavros hustles me even faster, but I don't need the encouragement. My feet fly up the steps.

If we can't get out of here fast enough, we might be slaughtered by the same people we raced in here to protect.

I don't know whether to be thankful or horrified that the scourge sorcerers' clay attackers took down enough of the guards that we're able to dash through the side hall without encountering even one. Does the king truly realize just how close he came to dying himself today?

We're almost at the main entrance when a yell carries from behind us. "There they go!"

We sprint past the fallen door and onward between the bodies of flesh and clay to the blasted gate—and run straight into a small herd of saddled horses in the lane beyond.

Rheave peers at us from the steeds' midst, his luminous blue-green eyes as eerie as always beneath his chocolate-brown curls. "I brought the horses like you told me to. Does the king need them?"

Casimir sputters a laugh. In the chaos, I'd forgotten that Stavros had sent the daimon-man to the stables in case the royal family needed to make a hasty getaway out the front of the palace.

"He doesn't," Stavros says grimly, catching one set of reins from Rheave. "But we do. Everyone, ride!"

# Two

*Ivy*

A snort brings my gaze to a stallion I know well. I snatch at his reins. "You brought Toast!"

"He's the one you like," Rheave says, as if it's self-evident that of course he'd know that. At a volley of shouts from the courtyard beyond the gate, he hefts himself onto a nearby mare.

Julita lets out a choked laugh. *It seems the daimon is good for something.*

The instant we're all mounted, Stavros kicks his horse to a gallop. We take off down the laneway with a clatter of hooves against the cobblestones.

For the first several minutes, we simply hurtle through the streets, following Stavros's lead. The citizens of the inner wards gape at our frantic passing. We're certainly not maintaining a noble standard of propriety.

We have to slow to a canter to avoid crashing into any pedestrians, but when we approach the ring of the old city walls that now mark the division between inner wards and middle,

Stavros nudges his stallion faster again. "Be ready to jump," he hollers back at us.

A curse slips from Alek's mouth. I'm not sure how avid an equestrian the scholar is.

I haven't been in the habit of sending my mounts over obstacles rather than around them myself. I tighten my grip on the reins, leaning forward to murmur to Toast. "If I'm going to stay on you, you've got to work with me now. No messing around."

The dark bay stallion is known as the terror of the college stables. He and I have come to a sort of understanding, but that doesn't mean he never tests my patience.

My steed gives a short huff, although I can't tell whether it's in protest at our renewed gallop or a dismissal of my concerns.

We veer along a curving road, and I spot the reason for Stavros's instructions up ahead.

Most people pass the old city walls through one of the many deteriorating gates. But the Crown's Watch likes to monitor those spots to watch for suspicious persons venturing into the hub of Florian's elite.

The former general must be hoping to avoid having any of the city's royal police force observe our frantic dash. So instead, he's aimed us at what's meant to be a dead end.

The stones of the old wall ahead of us are particularly crumbled. Only the base of the wall remains in an uneven line. But it's still about as high as my waist.

*Oh, dear,* Julita murmurs, and then seems to rally. *You can handle this, Ivy. Give that beast a good prodding.*

I sink lower into the saddle as if I can meld my ass and thighs with the leather.

To be honest, I've never jumped on a horse before. Hopefully Toast knows what he's expected to do here—and doesn't toss me right off his back in the process.

Stavros's stallion launches over the uneven row of stone blocks first. The black animal he took from those Rheave grabbed isn't his usual mount, but he still makes the leap look easy.

Casimir nudges the chestnut gelding he chose a little faster and soars over the stones with the same grace the courtesan seems to bring to everything he does. Then it's my turn.

Toast makes a sound that might be skeptical, but he pushes himself forward a little faster. With a soft grunt, he heaves himself up and over the low wall.

For a second in the air, I lift slightly off the saddle despite my best efforts. The wind whips my cloak's hood back from my hair. Then we're both thumping back into place—Toast's hooves on the road on the opposite side, my butt into its seat.

The breath jolts out of me alongside a shaky laugh. The rolling thunder of hooves behind me tells me Alek and Rheave have both managed to follow.

Stavros only races onward for another minute or two. He draws his stallion to a sudden halt in a small square where a few merchants peer at us from their shop windows.

We gather close together, my gaze darting over the buildings around us.

Alek swipes at the back of his neck and speaks before I can. "Where are we going?"

Stavros considers our surroundings, his expression tense. "We got a good lead, but we've made a lot of racket. It won't be hard for the Crown's Watch or the army themselves to track us."

Casimir's face has flushed from the ride, but his peachy skin pales again at those words. "You think King Konram will go that far in pursuing Ivy?"

"There are few things more important to him than stamping out the riven. He sees her existence as an affront to the gods—and sparing her as a betrayal of them." The former general cuts his gaze toward me. "It wouldn't have been a bad time for your divine guardian to throw in his sign of support."

I grimace back at him. "Kosmel makes his own rules. For all I know, he's enjoying this mess as long as I survive it."

The godlen of luck and trickery isn't exactly the predictable sort. All I'm absolutely sure of is that he'd like me to stay alive.

"Ivy knows how to hide in the city," Alek suggests.

Julita's tone perks up. *Yes, you're the expert on this part of Florian.*

My stomach sinks despite her optimism. "I know how to hide myself. All of us will be a little harder, especially with horses in tow."

I can't quite picture my sophisticated men scrambling up the side of the cloth factory building into my secret attic hideout.

"Our situation is particularly precarious while we're in the capital," Stavros says. "We could leave the city, find a place to regroup where we won't draw attention, and then work out how we're going to convince the king Ivy can be trusted."

He pauses, his head swiveling as he takes stock of our location, and points. "The nearest gate is that way. If we cut straight through the outer wards—"

A flash of light whips over the rooftops in the direction he indicated, and his voice dies in his throat.

Rheave tracks the same phenomenon from the edge of our group. "That was magic."

Stavros's voice darkens. "Yes. The palace is sending a message to the gates. No doubt ordering the guards to close them until we've been apprehended."

My ghostly passenger goes still in my head. *Curse it all.*

I swallow thickly. "They can't lock down the city for *too* long, can they?"

"For a threat as great as one of the riven?" Stavros shoots me an apologetic glance, his mouth slanted at a pained angle. We both remember all too well how badly he took the initial revelation of my magic, and he knew me far better than King Konram does.

Alek shifts in his saddle. "There's no way we can leave, then. We'll have to hide ourselves here."

While the king sends every available soldier sweeping

through the city in search—and the scourge sorcerers do gods know what else in the meantime? My skin crawls with the impression of the walls closing in on me.

I turn to Rheave. "Are the people who made you going to send more daimon after the king?"

The daimon-man frowns. "Everyone in the city was called to the palace. If you freed them all, they won't cause any harm."

Stavros studies him warily. "Everyone in the city, you say. What about outside the city?"

"There are many. I'm not sure of the exact number or what they might be doing at the moment on our creators' orders."

"Then the real threat is out there for now," I say.

Alek studies Rheave with his piercing gaze. "If he knows what he's talking about and he's not leading us astray."

The daimon-man cocks his head with a look of genuine puzzlement. "Why would I want to make trouble for you?"

Stavros lifts an eyebrow. "You were working on the scourge sorcerers' behalf for weeks, weren't you?"

"Because I was under their control. I've broken free from that magic—I want to stay as far away from them as I can."

Because he's afraid they'll destroy the body they created for him, and for whatever strange reason, the daimon has decided he likes his prison of flesh. He told us that much when he came looking for me.

My throat tightens at the memory of his earnest appeal for my help.

He *has* acted in my favor before, keeping quiet when he noticed me in hiding. And his concern for the injured butterfly that landed on him days ago couldn't have come from the conspirators—that was all him.

I glance around at my men. "King Konram would be dead if Rheave hadn't warned us. He isn't our enemy. And it sounds like our actual enemy is beyond the city walls. If we want to continue protecting the kingdom, prove to the king that *we're* not villains, and save our necks from the gallows, our best chance is leaving."

Casimir reaches to give my wrist a gentle squeeze. "That makes sense, but how are we going to manage it?"

Stavros's gaze settles on me with a tick to focus his damaged vision. "We can't count on your power to clear the way even if Kosmel would be willing to guide it this time. Not without doing enough damage that we *would* be villains. The guards at the gates and throughout the city will be alert to any sign of riven power—some of them have talents that allow them to detect magic."

Julita sighs. *I suppose he has a point.*

He does. And the trepidation in his voice reminds me of how much he distrusts the magic that flows through my broken soul in general.

Which is fair, because I hate my demanding, chaotic power too. As mercurial as Julita can be at times, she's a much more considerate lodger than the magic I was born with.

I pause. The fringes of the city are my domain, and I've navigated them without a spark of magic for years. I have to take the lead here.

My men's lives could rest in my hands as much as they held mine in theirs when they discovered my secret.

As I grope for the right answer, my gaze catches on a crow landing on a rooftop across the square. It looks like a perfectly ordinary bird, and it might not have anything to do with the godlen crows are associated with, but it lights a glimmer of inspiration in my head all the same.

I turn to the men. "I might be able to get us out of the city today, no sorcery required. But you'll need to do everything *exactly* as I ask."

Casimir nods. "Where do we start?"

The others wait for my answer without any sign of protest. I form a grim smile. "First we head to Tangleside."

# Three

Ivy

It feels like years since I last stepped through the broad doorway of the Frolic Theater. On the threshold, I restrain the urge to glance over my shoulder toward the derelict storage building where I had the men and our horses lay low for the time being.

The gang that rules Crow's Close keeps a close eye on comings and goings. I don't want to give them the slightest clue where I've left my allies.

This negotiation is going to require the most delicate of touches. I'm just lucky that one of the head honchos owes me.

*We're going into that den of criminals again?* Julita murmurs from the back of my head as I walk to the inner door with Kosmel's sigil carved over it. *Do you really think you can get them to help us?*

"We'll see," I whisper as if to myself, and slip down the musty stairwell into the darkness below.

A right turn beneath the stairs, then a winding pattern of steps in the passage where the darkness is thick enough to suffocate. I hurry out into the matching basement room and up

the stairs to the enclosed street that's Florian's biggest hub of criminal activity.

On the front step outside the theater's echoed façade, I pause to take in the strip. It's both less busy and less vibrant in the mid-day light, the kind of place that comes to life with the sinking of the sun.

The usual conjured illusions still shimmer over some of the doorways of the wooden buildings, though other shops haven't even opened for the day yet. Their owners are probably sleeping off last night's exploits.

A few disreputable-looking characters slink along the narrow dirt road, one ducking into the Brew & Dagger pub that'll have just opened. My gaze lingers on the sign with a pang of longing for one of their amber spritzes.

It would take the edge off all the tension of the day, but I've got urgent work to do here.

On the other side of the street to my left, the largest building in Crow's Close looms. The darkly varnished wooden structure holds three floors, the lowest one a public gambling den and the upper two dedicated to the private exploits of the most powerful crooks in the city.

Kosmel's sigil stands out in silver paint against the dark boards over the crooked doorway, framed by a carved crow on one side and a rat on the other. As I watch, one of the other stealthy figures prowling the street slinks through the entrance.

I just have to hope that Garom Rochimek has roused himself from his bed already.

I tug my cloak closer around me. The noble-style silk gown beneath it itches at my skin with the awareness that it's nothing like what I'd typically wear on a visit to this street.

Opulent clothes aren't totally out of place among the criminal element, but most of us prefer not to draw attention. It's a good thing I have a reputation to precede me. Otherwise I'd look like an easy target.

I stride across the road and beneath the divine symbols over the doorway, thinking a silent prayer at Kosmel. *How about helping me get out of yet another sticky situation? It does seem to be your specialty.*

He doesn't answer, but then, I don't really expect him to. The trickster godlen is fickle about how and when he chooses to communicate.

Plenty of clerics would be astonished to hear he ever bothered to speak to me with his actual voice in the first place.

As we step into the building, Julita lets out a soft hum. *Well, this is an interesting approach to worship. I suppose it's fitting to the godlen being honored.*

From the first glimpse of the interior, it's obvious the building is meant as a temple to Kosmel as well as its business purposes. Carvings of Kosmel's symbols and paintings of scenes from his legendary exploits decorate every wall of the expansive room that's a gambler's paradise.

And in the center of the space, the ceiling is open all the way up to the roof three floors overhead. A massive silver statue of the godlen stands in that column of open space, only visible up to his thighs from where I'm poised.

I've always wondered how the members of the Black Talons feel about having the trickster godlen staring right into their private quarters. Considering their typical moral code, maybe the gang members take comfort in the close proximity. Their illicit organization acts as the clerics and devouts of this temple.

The heads of three families combined forces to form the Black Talons ages ago. I scan the sprawl of tables around the statue for the specific figure I'm looking for, the current patriarch of the Rochimek family.

Only a few of the tables are in use this early in the day: a couple of rounds of cards going on at one side of the room and a cluster of gamblers trying their luck with dice at the other. The rattling sound bounces off the ceiling.

A couple of figures sit at the bar at the back of the room. A greasy, peppery scent wafts from that direction—the kitchen has gotten started on the fried goldrud root that gamblers consider a lucky snack.

And a middle-aged man with rumpled blond hair lounges by an otherwise empty table near the card-players, nursing a mug of ale. His baggy clothes give the impression of plumpness, a patchwork of stains and darning decorating the shabby fabric.

There's dressing down, and then there's outright slobbery. But in this case, I know it's all by design.

Keeping my expression cool, I smile inwardly and amble over to join the apparent vagrant.

I'd imagine Garom noted my arrival from the first moment, but he doesn't glance over to acknowledge me until I'm just a few paces from his table. As I lower myself into the chair next to him, he offers a reserved nod. "Ivy. It's been a while."

*You're on a first name basis with this vagabond?* Julita says with a note of disbelief. Apparently Garom's disguise has worked on her.

I figure it's best to cut right to the chase. He's a man who appreciates frankness.

"I wish I had a better reason to visit. I need to cash in the favor you owe me."

Garom's eyebrows rise beneath the messy locks of his supposed hair. He pushes to his feet. "I guess we'd better take this to my office, then."

He keeps up the vagabond act all the way to the staircase in the back corner, adding a shuffle to his walk as if he isn't totally steady on his feet. The moment we pass out of view of the gambling den, his strides lengthen.

I trail behind him up to the second floor. The torso of Kosmel's statue gleams at the other end of a hall that branches off into several rooms.

Garom pushes into one of those rooms. The moment the door has thudded shut behind me, he tugs off his wig.

The heads of the other two families in the Black Talons make regular appearances on the first floor in sharp suits and polished shoes that emphasize their success. Garom prefers to take a more subtle tactic. He hangs around the gambling tables regularly in the guise of an aging drunkard to observe how his patrons behave when they don't think they're being monitored.

The wig is necessary because of the typical sacrifice all members of the Black Talons families make. Beneath the fake hair, Garom's head is bald, a mix of shaved scalp and the scars where a cleric carved that scalp right off during his twelfth-year dedication ceremony.

Each member has a different pattern scored into the flesh over their skull. Garom's is made up of lines as chaotically woven as the streets of Tangleside.

I've heard people whisper that it's a maze with only one start point and end, not that anyone will have had the chance to test out that theory.

Garom drops into the chair behind his sturdy oak desk and studies me with keener eyes than he showed on the floor below. His gaze skims over my clothing. "You've gotten all dolled up for the occasion. I don't think I've ever seen you in a dress."

"It's a long story," I say. "And not really relevant. The king has closed all the city gates. I need a way to get past the walls, along with a few companions."

Garom's eyebrows leap up even higher than before. "Don't tell me the sudden commotion is because of *you*? I heard there was some kind of brawl at the blasted palace itself."

Of course one of his lackeys would already have caught wind and informed him. I should be grateful there was no one alive other than my men and the royal family to gossip about my confrontation with the king.

I have to choose my next words carefully. It's well-known that while all key members of the Black Talons sacrifice parts of their scalp by tradition, most make other, more discreet sacrifices so they can request a gift of sizeable power.

No one's sure what exactly Garom offered up alongside some skin and hair, but he's got a significant talent for separating truth from falsehood. And if he catches me lying to him, any sense of obligation he feels to fulfill his promised favor may evaporate.

I roll my eyes as if the suggestion is ridiculous. "I didn't attack the king. But having the gates closed is inconvenient for various other reasons. My associates and I are at risk of getting swept up in the search."

"And you want me to get you and—how many others?"

I would say three, because I barely know Rheave. He's barely even *human*.

But he did warn us when no one else could. He begged me to protect him from the scourge sorcerers.

If I leave him behind, will they get control over him again?

"Four," I say firmly.

"You want me to get five people out of the city while the Crown's Watch has Florian under a full royal lockdown." Garom's tone has taken on an incredulous note. "What kind of sorcery do you think my people can pull off?"

I manage not to wince at the s-word. "I think you're one of the leaders of the most powerful organization in Silana outside of the royal court, and if *you* wanted to be outside those walls right now, there'd be some way you could make it happen. So make it happen for me."

Garom leans back in his chair with a sigh. "I know I'm in your debt, Ivy. But *you* know that we're trying to keep the Crown's Watch off our backs. If you've gotten yourself mixed up in trouble as big as it sounds… that's a bigger ask than I was prepared for. I have to think about the security of everyone who works under me."

I fold my arms over my chest and fix him with my best defiant stare. "Really? Your daughter's life isn't worth that much? I believe your exact words at the time were, 'Anything you need, no questions asked.'"

Garom's jaw ticks at the mention of the job I did for him that earned me his favor. A few years ago, an upstart rival gang kidnapped his then-preteen daughter and threatened him with all the things they'd do to her if the Black Talons didn't kowtow to them.

I stole her back for him before he even had to tell the rest of the organization about his precarious position. Since he had the rival gang slaughtered, nobody much knows what went down other than me and him.

Unfortunately, that means *my* position is now precarious. If Garom refuses me, I can't turn to anyone else to enforce our deal. His colleagues aren't aware it exists.

But it's no secret that you don't become one of the realm's top crooks by playing by the rules. I came prepared.

He's still hemming and hawing. "Ivy, I'm going to see that you get everything you deserve for your help to my family. If it were in another week or two—"

I step forward and smack my palm against the edge of the desk. "I might not have a week. We need to go *today*. So let me make this easy for you. If I don't return to my companions with a plan for getting out of here before nightfall and see that plan through, I've arranged that the Crown's Watch will be informed of how to access Crow's Close, along with a list of who's responsible for all sorts of past crimes."

Garom stiffens, his face going sallow. He can tell I'm telling the truth. "You wouldn't— If they break into this place, they'll ruin everything. You'd side with those pompous assholes over *your* people?"

"Of course not." I smile tightly at him. "I don't *want* to tell them anything. I knew you'd be good to your word and I'd be able to stop the message before it's triggered. I just figured you might need a little reminder of just how much you do owe me first."

Garom studies me with warier eyes. I'm sure right now he'd like to slit my throat and toss me wherever bodies disappear in the Close, but then he'd be screwing himself over.

If I don't return, Rheave will deliver the sealed message I really did write to the palace. It'll be trickier to ensure my failsafe works if Garom's people turn on us in the middle of our escape, but he doesn't know that.

And if we make it out of the city safely, I'll burn the missive without anyone setting eyes on it.

A scowl darkens Garom's face. He can tell I was being honest about the rest of what I said too—that I don't want to do it, that I believe he'll come through with the proper motivation.

Sometimes I think perceiving truth and lies might be more of a curse than a gift. It'd make it a lot harder to lie to yourself when you'd like to.

The gang boss drums his fingers on the table and lets out another, rougher sigh. "I think I might be able to set something up. We made a recent acquisition—I had other plans for it—but you're right. I wouldn't trade Luzia's life for a business opportunity."

"I'm sure she'd be glad to know that," I say dryly, and prop myself against the edge of his desk. "Tell me all about this 'acquisition.'"

# Four

*Ivy*

I stare at my reflection in the cracked mirror for a few moments, taking in the results of my efforts at disguise. The dye Garom included in the supplies his people brought us has darkened my reddish-blond hair to a chestnut shade that makes my skin look even more sickly than usual and my blue eyes stand out starkly.

But not as unnervingly brilliant as the sea-green irises of the daimon in our midst.

Rheave comes up beside me and peers over my shoulder into the glass. I'm still not sure how much of the initial attitude I saw from the false guard is part of his personality or something imposed on him by the scourge sorcerers. There's a much more open vibe to his comments now.

"Humans can change their appearance so easily," he remarks studying my reflection, his tone awed.

Casimir lets out a soft laugh from the other end of the room where we're making our final preparations for our escape. "I suppose daimon don't have much of an appearance to change in the first place."

Rheave tilts his head to the side, watching his own reflection next to mine. "We don't normally need one. But it's interesting having that too."

He touches the face I've always thought was far too beautiful to belong to a soldier. "I wonder how I would look with pale hair."

I nudge him gently with my elbow. "We don't have time to find that out now. You can experiment with makeovers when we're out of this mess."

My jacket shifts around my scrawny form. Casimir carefully pinned it so it looks like almost a perfect fit, but I can still tell it's too big for me.

Rheave is the only one of us who came by the clothes he's currently wearing honestly. We simply left him in his typical guard uniform.

Garom has supplied the rest of us with a set of Crown's Watch uniforms he came by through means he wasn't willing to share.

I glance down at the smallest of the uniforms—the one I donned. I checked over every detail in comparison to Rheave's sapphire blue jacket and trousers, and Stavros examined them too, and as far as we can tell, they're perfectly authentic.

Perfectly designed to convince the guards at the gate that we're colleagues of theirs leaving the city on the king's authority. As Garom pointed out to me when he went over the plan, soldiers are the only people allowed to come and go during a lockdown.

I'm not loving the idea of marching out right under the noses of the people who most want to execute me, but I can't think of a better gambit.

Julita sounds as if she's suppressed a snicker. *I mean no offense, but I don't think military garb suits you.*

I snort in agreement and turn away from the mirror.

Casimir is just putting the finishing touches on Alek's face.

The scholar has his back to me, but I can see plenty of tension in the rigid set of his shoulders.

He hasn't gone without his leather mask covering most of his face in public for years. It was hard for him just to let me and Casimir see his scarred skin before.

But we know the king will have put out descriptions of us, and it'd be hard to explain him away as a *different* man with a dark brown mask. So he's tucked it away in one of the saddle bags and agreed to let Casimir cover the mottled area over his forehead, cheeks, and one side of his jaw as well as the courtesan's skills with makeup allow.

"There," Casimir says, stepping back. "It isn't flawless up close, but from the distance everyone outside our group will be seeing you, especially with the daylight fading, no one will notice anything unusual."

Alek turns hesitantly. When his bright brown eyes meet mine, a stutter runs through my pulse.

Julita gasps. *Cas really can work a kind of magic with that palette.*

Casimir has managed to paint over the ridges and streaks of reds, grays, and browns to match the smooth bronze skin that's Alek's natural coloring. Well, not quite as smooth as the unmarked side of his jaw, but awfully close.

I'm looking at the scholar as he would have appeared if he'd never let jealousy lead him down a vicious path that ended with a burning potion splashed in his face.

He's absolutely stunning.

But he's also not exactly the man I've fallen in love with. I'm torn between catching my breath at how striking he is and wishing I could wipe away all the makeup to see the real Alek underneath.

He's stunning with his scars too, just in a different way.

"It looks great," I tell him with a reassuring smile.

Alek's stance relaxes slightly at my words. "I suppose I need to see it as a different kind of mask."

"Exactly." Casimir brushes his hands together with a satisfied grin. "We're all going into hiding in plain sight."

Stavros lets out a grunt from where he's just finished darkening his hair with a black powder that's completely obscured the blood-red hue. Disguising him has been our biggest concern, seeing as the exalted former general is rather well-known among everyone with military inclinations.

"Some things can't be changed," he says, tapping his left wrist against his side—the left wrist that's currently just a stump.

He's removed his distinctive combat prosthetic, the loop of metal that's bent around into a hook-like shape, but his more realistic wooden hand is back in his quarters at the college. Even Garom couldn't come up with a believable replacement for that in the short time we have.

Casimir hums. "Keeping the stump hidden in your pocket should do the trick just fine. Plenty of soldiers ride around with just one hand on the reins."

The courtesan pauses to study the work he did on the former general's face. We couldn't adjust anything about Stavros's massive frame, which is stretching the largest of our borrowed uniforms, so we've tried to change as much as we can otherwise. Along with the darkened hair, Casimir has painted Stavros's light brown skin a creamy peach tone similar to his own, mottled by a broad scar across one temple and cheek as if from a vicious sword slash.

I'm not sure I'd recognize him at a glance if I hadn't watched Casimir do his work. We have to hope it'll be enough.

Rheave gives my face another once-over. "I'd still know you, even with the different hair color."

"You've seen me several times," I say. "You know what to expect. The king won't have been able to get out much more of a description than my hair and height."

Thankfully the latter detail is less obvious when I'm mounted on a horse.

I motion toward the doorway to the room where we've left

our steeds. "I don't think it's going to get any better than this. Let's pack up and get out of here."

As we squeeze the last few items into the saddle bags, Alek turns to Rheave. "Are you sure you want to come with us? The king probably hasn't realized you helped us. You could go back to playing guard at the college."

He speaks evenly enough, but I can tell from the hesitation in his stance that he's not convinced bringing the daimon-man along is a great idea.

I brace myself to defend the decision I made, but Rheave speaks up first. "The people who made this body—the scourge sorcerers, as you call them—they'd find me there. They'd break me." He pauses and smiles at me. "And if I can protect myself while protecting Ivy as well, that's even better."

When he looks at me like that, talks like that, a flutter passes through my pulse even knowing what he really is.

Stavros props himself against the doorframe, his eyes narrowing. "You were very set on coming to Ivy for help in the first place. Why her?"

The daimon-man pats the neck of his mare with a vaguely bemused expression that turns more solemn when he returns his gaze to me. "The scourge sorcerers assigned me to watch her. Because they wanted to make sure it was safe for her to join their group."

A finger of ice runs down my spine. The possibility that he was spying for them had occurred to me, but it's different hearing him confirm it. "So that's why you seemed to be around so often. What did you tell them?"

"There wasn't very much to tell. They wanted to know if you seemed friendly with any of the other guards, and I said no. They wanted to know if I saw you doing anything unusual, but they didn't seem worried about the stargazing."

He stops for a moment in thought. "And the man who gave most of the orders at the college—Torstem, the one you got rid of—he brought me when they put you on trial. He asked me to sense if a divine force blessed you."

Gods above, the scourge sorcerers were testing me even more than I realized. As I tighten the girth on Toast's saddle, I swallow thickly. "What did you say about that?"

The daimon-man offers me a softer smile that only makes me feel more jumbled up inside. "I felt the connection when you shot the arrows. Someone was watching over you. That's how—that's how I knew I could trust you. None of the rest of them ever called down any kind of influence from the ones you call godlen."

Stavros guffaws. "Did you mention that part to them?"

"They didn't ask. About that or what other supernatural forces might be working through Ivy."

Alek's head jerks around. "You knew she was riven?"

Rheave lifts his shoulders in a casual shrug. "I thought so. I only felt it a little, that one time."

It's a good thing I kept my magic so tightly under wraps, then. If there were more clay-captured daimon around during any of the other rituals, they might have tipped off the scourge sorcerers.

I have no idea whether the murderous psychopaths would have been excited to exploit my power or seen me as just as much of a threat as the king does.

I heft myself into the saddle, which puts my back to the daimon-man. "Is that why you came to me? Because you figured I was powerful enough to stand up to them?"

"No," Rheave says brightly. "I came to you because you helped me with the butterfly. Even though I could see you were nervous about being near me, you helped. And I could sense by then that you didn't really like what they were doing. I didn't tell them that either."

I can't help glancing over my shoulder at him. His beautiful face is utterly placid, as if he doesn't find anything about what he just said all that meaningful. But my chest has constricted around my heart.

He isn't wrong, is he? I lent him a hand with the injured butterfly that'd landed on his sleeve—because it realized he was something more than human?—for pretty much the same reason I haven't yet told him to take a hike.

My monstrous magic has left me with one firm principle I've never strayed from. If I can do some good for the people around me, balance the scales of the harm I've dealt and might deal in the future a little, then I do it.

*Well,* Julita says doubtfully. *I suppose that makes a certain kind of sense.*

Casimir lets out a soft laugh. "I think he sees the same things in you that we all do, Kindness."

I shoot him a teasing grimace at the nickname, but before I can say anything in return, a slim figure bursts through the doorway.

"There's a patrol coming this way," Luzia says breathlessly. "They'll be here in less than five minutes. You'd better get going."

She gives me a hasty but encouraging nod. As soon as she heard that her father had agreed to help me, she insisted on pitching in.

The men clamber onto their mounts, and we hurry out onto the street at a trot. If we go any faster, we'll only give away that we're fleeing rather than a patrol ourselves.

Clouds have congealed overhead, dimming the sun. A distant rumble of thunder sends a quiver through my nerves.

I set up our escape. My men are all counting on me.

What if Garom's tactic fails, and we end up arrested?

I've been prepared for that final fate for years. It won't feel so much like a tragedy as an inevitability.

But if I drag the men I've come to care about so much down with me…

Shaking off my worries, I will myself to stay focused.

We take the first side street and continue on a winding path to ensure the soldiers behind us don't catch sight of our group. It's only a short ride to the outer walls.

Garom monitors the schedule of the guards at the city gates and knows that they usually change at the sixth bell. If we get there right before the current sentinels are due to be relieved of duty, they'll be at their most restless. Eager to get on with things so their work can be done.

As we come out onto the main thoroughfare that leads to the gate we're aiming for, we arrange ourselves into a more formal procession. Rheave, who's still technically an actual guard, takes the lead with Casimir and I behind him. Stavros and Alek, in their heavier disguises, bring up the rear where they'll be less visible.

I hold my posture stiffly straight, as if I can add a few inches to my meager height, and form an expression with the sort of arrogant disdain I've witnessed on dozens of Crown's Watch soldiers in the past. With my chin raised, I peer down my nose at the pedestrians we pass.

There's a line of civilians along the right side of the road—mostly merchants with carts or wagons of goods they're hoping they can still take out of the city today, as well as a couple of carriages. They've been waiting long enough that many of them have perched amid their merchandise to talk with their neighbors in line. The muttering intensifies as we trot by.

Then a voice catches my ears, one I haven't heard in years but so familiar it cuts right down the center of me. "Oh, we were supposed to have these tracts to the Temple of Sunlit Skies three hours ago. I don't see why they can't let legitimate business people like us through."

My gaze flicks to the side before I can catch it. And there she is.

My mother perches on our old cart next to several stacks of thin books. Her pale hair is wound back in one of her usual buns, as much gray as blond now. Her thin lips slant at the disgruntled angle I can still vividly remember deepening into outright fury.

A prickle runs down my back through the scars she inflicted with the regular lashes of her belt. My breath freezes in my lungs.

I yank my gaze away, but Casimir has already picked up on my reaction. He peers at me with concern, keeping his voice low. "Ivy, what is it? Do we need to divert course?"

It takes far too much effort to drag the humid air into my chest. I grip my reins and will my voice to stay steady. "It's fine. I just didn't expect—I saw my mother."

There's a rustle as Stavros shifts in his saddle behind me. His words come out in a dark mutter. "What? Where is she?"

Alek speaks in a similarly hardened tone. "The cart with the books, I'd imagine? *That's* the woman who—"

He cuts himself off with a muted growl.

Their obvious agitation only rattles my nerves more. "It's not like you can do anything about it right now. It's not as if I'd *want* you to."

Rheave glances back at us. "What's wrong? Why's everyone upset?"

Casimir manages to make the explanation simple. "We passed by a woman who used to hurt Ivy when she was a child."

Rheave's posture goes rigid, his eyes flashing as he searches the line. "Where? Why hasn't she been punished?"

The fierceness of the words makes my heart skip a beat. "Gods above, not you too. It's my mother. We're not doing anything."

The daimon-man catches my gaze with a frown, his hands still balled into fists around the reins. "If she hurt you, then she's an enemy more than anything else."

Alek lets out a low, raw chuckle. "Hear, hear."

I aim a glare around at all of them. "In case you've forgotten, we've got much bigger enemies to worry about. Can we please focus on getting through that gate alive?"

Rheave makes a chagrinned expression and tugs his body back around. Stavros growls something under his breath that I don't ask him to clarify, but no one makes any further attempts to inflict justice on the woman who raised me.

*Men,* Julita murmurs with a hint of amusement. *I suppose it's a good thing for both of us they're so committed to defending you.*

It's a good thing they've remembered the larger problem, because we're just a few buildings from the gate now. I inhale and exhale slowly, gathering myself.

We're not fugitives. We have every right to pass through. We carry the full authority of Silana's military order.

Ha.

Normally there are only two guards monitoring each gate, maybe one on the wall overhead. Today, four blue-uniformed figures stand in front of the barred doors, with three others monitoring the situation from above.

My throat constricts, but I lift my chin again with my false haughty airs. More thunder rumbles in the ever-darkening clouds overhead.

Rheave rides right up to the row of soldiers as if he can't imagine them stopping him. At least he knows how to play this part well.

"We need to get through," he says in a commanding tone. "We have orders to search the countryside."

The woman in the middle frowns. "The lockdown hasn't been lifted."

The daimon-man lets a more urgent note creep into his voice. "There are concerns that the fugitives may have escaped before it was enforced. If that's the case, we must track them down quickly."

She still looks hesitant, and her colleagues peer along our procession, eyeing the bunch of us with critical gazes. My skin itches with apprehension.

The longer they take to ponder our story, the harder it'll be to convince them.

I nudge Toast half a step forward and summon all my memories of past Crown's Watch soldiers who've sneered and stomped their way through the outer wards. "We've been delayed enough already! Let us through, or the king will have your heads for your idiocy. We have a job to carry out even if you're struggling to do yours."

The guards stiffen, but my domineering attitude appears to do the trick. The woman mutters an apology and reaches with one of the men to heave open the crossbar.

My heart thuds ever louder as the doors swing open. We tap our horses into a trot, Rheave passing beneath the arch in the wall first, then Casimir and me. The hammering against my ribs doesn't start to ease until I hear the clops of Stavros's and Alek's steeds emerging behind me.

Then, in a deafening warble of thunder, the clouds open up with the first deluge of rain.

The drops splatter across our bodies. I spare a panicked glance behind me in time to see the make-up running on the faces of both of the men at my back.

And I'm not the only one who sees it.

"There's something wrong with them," one of the guards atop the wall hollers to his fellow soldiers. "They were disguising their faces!"

"Halt!" someone bellows from behind us, just as Stavros barks out, "Ride!"

We all prefer the former general's suggestion. I dig my heels into Toast's sides, and he takes off like his tail's on fire.

More rain pelts down on us, pounding almost as loud as the horses' hooves. Stavros urges his stallion to the head of the group, veering to lead us toward the nearest stretch of forest where we can disappear from view.

With an unnerving whine, an arrow shoots through the air just inches from his shoulder. It thuds into the grass instead.

"Faster!" Alek calls out raggedly.

I don't think Toast can gallop any harder than he already is.

Clutching the reins, I sneak a peek over my shoulder in time to see all three of the guards on the wall drawing bows, with more soldiers racing to join them.

The arrows careen through the rain. Two fly wide, but the third is shooting straight toward Stavros's back.

Panic jolts through my veins with a chill that has nothing to do with the water seeping down my back. My magic leaps up alongside it.

Before I can second-guess the decision, I fling my arm out.

Like with the king this morning, there's no time to beg Kosmel for guidance, no time to even question the decision. I can't stand to see Stavros killed over my mistakes.

So possibly I make another.

My power slams the arrow to the side. It hisses harmlessly into the grass.

And on the wall behind us, a cry of pain rings out.

The backlash of my magical shove must have struck one of the guards. My head is whirling too fast for me to rejoice or regret the act.

I duck low against the growing downpour and hurtle between the welcoming trees.

# Five

*Ivy*

By the time Stavros slows his stallion ahead of us, I think I'm drenched right through to my bones. The rain has started to ease off, but a steady drizzle continues flecking my cheeks through the gloom.

The former general wheels his stallion in a small clearing and looks to me first. His face is taut with worry. "Are you all right?"

I restrain a shiver and paste on my best unflappable smile. "I'll survive. What do we do now?"

Stavros lets out a rough breath. "We've covered a lot of distance quickly. As unpleasant as the rain has been, it'll have covered most of the signs of our passing. I brought us around the city and onward in nearly the opposite direction from where the guards last saw us, which should help keep us beyond their initial searches."

Alek wraps one arm around his chest over his sodden uniform, which is plastered to his lean frame. "They aren't going to give up any time soon, though. Not as long as the king is afraid of a riven sorcerer on the loose."

Casimir taps his gelding to bring it up beside me and rests a comforting hand on my arm. "The royal family does have plenty of other things to focus on at the moment, though. I'd imagine the attack on the palace will be their most immediate concern."

"Unless they're going to blame that on me too," I mutter, with a shudder I can't suppress at the memory of King Konram's accusing question.

Julita sniffs in disdain. *That's ridiculous. Surely the king has at least enough of a brain to realize you weren't responsible for that. Why in the realms would you have protected him from attackers you'd sent to murder him?*

A very good question, and one I'd like to hope will occur to Konram when he's had time to think things through.

Rheave glances around us, his eerie eyes gleaming in the thickening darkness. "This body is hungry. None of you have eaten much today—you must need the energy too. Can we stop for long enough to have a meal and relieve ourselves?"

Part of me wants to cling to Toast for dear life and ride to the very edge of Silana, but even as the urge passes through me, my stomach gurgles.

Alek's gaze twitches to me. "Yes, we should eat. If we get back under the trees, they should keep most of the rain off."

The muscles in my legs protest as I dismount. Toast shakes his mane with a snort and ambles to the edge of the clearing to snack on some grass.

Casimir retrieves a bundle of food from his saddle bag, and we gather under the denser branches. As he hands a cheese-stuffed roll to me, another shiver ripples through my body, too intense for me to suppress it.

The courtesan pauses. "You're freezing. Your cloak is in one of the bags, isn't it? You could change back into your dress and—"

I cut him off with a terse laugh. "And get that drenched too? No. I'll put on my cloak when we set off again, but I've been through worse."

The tightening of Casimir's jaw suggests he isn't happy to hear that, but he glances around at the others. "We should all put on our cloaks for the rest of the ride. There's no need for the journey to be completely miserable."

Stavros tips his head obligingly, looking faintly amused by the courtesan's concern.

I bite into the roll, even though I can't summon much sense of appetite despite my gut's grumbling. As I swallow the sticky lump, thoughts of everything we've been through in the past day whip through my mind.

My spirits sink like the fading of the daylight. I force down the rest of the roll, but it sits like a boulder in my belly.

"This is my fault," I say.

All four heads swivel toward me. Alek knits his brow. "What do you mean?"

I wave my hand vaguely. "I showed my magic in front of the king. Now he wants all of you imprisoned—or executed. You've had to run for your lives; you've had to leave everything *in* your lives behind…"

A pang of guilt brings a burn to the back of my eyes. "I think I hurt one of the guards while we were escaping. King Konram is going to be even angrier with me, which means the same for you too."

"Ivy…" Casimir slips his arm around me and presses a kiss to my temple. "I have no regrets at all about being here with you. The only alternatives were letting the scourge sorcerers slaughter the royal family or turning on you."

"And neither of those are remotely acceptable," Stavros says. He takes a step closer to me and hesitates, his dark gaze searching mine through the dimness.

It's only been four days since the former general and I finally made a real peace with each other. Since he told me he loved me… and I found I could trust him enough to believe it.

We haven't had much time on solid ground before our equilibrium was upended all over again.

Stavros's jaw works before he goes on. "You fought for the royal family with all the loyalty they could deserve. You put your life on the line over and over to infiltrate the scourge sorcerers and end their conspiracy. It is my honor to be standing with you, ensuring you'll get all the recognition you deserve."

I wish I found it easier to accept those words. How do I shake thirteen years of seeing myself as a monster because of my magic and the harm it's done?

Then Alek eases past Stavros to stop in front of me. A little hope quivers into being at the determination etched on his scarred face.

He touches my cheek, his gaze intent on mine, his voice equally intense. "You know I've made more than my share of awful mistakes. I can say beyond a sliver of doubt that the only one I've made today was failing to convince King Konram of who you really are while I had the chance."

A lump rises in my throat. "I don't think anyone could have."

"And I don't see any way you could have handled what happened today better than you did. What did I leave behind? Books and papers? I'd rather have you still in my life than the entire royal library."

A laugh hitches out of me even knowing how huge a statement that is from the scholar.

Alek captures the sound with the press of his lips against mine. More warmth flows through my chilled body, washing away the worst of my anguish.

When he draws back, I lift my hand to echo his caress. My fingers trace the ridges of now uncovered scars that ripple across his cheek. "In case you need the reminder, I like you best without any kind of mask."

Alek smiles at me so brilliantly that I could almost believe everything is already fine. But as he drops his hand, Rheave shifts on his feet.

The daimon-man focuses on Stavros. "How intently will the Crown's Watch continue pursuing Ivy even while they have their other enemies to deal with?"

Stavros swipes his sleeve past his mouth. "We probably have at least a few days before a particularly invasive search begins. The Crown's Watch won't venture very far beyond the city. It'll be the wider army we'll be contending with. But with the attack on the palace, standard protocol would be for all soldiers in the area to ensure the royal family's safe passage to one of their secondary residences before anything else."

"King Konram will be leaving the city too?" I ask.

"It's possible he and his family already have. There are secure routes out of Florian that are accessible only to the royals and their guards." Stavros exhales in a rush. "After that, I suppose it depends on how large of a menace the scourge sorcerers continue to present themselves as."

Casimir turns to the daimon-man. "Rheave, you'll know more about that than we currently do. You indicated that the leader of the conspiracy is still alive."

Rheave nods, his chocolate-brown curls swaying with the movement. "Not the one Ivy knew who worked in the college."

A fresh chill washes over me. "Ster. Torstem." The man we thought was running the entire so-called Order of the Wild.

He really did sacrifice himself to the fire so that his followers would keep faith in the conspiracy, then. Because he truly believed in the cause himself? Because he knew whoever commanded him would continue their efforts?

"Torstem gave out most of the orders for what happened in and around the college, but he was getting his orders from someone else," Rheave says. "There was someone overseeing the workshop where this body was made."

He touches his chest as if he still sees his human body as an object that's not entirely *him*. "I didn't see that man, though. When he came to the workshop, I was already trapped in the body, but the sorcerers hadn't fully animated it yet. I had no sight."

Alek perks up with an air of keen interest. "Would you recognize his voice if you heard it again?"

The daimon-man's forehead furrows as he considers. "Possibly. The sounds traveled strangely when I was encased in the clay, before it became flesh."

"Do you know where that workshop was?" Stavros asks.

"No. It was a fairly long journey to the city. We were kept in boxes, nothing but darkness." A slight tremor runs through the daimon-man's muscular form that makes me want to clasp his hand, as if I can offer some comfort.

"But this leader," Alek says, "he could still talk to you directly? You indicated that you sensed him calling all the daimon he'd harnessed to attack the palace."

Rheave hums thoughtfully. "It wasn't quite talking. It was more like a tug or a push. But I could understand what it was tugging or pushing me toward. My first few weeks guarding the college, I simply had to go along with those tugs and all the other orders they'd imbedded in me."

Casimir's mouth curves up into a fond smile. "Until Ivy inspired you."

The daimon-man's gaze veers to me. "Something like that. I wasn't really thinking about what I was doing, just following the orders and wishing I could break out. But Ivy talked about things I couldn't help wondering about later, and I started noticing what I liked about having this body. And when I questioned the people controlling us at the college about their orders, they didn't like it."

I wince. "They threatened to destroy you."

"Yes." Rheave's unearthly eyes remain fixed on my face. "But I knew if there was anyone who would stop them from doing it, it was you. And I was right. If it won't trouble you to have me around, I'd like to stay with you, wherever you're going. I know that's the best place for me to be."

A strange pang reverberates through my heart. I'm not sure how to be a figure like that in anyone's life, especially a daimon who's not used to having a mortal life at all.

But I can't think of any other answer I could possibly give. "Of course you can stay with us. We'll need all the help *we* can get."

Stavros grimaces, but he refrains from arguing for now. "The more information we have about what we're up against, the better. Do you know who arranged for you and the other daimon to be hired on as guards? Is there anything else you learned about the scourge sorcerers' plans, what they intended to do beyond the attack on the city?"

Rheave's gaze goes momentarily distant. "I'm not sure about hiring us. But for their larger plans—they were making their own army. I heard a few of them say that in the workshop. Building numbers, preparing to overthrow the Melchioreks… But I didn't hear anything more about it after I got to the city. The others might know more."

"The others?" I say. "You mean the other captured daimon? You said there were many more. Where?"

Rheave shakes his head. "I'm not sure of that either. Only a small number of us were sent to the city, but where the others went, I wasn't told. I think the attack on the palace was a sudden decision provoked by the arrests and Torstem's death. It wasn't the main thing they were working toward."

The rest of us exchange an uneasy glance.

"A small number," Alek repeats. "Just how many daimons did they stuff into clay bodies like you?"

Rheave's eyes widen. "More were always going out. But the workshop was big. In the week while they were making me, there were at least a hundred others they were animating."

Casimir pales. "And most of them have been gathering somewhere else? There could be an army of thousands by now."

The bottom of my stomach drops out. "And who knows how many scourge sorcerers egging them on."

The conspiracy seemed horrifying enough when I thought it was merely a few dozen villains scheming around the city. If the Order of the Wild stretches right across Silana… how in the realms are any of us going to stop them?

# Six

*Ivy*

For all Casimir's concern about keeping us warm and dry, he's the one sneezing when we finally stop for the night.

"I'm all right," he tells me when I go over to check on him, but his voice sounds unusually rough. His face has flushed with what might be the start of a fever.

Guilt and worry tangle in my gut. I caress his cheek and grab another roll from our stash of provisions. "You should get a little food in you and then rest."

He grimaces. "It's only a little cold." But when I drag him into the tent after Stavros and Alek get it set up, he sinks onto his sleeping bag as if it was taking all his energy just to stay standing. His breath rasps out of him as it slows with sleep.

Cuddled up next to him, I only manage to drift off when I'm sure he's completely out. My heart keeps aching until slumber rolls over my mind.

I wake up to the warble of the night breeze passing over the fabric of the tent and a twinge in my bladder.

Casimir is still deep asleep beside me, the hoarseness of his

breath smoothed out enough that no fresh worries grip me. Alek has tucked himself close at my other side, our shared body heat stopping us from freezing during the chilly autumn night. I can't really complain about having only one tent.

The scholar's cool citrusy scent has mingled with the courtesan's honeyed sandalwood into a complex perfume. I wish I could wrap it around me always.

I close my eyes, but my bladder protests more emphatically. Julita lets out a soft chuckle. *One of the few things I don't miss about having a body.*

Scowling, I ease myself up between the two men. I need to be able to get back to sleep if I'm going to be rested enough to ward off whatever illness Casimir has caught.

Moving slowly and carefully, I manage not to rouse either of my lovers or the daimon-man who's sprawled back-to-back with Alek. I slip out from under the two wool blankets we layered across our sleeping bags and step through the tent's flaps.

Stavros glances up from the log where he's been keeping watch. He'll have traded off with Alek a little while ago, and he's meant to switch with me in another hour or two. I don't think he trusts Rheave to take on guard duty alone at this point.

Like the rest of us, the former general has traded his stolen soldier uniform for the more discreet tunic, jacket, and trousers Garom supplied us with as well. The rain washed the black from his hair like it's mostly rinsed the temporary dye from mine, though the dark red strands still look almost the same shade in the faint moonlight that penetrates our campsite.

He arches his eyebrows at me in question, but his expression tenses with concern at the same time.

I wave toward the trees, pitching my voice low to avoid waking the others. "I just need to relieve myself."

Stavros's stance relaxes in a way I don't totally understand until he says, in a matching low tone, "No nightmares?"

I choke up for a second at the history implied in those two words. Stavros knows as well as I do that he was the starring figure in most of my recent nightmares, wrenching a noose around my neck as he once thought he might need to do in reality. He even instructed one of his students to partly strangle me with a rope to test my control over my magic.

But we've come a long way from there—both of us.

I walk over to the log. "No bad dreams at all."

Drawn to the mix of affection and anguish in his eyes by the same emotions coiled inside me, I bend down to kiss him.

Stavros meets the press of my lips with an encouraging hum and teases his fingers into my hair. When I pull back a few inches, he gazes up at me with a hint of his old cocky grin. "Trying to distract me from my duties?"

I snort softly. "Trying to show you how much I appreciate you watching over me."

"Hmm. I think I'd better appreciate you a little more, then."

He tugs me back down and claims my mouth with enough passion to leave my head spinning.

We both know this isn't the time or place for a lengthier interlude. I squeeze his shoulder before weaving off between the trees for a little privacy.

As I squat behind a bush several paces away, Julita speaks up with no apparent concern about what I'm up to. Really, privacy isn't a concept that can exist when you've got another person's soul residing in your head.

*Where do you think we go from here?*

I gather the skirts of the plain woolen dress I changed into and take a few steps from my makeshift latrine. The rustling and buzz of the forest life around me stir up memories of my ventures into the campus woods to join in the scourge sorcerers' rituals and spy on them.

We rode another few hours from the spot where we stopped to eat yesterday evening, to an isolated stretch of land Stavros says is along the border between two provinces. With no towns or roads nearby, it's unlikely anyone will stumble on us.

But clearly we can't simply camp out in the woods for the rest of our lives.

"I don't know," I murmur. "I guess we'll come up with some kind of plan in the morning after we're properly rested."

*What a plan it'll need to be.* She huffs. *We were supposed to be* done *with those fiends. I can't believe they've managed to spread their toxic magic across the whole country.*

Horror colors the noblewoman's tone. She's more familiar with the brutal side of scourge sorcery than the rest of us, having been subjected to blood-letting experiments by her brother and his best friend as a child in their fumbling attempts to enhance their magical talents.

I grimace in answer. "Rheave might be mistaken about just how far their operations have expanded. But it does sound as if it's a much bigger mess than we had any idea about."

My ghostly passenger shudders. *When I set you on this mission, I never thought it'd ask anywhere near this much of you, Ivy. I never thought it'd ask this much of* me. *And now the king wants your head too… I'm sorry.*

Does she really think this disaster is somehow her fault?

I wrap my arms around my waist, wishing I could touch the woman I now consider a friend, look into her eyes, make sure she accepts how much I mean this. "You didn't launch the Order of the Wild. You never asked me to use my magic. I'm still glad to have a friend through all this chaos, as long as you can stick with us."

I think the tickle of Julita's presence at the back of my skull gentles a little. Her voice comes out softer. *I'll stand with you until the end of it—as well as I can actually stand.*

The corner of my mouth ticks upward, but the unsettled mood the conversation provoked lingers. Pulling my cloak closer around me against the breeze, I peer through the night-cast woods.

A flutter of movement catches my eye. Was that a crow taking flight from a branch overhead?

I hesitate and then step toward that tree. Gazing up at it, I can't see any further sign of divine presence or anything else.

Did Kosmel know all along that he was sending me on a collision course with a murderous conspiracy that extended far beyond the college's walls? Have I offended him as much as I did the king with my impromptu shows of magic?

I was already in over my head at the college. Now I'm so deep underwater I can barely see a glimmer of light through the churning surface overhead.

How is a street-rat thief supposed to challenge a kingdom-wide, hundreds-strong plot to overturn the very fabric of our society?

For a moment, the drowning sensation overwhelms me. I close my eyes and sink to my knees at the base of the tree trunk.

I know what the clerics would say I have to do if I want to call on him properly.

Open myself up. Prove that I welcome his guidance.

Because I do need it now, more than I ever have before.

I'd started to take comfort in the trickster godlen's interest in me. Knowing he was on my side and supporting me helped me stand up to Ster. Torstem and deal with the conspirators my way.

Please, let him not have abandoned me.

I close my eyes and bow my head, thinking out to the divine powers that flow through our world. *Kosmel, if you're still watching over me, I could use some advice. Our enemies are so many more than we realized. I have no idea how I can even start to tackle the rest of the scourge sorcerers. And the king's soldiers will be hunting me too… If there's any direction you can offer, I've never needed it more.*

I wait, cold seeping into my knees from the dirt, leaves hissing against each other overhead.

No voice comes to me. No sense of a divine presence grazes my skin.

After a few minutes, I push myself to my feet. A hollow

sensation has formed in the pit of my stomach, but I ignore it as well as I can as I head back to the tent.

I've gotten through plenty of sticky situations in the past without any godly assistance. We'll figure something out.

Stavros nods to me as I pass him. I tuck myself back under the blankets between my other two men and soak up their warmth until it takes the edge off the ache inside.

The sleep I fall into this time is full of jumbled images that don't quite form a dream. Shadows whirl, and jagged shapes brush against my limbs.

Then I'm perched on a tree branch in the midst of the woods, the light of a full moon beaming over me… and a strange figure balanced on the branch across from me.

At first glance, I think it's a gigantic crow. Then the creature raises its head, and the eyes of a man stare back at me—pale but fathomless eyes as if I'm staring straight through a star.

My pulse hitches, and I jerk my gaze away, over the body that's feathered and winged but with a man's legs, leather boots braced against the branch's bark.

A low chuckle reverberates around me. "There are many ways I can appear. I promise you'd find most of the others more disturbing."

"Kosmel," I mumble. Am I still asleep?

The godlen doesn't bother to acknowledge his name. "You know I can't tell you what to do, my wayward rogue. Some of my siblings feel I've meddled too much as it is."

But he's here. He's reached out to me after all.

"I can make my own decisions," I say, remembering the things he's said to me before. I can't quite keep my voice from shaking. "I'd just like to do it with a better understanding of what we're up against. You want all the scourge sorcerers stopped, don't you? But I don't know how much I can risk using my magic without becoming just as big a problem as they are…"

Kosmel is silent for long enough that I'd think he might have vanished if I wasn't staring at his boots. The awareness of his divine energy prickles over my skin.

"It's a complicated journey you've found yourself on," he says finally. Like when he speaks in my head, his voice resonates through every particle of my body, quivering into my bones, scattering my pulse. "Being cautious is not my natural state, but things end in catastrophe when gods impose too much of their will on mortals. You've already suffered enough from those consequences."

I'm not totally sure what he means about my 'suffering.' I grope for the right thing to say. "You must have wanted to tell me *something*, or you wouldn't be here."

The godlen makes a rough sound that's as much caw as grunt. "I heard your plea. I didn't want you to think I've forgotten you. But this may be the last time we speak."

For a second, I feel as if the branch beneath me has disintegrated. I wobble, fighting through the sensation of freefall, of the one bit of security I clung to slipping through my fingers.

"But—my magic—if I need to use it again, will you help me guide it? I didn't want to let it loose without your direction; there just wasn't time—"

"Don't fret like that," Kosmel interrupts. "It doesn't become you." His dry tone gives no indication that he's upset about how I used my power in the past day.

He pauses and then clicks his tongue. "You should have guidance of some sort. I can offer better than my own, in this one case. To mend some of what was marred."

I shouldn't be surprised when the godlen of trickery speaks in half-riddles rather than plainly, but it's frustrating all the same. "Better?"

He adjusts his position with a ruffling of his crow feathers. "Walk with the sun at your left in the morn and your right after noon until you see the silver peak through the trees. Climb straight to the crossed trees, then continue to the left until you reach the waterfall. Announce to the sky that Kosmel led you there and expects you to receive a riven's welcome. Then listen well."

Listen well? Another question tumbles out. "If there's more I should know, can't you—"

Kosmel cuts me off with another raspy caw. "Mortal business is between mortals."

His wings sweep past me in a blur of black feathers, and I really do lose my balance. My boots slip on the branch. My clawing fingers catch only air.

I plummet down and down and—

My eyes pop open as if with a smack of impact. At my gasp, the men around me stir.

Casimir blinks sleepily with a hint of a sniffle and touches my arm. "All right, Kindness?"

I stare into the darkness, the dream echoing through my head. "I think so. I know where we need to go."

# Seven

*Rheave*

The soft blades of grass tickle my palm. I turn my hand over, taking in the difference of how they feel against my knuckles.

There are so many tiny experiences that make up the essence of bodily life. So many sensations it never occurred to me might exist when I barely brushed against the physical world.

Flowers of different shapes and colors bloom between the green blades. Their petals graze my fingers with a different texture.

A glimmer of curiosity lights inside me. I pluck up one blossom and then another and another before pausing to admire how the hues intensify when placed next to each other.

With a second quiver of inspiration, I crack little notches into the stems and start fitting them together. A smile crosses my lips at my handiwork.

As a pure daimon, I danced through the city streets and the fields beyond, stirring up the energy of everything around me when the impulse caught me. Now I can spark amusement and surprise more directly.

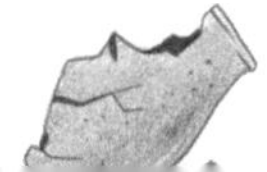

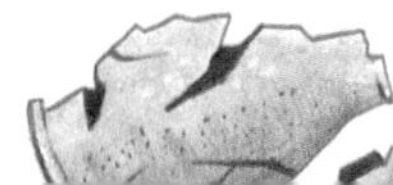

Stavros's commanding baritone carries across the field where we stopped to let the horses graze. "Rheave, why don't you join us? It'd be good for us to know how you could best contribute in a fight."

Sounds hit me much the same in this form as when I breezed along as a ball of spirit energy, only sharper and with a distinct impression that I should pay attention to them. It was easier to ignore humans talking in my previous state.

I glance over at where Stavros is standing with the other two men who are Ivy's dedicated companions. Stavros has drawn his sword, and Casimir and Alek are both holding daggers.

While we rode this morning, the big man said something about teaching the others more combat skills. Making sure they're prepared for whatever we might face on the road.

I didn't realize he meant me too.

I hesitate, reluctant to leave off my current occupation. Many humans seem to be fond of smacking and stabbing each other. It didn't appeal to me when it was the ones they call scourge sorcerers jostling each other around, and I'm not eager to be a part of any similar games with this bunch.

A few paces away from me, Ivy lifts her head by the buried firepit where we're roasting a couple of rabbits that Stavros caught in snares overnight. The earthen cover over the flames ensures that no smoke escapes to give away our location.

It's an old army trick, he said. Fascinating.

Ivy is exempt from his training, but I think that's only because she doesn't need it. It was also fascinating watching the deftness of the knife in her hand as she skinned the rabbits. The shifting of her fingers against the handle, the way the sunlight glinted off the blade…

"That's right," she says, her clear voice cutting through my reverie. "The scourge sorcerers put you in place as a guard—did they train you at all for the position first?"

I don't like thinking about the first couple of weeks as I

learned to operate the body that felt like a heavy cage around me at the time.

My mind skims through the memories. "They made sure I could move and speak well enough to pass as a regular human. I think we were supposed to rely on strength rather than skill when they called on us to attack."

Alek considers me with a gleam of interest in his eyes. His blotchy face is fascinating too, so different from any other complexion I've seen.

He doesn't seem to like it, though. Ivy swatted me this morning when I must have been studying the interplay of color and texture for too long.

"What about the supernatural power the other daimon used in their clay bodies?" he asks. "It looked as if they were summoning bolts of lightning from their hands. Can you do that?"

I look down at my pale hands beneath the strand of flowers draped across them. Callouses are forming from gripping my horse's reins. I'm lucky the creature seems to like me, or I'm not sure I could have stayed on it.

"I don't know," I admit. "I never have before. I never tried."

Stavros waves his sword. "Well, come on. We'd better find out before you fling it around at the wrong time or place. And Casimir could use a break."

The courtesan makes a sound of protest, but then he starts to cough. With a disgruntled noise, Ivy gets up and yanks him over to sit near the fire. "You should be taking it easy."

Casimir wipes his nose on a scrap of fabric he's turned into a handkerchief. "I might need more than my fists if we encounter a whole army of daimon."

"You won't be fighting any which way if you're too stuffed up to breathe."

Stavros is still watching me with the evaluating look that makes my skin prickle. I can't tell whether he's happy that I might be able to help or studying me like a potential enemy.

But Ivy glances over at me too with an expectant air. All of the others are working at being better protectors.

How can I ask for her help and not offer my own in return in as many ways as possible?

I get to my feet and bind the last of the stems as I cross the field. "First, for you," I say, setting the ring of flowers on Ivy's head like a crown. A renewed grin springs to my lips. "The colors look wonderful against your hair!"

"Oh." Ivy touches the garland tentatively, a faint blush coloring her cheeks. "Um, thank you."

As Casimir chuckles, I force myself to walk toward Stavros and Alek next. A niggling sensation runs down my back with the awareness that I'm leaving Ivy farther behind.

It's because of her that I'm here. I should stay close to her.

I want to understand her and all the little, unusual things about her that helped me snap out of the scourge sorcerers' control.

But the other men who hover around her seem to think she's *theirs*. That it's up to them to protect her and watch over her.

Maybe if I swing around a blade to their satisfaction, they'll start to see that I can look after her too. That I have just as much right to follow her on her quest as they do.

When I'm a few paces away, Stavros motions for me to stop. "Stay there and watch. I'll run through the exercises with Aleksi first, but you'll give them a try afterward."

The other man pauses and gives Stavros a lopsided smile. "You know, you could simply call me Alek at this point. Almost everyone does other than the professors. I think being on the run together puts us on a slightly less formal level."

It hadn't occurred to me to wonder why Stavros said the name a little differently, but Stavros looks chagrinned.

Casimir tsks his tongue playfully. "The scholar has a point."

"All right," the big man says, with a hint of a smile of his own. "Let's see how much you've learned so far, Alek."

He talks Alek through a series of jabs and parries. I watch for a couple of minutes, but my attention slides back to Ivy.

She's tucked a blanket over Casimir's shoulders and ambled over to the horses. When my gaze settles on her, she murmurs to the stallion she's most fond of while she brushes his neck. The animal pauses in his grazing to lean into the strokes.

Stavros clears his throat, and my gaze jerks back to him. He's watching me with a stern expression. "You're not going to pick up much skill if you aren't even following the exercises."

"I don't want to attack *you*," I point out. "We're all on the same side. What's the point?"

Humans are so odd.

A dry note creeps into the big man's voice. "The point is that your body won't be used to fending off an actual attacker if it's never gotten any practice. Brute strength will only get you so far. Especially if we find ourselves going up against the king's soldiers rather than only other conjured men and women like you."

With that last sentence, his voice stiffens a bit, but I don't know why. I can see there might be some logic to his words, though.

I roll my shoulders, reveling in the feel of the muscles flexing and stretching. "All right. I'll practice. Whatever will work the fastest."

Casimir shoots me a softly amused smile from his spot by the fire. "You don't like the idea of an extended battle?"

"Daimon don't get into fights," I tell him. "We let each other exist without worrying about anyone except ourselves. Why make more pain?"

Alek rubs his jaw. "You do play tricks on people sometimes. Startle animals. Things like that."

"Nothing that does any real damage. Not when we're in control. We just liven things up where the energy gets too dull."

"Then I'll try not to bore you." Stavros gestures to Alek. "Let Rheave use that dagger for a bit. Come on, daimon, let's see what you can do."

It's hard to put my full commitment into the imitation of fighting he leads me through. I push the dagger through the air as he instructs, but none of the movements feel natural, like how I'd want to move if I actually needed to deflect an attacker.

My fingers curl awkwardly around the weapon. Once, when Stavros blocks it with his sword, I fumble and nearly drop it.

The big man lets out a grunt that suggests he isn't entirely happy. "What about that burning magic the other daimon used? Can you send a little of that into this tree?" He taps a nearby maple.

I stare at the looming plant, but I can't summon any sense of power inside me. No part of me wants to burn this living thing that's doing nothing but growing peacefully.

A shiver runs through my limbs. That's the kind of thing this body's creators would have ordered me to do. They're the ones looking to destroy whatever they can.

To show I'm trying, I walk over to the tree and rest my hand on the bark. The texture presses into my skin to delightful effect. I want to trail my fingers over the surface, not sear it away.

"I don't know how to make it happen," I say. "Maybe it's something the scourge sorcerers channeled through the others, not something we brought."

"I suppose that's possible." Stavros ambles back toward the fire. "Those rabbits should be just about done. Let's see if we can't get in a little more—"

He cuts himself off with a wrench of his head in my direction. His metal prosthetic hand leaps up to point at a spot behind me. "Quick! One of the riven-hunters has snuck up on us—they'll be after Ivy!"

His words and the urgency coursing through them have my body whipping around before I make a conscious decision to move. My gaze snags on a bush just behind the maple tree, the twigs shuddering as if someone's about to spring past it.

I lunge first, a growl lurching up my throat. My arms shoot forward, the dagger dropping from my hand.

No one's getting to Ivy. No one's going to damage one fragment of her skin, one strand of her hair—

Fear and anger collide to set off a flare in my chest. I launch myself right over the shrub, snatching at the first movement my gaze catches.

The need to obliterate the threat crackles through me.

I thump to the ground and roll to the side. When I heave back to my feet, there's no one there.

No riven-hunter. No person at all other than the men and Ivy all watching from the field.

The frantic haze clears from my head. I look down at my hands and find myself clutching the blackened body of a bird.

When I adjust my fingers, its burnt feathers disintegrate into chalky powder.

"Well," Stavros says in a deadpan tone, "that answers at least one question."

My gaze flicks over to him. "I didn't want to kill a bird. I thought there was an enemy—you *said* there was."

"I was simply wondering what might happen if you were sufficiently motivated."

He's eyeing me, giving his head the little shake that I've come to understand means he's focusing harder. His face gives away no emotion now.

Is he pleased by how well I'd have tackled the supposed threat… or upset that I'd have gone so far?

Humans don't make any sense. But if this one decides I'm a problem, he'll campaign to leave me behind.

I don't know what he wants from me. I can only say the truth. "If Ivy needs protecting, I'll protect her."

"And that's good to know," the woman in question says from over by the firepit. "Plus now we have a little extra for lunch. Why don't you bring that bird over here, and we'll see if there's any edible meat on it?"

Her easy smile makes the men around me seem to fade. I

stride over, holding out the bird, grateful for the chance to return to where I'd have preferred to be all along.

Ivy slices into the bird I apparently charred without any sign of concern about the power I inflicted on it. Her exclamation of victory when she finds cooked flesh within settles my nerves more, even though I can sense Stavros still examining me from a distance.

What I told him was true. I'll protect Ivy from any danger that comes our way, however I need to.

Because I need her. Her strange remarks and unusual attitudes shocked me out of the spell the scourge sorcerers had me under. They gave me my first taste of how wondrous living in this body I didn't ask for could be.

If I'm forced apart from her—if I lose her… how easily would my former captors make me their prisoner all over again?

# EIGHT

*Ivy*

"Are you sure he said the 'crossed trees'?" Stavros asks, pausing to swipe the sweat from his forehead.

The breeze licks cold across my own dampened skin. I rub the back of my neck, dislodging the strands of hair that've stuck there.

We spotted the peak of the mountain this morning, shining like silver where it jutted up just above the tree line. The sun was directly overhead by the time we reached the mountain's foot, and we've been climbing for what feels like hours.

I can't be sure of the exact time, since we've found ourselves in a part of Silana so remote that the peal of the nearest town bell was little more than a distant chime even before we started the climb.

The air has cooled as we've ascended, but the exertion has warmed us at the same time. The last section of the trek has been up terrain so steep we had to dismount and lead the horses in our weaving path across the rocky ground.

I peer through the brush around us for any sign of trees that

would fit Kosmel's description. "Yes. I remember every instruction he gave perfectly."

Apparently dreams provoked by godlen don't fade into vagueness like the regular sort. His divine voice burned itself into my memory.

Alek swipes his fingers through his thick hair, glancing around us. "The forest is dense enough that we can't see very far through it. We could have already passed the trees by."

I grimace. "He said to 'climb straight.' We set off from the exact spot where we reached the mountain, and we've only been veering a few paces from side to side. I don't think it could be that far off course."

Casimir hums to himself and then lets out a few coughs. Guilt jabs through my stomach as I turn to him.

"We should take a few minute's rest anyway. Look, there's a log over there where you can sit."

The courtesan gives me the bemused look that's become more common in the past two days. His voice is still hoarse from his cold. "I'm not worn out yet."

"We shouldn't wait until you're totally exhausted." I prod him over to the log, touch his forehead to check his temperature, and turn to the horses. "Where are those berries we gathered this morning? Those seemed to help soothe his throat a little."

Stavros has already moved to his stallion's saddle packs. "Right here. It's not a bad thing to pace ourselves."

He hands me a bundle of the plump purple berries, and I hustle back to Casimir. After he accepts the snack, there isn't much else I can do for him other than sit on the log and massage his back with slow circles of my hand that I hope soothe his muscles too.

Casimir swallows a couple of the berries and tips his head toward me. "You don't need to worry about me. I've had colds before—it's hardly serious."

I let out a humph. "You've pampered me plenty of times

when I was perfectly well. Let me return the favor as well as I can."

The flush that creeps into his cheeks at those words looks more pleased than feverish. He presses a kiss to the side of my head. "You're doing a wonderful job."

Alek leans against a nearby tree, looking equally glad for the brief rest. "Did Kosmel give any indication at all of *why* we should come up here? If we had a broader sense of what we're trying to find..."

"That would make it easier, I know. I don't think he was going for easy." I sigh. "He mentioned it after I asked him about whether he'd still help direct my magic. He claimed coming here would 'mend some of what was marred,' but I have no idea what that means."

For the first time in ages, Rheave speaks up from where he's standing at the edge of our group. "If a godlen said it, it'll be true. They don't tend to explain things thoroughly, but they don't lie."

I look back at his smooth face. His eerie eyes gleam with unshakeable confidence.

How much do daimon know about our deities? They're considered divine creatures, closer to godly than mortal, but they're a far cry from being even lesser gods themselves. More like the stray cats and dogs of the unearthly realm.

Although I guess that means they probably still know more than any of us mortals do.

He peers around at the rest of us with an air of avid curiosity I'm seeing more and more of over time. "Have any of the rest of you talked to the gods? I didn't think they touched humans that directly often."

Casimir laughs. "They don't. Only Ivy has had that honor. Kosmel obviously sees something particularly impressive in her."

The daimon-man's gaze returns to me, even more avid. "She is special. But you two have gifts." He nods to Casimir and Stavros.

"One I can't use anymore," Stavros says brusquely. The injury that lost him his knack for catching glimpses of the near future is still a bit of a sore subject for him. I don't imagine he wants an inhuman near-stranger prodding about it.

As if to intervene, Casimir pops the last of the berries into his mouth and stands. He gives his gelding an affectionate pat. "I'm good to continue. Let's push on."

I adjust my grip on Toast's reins as I study the terrain around us. "Maybe we should split up to cast a wider net. We have our lockets—whoever finds the trees first can signal the rest of us."

Rheave frowns as if he doesn't like the idea of breaking up the group.

Julita chuckles in the back of my head. *The daimon would probably insist on coming with you. I swear he's even more stubborn than the others. You didn't even give him any offerings, and he's stuck on you like a hound to its master.*

The stray dog comparison might be even more apt than I realized. I did give Rheave something, without realizing it: honest answers and a little compassion.

A meal he needed more than the standard daimon offering of scraps of food on a plate, it appears.

There's no denying his commitment to his newly formed loyalty. The way he charged at that bird in the bush yesterday when he thought I was threatened… He was more attack dog than hunting hound then.

An attack dog capable of roasting a starling in an instant.

Really, I should simply be glad he's aimed his loyalties at me rather than the scourge sorcerers who made his human body.

Stavros guides his stallion toward a path through the underbrush. "I think we should keep together for now. We can reconsider later if we still haven't found the spot."

Toast grunts in protest, but he clomps onward up the slope at my gentle tug. Pebbles rattle away under my feet.

The sun dips lower, our shadows lengthening. The wind picks up and tugs at the hood of my cloak.

I'm just starting to worry that the climb will get so steep we'll have to leave the horses behind when I lift my head and spot a strangely angled trunk through the forest above.

My heart leaps. "Is that…?"

I do leave Toast then, though only to clamber through the clinging shrubs and over jutting tree roots as quickly as I can. A twig scrapes across my palm, but I barely feel the sting.

I come to a stop in front of the trunk I spotted, and a smile stretches across my face.

Somehow or other, a massive birch ended up growing on a slant. Its papery white bark makes it stand out like a slash against the trees behind it.

It looks as if the tree leaning against it was struck by lightning in a storm. The charred trunk toppled to the side—and caught on one of the birch's boughs. The pale tree holds the dark log against it in an arboreal embrace.

The tops of the trees veer past each other, stretching off into the forest. Forming a shape like a mismatched X in the midst of the woods.

Alek comes to a stop beside me with a breathless laugh. "The crossed trees. We head to the left from here?"

Of course the scholar would have memorized all of Kosmel's directions the moment I shared them.

I nod, my spirits lifted despite my fatigue from the climb. "I don't know how much farther it is from here. But I don't think we can miss a whole waterfall."

I turn to scramble back to Toast, but Stavros has caught the reins to lead both stallions up together. As the former general studies the crossed tree trunks with a wary expression, I give my steed's jaw a good scratch in apology for temporarily abandoning him.

We head left through the brush. Fading sunlight filters through the trees and sets off glints amid the vegetation.

I pause to examine a particularly glittery spot and find the rocks jutting from the soil are flecked with some kind of sparkly mineral.

"Mica," Alek says, and pauses. "The peak must be coated with the mineral to shine the way it does. You don't usually see deposits quite that big."

Casimir pats a nearby tree. "It's a godly place. Some of them enjoy a certain grandeur."

I wouldn't have thought Kosmel was one of those, but then, this mountain might not be his domain. He was sending me to seek help other than his own, after all.

A pang of hunger ripples through my stomach, but we're too close to our goal now for me to suggest another stop. As if sensing my mood, Stavros pulls out the apples we liberated from an orchard we skirted yesterday evening and passes them around so we can eat while we walk.

As we tramp onward, the daylight stretches farther with the sinking of the sun. Where the trees briefly thin, Stavros surveys the landscape beyond the mountain: mottled fields and forestland with a few isolated buildings in the distance.

"No sign of soldiers on our trail," I say.

He smiles grimly. "No. But gods only know what the scourge sorcerers have been up to since we left."

The uncertainty gnaws at me too. How long will whoever else makes up the Order of the Wild wait before they unleash more of their horrific magic on Florian… or the rest of the kingdom?

Kosmel knew that stopping the conspiracy was my greatest concern. I was under the impression he was awfully concerned about the scourge sorcerers himself.

Surely wherever he's sent me, it'll help us in our mission to stop them?

The trek along the side of the mountain is less strenuous than climbing upward, but we walk long enough that the ache in my calves spreads all the way up to my hips. The sunlight starts to dwindle completely.

I'm just debating suggesting we camp for the night when the warble of tumbling water reaches my ears.

I tug Toast faster. "I hear the waterfall!"

We hustle the horses along until we come into view of the stream that courses down the side of the mountain. Right in front of our path, it careens in a sheer drop maybe ten times my height before pooling on a rocky ledge a short distance beneath us and gurgling onward.

Stavros steps forward to splash some of the water on his face and then cup it to his mouth for a drink. We haven't had fresh hydration since the creek where we filled our canteens this morning.

I follow suit, shivering in delight at the chilly liquid rinsing the sweat from my skin. It's too cold for a full shower to be appealing, but the gulp of icy water I swallow snaps me back to total alertness.

I step back from the waterfall as the other men take their turns refreshing themselves. A faint tingle seeps through my awareness at the same time.

My body stiffens as I take in the sensation.

"What is it?" Casimir asks softly.

I swallow hard. "There's magic here. I can't sense much yet. I don't know where it's coming from."

Maybe that isn't surprising, given who sent us here. We can probably find out what's going on soon enough.

Kosmel said I was supposed to announce myself.

The words the trickster godlen gave me reverberate through my mind. I lift my voice to carry, ignoring the hitch of my pulse at forgoing caution. "Kosmel led me here and expects me to receive a riven's welcome!"

*And a better riven's welcome than the king offered*, Julita mutters.

We stand in silence for a few minutes, nothing reaching my ears but the hiss of the water. Alek eases closer to me. "What was supposed to happen now?"

I shake my head. "Kosmel didn't explain. He just told me that I should 'listen.'"

The scholar slips his hand around mine and squeezes my fingers. I grip his hand tightly in return, my heart thumping in anticipation.

For all I'm watching and listening, it's Rheave who notices first, with an urgent sound low in his throat. "There's a woman up there."

My gaze jerks to the point he's looking at just as a form moves into view, made tiny by the distance. The figure vanishes into the brush again, but I keep my head tipped up, so I see her as soon as she re-emerges by the top of the waterfall.

She's still too far away for me to make out the finer details of her appearance, but she looks to have at least four decades behind her, perhaps five. The streaks of pale gray woven through her black hair remind me of the crossed trees. She moves a little stiffly, not with the full limberness of youth.

Her plain brown dress and matching cloak cover everything but her hands, boots, and face, helping her blend into the forest. As she stares down at us, her posture stiffens even more.

She backs up a step as if she thinks we could threaten her from all the way down here.

"Which of you called me?" she demands in a gravelly voice she projects down the mountainside.

I raise my hand. "I did. But we've all come together. These men are with me."

It's hard to decipher the woman's expression, but she sounds incredulous. "And you brought them *here*?"

"I don't even know where 'here' is. Kosmel gave me the directions, and I followed them. He didn't say anything about needing to come alone."

He didn't say I should have the men with me either, but I don't see any point in mentioning that. It's not as if the godlen couldn't have figured out that if he didn't specify one way or another, I'd be bringing them along.

The woman hesitates. I'm not sure what she's waiting for.

"They know what you are?" she says in the same disbelieving tone.

Stavros speaks up in his commanding general's tone, sounding as if he's trying to rein in his impatience. "We're aware of her magic, and we have no interest in extinguishing it. In fact, we're quite devoted to ensuring she remains alive in spite of other opinions to the contrary. If that's all you're concerned about, there's no need to worry. Maybe you could explain why the trickster godlen would have pointed us here?"

The woman is silent for a long moment. Her lips move, but she must have murmured something to herself, because I can't make out the words.

A more potent quiver of magic passes by me from just behind, coursing up the mountain. Casimir lifts his head—he must have used his gift, sought out a sense of what he could do to make her happiest right now.

The courtesan offers one of his gentle smiles. "You have nothing to fear from us at all. We simply want to see Ivy safe and well. We've taken every care to ensure no one could track us here, so your own security shouldn't be disturbed. But if there's been some mistake and we aren't welcome at all, we can take our leave."

Something shifts in the woman's face. Another supernatural quiver tickles through my nerves, one I think came from her.

What gift is she casting over us?

Whatever it is, between our words and her own observations, she makes up her mind. Her posture relaxes incrementally.

"Tie your horses there for now. I'll come to lead them the long way around after we've had a chance to talk properly. You'll find a sort of staircase of stone between the trees a little to your right."

I glance over, and the rocky stairs show plainly through the brush—so clearly I don't know how I could have failed to notice them before.

Unless they were hidden by the magic I sensed.

My pulse kicks up a notch, but I start scaling the rough staircase. The woman was obviously more nervous about my companions rather than me. It's best if I face her first.

By the time I reach the top of the waterfall, I'm sweating again. The woman stands on the rocky outcropping waiting for us.

Once we've all arrived, she turns toward the trees and sets off on a path between them.

I hurry to keep pace with her swift strides. "Who *are* you? Do you know why Kosmel would have sent me here?"

She doesn't bother looking back. "My name is Sulla. And I'd imagine the godlen guided you here so I could teach you how to work with your magic."

I lose my breath for a second. "You can do that? I thought that was impossible."

She shoots a faint smile over her shoulder at me. "I can, because I'm riven too."

# Nine

*Ivy*

Even after spending the night on the mountain, I haven't gotten used to this place.

We're sitting on plump cushions around a low table—a little squashed together because the dining area obviously wasn't built with six people in mind and we're trying to give our host enough space to be polite. Sunlight filters through translucent panes in the rocky ceiling overhead, drawn there by magic. It streaks over us in a golden glow.

The table's wood shimmers with little carvings that move if you pause to watch them. Near my end, there's a fish that leaps out of the wavering water of a stream and a deer that gambols along a stretch of trees.

Rheave taps an etching on the corner of the table in front of him and laughs with delight at whatever effect he provoked. Casimir leans over to watch with a friendly smile.

*It's incredible,* Julita says, watching through my eyes. *Like the work of a master artist.*

If that wasn't enough magic, Sulla has a whole array of supernaturally enhanced tools at her disposal. Despite the fact that this room is carved into a mountainside, running water flows to her sink. I watched her fill a kettle from the tap only for the vessel to immediately start to steam.

The plates our meal of fried eggs and buttered rolls are sitting on exude warmth to keep our food at the perfect temperature. I only had to reach for the saltshaker before it leapt the rest of the way into my hand.

I've never been surrounded by so many objects imbued with power before. My skin quivers with a constant tingling as my cracked soul resonates with the magic.

I dab the corner of my roll in the runny egg yolk and pause to savor the mingling of savory and nutty flavors on my tongue. I've never had this kind of bread before either.

Julita hums alongside my contentment. *And the food is rather delectable too.*

It's a far cry from the typical elaborate spreads at the royal college, but it beats the bare bones fare we've been reduced to while on the run.

Despite my enjoyment of the meal, curiosity itches at me. Last night, Sulla hustled us into a bedroom and supplied us with down-stuffed mattresses and blankets for our slumber on the stone floor. She deflected all our questions with the promise that she'd get into everything in the morning.

I think she wanted a little more time to take stock of our unexpected arrival. She has to understand that we want to take stock of *her* just as much.

And it is morning now.

I study a carving of a woman in a dress who twirls on ever-shifting feet and then lift my gaze to meet our host's. Now that I've seen her up close, I'd put her in her late forties or early fifties —older than my mother. Her silver and black hair winds from her temples in two thick braids that she coils together at the back of her head. The even lines at the corners of her eyes and mouth make her face look serene, as if she hasn't smiled or frowned all that often.

I've never heard of a riven sorcerer this old. Sometimes they manage to go unnoticed for a couple of decades, but usually their increasingly ambitious manipulations draw notice before they reach their thirties.

And then there's the fact that she doesn't appear any less sane than I am.

I motion to the table and the glowing panes overhead. "Did you create all this with your magic?"

Sulla lets out a light chuckle. "Oh, no. The Haven has been a home to riven sorcerers for ages longer than I've been alive. We all contribute a little. It adds up over time."

Stavros shoots her a wary look. He's come to accept that *I'm* not a monster just because of my magic, and I suppose he can't help seeing that Sulla is hardly a raving lunatic either, but his past experiences with the riven have left him with more scars that you can see.

Accepting her hospitality and not overwhelming her with demands for answers has to be harder for him than the rest of us.

"Are there others living here?" he asks carefully, with a tick of his eyes so he can focus on her reaction as she answers.

"Not at the moment." Sulla lifts her teacup to her lips and takes a sip before going on. "There aren't many who make it to the Haven. I arrived at fourteen, and the two sorcerers already in residence then were nearly as old as I am now. They've since passed. I've been on my own here for nearly ten years. I was starting to think I'd be the last of us."

In my head, Julita shudders. *Ten years! It's a wonder she didn't go insane just from that.*

I try to imagine living somewhere—even a spot as magically animated as this one—for a decade without any human contact and have to suppress a shiver of my own. "Do you never come down the mountain to get supplies or… or anything?"

Sulla shakes her head. "We're only safe as long as we stay out of sight. If word got out about an odd woman who lives on the mountain, people would start poking around out of curiosity. And then it might all be ruined."

I'm starting to see why she was so unnerved by the five of us showing up together.

Alek glances around the room. "How have you kept yourself occupied all that time?"

"There's plenty to do. The sorcerers before me enchanted various entertainments, and we've amassed a collection of books —many written by the Haven's residents. There are gardens and animals to tend to. And one of the best things for a riven sorcerer who wishes to live in harmony with their power is meditation."

The scholar's eyes light up at the mention of books, but Sulla doesn't seem to notice his reaction. She scoops the last bit of her egg into her mouth and pushes to her feet. "Speaking of which, I should begin your training, Ivy. It's shocking that you've remained sane as long as you have without any guidance."

My stomach knots. I didn't get much out of Sulla last night, but she insisted on hearing the basics of my history, at least in relation to my magic. "I had a lot of motivation to keep my powers in check."

But my efforts haven't been without their problems. I remember Sulla wincing when I told her about the way my magic has lashed out—the pain that's seared itself through my lungs and gut so many times—and gulp the last of my roll. "I'm ready if you are."

If I can live to be as old as she is—older than many people in Silana who *aren't* riven become—without going mad with my power, I'd do just about anything.

Stavros catches my gaze, his eyes with their mix of brown and blue darkening with concern. "Take it easy. You know how to judge your magic's reactions best."

To judge whether it might slip my control, he means. He trusts my commitment to keeping my power in check, but not my power's demands to be unleashed.

"I'm sure we'll start slow." I turn to Casimir. "Did the tea help?"

When Sulla noticed his symptoms, she offered him an herbal brew last night and again this morning that she said should ease them. I haven't heard him sniffle since he woke up.

The courtesan beams at me and then at our host. "I feel much better already. Thank you. Sulla, I don't want to intrude on your privacy, but is it all right if I explore a little? I'm already intrigued by the many wonders you and those before you have created."

Rheave's face brightens. "Yes, I'd like to see them all too."

Sulla dips her head. "Feel free to wander within the boundaries of the Haven that I showed you last night. I only ask that you don't venture beyond them without me there to ensure we stay concealed."

"That's no problem at all," Casimir says.

Stavros motions to Alek. "I can run you through some more of our own training exercises. Ivy shouldn't be the only one honing her skills."

As Alek appears to restrain a grimace, Rheave pauses with a conflicted expression. "Maybe I should train too. In case there's any trouble for Ivy here."

His gaze follows me as I join Sulla by the doorway.

Sulla shakes her head with a light laugh. "No trouble will find us within the Haven. But you can pass the time however you wish."

She ushers me out of the room. As she leads me down the hall past the bedroom where we slept, her voice drops to a murmur. "Your companions do seem very devoted to you. I… I've never seen those who aren't riven themselves accept someone like us to that extent."

I give a rough chuckle. "It didn't happen instantly. And it helped that they'd known me for a while before they found out—and that Kosmel showed he was on my side."

"Still, it's a rare thing. Almost magical in itself. You're very lucky."

A twinge runs through my chest thinking of her many years of isolation. "I know. Most of the time I have trouble believing how lucky I am."

Julita huffs. *Not just luck. You earned every bit of devotion they offer you and then some.*

My mouth twitches in a smile of gratitude, but I don't pass on her comment to Sulla. We haven't seen any point in mentioning my other supernatural oddities.

The floor slants upward through the mountainside. We pass other rooms with door-less entrances, and I catch glimpses of the books she mentioned as well as various other collections of objects and storage containers.

I don't realize that we've wound around back to the surface until Sulla pushes open a door and the cool autumn air washes over me. We climb a winding path of stone steps past several slanted gardens with a variety of crops.

Magic dances in the air; little spurts of water erupt to dampen the soil.

Sulla escorts me through another doorway into a smaller interior structure that's no less fascinating than the first. A large bucket with a strange lid appears to be shearing grain off a set of stalks of its own volition. Drying herbs rustle as the thread they're hanging from creeps in a steady rotation.

"Most of the time I have far more food than I need," Sulla says. "But we've set up good systems for preservation. It serves us well when a newcomer finds their way here—and during the winter months when we haven't enough magic in place to grow very much."

We pop out into the mid-morning sunlight for another short trek past more gardens. Sulla points out a few shrubs in a cluster near the next doorway. "Mirewort, if you need it. We made sure to cultivate a few plants… This isn't any kind of a life to bring a child into."

I dip my head in agreement, taking note. In our hasty departure from the college, I left behind the small stash of the contraceptive herb that Alek procured for me.

I'll have to keep a supply close by from now on. It's not something I want to risk going without.

When we step through the next doorway, it becomes clear why the inhabitants of the Haven chose that particular spot to grow their mirewort. More golden light washes over the hallway and the rooms branching off it, which do have doors though those are currently standing open. Conjured warmth emanates from the rooms on the other side.

"These are typically the sleeping quarters," Sulla explains. "I've gotten into the habit of taking my rest in the base building since that's where I spend most of my time anyway, but you and your companions could retire here for the nights if you'd like. There'd be more room to spread out across. If that's something they're willing to do."

She shoots me an amused look that brings a flush to my cheeks.

"Then we wouldn't be quite so much in your hair," I say. I'm not sure how pleased she is to finally have some company, but she must have gotten used to having a lot of peace and quiet.

"It's fine. You're where you need to be. The gods saw to that. And this is where we'll do our most important work."

Sulla nudges open one final doorway, and we climb a dozen stone steps carved between two rocky walls. When we emerge onto the plateau above, I lose my breath.

We're nearly at the mountain's peek. Mica-laced stone glints all around me under the shining sun.

The tops of the nearest trees rise to the level of my knees. Over them, I can see all across Silana to where the vibrant green and mottled autumn leaves of the land meet the crystal blue of the sky.

Julita makes a sound with a sharp inhalation. *Wow.*

It takes me a moment to find my own words. "That's quite the view."

"I'm rather fond of it."

I tear my gaze away to take a closer look at the flat platform we're standing on. It's about ten paces across in a near-perfect circle, with the All-Giver's and each of the godlen's sigils carved along the edges.

Even though one of those godlen sent me here, my pulse gives a brief hitch at the call to the divine powers.

Sulla marks my reaction. "We ask them to have mercy on us and guide our way. Although you're the first I've heard of who's been guided quite so blatantly."

She motions for me to sit across from her. "Let's start with you telling me everything you can about how you've controlled your powers in the past."

Shaking off my qualms, I sink onto the smooth stone and lean back on my hands. The warmth of the sun and the crisp forest scents contrast sharply with the twist of discomfort her question provokes.

"I touched on it a little last night," I say. "It's hard to explain. I feel my magic clamoring to get out, get a sense of the things it could do, and I simply… refuse. I guess I tighten up my body against the urge. But mostly it's seemed to be willpower. The times when it slipped away from me have been more about mental distraction or haziness than anything else."

Sulla nods as if this doesn't surprise her. "Have you used any specific mental tricks? Imagery or similar?"

I reach back through my memories. "I instinctively picture my refusal as a sort of clamping down, like I'm shutting the power away, putting up walls around it. One time when I was really struggling, I imagined I was like a tree with a thick layer of bark that it couldn't break through."

"You should continue choosing concrete visuals that resonate with you and draw on them when you're tamping down your magic. We've all found that approach the most effective strategy." She pauses. "You also mentioned that suppressing it has led to some physical pain and possible injury."

I grimace. "Yes. For a little more than a year now, it's felt as if my power is attacking me from the inside when I refuse to use it. It only hurt mildly at first, but at its worst, the pain was so bad I couldn't stand, and I coughed up blood a couple of times."

Sulla sighs, the solemn cast that comes over her face making her look even older. "That's the most treacherous part of the magic that flows through our souls. If too much of it builds up inside us without being given a chance to act on the rest of the world, it'll act on us instead."

I run my hands over the warm stone. "But when riven sorcerers use their magic, they start to go insane. Isn't that true? I mean… I've never met any others besides you, but I can't imagine so many would have been hunted down if they weren't acting bizarrely enough to get noticed."

And Stavros has encountered at least two brutally violent riven firsthand.

Sulla's mouth slants at a pained angle. "Yes. It's a difficult balance we must all walk. We must use our power regularly to conserve our own bodies, but not so much that it starts to addle our thoughts. That's the main thing I can teach you."

My spirits lift higher than I've dared to let them since we arrived here. "So you've found that balance? You use your magic, and you manage not to harm anyone in the process?"

And not to go mad either. She's been aware of her power for more than thirty years, as far as I can tell, and she seems perfectly sane to me.

The older woman offers me a reassuring smile. "That's the most basic goal of the teachings we pass on here. I'm glad I'll have the chance to share what I was fortunate enough to learn."

My magic stirs in my chest as if it's picked up on the fact that it might get to play today.

I swallow thickly. "How do I start?"

Sulla smooths her hands over the skirt of her dress where it's gathered around her crossed legs. "One of the main principles is to keep the effects small. Just a little magic here and there. That makes it easier to keep a handle on both the external consequences and how the power affects you. Any of the more complex enchantments you see around the Haven are layers of smaller efforts that've been built up over time."

A laugh bubbles up my throat. "So you don't have all those augmentations just for your convenience. It's a way of channeling your magic into something useful, since you have to use it somehow."

"Exactly."

"But even letting a little out, there'll still be some kind of backlash."

"Yes," Sulla says. "That's inevitable. But using similar techniques to how you contain your magic, you can control both sides of the equation."

My eyebrows shoot up. "How? I've wanted to, but… it always feels impossible."

"That's the part requiring the most concentration and forethought. You should always plan both the impact you want to make and how the consequences should play out before you bring your magic to bear."

Sulla tips her head toward the sigil nearest to her, Jurnus's curving lines. "Let's say I wanted to carve this mark a little deeper. I need to think of what the obvious counteraction would be—if I'm reducing a little rock, something else would need to grow. And then I decide what I wouldn't mind seeing grow. Maybe the leaves on that shrub there."

She points to a spindly bush clinging to the edge of the platform.

"It's that simple?" I ask, barely able to believe it.

Sulla chuckles. "Not exactly simple. Not every effort you might want to make will have such a clear counter. And you need to imagine a reaction that's big enough to fit what you're trying to accomplish. That's why keeping things small is particularly important."

My heart is thumping even faster than before. "And once you've decided on all that…"

"You center yourself and ensure your mind is clear and your concentration steady. Then you picture both the action you want to carry out and how the countering energy should behave at the same time, as vividly as you can."

She closes her eyes, resting one hand on the sigil and the other on her knee with her fingers pointing toward the shrub. Magic quivers through the air.

As I watch, a few of the shrub's leaves tremble and stretch just a little longer.

When Sulla raises her hand, I can see that the etching digs deeper in the rock. She brushes a few bits of grit from her fingers.

"It only works if your choice of counteraction is appropriate," she warns me. "If you try to balance out your intentions with something unsuitable, the magic will act otherwise however it sees fit."

*Keeping it small definitely sounds like a good idea, then,* Julita remarks. *But, Ivy, if this works… you could do just about anything!*

Anything small. I'm not going to defeat the scourge sorcerers by carving little lines into stones.

But the idea that I could work with my magic even in this small way sets my pulse thumping giddily.

"Should I just… try it?" I ask.

"Why don't you borrow my example for your first few attempts?" Sulla gestures to the arching lines of Kosmel's sigil. "You could start with the godlen who guided you here, since he deserves some recognition for that. But take some time to simply meditate on your intentions and how you want them to play out first."

"Right."

I scoot over so I can rest my hand on Kosmel's sigil. Closing my eyes, I picture its shape in my mind.

I also imagine the shrub on the other side of the platform. The breeze licking over the leaves I'm going to channel the backlash into. The sun gleaming off their pale green surfaces.

Breathe in, breathe out. Steady the thunder of my pulse. Convince myself that I really can harness my magic.

It's only one small act. Even if I screw it up, no one should get hurt. But it doesn't even sound that hard.

When I've built up enough certainty inside me, I form the images in my head—the grooves of the sigil digging deeper into the stone, the leaves on the shrub growing bigger in return.

My magic tugs at me, eager to join in. I crack open the walls around it just slightly.

Just enough for a faint tingle to shoot through my arms, shaped by the pictures I've drawn in my mind.

My pulse skitters, and the images waver. In a sudden panic, I jerk my power into me so forcefully I rock backward.

When I lift my hand, the sigil looks lopsided. I pressed one side of the symbol a little deeper but didn't manage the whole thing.

One of the shrub's leaves has expanded about twice as large as the others. It looks rather ridiculous.

*It's all right,* Julita says. *It was great for a first try.*

I let out a bark of a laugh, but Sulla takes on a reassuring tone too. "That was an excellent start. See if you can hold your will firmer next time."

After periods of steadying meditation, I attempt my carving twice more. The second time I manage to even out the sigil, but I crack the tip of one of the curved lines.

Sulla has me focus on sealing the crack while snapping a twig off the shrub. I'm not sure I've ever felt as victorious as when the rough edge beneath my fingers vanishes alongside a light crack of broken wood.

I glance around the platform, newly energized, but Sulla

holds up her hand. "That's enough for one session. Even minor magic adds up. We'll find other ways to occupy ourselves for a few hours, and then we can return to practice in the afternoon."

I clamp down on the impulse to protest. She knows the safe limits of our magic far better than I do.

And the fact that I'm excited to keep going is a warning in itself.

HISTORIA

# Ten

*Alek*

The impact of Stavros's sword clanging against my dagger rattles through every bone in my hand. Possibly my entire arm.

I restrain my flinch as well as I can and sidestep the way he's shown us. The goal is both to block the blow that might follow and to put myself in a better position to find an opening.

My feet stumble on the rocky terrain. My arm whips out to steady myself, but I realize I've left my torso completely open with the same motion.

Stavros pauses, lowering his sword. "I think that's enough for today."

I straighten up, flushing with shamed relief and the lingering exertion. My hair clings to my forehead and the back of my neck, damp with sweat. My skin feels sticky beneath my shirt despite the cool mountain air.

I need to learn how to fight. It might be the only useful thing I can do out here without a vast library and records to turn to, without much in the way of practical skills beyond my ability to glean information from a page.

How could I stand against an army of scourge sorcerers with only book learning anyway? There are so few records that give even brief accounts of the old practices of the illicit magic.

But knowing how to do a thing and teaching one's body to actually do it are leagues apart.

I swipe at the perspiration on my brow, managing not to cringe at the texture of my uncovered scars, and glance toward the main Haven building. My relief deepens when I see that Ivy isn't even watching our current sparring match to have noticed my stumble.

She's standing with Casimir and Rheave, the latter of whom is examining a quiver of arrows he must have found in the Haven's many storage rooms. My chest tightens a little at the thought of him aiming those projectiles at targets around him.

How much can we really trust the daimon in our midst? How long will the dogged devotion he's shown to Ivy even last?

There are no records at all about spirit creatures inhabiting human forms.

As Stavros and I both amble over to join them, the daimon slides one of the arrows out of the quiver and then picks up the bow he rested against the outer face of the building. "I've seen these used before. You pull it back with the string, and it flies?"

Ivy lets out a wry chuckle. "I'm not the right person to turn to for archery advice."

Casimir holds out his hand. "I won't say my aim is fantastic, but I can show you the gist."

When Rheave hands the weapon over, the courtesan notches the arrow, looks around, and launches it at one of the broader trees along the edge of the small clearing. The head thumps into the bark a little right of center.

"Better than I could manage," Ivy mutters without any rancor.

Rheave's bright eyes have widened. He takes the bow back and grabs another arrow. "I like this. Better than swinging around a blade in the hand."

He positions the arrow exactly as Casimir did—a quicker study than I've proven to be with weaponry. With a twang of the string, he sends it soaring between the trees to smack into a more distant branch.

Ivy arches an eyebrow at him. "Are you sure this is your first time?"

"It makes sense," Rheave says with obvious excitement, snatching up another arrow. "The arc and the air and the tension in the string…"

He shoots a glance at Ivy, with a flare of fierceness in his gaze that somehow sparks both approval and uneasiness in my chest. "I can protect you from up close and from far away."

"I'll be very safe from any murderous trees that descend on us," Ivy says, but she pats the daimon's arm at the same time. "I'm glad you've found a form of combat you like, if only so you and Stavros don't need to squabble so much."

Stavros glowers at her with obvious affection before turning to Rheave. "Unless you want to climb those trees to get the arrows back, I'd suggest you stick to targets that aren't quite so distant. I don't imagine there's a huge supply of weaponry here."

Rheave hums thoughtfully. "How would a soldier practice?"

Naturally, Stavros knows all about that. He motions Rheave over and sets about constructing a couple of suitable archery targets at the edge of the woods.

I sit down on a stump that's been carved into a stool, finding a strange enjoyment in the graze of the cool air over my bare face. It's been years since I stepped outside without my mask.

My pulse still lurches from time to time when I remember that my scars are exposed, but none of my current companions react to them. There's nothing to really stir my insecurities.

It's unexpectedly freeing not having that small but constant weight against my skin.

Rheave works through the quiver of arrows with swift efficiency, landing all of them in the inner three circles of the makeshift bullseye Stavros created. I can't deny that the daimon has some strengths—and that his eagerness is admirable.

While Stavros offers a few tips, Casimir disappears into the building. The courtesan returns holding a metal flute that flashes as it catches in the sunlight.

He props himself against the wall and starts to play. The lilting tune winds through the air, drawing Stavros's and Rheave's attention.

The daimon bobs with the melody as he yanks the arrows from the target. "Music is better than shooting," he declares.

A laugh escapes Stavros that he then looks startled by, but he allows Rheave a small smile. "I suppose that depends on whether you're under attack."

He pauses, his gaze settling on Ivy with a brief tick of his head. The intensity in his expression has me bracing myself, but there's no hostility behind it now.

He steps toward her, holding out his hand. "Seeing as we're not under attack at the moment… I missed the chance to dance with you at the one college ball you were able to attend. I wouldn't mind remedying that oversight."

Ivy gives a laugh of her own, a blush touching her pale cheeks as she takes his hand. "I could probably use a little more practice at dancing like a lady, in case I need to play one again."

Stavros offers her a sly grin. "Who says I want you to dance like a lady?"

Ivy casts her gaze toward me for a moment, catching my eyes with a quick smile that I can read easily enough. She's telling me that I'm included too. I'd imagine I could have the next dance if I ask for it.

Of course, I'm not much more graceful a dancer than I am a sparring partner.

As Casimir keeps playing, an unexpected sense of peace settles over me. Stavros turns Ivy with the music, Rheave sways in his own sort of dance, and the mid-day sun beams down on all of us as if we're part of a strange new family.

And I'm on the outskirts of that family, even though I've been by Ivy's side for far longer than the daimon has.

The serenity I felt disintegrates. I don't want to feel like an outsider in this unnervingly immense mission we've found ourselves on.

The ground has shifted beneath all of us, and I need to get my footing.

The cotton shirt I wore for sparring has stiffened against my torso with dried sweat. I duck through the nearby doorway and make my way up to the sleeping building where I left my regular clothes.

Sulla has managed to provide us with a couple of spare sets, washing what we've discarded despite our insistence that we could take care of that ourselves. It was easier to stop protesting when she showed us the washer tub that churns the clothing all by itself once it's filled with soapy water.

I'm not sure where our host has gone off to at the moment. She seems to prefer to give us our space—or to recover her own—outside of meals and her training sessions with Ivy.

But she did give us permission to explore all of the Haven's buildings. I don't think she keeps even her own bedroom locked.

Not that bedrooms are on my mind right now. After a quick shower thanks to the magic conveying the mountain stream's water through the Haven, I head back to the main building where I found one particular spot I can put the skills I've already cultivated to use.

A room down the hall from the dining area has built-in shelves on either side. One set holds various sources of entertainment: wooden board games, a couple of faded sets of cards, toys that suggest some of the Haven's inhabitants arrived here at an even younger age than Sulla did, and a few musical instruments. I assume this is where Casimir found the flute.

The other set of shelves holds a varied assortment of books, many of their covers crumbling with age.

I've already perused the contents a few times in the past

couple of days. Most are fiction, either books of tales past residents brought with them or stories they wrote themselves. I found a journal kept by a sorcerer who lived here nearly a century ago, which I spent a few hours yesterday carefully paging through, but he mostly talked about his efforts cultivating new crops through both traditional means and magic in the Haven's gardens.

So far, I've avoided the oldest volumes in the collection, mostly out of respect. I'd be a horrid guest if I destroyed the Haven's archives by having the ancient texts fall apart in my hands.

The books stashed away here haven't benefitted from the professional archival efforts of royal or temple librarians. I can see signs of rot in the leather, scraps of paper that've already cracked off their brittle pages.

But there's nothing else left for me to check. And those aged volumes are the ones most likely to contain some piece of information I don't already know.

Something that'll help us convince the king of Ivy's worthiness or defeat the scourge sorcerers? That might be too much to hope, but I have to try.

I ease one of the older books off the shelf, wincing as the leather binding crumbles more against my fingers. Sinking into one of the two armchairs set against the wall between the shelves, I open the pages as carefully as I can.

This one is handwritten, and it took some water damage before it arrived here. Many of the words are lost to splotches. Some of the paper sticks together too tightly for me to risk cracking it apart.

What I can read appears to be instructions for various games I've never heard of, with other pages holding tallies of scores. New entertainments that past inhabitants made up to pass the time here?

I set that one back in its place and lift another book that looks more professionally bound. It turns out to be printed, with ink that's held up fairly well over the years, but it's a guidebook to the animals of the Abandoned Realms. Interesting but not particularly useful to my purposes.

I work my way through several more books until I reach one with thick leather binding and an attached strap. The strap snaps in half when I loosen it, and in my horror, I almost put it back.

Leaving it alone won't fix the damage, though. I take a deep breath and peel back the cover ever so delicately.

This is one of the books where the pages have started to fragment. Chunks are missing along the edges in an erratic pattern.

What's left of the pages is hand-written in a scrawling, disjointed style that I'd find difficult to decipher even without pieces missing. Staring at it, I almost give up again.

Then my eyes catch on the word *riven* in the midst of the mess.

Girding myself, I study the letters closely.

*They call us riven… don't know what that… something happened to us… I want to keep a record… went through the Great Retribution… but when the fire came…*

My heart beats faster. Is this the writing of one of the original riven sorcerers, born in the wake of the Great Retribution? They might know more about the scourge sorcery that brought down the All-Giver's rage than we do.

I peer at page after page until my head starts to ache from deciphering the messy scrawl and the fractured sentences.

As far as I can determine, the writer was alive not long after the Great Retribution. They saw the effects of the destruction and kept their magic hidden because of a few early experiences where people reacted with horror.

There's no mention of scourge sorcery, though. I suppose the writer had enough of their own problems without accounting for anyone else's illicit magic.

Then I come to a page that's nearly whole, just ragged along the edge.

*...never asked for this. Did I want our world torn apart by those who use death for their own gain and seek to bend the entire continent to their will? Of course not. But to be turned into a vessel for the gods' power—to be used like a weapon with no will of my own so they can defeat those villains, bringing down a hail of fire and destruction—and then left with my soul cracked open now that they no longer need me... Why have I been punished for serving our deities as they chose?*

I stop at the end of the page and simply stare blankly, my breath halting in my throat. The writer can't really mean...

It sounds like they're saying the gods used *them* to fight the scourge sorcerers. That the effect of the divine power is what cracked their soul.

Not born that way as a lingering punishment, but purposefully created as a tool.

That contradicts everything I've read before about the origins of riven magic. Why would the gods let people who served them be shunned and driven to insanity?

Maybe this one was already going mad and had delusions clouding their mind. Or maybe they convinced themselves of this story to justify other destruction they caused with their magic.

I turn the page with a shaky hand, but the next few only vent about the hardships of a trek on the road between towns with no mention of magic at all. The several pages after have lost too many chunks for me to glean much of the subject. There's a brief account of seeing the silvery mountain top and deciding to try to reach it.

And then I arrive at the end of the journal.

There's nothing definitive, nothing to confirm his stories. They're as likely to be the ravings of a near-lunatic as anything we should put any stock in.

What good would it do Ivy to bring up the possibility when I have no reason to believe it isn't utter nonsense? I can't trust a word of it unless I find other accounts that corroborate the writer's story.

As I get up to search the shelves for any records that might give a clearer picture, a thud in the hall brings my head jerking around. I dash over to the doorway.

Rheave is kneeling on the floor a few paces down the hallway, his hand braced against the wall. He's frowning at his knees, but he looks up at my arrival.

"I… My feet moved the wrong way," he says. "I tripped right over them."

I offer him a hand to help him back up. He shifts his weight tentatively and then stiffens.

"What?" I ask. "Are you all right?"

His frown deepens. "I think the creator of this body is trying to call me back."

The daimon's gaze darts up to meet mine again, panic flickering through his expression. "It's only a faint tug right now, but what if they pull harder? How can I stop them?"

That… is a very good question.

I open my mouth and close it again, realizing I don't know what to tell him.

Until a few weeks ago, I wouldn't have believed it was even possible for magic to create a living body to house a daimon that could pass for a human being. How would I have any idea how they might control it?

But the fact that he's asking at all, that he cares this much, makes me want to help him. Is this how Ivy felt when she agreed to have him join us?

Gods above, how many other types of magic have I read about? I should be able to give him some sort of answer.

As I grope for the right thing to say, Rheave adjusts his posture in that slightly alien way that reminds me he isn't used to having a body at all. He's a creature of pure spirit trapped in a physical cage, as much as he's come to enjoy his new home.

Perhaps the answers aren't in the magic involved, but in the rights of possession. I watched my parents haggle with customers often enough to know that negotiating any kind of deal centers around claims of ownership.

My thoughts whirl and come together with a quiver of inspiration. "It's your body they're trying to take back, not your spirit, isn't it? They can't control what you think or feel?"

Rheave nods. "The body is the part they made."

I tap his chest lightly. "But it's yours now. They gave it to you. The more you can convince yourself of that, the more you may be able to pull away from their hold."

The daimon peers at me. "How do I convince myself?"

"Think about all the ways you control that body now. All the things you can do with it. Move it around to prove that you get to decide what it does."

Rheave looks down at his well-built form. He claps his hands together and stomps his feet against the stone floor, and a grin springs across his face. "Yes. Yes, it is mine now. They can't have it back."

He bounds off down the hall with renewed energy. I watch him go with a tendril of dread winding through my gut.

I hope he's right about that.

What will it mean for the rest of us if my little trick isn't enough?

# Eleven

*Ivy*

The petals unfurl above my fingers. My pulse flutters at the incredible feeling of their velvety surface blooming with life.

Of course, my magic is dealing out death as well. I chose a twig on one of the hunched saplings around the stone platform to shrivel as the bud blossomed.

When I open my eyes, the yellow flower beams up at me. A glance at the twig confirms that it's turned wizened, its beige bark transformed into dark gray.

I slump back against the stone beneath me. The act has left me depleted even though I've created much vaster effects with my power before.

The concentration needed to moderate both the intended effect and the consequence drains me faster than simply tossing my magic out into the world.

That and the increased clamoring of the magic I *haven't* let out.

I turn to the imagery I've found resonates most with me: a leafy vine wrapping around me, like the plant I took my chosen

name from clinging to the oak in Ewalin's yard in Slaughterwell. As I picture it winding densely together, shutting away the thrum of energy inside me, my power gradually settles.

But it's still simmering there, eager for me to stretch its capabilities more.

Sulla smiles with a crinkle at the corners of her eyes and pats my shoulder. "You've been doing very well. I think tomorrow we can start making minor adjustments around the rest of the Haven. More practical matters and slightly larger effects that could sustain you for longer before your magic becomes demanding."

My mouth goes abruptly dry. "Really? You think I'm ready for that?"

This is only my fourth day of training. I haven't slipped from my intentions since the second afternoon, but the single flower I've just invigorated is the most potent act I've carried out.

And nothing I affect up here matters all that much. If I crack the stone or snap a twig I didn't mean to, no one suffers for it.

If I falter in my control around the rest of Haven, I might ruin a treasured relic or valued tool that the sorcerers here created over decades of work. I could hurt Sulla or one of my men.

"I'm sure of it," Sulla says without a hint of hesitation. "You can still come up here to meditate and ground yourself, but it's important to get comfortable working your magic in everyday settings. Especially if you still intend to leave the Haven once we've finished your basic training."

I know she doesn't approve of that goal. From what she's said, I may be the first sorcerer to train here and not stay on. But the scourge sorcerers and their unknown leader, whoever stood even higher than Ster. Torstem in the Order of the Wild, are still out there, wreaking havoc or planning to.

I can't just sit on my ass while the rest of the world falls to ruin. That would be almost as bad as carrying out the destruction myself.

When I get to my feet, energy continues humming through my chest and limbs. I might not have done anything spectacular with my magic during our twice-daily sessions up here, but I've used it more times in the past four days than I have in my entire life before.

My power feels primed now, ready to spring out of me at a moment's notice even though there's no threat to provoke it. The sensation makes my gut twist.

I picture the vine tamping it down again and take a deep breath to steady myself.

I'm in control. I decide how I use my power.

Sulla says that once the habit of using it in minor ways becomes familiar, I'll find its presence reassuring rather than unnerving. I'll know that my defenses won't allow any power to slip free without my permission.

It's hard to imagine that level of comfort right now.

Thankfully, as we walk down the mountainside through the network of buildings, the movement of my body pushes my awareness of my magic into the background. The woolen dress I've customized with slits to my thighs swishes against the loose trousers I've turned into an underskirt.

Out here, away from noble society, I could simply wear pants and tunics like I used to on the streets. But I've come to appreciate how much easier it is to keep my blades close at hand but concealed with riding-style dresses.

While we descend, Julita stirs at the back of my skull. *Hmm. I wonder what you could do first? Add a little picture to the walls? Try to fix up one of those old books Alek's been obsessing over?*

Both suggestions sound potentially complicated. I lift my shoulders in a slight shrug.

By the time we reach the main building, I feel almost like myself. Sulla drifts off to tend to her gardens, and I head toward the sound of voices carrying from the dining room.

Rheave is sprawled across a couple of the cushions by the table, plucking slices of pear out of a bowl. Casimir sits across from him with a cup of tea, and Stavros is pacing as much as the short width of the room allows.

"—what they'd do next," he's saying as I reach the doorway. He halts both his pacing and his remarks at the sight of me.

His restlessness sets my heart thumping at an uneasy pace. "Is something wrong?"

The former general offers me a crooked smile. "Not that we're aware of." He pauses. "Can you see much from that perch where you do your training?"

The memory of the view swims up in my mind. "I can see a lot, but it's mostly wilderness other than a few farms farther off. Why?"

Stavros sighs. "I wish we had more of an idea what's happened since we left Florian. I know what the king's first steps would have been, but without any sense of what the conspirators' continuing plans were…"

The twist in my gut tangles into a series of knots. It's because of me that we're here—because of me that we've been totally cut off from the rest of the world for days.

In all the time we've already spent here, I've only gotten the slightest grip over my magic. How long will it take me to harness the vast stores of power that can flow through my riven soul?

My throat constricts against the words, but I have to say them. "You don't need to stay. If you want to go back and start helping with the military efforts—"

Anguish flashes across Stavros's chiseled features. He steps forward and grasps my arm to stop me. "Ivy, that's not what I meant. I'm not leaving you. You should have us supporting you while you grapple with your magic."

His voice still tenses slightly when he speaks of the practice I've been doing. He can't help seeing my use of my potentially destructive power as a different sort of battle.

I paste a smile onto my face, willing my voice to stay even. "I'm taking things slow, so you don't need to worry about me. If it would make sense—if you could help more that way… I don't want to feel like I'm holding you back."

"You're not. We're here so you can be properly prepared for all the threats we're facing, and then we'll have the best chance of overcoming them together." He lets out a rough chuckle. "I'd simply like a better idea of what exactly we're facing so I could prepare more in the meantime."

Rheave pops one last bit of pear into his mouth. "Is there any way you could find out without going far away? Humans have ways of passing news along, don't they?"

Stavros rubs his jaw, appearing to give the daimon-man's suggestion his full consideration. "Not to random farmers, I wouldn't think. But I suppose…"

He glances toward the map he found in one of the Haven's storage rooms that he was poring over last night. "I'll have to think on it. There's no point in taking a risk if the benefits wouldn't justify it."

I swallow down the lump of guilt. "If you come up with a plan, I'm sure it'll be a good one."

"Thank you for your unconditional confidence," Stavros says dryly, but he leans in to give me a quick kiss.

It's the most public he's been with his displays of affection, the heat of his mouth reassuring and thanking me, and gone sooner than I'd like. When he draws back, Rheave is watching us avidly.

I flush at the daimon-man's intense attention, but he shifts it completely to Stavros a moment later. "If you don't have any other plans right now, you said there were more advanced techniques with the bow and arrow. Would you show me?"

Stavros chuckles. "I suppose that's as good a way to pass the time as any. We'll have you toppling scourge sorcerers in no time."

Julita snorts. *It figures that he'd get friendlier as soon as military skills were involved.*

My mouth twitches with amusement. Regardless of the

reasons, it's nice to see that the former general seems to finally be warming up to our newest companion.

As Stavros motions for Rheave to follow him, Casimir takes one last sip of his tea and gets to his feet too. The courtesan ambles over to join me while the other men stride off to continue their combat training.

"Where's Alek gotten to?" I ask.

"Oh, he's buried in the books he's found." Casimir grins fondly. His voice is back to its usual smoothness now, all traces of his illness gone. "I don't think he's in any hurry to return to the rest of the world."

I try to laugh, but it comes up in a hitch. "At least that's one of us."

Casimir studies my expression, his hand rising to stroke up and down my back. "Are *you* all right, Ivy? Sulla's mentioned that your sessions with her are going well, but you've seemed more and more tense the past couple of days."

I give my body a little shake as if I can shed the worries that've gnawed at me. "I *am* getting better at controlling my magic. There's just so much of it to contend with. I feel like I've only just learned how to stack pebbles and I've got a whole mountain looming inside me."

"If there's any way any of us can help..."

"I know." I lean into his touch, unable to hold back a sound like a purr when he trails his fingers right up the side of my neck. "Unfortunately, since the magic flows through *me*, it's really up to me to handle it on my own."

"That's a lot of responsibility for any one person to have to take on." Casimir caresses my cheek and teases his fingers into my hair, sending tingles over my skin. "It's been weighing on you. Hmm. You're done with your training for the day, aren't you? How would you like to take a break from having to be in control?"

I peer at him through lowered eyelashes, swaying with the pleasure his touch provokes. "What do you mean?"

The courtesan offers a smile of promise that sends another tingle straight down the middle of me and clasps my hand. "Come with me, and I'll show you. It's been too long since I got to do any real pampering."

*Ooh,* Julita murmurs. *I want to see where he's going with this, but then I'll give you your privacy.*

I'm not going to deny my ghostly passenger a little taste of the bodily pleasures she can no longer experience herself. She never sticks around for very long when things heat up with my men.

Casimir leads me through the Haven to the building where we've been sleeping. Most residents have made do with plump mattresses right on the floor, but one of the rooms has a full if low wooden frame. After we first explored the rooms, the men insisted I take that bed.

"Wait here for a moment," Casimir says. He vanishes down the hall and returns holding a bundle of silky fabric. He tugs the door shut behind him. "Let's undress you first."

"Just me?" I ask as Casimir sets the fabric down on the bed and reaches for my plain dress. "Shouldn't the nakedness go both ways?"

"I'll take care of myself and you. All you're going to do is enjoy the experience."

Julita giggles. *Well, I think that's my cue to go.* She dwindles into the faintest of tickles at the back of my skull.

I'm not sure I'm totally on board with Casimir's goal. The courtesan has a habit of putting everyone else's needs—and pleasure—over his own. But for the moment, I gamely help him strip off my dress and underclothes, everything except the ribbon I keep tied around my upper arm in memory of my little sister.

The magical warming system in this building takes the edge off the autumn chill. Casimir nuzzles my cheek with a gentle kiss, his closeness warming me even more, and then nudges me over to the bed. "Lie down on your back."

The cozy fabric of the blanket cushions my old scars. As I comply, Casimir picks up his bundle of silk and unravels it into a few separate strips of fabric. He winds the end of one around my ankle and glances up at me to judge my reaction.

My heart skips a beat. "What exactly are we doing here?"

Casimir dips his head to press his lips to the top of my foot. "Making sure you're fully aware that you're not in control of this interlude—and you don't need to be. What do you think, Kindness? Can you let me completely take over?"

When he says the words in that heated tone with the gleam of desire in his eyes, it's hard to imagine why the idea should unsettle me. Of all my men, Casimir has never hurt me even unintentionally.

I trust him with my life. Trusting his skills with my body is nothing compared to that.

Still, my limbs have tensed at the idea of being bound. Casimir strokes his fingers over my calf, watching me.

"We don't have to do this. But I think it might be good for you. Offer you a chance to remember that you can give up control without any kind of disaster. If at any point your feelings become too intense and you want to stop, all you have to do is say so."

I drag in a deep breath, anticipation and my own desire overcoming my instinctive reluctance. "Okay. Keep going." I let my gaze rove over his lean, graceful frame in the simple tunic and trousers he's wearing. "But you did promise I wouldn't be the only one undressed."

Casimir chuckles and obligingly strips off his shirt and pants, leaving only his drawers. While I ogle his deliciously toned body freely, he ties the end of the cloth around my ankle to one side of the footboard. Then he repeats the process with my other ankle on the opposite side.

He's left me spread open, my sex bared—and dampening with a heady heat as he flicks his hungry gaze over it.

But the courtesan isn't finished preparing me yet. He moves

to the top of the bed and binds my wrists together over my head, just snugly enough that I'd struggle to release them but not to cause any discomfort. He attaches that strip of fabric to the middle of the headboard's slats.

"There you go," he murmurs, bending over me. His lips graze my cheek, my jaw, my throat. "There's nothing you can do. Nothing you *need* to do. I'm the one in charge here, and I'll play with you as I see fit."

I haven't heard Casimir sound quite so domineering before. His tone sends a giddy quiver down my spine.

He swings his leg over my waist to straddle me and captures my mouth. I give myself over to his searing kiss.

Part of me still wants to resist. My arms flex against their bindings with the urge to wrap my arms around my lover, to run my fingers down his chest.

A tremor of my magic reverberates against my ribs, offering to release my restraints.

I focus on the sparks of delight conjured by the press of Casimir's lips and the caress of his hands down my torso. It's not up to me what happens here. I don't *have* to decide. I don't have to try to keep up or give back equally.

As I sink into that acceptance, it's a weirdly freeing idea.

Casimir nibbles his way along the edge of my jaw and down to the crook of my shoulder. Bliss flows over my skin from every place his lips mark with their delectable heat.

When he nips my collarbone, my hips jerk of their own accord. Casimir's tongue darts out to smooth over the spot. "Oh, we're just getting started, my darling."

As he continues to tease his mouth along my upper chest, he strokes his fingers up from my belly to cup my breasts. He swipes his thumbs over my nipples in tandem, bringing a gasp to my throat at the combined jolts of delight.

Casimir works several more increasingly urgent sounds out of me with every skilled swivel of his hands. He kisses his way down my sternum, pulling backward so he kneels between my splayed legs.

The erection tenting his drawers brushes against my core, and I can't help arching toward him with a needy whine. Casimir hums and laps his tongue over one stiffened nipple, letting the vibration of the sound carry through the gesture.

"We have lots of time to get to that. I won't be satisfied until you're absolutely drenched for me."

A strangled noise escapes me. "I think I'm already there."

"But I still have so much to enjoy here." He slicks his tongue over the other nipple to set off a renewed pulse of pleasure. "You're at my mercy, Ivy. I decide when you're ready."

My disgruntled huff breaks into a moan when he sucks the tip of my breast right into his mouth.

He strums it with his tongue and then scrapes the tips of his teeth across the peak. All I can do is writhe against my bonds with bliss.

He teases and suckles that breast until my head is hazed with the sensations, running his fingertips up and down my sides at the same time to spark even more delightful quivers. With another satisfied hum, he turns his attentions to my other breast.

One hand slides over my belly to delve between my legs. His hot breath spills over my breast in an approving sigh. "That's what I like to feel. And I'm going to enjoy it fully."

I understand what he means when he eases farther down the bed and lowers his head to where his fingers were just fondling me. The first swipe of his tongue over my clit makes my hips buck to the limits of my restraints.

The courtesan shoots me a pleased grin and buries his face between my thighs.

With every movement of his lips, every swirl of his tongue and graze of his teeth, ecstasy floods me. It washes over me in waves, until I can't stop myself from straining against my bonds, rocking into his mouth to urge on my release.

Casimir sucks hard on my clit and curls two fingers into my

channel to stroke me from the inside. But just as I shudder to the edge, he pulls back a few inches.

I growl in protest, my sex aching with need.

The courtesan licks my arousal from his lips and glides his fingers over my inner thighs. "You'll come when I decide."

"Fuck," I groan.

But when he laps his tongue over me again, I have to admit the pleasure spikes through me even more forcefully. The burn of need deepens into a searing sensation that spreads all through my body.

Casimir works me over just as thoroughly as before. He thrusts a third finger inside me to fill me even better while he teases my clit with his mouth.

Every nerve in my body trembles giddily. I sway with the movements of his tongue and hand, spiraling toward my peak—

He pulls back at the last second again with a low chuckle that could almost make me come on its own.

A sound slips from my lips that's almost a sob. Casimir presses a tenderly apologetic kiss to my hipbone and tugs off his drawers.

My pulse skips eagerly at the sight of his rigid cock. He rubs it across my sensitized folds in careful strokes until I really am sobbing… and then he plunges into me in one smooth thrust.

The sudden pressure sets off a chain reaction inside me. Pleasure crackles through my nerves and bursts through my body.

I bow my head against the pillow, crying out with the force of my climax.

Casimir holds still while my channel clamps around him, his skin flushing with restrained desire. When the haze clears from my vision, he smiles wickedly down at me. "We're not finished yet."

I'm too wrung out with bliss to argue. And not a single part of me *wants* to argue when the courtesan starts to rock into me.

He has to lean close to hit the right angle, clasping my hip with one hand and bracing his elbow next to me so he can caress my breast with the other.

He builds up his pace so gradually it would be torturous if I hadn't just come. As it is, the ache of bliss builds slowly and steadily with every thrust until it's radiating all the way to my toes and fingertips.

Casimir hits just the right spot to send an extra jolt of pleasure up the center of me. I let out a ragged moan—

And the bedroom door slams open.

Stavros jars to a halt on the threshold, his stance stiffening at the sight of us. As Casimir tilts farther upright to glance over his shoulder, a ruddy cast creeps up through the former general's light brown skin.

He takes a step back. "I—I heard you cry out. I didn't mean to interrupt."

My whole body has flushed hotter, first with embarrassment and then with a thrill at the matching heat that's sparked in Stavros's eyes.

He's never seen any of the other men do more than kiss me before. His hand has closed into a fist as if he's tempted to punch the courtesan right off me, but hunger blazes in his eyes.

Maybe I'm just high on the pleasure that's already flowed through me, but it seems like a good idea to say, "You don't have to go. You could join in."

The next instant, my gaze darts to Casimir. I've immersed myself in his control enough that I'm not sure if I've stepped out of line.

He beams when he sees me check with him, flicking his thumb over my clit as if in reward, and looks at Stavros again. "Yes, you could. I'm teaching our lady a lesson in letting the rest of us take on some of the responsibility around here. She might pick up the material even faster with a professor pitching in."

Stavros wets his lips. Part of him is still hesitating, but his gaze smolders hotter.

With a strangled groan, he hurtles across the room and

drops down at the edge of the bed by my shoulder. His fingers trail through the sweat that's formed along my clavicle and up my neck to tip my chin toward him.

Then his mouth crashes into mine with all the ferocity I expect from this man.

As Stavros's kiss consumes me, I notice a light tug and a loosening at my ankles. Casimir has adjusted the strips of silk to increase their length without completely freeing me.

He guides my knees into a mild bend and then lifts my ass so he can ram into me while staying upright. When I gasp against Stavros's lips, the former general only kisses me harder.

The courtesan picks up his pace, filling me over and over again. The head of his cock strokes the most sensitive spot deep inside.

At my next moan, Stavros tears his mouth from mine to scorch a path to the crook of my jaw. His hand teases over my chest to cup one breast.

His cocky drawl, turned nearly liquid with lust, resonates into my ear with a tingle of his breath. "You like letting him take you, hmm, Lady Thief? How much can you open yourself up? Let's see you give him everything."

I thought I already was, but the words make me whimper with the desire to comply. Somehow I manage to splay my hips even wider, to buck even more eagerly into Casimir's thrusts.

The courtesan groans in approval and rests his thumb on my clit. He fingers me as deftly as if he's playing a song on my body while he pounds into me ever faster.

Stavros nips my earlobe before his darkened voice reaches me again. "So obedient for once. See how good it can be when you let someone else call the shots? Next time it'll be me driving into you, taking you right over the edge."

The combination of the promise and Casimir's talented thumb sends me careening into ecstasy with the courtesan's next thrust. As the blaze of my second orgasm roars through my body, a ridiculous stream of sounds tumble out of me.

Stavros's mouth brands the side of my neck, his fingers stroking my breast through my release. Casimir's grip on my ass tightens, and then he's bowing toward the other man as he loses himself to his own climax.

We linger there for a minute, breathing heavily, coming back to ourselves.

Casimir slides out of me with all his usual tenderness and caresses my thigh. "You can always count on us to take care of you, Ivy."

"In every way we possibly can," Stavros adds in a raw voice.

Casimir unties my ankles and then my wrists. My hands immediately dart out to slip around the backs of their necks, drawing one lover and then the other in for another kiss.

As we nestle together for a moment, still coming down from the high, a pang reverberates through my chest.

Casimir made his point. I know not everything here depends on me.

But gods above, do I wish nothing at all depended on any of us. That we could stay here in this cocoon of peace for the rest of our lives.

What's going to become of the trust and understanding we've forged when we have to face the judgment of the outside world once more?

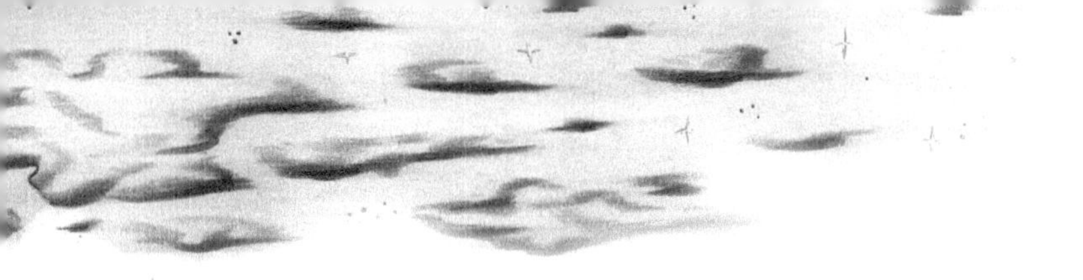

# Twelve

*Stavros*

The sun is sinking by the time I spot the crossroads up ahead. I turn my stallion to the left before I reach the marker, a mix of trepidation and relief congealing in my gut at the sign that my destination is close at hand.

I've been riding for hours, but I've made it here in about the time I expected. I wanted darkness to be falling before I approached the small fort where one of my old colleagues has been posted for the better part of the past year.

I tie the horse well out of view of any road and make the rest of my approach on foot.

There hasn't been much military activity in this part of the country in years, so I don't encounter any sentries patrolling the grounds around the building. I'd imagine Major Pawlem has gotten a little restless while overseeing this post. But it's not far from the Icarian border to the southwest, and they could rush to help if Darium came at us across the Seafell Channel to the east.

The forest has been cleared around the stout stone building with its high surrounding wall. The fort will house the major, a captain or two, and perhaps thirty infantry prepared to run a

first line of defense against an attack. They'll mostly have been occupied with tracking down local bandits and highwaymen.

I stop at the edge of the clearing where the shadows of the trees still conceal me, the tart scent of the autumn leaves filling my nose. Lanterns gleam in several of the windows. The soldiers may be just sitting down to their dinner.

I spot a figure in the tower that juts up over the arched doorway and two others standing guard on the ground on either side of the gate. As I watch, one makes a brisk circuit of the wall. They talk in low voices for a few minutes, passing the time with idle conversation, and then the other makes his own circuit.

Pawlem will be inside. I don't fancy marching into the midst of a squadron that may have gotten orders to arrest me on sight, so I need to contrive a reason for him to come out here.

I considered the problem for the entire ride out here, but I still pause and work through it in my head before stepping forward. One misstep, and this errand I decided to attempt will put everyone I care about at even more risk than before.

The two soldiers on the ground snap to attention the moment I've taken two paces from the trees. I stop before one has even hollered, "Who goes there?"

I keep my prosthetic tucked under my cloak so they can't identify me by it. The cloak's hood and the thickening dusk should hide my next most distinguishing feature: my hair.

I can't do anything about my face or size, but it's relatively unlikely that either of these two will have encountered me in person for any significant length of time. The plain trousers and jacket I borrowed from the Haven won't fit their image of the great General Stavros.

"I'd like to speak with Major Pawlem," I say evenly. "I assume he's still stationed here? But I'd prefer to keep the conversation outside for discretion's sake. If one of you go in and tell him the man he always beat at three-snap has stopped by, I'd imagine he'll come."

I've kept my tone mild, with just a hint of the commanding

air I'd have projected if I had any real authority here. The pair draws themselves even straighter, studying me with more intense concentration.

I'd imagine they're not quite sure what to make of a man who dresses like a peasant, speaks like a noble, and refers to their superior officer with such familiarity.

The woman replies first, with a stern expression to offset her obvious confusion. "I think you'd better come inside. If the major is willing to speak with you, you should see him there."

"For the security of the country, I feel that would be unwise." Really for my own security, but a call to patriotism should work better as motivation. "Pass on the message. If he refuses, we can worry about alternate arrangements."

The soldiers step closer to each other to murmur in private conference. Their hands rest on the hilts of their swords at their hips. I keep my hand loose at my side, well away from my own blade, but I'm ready to retreat into the woods if they decide to take an aggressive approach.

They're good infantry, looking out for their commander and the safety of the fort. Watching them sends a twinge like homesickness through my chest.

It's been over a year since I last commanded anyone other than the students at Sovereign College. I never felt anywhere near as alive in the classroom or the courtyard as I did planning strategy, giving pep talks, and leading forays along the borders.

My vision fogs, reminding me of why I'm never going to take on that role again. What I'm doing right now is the closest thing to fighting for my country that I'm capable of anymore.

Before I can wallow in the loss, one of the soldiers ducks into the fort. The other remains, eyeing me warily. I keep my careful distance from the building, both so I don't appear a threat and so they can't pose much of one to me.

The last glow of sunlight fades from the sky. I shrug my cloak closer against the bite in the wind—and the gate swings open.

Major Pawlem looks much the way I remembered him: keen eyes wide set in his tan face, sandy hair pulled back in a short ponytail at the nape of his neck, average height made more impressive by the assurance with which he carries himself.

He strides a few paces from the doorway and stops there with an expression of disbelief I catch in the moment before my vision hazes again. "Gods above. What in the realms are *you* doing here?"

I note with relief that he hasn't brought any additional soldiers with him, at least not right out of the fort. Knowing Pawlem, he has at least a few waiting on his call just beyond the gate. His cleverness didn't only extend to card games like three-snap.

He's also been circumspect enough not to name me in front of his charges. Which means he isn't yet sure whether he should report my presence here or not.

I smile grimly. "I'm trying to avert a nation-wide disaster. And I was hoping we spent enough time together that you know I *would* be on the side of averting it rather than causing it."

He lets out a huff of a sigh and motions to the soldiers at the gate. They hang back while he ambles toward me, but their gazes stay glued to me, watching for any threatening movements.

Pawlem wears a sword of his own, his hand resting casually on his belt within easy reach of it. He comes to a stop about halfway between the fort and my position near the trees.

He doesn't want to open himself up to an easy ambush either. That's perfectly fair.

I walk to meet him, watching for any trickery on his end. No one else stirs around the fort. A raucous laugh filters faintly through one of the lantern-lit windows.

The soldiers are having a little ale with their dinner, from the sound of it.

I draw up a couple of paces from my former colleague: close enough that we can speak without his underlings overhearing, far enough that he'd have to lunge to stab me.

I pitch my voice low. "I'm sorry to come to you like this. You're probably aware that my situation has become rather... fraught. I won't take much of your time. I've been cut off from my usual sources of information—I wanted to confirm that the royal family is still safe and find out whether there've been any additional attacks since the assault on the palace."

Pawlem lets out a rough chuckle under his breath. "You have missed a lot. Is it really true, Stavros? You've given your loyalty to one of the *riven*?"

I manage to work a wry note into my next words. "Strange as it might seem, it turns out there's more to them than their powers, just as there is with every other human being. And this one happens to be the key to fulfilling my loyalties to the Crown, as hard as the king finds that to believe at the moment."

"I'll say. By rights, I should arrest you. He's calling you a traitor."

I grimace. "He didn't give me much of a chance to explain myself. But I swear to you, Pawlem, on the souls of all the men and women we saw fall in battle, I'm serving him as well as I know how, whether he can understand my methods or not."

The major takes a few moments of silence. Even without twitching my head to clear my vision, I can feel him studying me.

He wasn't one of the officers I worked most closely with, but he rode out under my command enough times for me to have felt this visit worth the gamble. There was a time when the man in front of me trusted my word implicitly.

He once helped lead our squadrons on a rambling hike through icy wind and drifts of snow because I said it was the best route to come at our opponents' flank. On another occasion, he had his cavalry charge straight through what looked like a wall of fire after I assured him it was only illusion.

But now he isn't sure he can even talk to me.

Pawlem swipes his hand across his mouth. His gaze darts from me across the nearby trees. "Is she here?"

I don't need to ask who he means. "No. I came alone. For *her* safety."

He sighs and shakes his head. "I never thought I'd see this day. There are patrols sweeping the countryside looking to hunt you down like a common criminal, you know. Have you gone as mad as the riven do, throwing everything you've worked for away for some woman?"

It takes all my self-control not to bristle. "If you knew her, you'd realize she's more than that. And as I said, my decision has to do with what's best for our entire country. I can understand that's hard to accept. You don't have to believe it. But what would it hurt to answer the questions I asked?"

Pawlem appears to deliberate silently with himself. Then he makes a flippant gesture as if to say, *Why not?* "I'm not going to tell you where the king and his family have settled for the time being, but the last I heard, they were all still alive and uninjured."

Thank the gods.

I take a deep breath. "And the miscreants who attacked them? Has anyone significant been apprehended? Have they made any further moves?"

Pawlem's jaw works as if he isn't sure he's comfortable telling me. Or maybe he's simply uncomfortable with the fact of what he has to say.

His voice comes out strained. "There's been a rebellion in one of the northern provinces up near the Bryfesh border: Eppun."

My heart lurches. "*What?*"

Pawlem scowls. "We've only gotten information in dribs and drabs out here. But it seems some group claiming they know the gods' true will has inflamed the commoners and displaced the local counts and countesses. The heir to the seat of Coliz up and murdered his parents to stake a claim for what they're calling the 'Order of the Wild.' There's been heaps of turmoil in Nikodi and Selce as well."

I resist the urge to reach for my sword, as if I could cut down the traitors from the other side of the country. Frustration sears through my gut.

The scourge sorcerers have managed to gain that large a foothold—to commandeer an entire province? How long have they been laying the groundwork for this uprising without us realizing?

"And they've swayed enough civilians to their 'cause' to hold the territory?" I ask.

Pawlem's scowl only deepens with shared frustration. "You know what the outer provinces can be like. Always thinking the capital isn't doing enough for them. They feel left out, so they decide the sophisticated ways of the urban nobility are suspicious. It'd be easier to win them over with seditious ideas than anyone else."

It would indeed. My hand flexes at my side with tension I don't give in to. "The king can't let that kind of mutiny stand."

"No. But they're giving the army a difficult time. From what I understand, the traitors haven't tried to march any closer to the capital yet. I suppose they learned their lesson with their attack on the palace in Florian. Instead, they've been challenging the king to come and face them himself. But it's not as if they're standing on a field waiting for a charge. The first few squadrons sent up that way were ambushed and handed their asses."

"They want to pick away at our forces, wear us down until they see an opening," I mutter. It's the kind of tactic many Silanians turned to during the uprising against the Darium empire several decades ago—a solid tactic, even if I hate knowing it's being used against us now. "And the more soldiers the king sends out there, the fewer he has protecting him."

Pawlem nods. "That's about the size of it. Bad business all around. I'm sure we'll quash them eventually… but I don't like how much it'll cost us along the way."

I can't share his certainty about the first part. He hasn't

witnessed scourge sorcery firsthand—he has no idea how fanatical this Order of the Wild can be.

They mean to see King Konram burn one way or another.

"Thank you," I say to Pawlem, because I am grateful for the intelligence even if I'm horrified by it as well. "I'll do whatever I can to see our country set to rights."

He raises an eyebrow. "Not with riven magic, I hope."

An uneasy twinge runs through my gut at the thought of the power Ivy's been working at the Haven. Practicing the vicious magic that's hurt her as much as those around her, attempting to tame it.

Gods only know how much it'll ruin—including the woman I love herself—if it yanks free of her hold.

I force a small smile. "I would never rely on just one trick, my friend. And I never risk more than we stand to gain."

When I tick my gaze away and back, I can see enough tension in Pawlem's stance and expression to recognize that he doesn't fully trust my judgment now. He isn't really my friend, even if he played along with me for now.

He thinks he has something more to gain here too.

I don't want to assume the worst, but present circumstances require expecting it. And I promised Sulla I'd take every precaution to ensure no one finds out where I've been staying.

I bob my head to Pawlem. "I'll take my leave of you, and I won't bother you again. I hope our next meeting is under better terms."

"So do I," he says as I turn away.

I walk into the forest in the opposite direction from where I left my horse. After several minutes, I stop at a particularly dense stretch of brush and sink back against a tree trunk.

It doesn't take long before I catch the crack of a twig and the rustle of boots through fallen leaves. What little hope I had left deflates.

Pawlem sent people to track me. No doubt he imagines he'll

turn me and all my treacherous companions over to the royal patrols for much reward.

My gift might not work with my damaged vision, but I can still see some moves before they're made.

I stalk onward through the woods as if I'm being cautious but unaware of my pursuers. When I reach the farm I spotted on my way here, quiet with the fallen night, I ease into the barn and select the largest of the horses.

With a silent prayer of apology to Prospira for disturbing this family's livelihood and a request to guide the animal home safely, I lead it out around the back of the barn where the soldiers won't have followed too closely yet for risk of being seen. Then I whack the horse on the rear hard enough to send it galloping over the nearest hill.

There's a scuffle of hasty footsteps from the woods as the soldiers must rush off to alert companions hanging back on steeds of their own. I wait until I've watched two stealthy soldiers on horseback crest the hill before trekking back to my actual mount.

By the time they find the horse and realize it's riderless, I should be well out of easy tracking range. And I know all the techniques to ensure they can't follow my path by more complex means either.

But as I swing into the saddle and set off, all I can feel is the weight on my shoulders.

The Order of the Wild is claiming our kingdom, including the county Julita once expected to rule. Even so, King Konram wants Ivy's head—and the rest of ours too—on a platter.

There's truly no one we can count on across the entire kingdom except ourselves.

# Thirteen

*Ivy*

An unexpectedly homey atmosphere has developed in the Haven's dining room. As the five of us gather around the table, I try to let the warmth of the company I have distract me from worries about the man who's not currently with us.

Even if all went well, Stavros wasn't sure he'd return before noon. There's no reason to fret.

As Sulla sets the dishes she prepped last night on the table, Casimir reaches for the tea pot. He's gotten into the habit of pouring out the tea for all of us—remembering that Alek likes just sugar in his, I prefer only cream in mine, Rheave wants both, and Sulla takes neither.

As the pale cream swirls with the darker tea, the daimon-man leans over next to me and tips the end of his spoon into it.

"Watch," he says eagerly, and gives the metal handle a little wiggle. Somehow he creates an image like a spinning leaf in the tea's surface for a few seconds before it wisps away.

The playful gesture distracts me a little more. I smile at him

gratefully and tune out the skip of my pulse when his face turns even more stunning with his smile in response.

I pluck up an egg and pass the platter to Alek, because I know he'll want at least two. As I gulp down my own, Casimir nudges the basket of biscuits toward me.

I've just taken my first bite of the rich, nutty dough when footsteps thump into the hall. Before I can do more than swallow, Stavros appears in the doorway, hair windblown and expression fraught.

His voice comes out rough. "The scourge sorcerers have already struck again."

Alek's eyes widen. "What? How?"

With a grimace, Stavros launches into a recounting of his conversation with his former colleague.

By the time he's finished, the biscuit I was eating has crumbled between my clutching fingers. I can feel it disintegrating in my hand, but all I can do is stare at Stavros.

My voice rasps on its way up my throat. "They've taken over an entire province?"

Stavros bows his head in acknowledgment. He must be exhausted—I don't think he could have slept at all since he left yesterday morning, expecting to reach the fort where a friend was stationed by the evening.

But all I see on his handsome face is horrified determination.

"The better part of Eppun, at least," he says. "And the major's information would be at least a couple of days behind."

Julita speaks in a strained murmur. *They took Nikodi… What have they done to my parents?*

It's obvious that Stavros doesn't know more than he's already told us—and that his uncertainties are gnawing at him.

Casimir reaches along the table to squeeze my forearm. At his reassuring touch, I finally drop the chunks of decimated biscuit, brush the crumbs from my fingers in a daze, and turn my hand to clasp his.

The courtesan manages to keep his voice calm, though the

grip of his fingers betrays the tension he's holding back. "It sounds like their goal is the same as it's always been: destroy Silana's rulership and establish their own."

Alek's lips have tightened. "The heir who's taken over Coliz —who murdered his parents to do it—he was an entomology club member under Ster. Torstem before he graduated three years ago."

He glances at Rheave. "Does this uprising line up with anything you remember hearing or orders you were given?"

The daimon-man shakes his head, his forehead furrowed beneath the fall of his dark curls. "I don't think so. That could be where most of the others like me were sent—to the north. But I never paid attention to names of things like counties and provinces in my natural form."

Why would it matter to a spirit-creature what lines humans drew on a map or what they called the territories on either side?

I swallow thickly. Any appetite I had left has fled. "The people who are standing with the Order of the Wild can't know who they're really supporting, can they? They wouldn't push for scourge sorcerers as our new rulers."

*I should certainly hope they can see through the degenerates' lies,* Julita says hotly. *It'll be their kids the fiends are carving up next. Great God help us, what if they've already started?*

My stomach lurches with horror echoing her own. If the conspirators could get away with hiding their sacrificial accomplices right under the Crown's Watch's noses within Florian's walls, how much easier would it be in a far-flung province?

Stavros's mouth twists. "I'd imagine they've hidden the source of any powers they've displayed. They'll be presenting themselves much as they did to new recruits like you supposedly were—as true believers who want to bring the country back into harmony with the wishes of the gods and unseat greedy despots who've abandoned real faith."

Casimir swipes his free hand over his face. "And the people

of the border provinces will have taken to that message much faster than anyone in the city. A lot of them are already inclined to see the rest of us as selfish prigs."

"The king should be able to expose the scourge sorcerers," Alek says. "He knows."

Stavros sighs. "Maybe he's tried. We don't know what's going on out there. But the conspirators have captured the people's attention first. They can claim he's telling tales to discredit them and protect himself."

I wrap my arm around my churning stomach. "The members of the Order of the Wild might even believe they *aren't* scourge sorcerers. I never heard any of them refer to their magic that way. And they don't seem to think the All-Giver would object with another Great Retribution. Maybe they've convinced themselves that they're different—that it's acceptable magic as long as they aren't outright killing anyone in sacrifice."

Who knows how those sadistic psychopaths think?

And now they're filling the heads of tens of thousands of people with their nonsense. How many ordinary civilians will march with them the next time they strike directly at the royal family?

Gods help us, where will we be if they manage to take over all of Silana?

Sulla has been watching the conversation in silence from her spot at the head of the table. She clasps her mug between her hands. Her knuckles have paled.

"It's a long way from here," she says evenly. "And all will end as it should. The entire army will be defending the king."

The entire army other than the soldiers he's sent to hunt me down.

"They aren't providing a very effective defense, from the sounds of it," Stavros says. "Guerilla tactics are difficult to stamp out. And we still need to defend our border with Darium, or the emperor will take advantage of the lapse to attack. If the conspirators spread our forces too thin…"

He can't help speaking about the army as "we" rather than "they" even a year after losing his position. The frustration in his voice wrenches at me alongside my nausea at the thought of the atrocities the scourge sorcerers have committed.

The words spill out before I've thought them through. "We have to go."

Every head around the table jerks toward me, including Sulla's. Casimir's grip on my hand tightens. "Ivy—"

I sit up straighter, conviction swelling in my chest. "We know better than anyone what the scourge sorcerers are like. We know their attitudes and their tactics. And we have an ally who can identify other captured daimon." I tip my head toward Rheave. "We could speak to people who are hesitant about the Order of the Wild, build up a local resistance, pick away at the uprising in ways the army couldn't."

Rheave perks up. "I'll help you any way I can."

Even Julita seems to liven up. *I know many people in Nikodi, especially those living near our estate. I'd be able to help you make contacts and determine who's taken charge.*

Stavros's stance appears to firm at my words, but his gaze darkens. "We'll have to cross most of the country—if any of the soldiers catch you, they'll kill you on sight."

I gaze right back at him. "Then that's a risk I'll have to take. I've been risking my life to stop these psychopaths from the start. I'm not going to risk *less* when they're hurting so many more."

Alek taps his finger against the table, his shoulders rigid with tension but his tone abruptly invigorated. "We could solve both of our problems, couldn't we? We already thought that dismantling the conspiracy was the answer. What would prove our loyalty to the king more than putting down the uprising? No one could argue that Ivy's a threat if she's just saved the entire country from a scourge sorcerer coup."

Stavros pauses and then nods slowly. "We could request a

royal pardon. The locals we collaborate with would speak up for her too."

"For all of us," I put in, in case he's forgotten that there's a bounty on his head as well. "But that's not the most important part. We *have* to stop whoever's leading the Order of the Wild —soon, before they destroy even more than they already have."

Sulla's voice breaks in, a slight quaver running through it. "You can't."

The mug trembles in her hands. As she sets it down, I stare at her. "Why not? We can't wait while they take over the entire country."

"It's too dangerous." Sulla thumps her fist against the table. "You haven't been training even a week yet. It could take years to fully master your power, especially when you've gone so long without guidance. You want to help—what about the harm you could do?"

The question lances right through the middle of me.

As I grapple with my words, I see Stavros hesitate.

But Casimir speaks up first. "Ivy's kept control over her magic on her own for all those years. I'd say that's more than enough proof that she can avoid unnecessary harm."

"And this might be her only chance to convince the king that she deserves to have a real life," Alek adds.

Most of the color has drained from Sulla's face. "The riven don't get to have those kind of lives. We stay here where it's safe for both us and the rest of the world."

I manage to push my voice past the lump in my throat. "You knew I was planning to leave. This is just a little earlier than I expected."

"Too early. I can't condone it."

*Who says she gets a vote?* Julita mutters. *This woman barely knows you.*

Casimir speaks again in his gentle way. "You could come with us. *You've* had years of training, so your control over your powers must be impeccable. And you could continue guiding Ivy along the way."

A rush of hope fills me. I smile at Sulla. "Yes. You could be so much help with your mastery over your magic. We can find another horse for you—we'd make sure—"

"No!" Sulla cuts me off with a scrape of her chair legs as she springs to her feet. "Neither of us should be going anywhere. Maintaining the right balance in a carefully controlled setting is nothing at all like dealing with a war like what's sparked out there."

I stare at her. "Then we'll figure it out. We'll be careful about bringing our power to bear. It's better than doing nothing."

Her gaze burns into mine. "You don't know that."

A little anger prickles through my disappointment. Julita's right—Sulla doesn't really know me. Maybe she doesn't care if Silana descends into a mass of torment and suffering, but she should at least be able to understand why it matters to me.

I push myself to my feet so we can eye each other on an equal level. "You don't have to join us, as much as I'd like you to. But we need to do this. *I* need to do it. It's my country too, no matter what most of the people in it think of me. The last thing we need is another Great Retribution."

Which could mean even more riven, more sorcerers torn between unbridled power and madness. Has she even thought about that part?

If she's thinking it now, she doesn't care about those consequences either. Sulla lifts her chin in a stance haughtier than I've ever seen from her. "You won't listen to reason. Who knows what blunders you'll make."

Before I can protest, she sweeps out of the room.

Casimir stands next to me, stroking his fingers up and down my arm in a soothing gesture. "She's upset, but it's not her place to choose what's right for you. Kosmel always supported your quest against the scourge sorcerers."

"He did," I say, the thought bolstering my resolve.

Alek looks at Stavros. “How long will it take us to reach Eppun on horseback?”

Stavros’s gaze goes distant with thought. “The college horses are good stock, and they’ve had plenty of time to rest. Depending on the weather and how many diversions we need to take, I’d hope we could cover that ground within a week or so.”

My pulse hiccups at the thought of all the things that could go wrong in a week of scourge-sorcery-driven warfare. “We need to get moving right away, then. It shouldn’t take long to—”

A clatter from the hall outside interrupts me. We exchange a glance and hustle out of the dining room in a mass.

Sulla is just tossing a shape I recognize as Rheave’s quiver of arrows into one of the smaller storage rooms. As we hurry toward her, she tosses the dagger Alek was training with and the camp pot we used during our trek after it.

“What are you doing?” Rheave demands, rushing to the front of our group.

Sulla holds up her hand to stop him while shoving the door closed with the other. A tingle of magic in the air tells me she’s sealed the room with more than physical force.

She swings her hand toward the far end of the hall as if to lock the door that leads to the higher buildings as well.

“Whatever you brought here is part of the Haven now,” she says in a ragged voice. “You’re not taking any of it with you. And you’re not getting very far without your equipment.”

She’s trying to force us to stay.

My heart plummets. How are we going to get by on a week-long journey without most of the supplies we arrived here with?

How much farther will she go to stop us if we linger any longer? If we’re leaving, we have to go *now*.

Stavros’s expression has hardened. Any doubts he might have had about the validity of her concerns appear to have vanished.

He marches toward the sorcerer. “This isn’t your decision to make.”

Casimir tucks his hand around my elbow and leans close so

only I can hear him. "We left a few things in the saddle bags down where the horses are stabled. I don't think she could have grabbed anything there yet. We'd better get to them first."

Sulla's head swings toward us. Her mouth sets with determination.

She must have come to the same realization we just did.

I bolt for the nearby doorway, the one she hasn't sealed yet. It's a short scramble down the stone steps built into the mountainside to the covered wooden shelter where we've been keeping the horses.

The men hurtle down the steps behind me. Sulla's cry carries after them. "No! I can't let you do this. You're meant to be here."

At the base of the stairs, I dart to the side, letting the men charge past me to prepare the horses. Toast nickers, either in greeting or to protest that I'm not attending to him myself.

Sulla scrambles after us, her eyes wide. She catches her balance against a hunched sapling just a few steps away from me and stares past me toward the makeshift stable.

Her hand rises again as if she intends to cast out more magic.

I step right in front of her, my own magic unfurling through my chest with an unnerving but potent vibration. "Is this really what you want to do, Sulla? You're going to protect the world from being hurt by my magic by hurting us with yours?"

The desperate look she gives me sends an ache through my heart. "You don't know what could happen."

I gather all my determination in my posture and my voice. "Neither do you. I know where I'm meant to be, and it's not locked away up here for the rest of my life. Not when there are good people down there who'll definitely be hurt if I don't step in."

Sulla looks down at her extended hand. Her arm shivers, and she lowers it to her side with a mumbled curse.

She's probably already let loose more magic in the past few minutes than she normally would in a week. I can't imagine she had enough time to think through the consequences. How much damage has *she* done to her own home?

Seeing her hopeless expression, I can't help giving her one more chance. "You could still come with us. We'll keep each other in check. I'd appreciate your guidance just as I have here. Please."

Sulla meets my gaze again. There's so much anguish in her eyes that my throat closes up.

"We're not meant for the rest of the world, Ivy," she says. "I know that. I pray that you realize it as well before too many others pay the price."

# Fourteen

*Ivy*

My mentor's words echo in my head long after we've left the Haven behind. With every step I take down the mountain, a boulder seems to sway in my belly.

Sulla saw my power firsthand. She knows more about the riven than anyone else I've encountered in my twenty years in this world.

What if she's right that I shouldn't trust myself? Tackling a province-wide uprising is going to challenge me a lot more than tangling with a small group of conspirators at the royal college.

My men have stayed mostly silent as we descend the mountain, concentrating on leading the horses well so none of us breaks a leg. As the ground between the trees levels out, Stavros draws to a halt at the head of our group and reaches for his saddle to mount.

The rest of us move to follow suit, but Casimir stops me with a touch of my shoulder. He trails his fingers up to my jaw and leans in to claim a kiss.

The heat of his mouth reminds me of all the ways he took charge the other day, of the fleeting freedom he offered me from

my responsibilities. Which maybe is his intention, because when he draws back, he says in a firm but tender tone, "We're facing this crisis together. If you need anything, we'll be right there with you."

I gaze up at him with a swell of affection. "I know. I couldn't do this on my own."

*And you shouldn't need to,* Julita pipes up in my head. *But I do look forward to seeing the bunch of you accomplish what the king's whole army hasn't managed. He'd better realize he never should have cast you out.*

As I haul myself into Toast's saddle, I appreciate my trousers and the slits I cut in my dress's skirt overtop more than ever. At least my legs will stay decently warm in the late autumn air.

Stavros glances back at the rest of us. "We should take stock. See what equipment we still have—what supplies we're starting with so we know what we might still need. I have my sword."

He taps the weapon at his waist that thankfully he wore on his trek to the nearby fort.

I look down at myself. "I've got two knives—one in my boot and one on my thigh. The other two, you were using for your combat training. Sulla must have confiscated them."

"We'll want more weapons then. Is anyone else carrying anything of use? What's in your saddle bags?"

We keep the horses walking at a sedate pace while we check the baggage attached to the saddles. My favorite noble dress that I was wearing when we rushed to the royal family's aid is still bundled up in mine, along with the military uniform and a few extra apples. The men all have their uniforms too.

Alek has the tent, which we haven't needed to use since arriving, and Casimir has one blanket. We brought the others up to the Haven buildings when we were first getting settled in.

We have two canteens between us, which Stavros and Rheave already refilled at the mountain stream. We all wore our cloaks coming down from the sleeping building, so we're not doing too badly for outerwear. Although I'm not sure just how cold it'll get in the north with winter creeping in.

Casimir finds the makeup he used to partly conceal Stavros's and Alek's faces, however much use we might get out of that. And the four of us have our enchanted lockets that we can signal each other with if we separate.

Stavros hums pensively when we've finished our accounting. "We can forage for food, but hunting won't be easy with just a sword and a couple of knives. We'll see how far we can get with my snares. It'll be a lot harder to start fires without the flint. And we're awfully short on blankets."

Alek glances at Rheave. "Could you start a fire with your daimon powers?"

Rheave peers at one of his hands. "I'm not sure. It seems to go straight to burning without any flames."

"We didn't see any fire at the palace, only scorch marks and charred things," I acknowledge, and hesitate. "I suppose we could… borrow a few things from one of the farms around here?"

The idea of stealing from farmers who are eking out a living sits much worse with me than pilfering from the overflowing coffers of greedy merchants.

I suspect Stavros can sense my reluctance. He knows my aspirations as a thief were to give to the commoners who needed it, not take from them.

He scans the horizon and turns his stallion a little to the right. The rest of us follow suit automatically.

He motions with his prosthetic toward the route ahead of us. "About halfway to the fort, I spotted a military marking that indicates an equipment stash nearby. The royal army has hidden stores across the country for emergency situations. There'll be food rations and weapons and probably some tools and the like as well."

Alek tenses in his saddle. "Will it be guarded?"

The former general shakes his head. "That would defeat the

purpose of hiding it. We'll have to be careful because of the patrols the major mentioned, but that's the case no matter where we go. And the stores aren't checked often. Supplies taken from one are much less likely to be noticed and commented on than a farmyard theft."

My uneasy spirits settle. "Let's make that our first stop, then. If scourge sorcerers taking over the country doesn't count as an emergency, I don't know what would."

We nudge the horses to a trot, not wanting to push them too hard when we have a long journey ahead of us. Alek lets his mare fall back closer to Rheave.

"When we reach the north, it sounds like there could be quite a lot of other daimon that the scourge sorcerers have turned into accomplices," the scholar says. "How close would you need to be to distinguish between them and actual people?"

I peer over my shoulder in time to see the daimon-man cock his head. "I think I'd just need to see them clearly. Someone in the same city square or across a clearing like the ones we've been in should be fine—there's a feeling I get."

"You'll let us know if you do see any?" I ask.

Rheave draws himself up straighter at my attention. "Of course, if it would be helpful. I'd like to know what's happened to the others like me."

"It'd definitely help," Stavros remarks from ahead of us. "At the very least, it'll let us know there are likely to be scourge sorcerers in the area."

Alek adjusts his grip on his reins. "And do you know any way to disable them or, well, free them other than killing them so the bodies imprisoning them turn back into clay? Or to break the scourge sorcerers' hold on them so maybe we don't have to?"

Rheave knits his brow. "I think… I think if the one who cast the magic that can command us died, the other sorcerers wouldn't be able to control us anymore. But the previous orders might linger for some time. And I don't know who cast the magic. From what I've seen, the bodies remain whole and living, containing us, as long as they're alive."

Alek was obviously hoping for a more useful answer than that. He lets out a mild disgruntled sound.

After a moment, he ventures another question. "How long have you been in existence anyway? Were you around for the Great Retribution?"

Rheave hums. "I've heard talk about that time for a while, but I don't remember experiencing the sorts of things people mention happening. My memories do become blurry fairly quickly, though. We don't pay much attention to the passing of time, only what we're doing in the moment."

"Ah." Alek pauses. "You said you could tell when Kosmel reached out to Ivy. Do the daimon interact with the godlen often? Have *you* ever talked to one directly?"

Why is he asking about this? Does he think Rheave might be able to plead for our cause with the other lesser gods, prevent another hail of vengeful fire?

If so, it appears we're out of luck. The daimon-man lets out a chuckle. "I sense when they come, but they don't usually pay attention to us. And we don't really… talk, even to each other, in our usual form." His tone abruptly brightens. "Maybe we should. Talking can lead to many interesting discoveries."

Stavros sounds as if he's restrained a snort, but Rheave's enthusiasm brings a smile to my lips for the first time since we left the Haven. He manages to find so much wonder in the world even in dire circumstances.

There *is* so much that's wonderful in this world, no matter how difficult the road ahead of us becomes. That's exactly why we need to save the world from those who'd twist it to their sadistic ends.

As the trees thin up ahead, the former general twists in his saddle, his voice low. "We should avoid any talking now unless it's absolutely necessary, until we're back in the cover of the denser woods. Our voices will carry farther over open ground."

Rheave clamps his mouth shut with an emphatic nod.

We cross the fields and weave through a stretch of forest beyond them. The sun is just past its peak, gleaming through the leaves, when Stavros motions to a small carving on a tree trunk.

It's Sabrelle's sigil surrounded by a circle with a few other, smaller etchings I don't know the meaning of. But Stavros clearly does.

He urges his stallion to the right, and the rest of us follow. Several minutes later, he turns left at another etching. It can't be more than a few minutes after that when we arrive at a small glade.

When Stavros dismounts, we all do the same and gather around him. He kneels to brush aside the fallen leaves to reveal a smooth, round stone. When he lifts that up, a steel hatch shines in the early afternoon sunlight.

The former general pauses. The center of the hatch holds the imprint of the Melchiorek family crest, like he had on his old sword that must be back in his chest in his quarters at the college.

He sits back on his heels with a faint growl. "Shit. I didn't think about that. Every officer carries a seal that could unlock this, but obviously I don't have mine. The entrance is locked with magic."

My power twitches in my chest. Casimir and Alek both glance toward me, as if the answer is inevitable.

Maybe it is, but my lungs constrict even as my magic squirms through them. None of my training with Sulla prepared me specifically to set my magic against a spell already in place.

I don't know how to counter that properly. I don't know what the consequences would be if I can't focus on a proper balancing effect.

Stavros is already uncomfortable enough about my magic without me screwing up on my very first attempt at using it since leaving the Haven.

Rheave shifts his gaze to me too. My hands clench at my sides.

We *need* what's down there. That matters more than anyone's opinion of me.

The backlash for opening a lock can't be *that* immense, can it?

I open my mouth, but before I can force out the offer, Rheave pushes in front of me and kneels by the hatch. "My power might be able to break the magic on it. Ivy should save hers for when no one else can help."

I stare down at him, not sure what to make of his declaration. Is he only thinking in practicalities… or did he realize how conflicted I was?

The daimon-man is directing all his focus at the hatch now. He rests his hands on the edge of the metal surface. "I think the rest of you might want to back away."

We all take a step back, apprehension rippling between us. Rheave leans closer to the hatch. He exhales in a soft hiss.

Energy crackles across the hatch in a burst of light with a metallic squeal. The daimon-man lurches backward as if shoved by the force he's exuded.

I leap forward automatically, ducking down to catch his shoulders before his head slams into the dirt.

The impact knocks me off-balance too. I tumble sideways, falling to my knees with the daimon's head landing on my thighs.

As I catch my breath, Rheave gazes up at me with his unearthly eyes. I'm still clutching one of his shoulders, close enough to his head for his glossy brown curls to graze my wrist.

He reaches up to brush his fingertips along my jaw, so delicately a flutter passes through my pulse. "Thank you, Ivy. You protected me too."

Before I can sort out the sudden clash of emotions inside me, Rheave sits up with a jerk and motions to the hatch. "Try it!"

Stavros moves first, hooking the end of his metal prosthetic around a small fingerhold in the steel circle. He tugs at it—and the hatch lifts with a faint creak. A trace of a burnt scent wisps through the air with the movement.

Casimir laughs lightly. "Now that's a use for daimon magic that I can approve of."

As Stavros peers into the blackness below, I slip between the other men to join him. "I can go down first. I'm used to finding my way in the dark."

The former general frowns as if he's about to argue with me, so I don't give him the chance. Spotting the glint of an upper rung, I plunk myself down at the lip of the opening and hop onto the ladder inside.

"Ivy," Stavros protests, but I'm already clambering the rest of the way down.

When my feet hit the earthen floor, I glance up at his looming form. "Why don't you move your massive self out of the way so I can get a little sunlight down here?"

I catch a muffled guffaw that sounds like Alek. Stavros mutters something about insolent ladies under his breath but draws back from the opening.

I choose not to remind him that I'm more a thief than a lady and study my surroundings in the beams of sunlight that streak past the hatch.

A few rectangular shapes that I determine are cots lean against the wall near the ladder. In case a few soldiers need to hole up here for a while?

Beyond them, the room stretches off into darkness, the light only catching on the edges of crates and chests. I step closer and make out the shape of an empty lantern propped up on one stack.

Squinting and groping, I find a set of shelves carved into the wall that hold, among other things, a tin of beeswax candles and a flint. In a matter of seconds, I have the lantern flaring. The sweet scent of the wax mingles with the loamy odor of the packed soil around me.

Stavros must catch the flare of the light. "Keep watch," he says to someone above and climbs down to join me with Alek following close behind. I guess he's left Casimir and Rheave on guard duty.

The lantern has illuminated the entire space, which is rather impressively large for a secret room no one much expects to use. There are houses in Slaughterwell you could fit in here.

It appears Stavros knows his way around. He strides past the shelves and the crates to the very back of the room, where the lantern's glow is now reflecting off several metal surfaces.

A sort of weapons rack is embedded in the back wall. The former general taps his fingers against the hilts of several swords that don't meet his approval and finally picks out a short one as well as a fighting dagger that I suspect is for Casimir and a hunting knife.

"Get over here," he says with a motion to Alek. "See if you can find at least one blade you'll feel reasonably comfortable with. Ivy, you can take your pick too."

Back in familiar territory, I pluck up the smallest two knives and fit them into the vacant sheaths in one boot and on one thigh.

As the scholar studies the weaponry with a grimace, Stavros hefts a bow and a quiver of arrows that was leaning against the wall nearby. He considers the other few quivers and shakes his head. "We can only carry so much. But the daimon will be happy."

While he carries our new arms up to the surface, I pry at the lids on a few of the crates. One proves to be full of various nuts, while another holds strips of dried bloodfruit.

I hold up one of those to show Stavros as he returns. "So many delicious meals ahead."

He raises an eyebrow at my sarcastic tone. "Better than starving."

*I suppose he has a point there*, Julita says, but she doesn't sound any more enthusiastic about the rations than I am.

Alek has shoved a thin dagger under the belt around his tunic and is checking the chests. "Here are some blankets," he announces. "There are spare clothes down here too, but they don't look any warmer than what we already have."

Stavros nods. "They stock what's appropriate for the area. If we want heavier wear, we'll need to find a stash up north."

I move to the chest to inspect the offerings. "We should each grab a set anyway. Two layers is warmer than one."

"Ah!" Stavros snatches up what looks like a ball of twine from a lower shelf. Closer to the lantern, I see it gleams like steel. "Wire will make for easier snares. You'll have something to eat other than nuts and bloodfruit, Lady Thief."

"Let us all rejoice."

We paw through the rest of the supplies, but Stavros is right that there's only so much we'll be able to carry. We have to balance equipping ourselves with our need for haste.

As it is, carrying our findings to the surface, we determine that we can't take quite as many blankets as I'd have preferred. We all put on an extra tunic now so that we don't have to find space for them in the saddle bags.

Stavros gives the hatch one last look before he moves to cover it again, with a tense expression that dampens my delight at our find.

This isn't how he would ever have expected to access one of these storerooms—as a fugitive, breaking in and technically stealing from it.

We really are criminals now. And we have a long road ahead of us before we can prove ourselves to be anything different.

# Fifteen

*Ivy*

Toast gives his mane a rebellious shake as he trots along, but his gait has turned more sprightly on the even ground. After three days of traveling through woodlands, we've decided we can risk taking one of the smaller country roads, at least as long as it's cutting through forests rather than fields so we can't be seen at a distance. It's hard to keep up a good pace picking through the brush.

Stavros is still taking the lead, since he's the one with by far the best idea of where we're going. A couple of times he's ridden ahead alone to check road markers, but mostly he seems to be guided by the sun and the occasional landmark.

We all scan the trees warily as we ride, our passage silent other than the clop of the horses' hooves. My ears are pricked for any other sound that could alert us not just to a patrol but local brigands as well.

Although with most of us visibly armed, in peasant-style dress, and carrying little cargo, we probably don't look like ideal targets for a robbery.

It's only when we stop for a brief break that we speak again,

in lowered voices. Casimir passes around handfuls of nuts and bloodfruit, and Stavros checks our steeds' horseshoes for stray pebbles while they graze.

Rheave drifts over to the trees while chewing on his dried fruit and trails his fingers over the leafy vine that's wrapped around one of the trunks. "Ivy," he says thoughtfully, and looks over at me with a glint in his eerie eyes that's almost sly. "Is it strange that you have the same name as a plant?"

I shrug. "It's not the most traditional name, but I've met people named after flowers. I picked it because it meant something to me."

The daimon-man blinks, and his face lights up with more curiosity. "*You* picked it?"

Julita's presence perks up in my head. *I didn't know that either. You've been holding back stories.*

She at least knows the basics of my history, things I'd rather not have to explain to Rheave too.

My stomach knots, and I pick my words carefully to skirt the worst parts of the tale. "Things were bad between my parents and me as I grew up. I left home early and picked a new name for myself. There was ivy growing on a tree in a neighborhood I often visited. It seemed like something resilient and a little sneaky, and I liked that."

A giggle bubbles out of Julita. *It certainly suits you, and I mean that as an absolute compliment.*

Rheave appears to consider my explanation. "Maybe all people should pick their own names. They would be more fitting that way."

"No one would know what to call us when we're too little to decide," Casimir says in an amused tone.

Rheave starts to chuckle. "And if you went by what babies look like, they'd all be called 'Potato' or 'Gourd.'"

I muffle a laugh of my own with my hand. The fact that I can laugh at all despite the tension hanging over our trek lifts my spirits and makes the day seem a little brighter.

Alek shakes his head with a short guffaw and shoots a tentative glance at me. "What *was* your birth name? Not that I'd call you anything but Ivy. But it might be useful to know in case it comes up somehow… In case anyone manages to connect you to your old life."

I guess that's true. I hesitate all the same, my body balking against forming the sounds I haven't heard spoken to me in more than eight years.

My voice comes out a bit raw. "Izabel. Izabel Milaeya."

Stavros makes a dismissive sound, as if casting aside the name and all the painful history entwined with it. "Ivy suits you much better. And you don't need a last name when the woman it refers to doesn't deserve to be honored."

*I completely agree*, Julita declares.

The former general pats his stallion's neck. "Come on. I'd like to cover a lot more distance today."

An unfamiliar voice pipes up from behind us. "I don't know if you'll accomplish that."

We all startle, Stavros's hand whipping to his sword as he whirls to face the source of the unexpected interruption.

A figure is standing in the middle of the road, just a few paces from the nearest of our horses. I have no idea how the man got this close without any of us noticing him approaching.

Especially given that he doesn't look like the nimblest of hikers. His shoulders are hunched within the layers of dark gray cloth that swath his body so erratically I can't tell whether they're part of a cloak or a thick tunic, or perhaps some combination of the two. He sways a little as we stare at him and clenches his hand around a gnarled walking stick.

His face is gnarled too, a sharp nose jutting from his wizened brown face. Wisps of white hair peek from beneath his hood.

But his eyes are perfectly steady. He peers right back at us with a fathomless gaze, his irises so dark I can't tell where his pupils end and they begin.

Julita shivers. *Who in the realms is* that*? And did no one ever tell him it's impolite to sneak up on people?*

I'd hardly take the man for a threat if it wasn't for his abrupt arrival. Stavros's tensed stance suggests he's unnerved too.

What on earth is anyone doing traveling this isolated road alone and on foot? Does he live on a farm nearby?

The former general motions to the old man with his prosthetic, his hand of flesh still resting on his sword hilt. "What do you mean, we might not accomplish it? Who are you?"

The man rocks on his heels, making his head bob in an unsettlingly bird-like motion. "Many people make plans. They don't always turn out as they hope."

He ignores the second question completely. I glance at Rheave, but the daimon-man shakes his head. "Not like me," he murmurs. "Just a man."

"Where are you headed?" Casimir asks cautiously.

The old man hums to himself, his expression turning distant. "I simply need to find it, and then I'll know…"

He seems so out of sorts that I can't keep quiet. "Are you all right?"

His unsettling gaze snaps back to me. A chill washes over my skin.

"There are a few coming who would like to set their swords through all your hearts," he says in the exact same tone as before.

The instant his last word fades in the air, the sound of far-off hoofbeats carries on the wind.

Stavros stiffens and motions us toward the trees. He pitches his voice ominously low. "Take shelter. Pull as far back into the woods as you can, but be quiet about it."

I snatch Toast's reins and tug him with me between the trees. The stallion huffs in dismay but follows, shuffling through the brush.

The men guide their own mounts on either side of me. But we've only pushed about a single horse-length into the forest before Stavros jerks up his hand to stop us.

I glance toward the road—and spot a flash of rich blue fabric that makes my pulse stutter.

Three soldiers in the standard military uniforms are riding around the bend in the road maybe a quarter mile distant. The thudding of their horses' approach reaches our ears even more clearly now.

Shit. It's got to be one of the king's patrols.

If we keep tugging our steeds along, they'll hear us rustling through the forest now. They'll be able to see us in a matter of seconds.

But if we abandon the horses to walk more stealthily, the animals will still give us away. At best, we'll lose all the supplies we've gathered.

At worst… our blood might water these trees.

Stavros's face has gone taut with tension. He gestures for us to ease our horses down to lie on the forest floor.

I touch Toast's muzzle in the hopes of keeping him calm and sink to my own knees. The stallion gives me an incredulous look but follows suit with just a brisk shake of his mane.

We're more concealed by the bushes now, but I'm not sure it'll be enough. The pale gray hair of Rheave's mare stands out amid the vegetation even in the shadows.

Are we going to have to fight these men? Kill them so they can't stab their swords through us the way the old man suggested?

My stomach churns at the thought. I left the Haven to stop people from dying, not to add to the death toll.

At the thought, my magic flares in my chest and quivers through my limbs. There are so many things it could do to protect me.

I hesitate and then slowly consider. *Is* there something I could do that wouldn't hurt anyone?

Maybe it's time I put Sulla's teachings to use. Now, while I have a few moments to gather myself, rather than in a desperate jab if this comes to a battle.

Soon I might not even have the choice.

My heart thumps faster, but I can't back away like I did about opening the underground storeroom. Eventually I need to find out whether I can count on my control when it matters most.

The soldiers don't know we're here. All I need to do is ensure I keep it that way. Something concrete with a clear counteraction.

An idea forms in my head. My hopes rise with it.

I glance around at my men, confirming their positions in the forest around me. My heart aches at the thought of any harm coming to them.

I simply can't let that happen. They came all this way to defend me, and now I need to return the favor.

Girding myself, I let go of Toast's reins to extend one hand in front of me while lifting my other arm toward the treetops. Guiding my focus with my body.

Julita's presence shivers in the back of my head, but she doesn't speak, maybe not wanting to distract me when she can tell I'm up to something.

I picture the effect I want to see and squeeze the power in me into the shape I've imagined.

Darkness condenses through the trees between us and the road. The shadows thicken and stretch, forming a wall no mortal eyes should be able to penetrate in the gaps between the trunks.

My breath hitches with the energy streaming out of me. Overhead, the shadows should be stripping away from the uppermost branches to balance out my magic. The remaining leaves and the branches they're clinging to will be glaring with unmuted sunlight.

But no patrol will see the blaze from the ground.

Through the thunder of my pulse, I will my cloak of shadows to hold steady. We all stay crouched in silence.

The soldiers trot by, their gazes skimming over the woods on either side of the road. For a second, one leans a little over in his saddle, squinting our way—

And then he's straightened up with a rough chuckle as if chagrinned with himself. The patrol rides on without stopping.

I have the impression of Julita clapping her hands. *Now that's a worthy trick.*

I keep pouring my magic into the darkness draped over us until the hoofbeats fade away and my head starts to spin. With a sharp exhalation, I pull my hands back to my chest, yanking my power in with it.

My magic squirms against my grasp, but half-heartedly. It settles into a soft vibration within my ribs that feels almost content, like a purring cat.

I sink back on my ass and swipe at the sweat that formed on my forehead. Relief surges up from my gut.

I did it. I worked with my magic instead of fighting it, all while keeping it on a tight leash. I stopped the consequences from harming anyone.

I really have harnessed it, and for once I didn't need a godlen's intervention to hold disaster in check.

An instinctive need to reassure myself of my men's safety grips me. I turn toward Alek where he's crouched across from me and pull him to me in a tight hug.

He returns the embrace with a rough noise in his throat. Casimir slips closer to me through the brush and wraps his arms around me in a hug of his own, as if to reassure me that he's grateful rather than horrified by my efforts.

I squeeze him back too and then look up to find Stavros standing over me.

"Are you all right, Lady Thief?" he asks. "The conjuring didn't rattle you at all?"

I drag in a slow breath. "No. I feel fine."

His mouth curves into a half-smile that's fond if restrained. "You did well. I think we just might make it to Eppun after all."

Alek grips my shoulder. "That was fantastic. And using your

magic a bit means it won't hurt you as much if you have to hold it back later, doesn't it?"

I nod, my nerves settling at their joint show of support.

As I get to my feet, nudging Toast to follow me, Rheave moves to join us. But he's looking toward the road. "Where did the man who warned us go?"

We tread carefully out from between the trees. The road lies completely empty of both soldiers and strange old men.

*He was… very strange*, Julita remarks. *I can't say I'm upset that he's gone.*

I can't say I am either.

"He probably moved off into the woods on the other side," Stavros says. "Whatever he's up to, it's no business of ours. Let's get going. We've had plenty of break time now, and I don't want to be here if that patrol decides to double back." He flashes another smile my way. "Let's not make our sorcerer save us all over again."

Despite the lightness of his words, I feel his gaze evaluating me. Watching to see if the use of my magic has had any ill effects on me?

As I heft myself into the saddle, a different sort of ache spreads behind my sternum.

I did save my companions… and I can only pray to whatever gods are watching over us that I can do it again without bringing even more danger down on us.

# SIXTEEN

*Ivy*

I wake at a gust of icy air slipping beneath the layered blankets.

Casimir follows the draught, returning from his time on watch. He must have swapped with Stavros, who was sleeping on that side of me the last time I was conscious.

Alek mumbles and pulls deeper under the blankets at my other side. It's just occurred to me that there should be one more man squeezed into the tent with us when Casimir speaks by my ear at a whisper.

"Rheave came out maybe half an hour ago. He's sitting off by himself under the trees, not even with his hood up. I tried to convince him to come back and warm up, but he didn't listen to me. He seems to pay more attention to you, if you want to try to convince him."

I muffle a groan and swipe at my eyes. Does the daimon-man want to turn the body he's so determined to keep alive black with frostbite?

Why would he want to be out there in the freezing dark anyway?

I can't really complain about the interrupted sleep. Since I used my magic the other day, the men have refused to let me take any of the watches. They want to ensure I have all the focus I need if another occasion arises, so I've been getting the most rest out of any of us.

I give Casimir a quick kiss and squirm out from under the blankets.

The nights have gotten increasingly chilly as we've continued north. We've mostly gotten through by cuddling close together to share body heat, which the small tent makes kind of necessary regardless.

I'm not sure what's been more torturous: the occasional wafts of frigid air that manage to reach us anyway or lying so close to my lovers without being able to do more than cuddle. Having Rheave sharing the space doesn't exactly set the right mood for an intimate encounter.

But I'm not going to let him freeze just for a little privacy with my men. Sighing, I pull my cloak close around me and tramp out onto the frost-laced grass.

Stavros is poised on a stone a couple of paces from the tent, his own cloak covering most of his massive form and his body tipped toward the smoldering firepit. He's partly buried it to limit the smoke, but it still emanates a faint glow and a little heat through the earth to take the worst edge off the chill.

He glances over his shoulder toward me with a sweep of his gaze over my form.

"Are you all right?" he asks in a quiet voice, taking a casual tone despite his obvious concern. He's been asking that question more frequently than usual since the day I called on my magic by the road.

I match his tone. "Just making sure the daimon doesn't become as much ice as clay."

Stavros gives a muted chuckle and tips his head to the left. Following the gesture, I spot Rheave's muscular form sitting cross-legged between two trees several paces beyond the edge of the clearing.

Like Casimir said, the idiotic daimon hasn't even bothered to raise his hood. His chocolate-brown curls are going to end up as frosted as the grass, which crackles under my feet as I walk over to him.

When I get closer, I see he has his bare hands splayed on his knees rather than tucked into his pockets like any sensible person would. Because of course he isn't a person, and also not especially sensible as far as I can tell, though I'm not sure what's typical for a spirit-creature.

Julita lets out a soft huff. *What in the realms is he doing? Attempting to transform into an ice sculpture?*

"I suppose I'd better figure that out," I murmur, treading between the trees.

Rheave doesn't stir as I come up beside him. His eyes are closed.

I peer at his hands and face in the dim moonlight, but I can't tell whether they're already turning blue.

"Hey," I say, unsure whether he's even awake. Can a daimon fall asleep sitting up?

Rheave's vibrant eyes blink open. He looks up at me and frowns. "Why are you out here? Isn't this your time to sleep?"

"Isn't it yours?" I retort. "I'm guessing you didn't sleep as a daimon, but I'm pretty sure that body of yours needs it. And it also needs to avoid turning into an icicle."

The daimon-man considers me with a gleam of curiosity rather than concern in his eyes. "Is that a thing that can happen to humans?"

What am I going to do with this guy?

My tone comes out dry. "Not exactly, but bodies of flesh *can* freeze if they do things like, I don't know, sitting out in the forest in the middle of the night with no heat source nearby."

Rheave shrugs as if the idea doesn't particularly bother him. "I was never cold when I was a daimon. Or warm. Or anything like that. It's interesting to feel it. Like the air is biting you, but not that hard."

The breeze blowing past us is definitely nippy. I tuck my own hands deeper under my cloak, out of its reach. "So now you've felt it. Why are you staying out here?"

"The way it feels keeps changing a little. Some parts tingled. Some stopped feeling at all." He taps his fingertips against his knees with apparent delight.

Panic jolts through my nerves. "How long *have* you been out here?"

I bend down to press my fingers to his cheek and then the back of his hand. The latter feels outright frigid.

My magic jostles inside me, clamoring to flood him with heat, push back the chill.

But where would that heat come from? Everything around us is freezing except me, my men, and the fire I don't want to snuff out.

I wrap my hand around Rheave's as if I can squeeze some warmth back into his skin and tug at him. "You've had enough trying out the cold for now. Come on—we need to get you warmed up before you do any permanent damage to yourself."

Rheave pushes slowly to his feet and looks down at our clasped hands. "I don't feel *bad.* I'm sure I'll be all right, Little Vine."

Is that what he's going to call me now? I might be 'little' compared to him, but I've still got the ivy resilience.

I step away in an attempt to drag him toward the tent, my throat constricting with worry. "That part where you can't feel anything? If you leave it very long, it becomes permanent. And then the bits with no feeling fall right off. Do you really want to start losing pieces of this body? I don't think the scourge sorcerers are going to build you a new one."

To my relief, my final comment finally rouses him to action. Rheave strides with me over to the tent, grimacing as he wobbles on legs that must have gotten stiff. "Mortal bodies are very fragile."

"That's right. How about you keep that in mind from now on?"

I push him into the tent, tug off his cloak which might as well be pure ice, and draw him down with me toward the blankets. Casimir is still awake, rolling over as I nudge Rheave toward him.

"He's already going numb," I whisper, wanting to avoid waking Alek too if I can. "We need to warm him up as quickly as possible."

Rheave makes a faint sound of protest, but he lets me push him closer to the courtesan. The two of us tuck ourselves against the daimon-man's body, even though I wince at the cold still seeping from his clothes.

"Put your hands in your armpits," I murmur at him. "Pull your face right under the blanket so it'll soak up the heat too."

Rheave ducks his head. His silky curls graze my jaw.

I pull the blanket higher over him and instinctively set my hand against his arm to reassure myself that he's still got some warmth in him. That he isn't totally frozen.

The constricting sensation in my throat has spread down through my chest. What if he *has* done real damage to himself?

The realization creeps over me so gradually but undeniably that my heart clenches up too. As exasperating as the daimon-man can be, I appreciate the brightness and wonder he's brought with him. I've enjoyed his company.

I don't want to lose him.

What am I supposed to do with that knowledge or the ache that's come with it?

Our breaths rise and fall together. Gradually, the heat we radiate penetrates the cold we carried with us.

Despite the tangled emotions inside me, I lift my hand to rest my palm against Rheave's cheek. It's still cool but not totally cold anymore. He's okay.

A rush of relief tinged with absurd humor passes through me. At least his ridiculously beautiful face shouldn't be marred by his embracing of the northern night.

I tap his jaw lightly to get his attention. "Let me feel one of your hands."

He adjusts his position, rolling onto his side to face me. I expect him to reach for my hand, but instead he places his palm against my stomach.

A flicker of an even more confusing emotion lights low in my belly. A deeper heat than his sunny smiles ever provoked.

I clamp down on it, mentally shaking my head at my reaction. This man is gorgeous and bizarre and makes me wonder about things I never did before, but he's also not really a man.

And I've got three other men I'm very much devoted to. Even Signy, after all her heroics, stopped at a trio.

I grasp Rheave's wrist the second enough warmth has seeped through my over-tunic and dress for me to be sure he won't be losing any fingers and ease his hand away.

Rheave lifts his head from beneath the blanket. It's nearly pitch black inside the tent, but I can feel him looking my way. Maybe he can make out my face even if I can't see his.

The second I let go of his wrist, he reaches for me again. He touches my shoulder and then slides his hand down almost to my elbow.

We've never slept next to each other before. My men have always insisted on surrounding me, and the daimon-man has settled for taking the spot closest to the flaps where he can still serve as some kind of protection.

I didn't realize he was going to be touchy-feely about our current position.

Julita lets out a giggle. *He is all about feeling new things, isn't he? If you could snap the rest of the scourge sorcerers' army out of whatever spell they're under, they'd be dopey as puppies.*

When Rheave speaks, he doesn't sound particularly dopey.

He keeps his voice low but steady. "Everything is back to normal now. My fingers were prickly for a while, but that faded away."

"Good. Then you didn't freeze them right off."

"I wasn't being careful. I'm sorry I worried you. I'm supposed to be looking out for you, not making you do that for me."

He sounds downcast enough that I stroke his cheek again in an effort at reassurance. "We all look out for each other. That's what… friends do. And you're still getting used to being whatever exactly you are now. It'd just be nice if you'd listen faster the next time I try to warn you. Or you could listen to the others. We all have a lot more experience in mortal bodies than you do."

"I know. But you're the one I'm sure will really listen to me. I'll try to be better about listening too."

He's silent for a moment, his fingers squeezing my arm lightly, and then he drops his hand to my waist. It flexes against my side as if he's testing some other new sensation.

"Ivy," he says, "why do humans press their mouths together?"

I think I hear Casimir choke back a guffaw. My cheeks flare. The courtesan should be the one fielding questions like this.

And if I have to, he could at least do me the favor of going to sleep so I don't have an audience.

I grope for a reasonable answer. "It feels good. It's a way to show you like being close to someone."

Rheave hums and dips his head toward me. I jerk my hand against his sternum before he can press right against me, tuning out the pulse of desire that sparked in my core.

"Are you trying to kiss *me*?" I demand as quietly as I can manage.

*I think you opened yourself up to that one, Ivy*, Julita says through another giggle.

The daimon-man simply sounds confused. "You said it feels good. I wanted to see. You kiss Stavros and Casimir and Alek."

Great God help me. “I know them a lot better than I know you. We have a different kind of relationship. Most people don’t get that close with each other.”

“Oh.”

Now he sounds outright despondent.

I grit my teeth at the twinge of sympathy that runs through my chest. Who’s ever going to want to kiss a man who’s not really a man?

At least, enough to allow themselves to go through with it. We won’t talk about the feelings I’m reining in as much as I have my magic.

Well, maybe we can compromise.

I turn my head away from him. “On the mouth, anyway. People who are just friendly could kiss each other on the cheek. That wouldn’t be so strange. It’s not quite the same, but you could try that.”

My earlier rejection seems to have shaken Rheave’s confidence. “Are you sure? I don’t want to do anything that would upset you.”

The twinge rises through my chest to solidify into a lump in my throat. I don’t like hearing his eager brightness give way to hesitance. “It won’t. Go ahead.”

He leans in, soft hair against my temple, hot breath drifting over my jaw. His lips graze my cheek and then press the skin a little more firmly.

Heat flushes my body from head to toe. I can’t blame it completely on the wash of his breath.

I’m not sure I ever noticed the daimon-man’s personal scent before. There’s a fresh, woodsy scent to him that makes me think of leaves dappled in dew under the morning sun.

He draws his head back, but then he wraps his whole arm around my waist, pulling me right up against him again. “Now I’ll keep you warm. You should sleep.”

It *is* warm in his embrace. I rest the side of my face against my arm and close my eyes, dismissing the emotions that have jumbled inside me.

It's the middle of the night. He almost froze to death. Of course I'm out of sorts.

It's not as if it means anything—or as if it even could.

The next time I wake up, sunlight is beaming through the walls of the tent and Rheave is stepping over me to push outside. As I rub my bleary eyes, Casimir takes the opportunity to scoot closer to me.

"Did you have a nice snuggle with your new friend?" he asks in a teasing voice.

I elbow him lightly. "Oh, hush. He's still figuring out what's normal."

The courtesan guides my mouth to his to claim the sort of kiss Rheave attempted to last night. Then he nips the crook of my jaw. "You were very sweet with him. He deserves the patience. I think he adds a little something to our group that we all benefit from."

Before I can decide whether to debate the issue, Stavros's voice carries from outside. "Rise and shine! Let's not waste the daylight."

We scramble out and gulp down the hasty breakfast that the former general passes around. Alek grabs the canteens to refill them at the stream we stopped near, as has become his self-appointed duty, and Casimir and I pack up the tent and blankets. After several days of trekking, we fulfill our roles with brisk efficiency.

When I go to saddle Toast, he snorts as if he's personally offended by the wintry weather.

"Just be glad it isn't snowing yet," I tell my cantankerous steed.

Apparently I spoke too soon, because a few fat flakes drift

down as we set off. Stavros grimaces at them and leads us even deeper into the woods.

We've stayed off the roads for the past couple of days now that we're close to Eppun. We wouldn't want to run into the Order of the Wild's forces or the king's marching to confront them.

We set a swift pace through the trees, marking time by the ringing of distant town bells. We've heard two when the forest thins up ahead.

Stavros motions for us to dismount. We slink the rest of the way through the woods to a small rise that blocks all view of what's ahead.

At the former general's direction, we crouch low to creep up the slope and peer over the top.

On the far side of the hill and perhaps a mile to our right, a road cuts through the fields of browned grass. A wooden post juts from the earth along its course, and a couple of men stand on either side of it.

At the sight of them, Rheave goes utterly still.

"Those are daimon," he says with total certainty. "I can feel it even from here. What are they doing?"

Stavros's mouth forms a grim smile. "Guarding the territory their masters have claimed, I assume. That post marks the border of Eppun."

"We made it," I murmur.

And now the truly hard part of our mission begins.

# Seventeen

*Ivy*

Stavros paces in front of the tent. "I can't simply sit here while the rest of you do all the work."

"You're not sitting," I point out helpfully. "And I'm sure we'll find plenty to keep you busy once we know what we're doing. But when we're simply going into the town to wander around and get the lay of the land, you'd stick out like a sore thumb. You're too recognizable."

Stavros growls, but he knows I'm right. It's doubtful that the conspirators know or care that the king wants our heads on a platter… which actually works against us with them.

If anyone from the Order of the Wild recognizes one of his former top generals, they'll assume Stavros is here under King Konram's orders, to stop them.

Alek touches my arm where he's come up beside me. "Just be careful. We don't know what exactly to expect here in Nikodi."

He's hanging back at our campsite too, for similar reasons. If any word has gotten around about the supposed traitors harboring a riven sorcerer, showing his scars or his mask will make him easy to identify.

We're only going on a scouting mission, after all. The point is to blend in and gather information, not to make any big moves.

I give Alek a quick kiss. "We should be fine. There's no reason for anyone to find us suspicious. And this is Julita's home territory—we have her to guide us too."

My ghostly passenger pipes up from the back of my head. *That's right. I'll keep you on the right track.*

Her attempt at a perky tone doesn't entirely work. Apprehension winds through it.

We're heading to her family's estate first. We have no idea what we'll find there, but I've gathered that she finds it hard to believe that her parents would have been won over by the Order of the Wild.

Which means the scourge sorcerers have likely taken over by force.

I offer Stavros a kiss for good measure, which he accepts with another disgruntled growl but plenty of heat in return. When I draw back, he studies Casimir and Rheave for a second, with less hesitation than he used to show the daimon-man.

Casimir picks up on the worry he's not expressing. "We'll make sure Ivy comes back in one piece."

Rheave draws his well-muscled form up straighter. "No one will get past us to harm her."

"Hey, I might be the one who ends up defending the two of you," I retort lightly.

A shadow crosses Stavros's expression before he seems to will it away. He keeps his tone even. "Better not to turn to your magic unless you have to, while you're still getting the hang of balancing the effects."

I smile even though my stomach knots at his cautioning. "Agreed." I pat my pocket where I've stashed my enchanted locket. "Signal us if any trouble finds you."

Stavros nods and turns to Alek. "I suppose we should keep

working on those knife skills of yours. I'll whip you into shape eventually."

Alek groans, but he gets out his dagger without further protest.

I wink at him. "Draw a little blood for me."

As Stavros snorts in amusement, I haul myself onto Toast's back. Casimir, Rheave, and I set off at a trot.

The ride to bring us within sight of the county of Nikodi's seat of authority takes about two hours. We pass it in silence and brief moments of hushed conversation, scanning the countryside as we go.

With each passing mile, my gut twists tighter. We don't really know what to expect up ahead. I've spent years picking up information from the streets of Florian, making my way through both the grittiest and poshest neighborhoods without drawing attention, but I've never had to navigate a violent uprising before.

I've got much more practice at subterfuge than any of my men, though. I have to keep them safe—both here and on a broader scale.

If we can't find a way to clear our names and prove ourselves to King Konram, they'll spend the rest of their lives like I've spent most of mine, just a couple of steps shy of the gallows. All because they've stood by me.

Julita alerts me to our arrival with a strained noise. *There's the house. You can see the roof over the top of that rise.*

I slow Toast to a walk and peer into the distance. She's right—just over the top of the rolling fields ahead of us, I make out a few peaks of a tiled roof.

"That's your family's manor house?" I ask her in a low voice.

*Yes. I suppose we should approach more cautiously from here. Once you reach the top of the next slope, you'll be able to see the whole estate and the city of Pima to the left.*

I pass her suggestion on to the men and dismount. We leave

the horses grazing lower down the rise and sneak to the higher ground on foot.

As soon as the house below comes into clearer view, I drop lower to the ground, setting my gloved hands in the frosty grass. The men follow suit. Our breaths puff out of us like smoke in the chilly winter air.

The building Julita grew up in is much broader and more sprawling than the noble homes I'm familiar with from Florian. Which makes sense, given that the nobles in the capital are restrained by being packed together in the city's inner wards.

The house below me looks as if it might have started as something more compact. The central structure around the main doors is symmetrical enough, looming three stories to a stout tower. But over the centuries various counts and countesses built the sides and back out with additional rooms until it became a bit of a mishmash of stone-block forms.

Julita lets out a ragged sigh without adding any words. It's been months since she was last home.

Now she'll never really be able to enter that building again, not as herself at least. I can't imagine how that feels.

I might have left my own family home, but there was nothing for me there anymore. And I *could* return if I really wanted to.

Julita lost the choice.

My gaze veers to the stretch of smaller rooftops to the left. A handful of tall structures—a few temples, what might be the city's main hall—jut up amid single and two-story buildings.

Compared to Florian, it's hard to call that habitation a city. It can't be more than a tenth of the size of the capital.

Julita did tell me once that all of Nikodi had maybe a quarter of the citizens Florian can boast.

Casimir makes a soft sound in his throat that draws my attention. I jerk my gaze back to the estate.

A couple of men have emerged from the orchard around the back of the property and are walking next to the low wall that surrounds the grounds. As I watch, another figure—a woman dressed in a simple jacket and trousers under her cloak like the men—walks out of the house toward the front gate.

They don't look like nobles even of Julita's backwater level. But they move with a menacing assurance I'm not used to seeing from household staff.

*We usually only had one man on watch,* Julita murmurs. *And he'd have been wearing a proper uniform.* The nervousness in her voice has grown.

I glance toward my companions. "Julita says her estate normally wouldn't have had so many people patrolling. Those could be people associated with the Order of the Wild."

Rheave is staring intently at the figures. His expression darkens with a frown. "They're all daimon."

Even though I was already assuming they weren't regular staff, my stomach drops. "All three of them?"

He gives a subtle nod. "In the conjured bodies."

Julita's presence shivers in the back of my head. *The scourge sorcerers have taken over my home.*

"We'll figure it out," I say in the quieter tone I use so the men know I'm talking to her rather than them. Then I raise my voice slightly to include Casimir and Rheave as well. "They could have her parents and members of the actual staff imprisoned inside, under watch. Or have driven them out. Or there's a chance the household is collaborating, whether truly willingly or only under duress."

Casimir is frowning too. "I suppose we can hardly go over and ask."

Julita sucks in a breath. *I hope they're all right. We might not have seen eye to eye on everything, but… they tried. They gave me opportunities even though Borys was the main heir.*

She was hoping to inherit the estate as countess at some point after she finished her education at the college. With her older brother going missing a few years back and presumed dead, it should have been possible.

But now the scourge sorcerers have upended not just her life but the rest of her family's as well.

"We'll figure it out," I say again. "What do you think we should do now?"

She pauses for a moment in thought. *It seems unwise to approach the estate. We'd draw too much attention and likely not get any answers regardless. Let's go into Pima and see what's happening in the city.*

I pass on the idea to the men, and we creep back to our horses. As we turn them toward the road into the city, an air of gloom has descended over even Casimir's gorgeous face.

We have a story prepared, but none of the people who observe us riding into the city bother to stop us, let alone demand to know why we're there. Rheave murmurs that a few of those hanging around at the outskirts are daimon.

I guess that others keeping watch are human members of the Order of the Wild. Either scourge sorcerers or ordinary civilians who've become wrapped up in their claims of restoring Silana to its former glory.

Merchants are still coming into the city with wagons of goods; shops and eateries are open; pedestrians circulate on the streets. But a thread of tension winds through the atmosphere, as if everyone is periodically looking over their shoulder to check for threats.

I know the impression isn't just in my head when Julita comments on it too. *It feels like life as usual… but not quite. Everyone's just a bit keyed up.*

Nikodi sits at the northern end of Eppun province, its farthest border rubbing shoulders with Bryfeen, so I doubt there've been any direct clashes with the royal army here. But obviously the effects of the revolt have rippled through the county.

As we tie our horses at one of the city's hitching posts so we can mingle with the townspeople, a sharp voice carries over the softer hum of everyday conversation. "King Konram and his court have bullied us for too long! Everyone should stand up for Silana and embrace the ways the All-Giver intended us to live!"

A woman with a cluster of followers is standing on a crate at one corner of a nearby square. She hands out pamphlets to everyone who passes nearby.

I pick up one that's been dropped on the street and restrain a grimace. The Order of the Wild has taken one of the old myths about Creaden supporting the first kings of the realms and twisted it to make it sound as if even the godlen of rulership would support their cause.

The very fact that there are no soldiers or local law enforcement around to shut down the woman's hostility toward the Crown shows how thoroughly the scourge sorcerers have taken over. I shudder to think what they've done to anyone who tried to stand up to them.

Julita's voice stays subdued as she takes all this in through me. *There was a pub around this end of town that the staff often talked about visiting. The Silver Stag. I went there a couple of times myself. It's possible we'll spot someone I know who'll talk to us there… I think if we take a right at that cross-street…*

We follow her directions through a few turns to a pub on the corner that's bustling with lunchtime business. Rheave's eyes light up as he watches the conjured illusion of a stag leap from one end of the sign to the other and back again.

When we slip past the door into a room smelling of fresh-baked bread and fried dumplings, almost all of the closely packed tables are full. So are the seats along the varnished bar where some people are having a more liquid sort of lunch.

I ease between the tables as if looking for someone I meant to meet, letting my gaze sweep over the patrons. None of their faces mean anything to me, but toward the back of the space, Julita gasps in excitement.

*There's Hanie! The woman alone at the small booth on the back wall—in the olive-green dress with the brassy hair. She's the head maidservant at our estate. Always making sure the newer maids were looking after my clothes and hair properly and keeping our rooms clean.*

I pause to study the woman Julita indicated from the corner of my eye. She's hunched over a bowl, her gaze flicking toward the rest of the room between bites.

If she was in Julita's house when the uprising reached Nikodi, she must have escaped it. She looks as if she's afraid her association with the county's rulers will be found out.

At the very least, I don't think she's comfortable with the shift in authority in the city.

*Go on,* Julita urges. *Talk to her. Tell her you're a friend of mine and see what she knows.*

I duck my head close to the men to tell them what's going on, and they follow me over to Hanie's table. When I reach her, she stiffens with one hand raised partway to her mouth and the other braced against the bowl of stew.

"Are you Hanie?" I ask, because technically I shouldn't know her for sure on sight.

The woman eyes me warily, lowering her spoon into the bowl. "That's my name. Can I help you?"

"I hope so. We're friends of Julita's. She told us who to look for… Would you mind if we join you so we can talk more discreetly?"

Hanie's eyes widen. She dips her head in agreement, tugging a strand of her brass-brown hair behind her ear as Casimir and I squeeze into the seat across from her. Rheave shifts position to block us from view from most of the rest of the room.

"Has Julita come back to Nikodi?" the maidservant asks in a hushed voice that betrays a mix of excitement and worry. As far as I can tell, she still cares about the family she worked for.

No one in Nikodi will have any idea what happened to the daughter of their count and countess. The story passed around the royal college is that Julita made a hasty departure for home, but I doubt anyone's bothered to check whether she completed that journey yet.

As far as anyone here knows, she's still studying away in Florian, not murdered and buried in an unmarked grave with her spirit stuck in someone else's body.

I shake my head. "She couldn't leave Florian yet, but she's been upset after hearing what's been happening here. It was easier for us to make the trip. We promised her we'd do whatever we can to help."

Hanie's gaze drops to her bowl, her expression morose. "I'm not sure there's much helping to be done. The past two weeks… It's been a nightmare."

Well, she definitely doesn't support the uprising. Good to have that confirmed.

Casimir's mouth twists in sympathy. He speaks up in the gentle voice that could soothe a thunderstorm. "We've had some dealings with the people behind this 'Order of the Wild' back in Florian. We've been able to prevent them from carrying out some of their worst plans."

"I think we can do the same here," I add. "We just need a better idea of what exactly they've been doing."

Hanie's shoulders come down a little. She glances around the room again and drops her voice even lower. "They stormed Julita's estate first—and the local Watch building. I heard all the soldiers in the fort farther south were slaughtered too. Since then, the Order people have mostly been talking about how they're going to put a 'real' king on the throne and pave the way for the All-Giver to return. And coming down on anyone who questions them."

I wince. "Have you seen any odd-looking figures with them? People who've made an unsettling number of sacrifices, or covered up so you can't even see their faces?"

"Knowing where they're gathering to make plans or keeping supplies would also be useful," Casimir puts in.

Hanie's expression turns distant with thought. She brings her knuckle to her lips. "I've noticed a few things around town… I try not to get too close. You'll need to be careful.

Anyone who's pushed back at all forcefully, they just disappear."

I swallow thickly. "We won't be blatant about it. But someone has to stand up to them before they do any more damage."

Julita squirms at the back of my skull. *What about my parents? She said the scourge sorcerers stormed the estate—what's happened to everyone else?*

I can't blame her for wanting those answers while she has the chance to get them.

I drag in a ragged breath. "And if you can tell us, so we can send word back to Julita—where are her parents now? Are they being held in the house?"

Hanie's face pales. I brace myself for the worst.

Her voice falls to a mere whisper. "They're gone. The brigands—they dragged them out of their beds and cut their throats."

Julita lets out a wail that resonates through my head. I close my eyes for a second, grieving her loss alongside her.

How much more blood is going to be spilled before we can stop these psychopaths for good?

# Eighteen

*Casimir*

The Petal's Pleasure brothel is one of the subtler establishments dedicated to the carnal arts I've observed in my time, at least from the outside.

That isn't to say it's outright discreet. The owner commissioned an illusionist to conjure an image of a woman's manicured hand stroking along the letters on the sign, and Ardone's sigil is clearly carved on either side of the business name. But the face of the building is painted a modest ivory, dulled in patches to light gray, with no additional decoration. The dark red curtains covering the windows obscure all hint of what goes on within.

What's going on right now may be more than indulgences in bodily pleasures. Julita's former maidservant mentioned that she's seen some of the more authoritative Order of the Wild members coming and going from this place regularly.

It could be they're simply looking to scratch an itch. But considering that the conspirators in Florian used at least one brothel to hide their sacrificial accomplices, we felt it was worth investigating.

And my observations from the past two days have only increased my certainty that Petal's Pleasure figures into the scourge sorcerers' plans in some significant way. Whenever the man who runs the place steps out in one of his elegant but slightly tatty suits, I can see the stress he's under in everything from his furtive swipes at his face to the stiffness in his slim frame.

Something is making him nervous. From the looks of his business, he's been in the trade for decades, so I doubt he's having misgivings about the official services he offers.

And when a few of the men and women we've identified as important members of the local Order stopped by last night, they came and went with attitudes much more resolute than leisurely.

So, we're taking a gamble, and we'll see if we can chip away at a little of the scourge sorcerers' power in Pima.

For a second, the thought of the uprising that's spread across the entire province squeezes my lungs. I'm used to dealing with people one-on-one, tending to their concerns with a personal touch.

I never expected to find myself tackling a horde of traitors with brutal magic.

My hands clench where I'm standing down the street from the brothel. Dragging air into my lungs, I will them to relax.

A personal touch may be exactly what's needed here. Hanie questioned whether we'd be able to make a difference, but it doesn't need to be a matter of bowling the conspirators over all at once.

We can try to undermine them with a few small, swift jabs that might seem minor but will make an impact as the effects ripple through their organization. They've only had a couple of weeks to set down roots.

We have to do everything we can to cut those fledgling roots out from under them. All of us working together, no matter how far we are from our usual endeavors.

Gathering myself, I stroll over to the brothel through the thin late-afternoon light. I hold my chin high and my posture straight like the conspirators I watched enter the building yesterday.

The hinges give a faint squeak as I open the door. Warm air washes over me from the hall, thick with the scents of vanilla, jasmine, and roses.

A narrow, cushioned bench sits just inside the hall. A curtain sections the front area off from the rest of the house. Sultry music and a burst of feminine laughter carry from beyond it.

Only moments after I've stepped inside, the slim man appears at the doorway of the one room on this side of the curtain, which I assume is his office. He looks me over with a calculating smile. "What can I do for you, sir? It's early—there are plenty of options."

I keep my answering smile reserved enough to hide the gem teeth in the back of my mouth that would give away my own status as a courtesan. "Actually, I'm here to do something for you."

As I speak, I nudge my gift toward him. A tingle spreads through my gums where I sacrificed the eight teeth to Ardone, and a rush of images and sensations floods my head.

Ah. Conveniently, what I can do that would make this man happiest is exactly what I came hoping to do.

His brow has started to furrow. I go on before he can question me. "You have something here that belongs to the Order of the Wild. We need to relocate them. I'll be taking them off your hands. You will, of course, receive the rest of your due compensation."

Relief flashes across the man's face before he can hide it. He bobs his head with the eagerness he's trying to suppress and motions for me to follow him. "I'm glad I could be of service to those who celebrate the All-Giver."

But he's even more glad not to have the responsibility hanging over him anymore. From the twinge of revulsion I caught in the gift-brought stream of impressions, I suspect he's caught at least a glimpse of what his unexpected lodgers look like under their shrouds.

I don't think he wants to know what the Order of the Wild plans to do with these mutilated people.

The brothel owner leads me down a flight of stairs at the back of the building, where the perfume smell gives way to dust and a trace of mildew. He unlocks the door to the right of the stairs and motions me toward the room beyond without stepping into it himself. His stance has already tensed.

Oh, he's definitely unnerved by what he's seen of the scourge sorcerers' sacrificial accomplices.

Keeping my expression mild, I cross the threshold into the dim space.

The room has no windows and barely any furniture. Four cots stand along the walls, a small table between them with plates still scattered with scraps of food.

Without arms to hold their food or eyes to see it, do the sacrificial accomplices simply lower their mouths to the plates and eat like animals? Have my supposed colleagues ordered the brothel owner to assist with their meals?

The shrouded figures look eerie even beneath the dove-gray cloth that conceals most of their mutilations. It's obvious to the eye that the fabric falls too smoothly across their heads, too narrowly along their bodies, where they've given up so much for whatever gifts they received that the scourge sorcerers are now exploiting.

I've been taught to see the beauty in every scar life can leave behind… but there's nothing beautiful about sacrifices made through manipulation. The scourge sorcerers cajoled these people into carving themselves up when they were mere children of twelve, with promises of divine glory.

That knowledge tells me how I need to cajole them myself without any need for my own gift.

The four of them turn their heads toward me where they're

perched on their cots. They won't be able to see me, but even without the outer shells of their ears, they'll still be able to hear.

"It's time for you to contribute to our cause," I say, speaking steadily despite the twisting of my gut. "You can serve our purpose in an incredible way tonight."

"Of course!" one of the shrouded figures says in a slurred voice, lurching to his feet.

The woman beside him bows her head. "We welcome the chance."

They all stand except the one figure whose shroud falls unevenly across his knees. He's missing the lower part of one leg, only the stub of a crude wooden prosthetic protruding from beneath.

I touch his arm so he knows I'm there and help him leverage himself upright. He sways but catches his balance.

"Our wagon will have drawn up right out front," I tell the brothel owner. "Thank you for your own contribution."

He trails behind us as we form a wobbly procession up the stairs and back down the hall. Without arms, the sacrificial accomplices sway even walking straight ahead.

I stay in the lead to guide them with my footsteps, watching to ensure there's nothing to trip them up. With every rasp of breath they emit and every hitching motion, horror swells inside me.

Do the scourge sorcerers tell themselves what they're doing isn't a crime because they haven't killed the people whose sacrifices they use to boost their power? Because it seems to me they've traded the brief cruelty of murder for a lifetime of torture.

I reach the door first and lean out to make a swift signal. Down the street, Rheave taps the horses to draw the wagon we commandeered from an abandoned farm in front of the brothel. The canvas arching over the cargo area will hide the accomplices we're stealing from view.

As I guide the shrouded figures out of the brothel, the canvas flaps at the back of the wagon part. Alek holds one side open while I usher the four figures inside.

He wanted to join us for this venture, but not out in the open while we travel through the city streets. The makeup I painted over his scars isn't a perfect cover.

He shoots me a quick, tight smile of welcome. Neither of us are happy about the state of the people we've come to free, but we're glad we can free them at all.

Even if I'm taking the lead role in this operation, I couldn't pull it off without both him and the daimon who's become such a devoted ally.

Once the sacrificial accomplices are settled on the benches within, I close and tie the flaps. Alek's even voice filters through the canvas as I come around to the driver's seat. "I want to make sure we position you properly for the best impact. What are each of your gifts?"

I pull myself onto the seat beside Rheave, who takes that as his cue to set the horses trotting forward. The brothel owner has already disappeared back inside his establishment, no doubt thinking, "Good riddance."

I pitch my voice low to murmur to the daimon. "We should keep a conservative pace until we leave the city so we don't draw suspicion. Once we're on the open road, we'll push the horses harder. We don't want to take so long that the accomplices start to worry."

Rheave tips his head in agreement, his expression calmly intent. He's really the perfect comrade for a bit of subterfuge like this—he's so unaffected by human insecurities that he doesn't have any nerves to hide.

I wasn't totally sure at first how he'd fit in to the dynamic that's formed between the four of us. Ivy, Alek, Stavros, and I have been through so much at the college before Rheave quite literally barged in. But somehow he manages to be both fanciful and steady when we could use more of both to bolster our spirits.

I sink back in my seat, letting my own nerves settle. It should be smooth going from here. Hanie vouched for a cleric at a temple of Prospira that's about an hour outside the city. We'll go there and surrender the sacrificial accomplices to his care.

Alek wanted to talk to the cleric too—something about investigating records about the Great Retribution. I'm not sure where he hopes that line of inquiry will lead him, but I trust the scholar knows what he's doing.

And now the scourge sorcerers will have four fewer victims to exploit to enforce their rule. All the brothel owner will be able to tell them is that one of their own came to—

"Hey, you there! Halt a moment."

A burly man with a sword at his hip steps into the street ahead of us, holding up his hands. My pulse hiccups.

We've only made it a few blocks from the brothel. Did someone realize what we're up to?

From the man's swaggering stride toward us, he's either a member of the Order of the Wild enforcing their will around the city or one of the locals doing the same to win the Order's favor. His imperious gaze sweeps over us.

"What's your business in Pima?" he demands. "I don't recognize either of you."

Probably a local, then, and one whose head has swelled with his newfound authority.

I keep my stance relaxed. "We came through town to do a little business. We're making the trip back to Valk now."

I pick a Nikodian town that's farther from the border rather than closer in the hopes that'll deflect any worries that we're involved with the king's forces. All I get in return is a frown.

The guard takes on a haughtier tone, ambling past the horses. "I hope your business supports our goals. Have you pitched in anything toward seeing a proper king on the throne?"

"We do what we can. What the All-Giver would want from us."

He pauses next to me and squints at Rheave. "Your business partner is awfully quiet."

Rheave peers at him in his unflappable way. "Is there something you wanted to ask me?"

His detached tone appears to raise the guard's suspicions. He glances at the rest of the wagon. "Maybe I should take a look at what goods you're peddling."

Gods smite us. I grope for the right words to temper his authoritative ego, but nothing comes to me.

I don't know what he really wants. But I do have a way to find out.

I inhale deeply, my teeth setting tight against each other. I wouldn't normally use my gift twice in such close succession—I'm not totally sure it'll work.

As I aim my attention more intently at the guard, pain splinters through my forehead. It condenses into a throbbing ache at the sides of my skull.

I keep casting out my gift through the pain. The impressions that reach me come in filmier fragments than usual, but I think I grasp enough emotion and ambition—and a single name—to piece together an answer.

Now I know what would make him happiest… and I'm going to do the opposite.

I set my hand on the seat beside me to offset the dizzying headache and raise my voice just slightly. "You're one of Artor's fellows, aren't you? He did say you were getting a bit big for your britches."

The guard jerks around, his shoulders going rigid and his face flushing. "You know Artor? He talked about me?"

I know from the glimpse I caught that Artor is someone who's given this man orders, who he desperately wants to impress.

I manage to nod despite the throbbing in my head. "Oh, yes. We've known each other since we were little. I told him it's impressive what you all have coordinated here, but he's concerned some have come on board to puff themselves up with bullying rather than to see that the gods' purpose is fulfilled."

The guard blinks, and most of the arrogance deflates out of him. He averts his gaze with a scowl. "I was only trying to do my job."

"I'm sorry if we gave you any reason for suspicion," I say in an arch tone that's more chiding than apologetic.

My heart doesn't stop thudding until he waves his arm for us to continue. "I didn't know you had those kind of ties here. Go on now."

"Thank you," Rheave says in a tone that's a little more chipper than the situation calls for, but to my relief, the guard doesn't shout after us as the horses clop onward.

I tip my head into my hand, rubbing my temple as the ache slowly wanes.

Rheave glances over at me. "Are you all right? You used your magic on him, didn't you? But I thought it was a regular gift—it shouldn't hurt you like Ivy's does."

I manage to give him a crooked grin. "It only does if I push it harder than is wise. As long as I don't try to peek inside anyone else's head today, I'll be fine."

He hums to himself, though I'm not sure if he fully understands what I'm saying. How can a being practically made of magic comprehend the kind of gifts we humans sacrifice for?

He turns to glance at the canvas covering behind us as if he can see through it. When he faces the road again, his face has turned solemn. "You got the people the sorcerers are using for extra magic?"

"Four of them."

He knits his brow. "It isn't any of them."

I shoot him a puzzled look. "What isn't?"

"The one who helped make my body—and the one who helped control it. Neither of them are in the wagon. Those two are still out there, making more like me."

# Nineteen

*Rheave*

I'm not sure whether I like the "apartment" Ivy's new friend found for us to stay in better than camping.

It is much bigger than the tent: two attached rooms, one with enough space for a table and set of chairs as well as a wood-burning stove that helps warm us, the other empty other than the blankets we've laid down to form beds. The walls hold in the heat better than the tent's canvas, so my fingers and ears don't get tingly and numb.

But there's only one small window overlooking the street. It's impossible to tell that anyone's coming up the stairs to the second-floor hall until you hear the boards creak, and equally impossible to know which of the three apartments they're going to unless they knock on the door.

We only have one way to flee if danger arrives, and it'll probably have to be right through the danger.

I understand we need to be in the city so we can make our plans effectively. The people who trapped so many of my kind need to be stopped.

But I miss the wide-open space of the forests and fields we kept to on our journey here. My spirit is used to roaming.

I don't think Ivy's friend likes being in this room either, at least not with me. Since we've been squeezed around the table, discussing our next steps to disrupt the scourge sorcerers, she's been shooting little frowns my way.

She didn't know I wasn't exactly human until the others told her, but I don't see why it should matter. Especially when it means I can be useful.

Because the main thing we've been talking about is how I can use the energy I seem to be able to generate to create a disturbance.

"What would be the best target for Rheave's daimon magic?" Ivy says, rubbing her chin as she studies a map of the city that Alek and Casimir were able to obtain. We've marked the known sites of major Order of the Wild activity on it.

Stavros folds his real hand over his prosthetic as he leans his elbows against the side of the table. "His energy appears to burn very quickly. We could destroy supplies they're relying on."

I consider the materials that I've observed humans require most often. "Food?"

Hanie jumps in with another of those quick frowns and a hasty protest. "If you mess with their stores of food, they'll just take from the rest of us."

"What about weapons?" Alek suggests, rubbing the edge of his mask. He put it back on when he heard Hanie would be coming to this meeting, although I don't know why he feels he needs to hide his interesting face from someone who's supposed to be our friend. "They aren't going to win many battles if they haven't got the tools to fight with. I'd bet Rheave could damage even swords and daggers."

I imagine the crackly energy that can flow out of me searing through metal blades and leather-wrapped handles. A grin springs to my lips. "Yes, I could muddle them!"

Ivy turns to Hanie. "Have you seen any place where the Order seems to be stashing that kind of equipment?"

The local woman shakes her head. She gestures to one area of the map where several buildings are marked. "They're mostly operating out of that neighborhood. I'd imagine any stores of supplies they've built up are somewhere in there. I don't—I don't want to risk wandering around too close without any real reason to be there, or they might assume I'm spying."

Casimir touches her arm. "It's all right. We can scope out the situation. You've helped a great deal already."

Ivy smiles at him as if she's the one he was speaking kindly to. Like he's done a wonderful thing.

If I can burn up a bunch of swords and shields, will she smile at me that way?

It's not that she never aims any smiles my way at all. But they always look a little... uncertain compared to how she is with the other men.

She helped me snap out of the spell the scourge sorcerers had me under. She led me to freedom.

I can't shake the feeling that I haven't done even half as much for her yet. But I want to.

I also want her to touch my face again like she did when I was out in the cold night. That was a special kind of warmth like nothing else I've felt.

But I don't have any wish to frighten her again like I did that time.

It's a complicated desire.

"We could ride through on the horses to take a look," I suggest. "Then we'd be able to leave quickly if anyone acts suspicious."

Ivy hums. "I think it'd be better if I sneak around and don't let anyone see me at all. It shouldn't take very long to figure out their operations."

Stavros turns to me. "You haven't seen any signs that they're producing clay bodies in the city?"

"No," I have to admit. "It was a big space where I first woke up. I'm not sure there would be room in a city."

"Well, that was a long shot anyway. Even if the production is happening in Eppun, Nikodi is only a sixth of the province's territory, and Pima a fraction of that."

The big man sighs and shifts backward in his chair. "We can continue monitoring the few other brothels in the city and watching for shrouded figures in general. The more accomplices we displace, the less power they'll have to maintain their authority."

Casimir nods. "The cleric we brought the others to said he'd be happy to take in more. He was horrified by what's been done to them. With Prospira's influence, we can hope he'll be able to help them grow beyond the near-slavery the scourge sorcerers consigned them to."

Alek clears his throat. "I should mention—my conversation with him was somewhat fruitful. It sounds as though there may be detailed records on certain aspects of the Great Retribution at a temple of Jurnus a few hours east of here. I think fully understanding how the godlen dealt with the original scourge sorcerers could be essential to challenging them now. I'd like to take a day or two to visit and go through the accounts, since I haven't been needed for much here so far."

Worry clouds Ivy's bright blue eyes. "You'd go alone? That doesn't seem safe."

"Who could you spare to come with me?" he asks, his normally flat tone softening the way it often does when he's talking to her. "This is the best way I can contribute. The scourge sorcerers won't be searching for solitary scholars on the road. They're watching out for armies."

His logic makes perfect sense, but Ivy's brow stays furrowed. She reaches across the table to squeeze his hand.

Another pang of that uncomfortable emotion hits me in the chest.

I don't think she'd look at me like *that* either. If I offered to go on a quest by myself, would she try to convince me to stay for my safety?

I wouldn't, though. I don't even like it when we're apart within this city, even though I can see why sometimes it's necessary to carry out our mission.

Everyone starts to get up from the table. Stavros tips his head toward Alek. "Let me go over some self-defense techniques for when you're on horseback, just in case. So our lady can worry a little less."

"Yes, you do that," Ivy mutters, but the look she gives the big man is undeniably fond too.

I nudge back my chair and push to my feet, still fascinated by the sensation of moving through physical space: the air shifting against my skin, the recalibrating of my center of gravity. I went through my entire past existence totally unaware—

A force wrenches through me like a rake hooking its prongs around my insides. As I stumble backward, bumping into my chair, a command that's as much felt as heard reverberates through my nerves.

*Come here,* the call says. *Come to me. Now!*

I have only a vague sense of where the magical command is directing me to go, but my body lurches around before I can get a grip on it. The chair clatters over on its side.

Ivy's voice reaches me as if from a distance. "Rheave? What's the matter?"

Then Alek's: "It might be the scourge sorcerers trying to regain control. They did it before. Remember what we talked about, Rheave!"

And then Hanie, panicked: "The sorcerers can still make him do things?"

I try to focus on Alek's words. Remember what we talked about—the advice he gave me back at the Haven.

Focus on all the ways this body is mine now. All the things I can make it do.

I try to stomp my feet against the floor so the impact will reverberate through them, but I nearly trip over them instead. A flare of my own panic crackles through me.

I can't let them manipulate me. I can't let them make me hurt anyone.

I can't let them kill me.

My hands flail out. One smacks into the wall; the other swings toward the table.

In my urgency, the energy I can call forth courses up my arm as if it can anchor me to the furniture. A bright streak sears across the wood, blackening the surface in an instant.

Hanie yelps. Stavros charges toward me, but Ivy darts in front of me first.

She grabs my face between her hands, turning my head so her face fills my field of vision. All I can see is her bright blue eyes, her skin turned even milkier than usual, her pale orange hair billowing around her.

"Rheave," she says. "You're staying with us. You don't belong to them anymore. You can fight them off."

I find myself swaying toward her even as the command yanks at me again. As if she's a tether holding me in place.

No, I don't belong to them anymore. I belong to myself—and to this woman who's always cared even when I couldn't do the same in return.

I set my hands against her forearms to help solidify the connection between us. From somewhere beyond her, I'm vaguely aware of Hanie saying, "I've really got to get going," and scampering out the door.

Ivy doesn't break eye contact with me. "Better?"

"Yes." Then I shudder with another magical tug. The rake prongs are digging in with little points of pain.

That's another sensation I never experienced as a pure daimon. Pain is fascinating but also unpleasant—especially when I know that the purpose of this specific discomfort is to break my will.

"Come here." Ivy guides me into the sleeping room and closes the door, putting one more barrier between me and the sorcerers attempting to repossess me.

"If you need any help..." Casimir calls after us.

"I think I've got this." Ivy slides her hands down to my shoulders. "Deep breaths. Feel your feet on the floor. Feel my hands squeezing you. You're here. They can't take you away."

I inhale and exhale, abruptly conscious of the act my body performs so automatically most of the time. It's easy to hone my attention in on the feel of her fingers against my shoulders, pressing through the fabric of my shirt.

She didn't want me to get *too* close to her that night she brought me in from the cold, but every particle of my being resonates with the need to get as close as I can. It's a demand loud enough to drown out most of the sorcerers' call.

I step closer and wrap my arms right around her. Ivy's breath hitches with surprise, but then she hugs me back.

"It's okay. You can stay right here with me, as long as you want to."

I'll always want to. I know that right down to the core of my being. With every word she says, every gesture she makes, every second I spend observing her, I know that wherever she ends up is the only place I want to be.

I don't know how to say that to her in a way she'll understand or accept. I turn my head and brush my lips against her cheek like she let me the other night.

A softer sound escapes Ivy, one that sends a very different jolt to the mostly useless appendage between my legs. A strange heat creeps over my skin, but she's already easing back.

She gives my arm one last pat and smiles at me—her usual cautious smile, not the one I want. "It's good to have you back with us. You just keep shutting the scourge sorcerers out. Practice those techniques even when they're not badgering you, and you'll be better prepared when they do. At least, that's helped with my magic."

"Thank you," I say, the heat from before prickling into a flush of shame. I'm supposed to be protecting *her*, and now she's had to do it for me again.

But the worst knowledge niggles at me as we walk back into the other room.

She grounded me. She drowned out my former masters' call.

What will happen if they yank at me that hard again—or harder—when Ivy isn't around?

# TWENTY

*Ivy*

Tucked into the shadows of the narrow alley, I point at a boxy wooden building a few storefronts down the street. "They're hoarding all kinds of weaponry and armor inside that inn. It doesn't seem to be operating as a proper business anymore."

The two men beside me study the structure in pensive silence.

Rheave knits his brow. "Why do they want to keep all of it together? Don't the Order of the Wild people need to use the equipment?"

I shrug, doing my best to ignore the sense of dread that's crept up inside me since I started monitoring the scourge sorcerers' activities here. "They haven't had any battles nearby so far. I'd imagine they're either gathering equipment in case the army pushes this far into the province, or they're planning on sending cartloads of it on to the front lines as it's needed."

Julita's presence gives the impression of a wince. *I don't like either of those options.*

Neither do I.

I'm about to suggest that we should set our own plan in motion when a horse-drawn carriage pulls up right outside the inn.

For a second, I think I've been mistaken, that the place is still receiving guests. But no one gets out of the carriage. While the driver waits with a bored expression, a couple of men emerge from the inn carrying crates that they stuff into the vehicle.

Casimir keeps his voice low. "It looks like they might already be moving some of their stash around."

I match his tone. "Maybe things didn't go as well as the Order would like us to believe in their clashes with the royal army over the past couple of days."

Several news callers have taken to the streets announcing victories against army squadrons the king has sent to try to stomp out the uprising. The conspirators passed around free ale and had minstrels playing in a celebration last night that was noisy enough to interrupt my sleep until well past midnight.

I'd certainly like to believe they're actually being squashed like they deserve. Taking them down all by ourselves is an awfully big undertaking.

I lean as close as I dare to the mouth of the alley and prick my ears. The men bring out a few final boxes, and one of them stops to pat the horse's flank.

"A bunch of us will be following in just a few days," he says. "Make sure everything's organized for the march to start."

The driver nods and prods the horse into motion. I draw farther back into the shadows as the carriage rattles by.

"It sounds like they're going to be moving people too," Rheave remarks once the carriage is out of sight.

I nod. "To march to the border of the province? They might have lost a lot of manpower on the front lines."

Casimir pauses, a frown shadowing his face. "Something about the way he talked makes me think it might be bigger than that."

*Gods, don't tell me this situation can get even worse,* Julita mutters.

I let out a shaky breath and square my shoulders. "Well, whatever they're planning, it'll be harder with significantly less weaponry. Are you clear on your part, Rheave?"

The daimon-man meets my eyes with an eager light in his. "Yes, I'm ready! I'll ruin everything in there that I can. I'm getting better at adjusting how much power I pour out."

He gives his fingers a subtle snap in demonstration, and a tiny spark jumps from them to tickle my neck. It sends a deeper shiver right down the middle of me that I refuse to acknowledge, but a little of my tension ebbs.

I smile at him. "All right. Give me a moment to cast the magic to conceal you. Casimir will tell you when it's safe."

I sit down on the grubby alley floor, taking the position of my training sessions with Sulla. It's easier for me to concentrate on directing my magic in the now-familiar pose.

As Casimir takes my place at the mouth of the alley where he's going to keep watch, I fix my gaze on Rheave. I take in his stunning face and muscular form—and imagine the dwindling daylight passing straight through him.

My power vibrates through my chest, sensing that I'm about to call on it. An image of Stavros's concerned expression when we confirmed our tactics floats up with it, but I push that away.

He trusts me to extend my magic this far. What am I even doing here if I don't bring the most useful skill I have to bear?

Although I can't help thinking that as much as my men like to compare me to Signy, the exalted Veldunian hero didn't need to sneak around in shadowed alleys or tap into illicit magic to get things done.

I close my eyes against all those distractions, holding the image of Rheave fading away in the front of my mind. I focus the rest of my attention on the consequence I'd like to counteract the spell.

Up on the rooftop above my head, light will bounce off

empty air as if the form of a man is standing on the shingles. If anyone happened to be up there, they might see a mirage of Rheave.

I let my weight sink into the ground to steady myself and slowly open up. My magic unfurls from my chest toward the targets I've pictured.

A choked sound escapes Casimir's lips. "It's working. I can barely—now I can't see him at all. Rheave, you should go, quickly. We don't want Ivy to strain herself."

My magic races after the daimon-man as he hurries down the road. A nervous jitter shoots through my veins at the sensation.

I haven't expended quite this much energy in a sustained way… ever.

As long as I keep focusing the backlash somewhere it won't hurt anyone or reveal our trick, it should be fine. I know what I'm doing.

It's *my* power, and it's going to obey me.

Casimir eases back and crouches behind me. He sets his hands on my shoulders. "I'm right here with you, Kindness. If you need grounding, you can focus on me."

The tenderness in his voice does help me stay centered in the midst of the magic flowing through me. I breathe in and out, channeling the power through me from the broken soul this man doesn't shy from.

As if from a much farther distance, a hiss and a warble of flames reaches my ears. Rheave's spent a lot of the past couple of days testing out his powers, and he thought he might be able to create the right sort of sparks to set the building outright on fire. It sounds as if he's succeeded.

Casimir shifts his weight with a soft rasp of his shoes against the ground and a gentle pressure on my shoulders. Shouts reverberate from the direction of the building.

My magic prickles through my flesh, contracting into me as

Rheave lopes to rejoin us. The second his feet thud into the alley, I yank all of my power back inside with a gasp of breath.

As my eyes pop open, the daimon-man solidifies into view in front of me. He's grinning wide, his eerie eyes sparkling. "I burned up everything I could—I even melted some of the metal."

Casimir straightens up and tugs his arm. "Wonderful. Now let's get out of here before they start searching the whole street for the culprits."

The courtesan holds out his hand to yank me to my feet as well. We dash down the alley the way we arrived, wind around the back of a few buildings, and emerge into a public square.

Most of the civilians we hustle out to join are peering over the rooftops. I spin to see smoke billowing up from the burning building, tainting the deep blue of the early evening sky.

Julita lets out a wordless crow of victory. *Ha! They'll be starting to see they can't get away with their degeneracy.* I get the impression she's spun around in my head with excitement. *You were amazing, Ivy. It's incredible what you can do now that you know how to work with your magic.*

I chuckle under my breath, not able to fully share her enthusiasm. Like when I pulled the shadows over us on the side of the road, the effort has left me a little dizzy.

I'm not sure I could do much more than this and stay focused.

But it is pretty incredible that I was able to help even as much as I did. I kept Rheave hidden so he could attack the scourge sorcerers in ways I wouldn't dare to attempt with my own magic yet.

We gape at the smoke for a minute like the other bystanders, just to fit in. Then Casimir tucks his hand around my elbow with a careful tug. "We should probably—"

His voice cuts off as we turn and find a cluster of five men and women closing in on us, their gazes unnervingly intense.

Rheave pushes in front of me in an instant, his hands rising defensively. I grab his sleeve to hold him back, though my stance has tensed.

The man at the front of the group holds up his own hands in a gesture of surrender. "We're not with… *them*. We just want to talk."

The woman next to him folds her arms over her chest beneath her long cloak. "And it seems we have a lot to talk about."

Julita's presence stirs uneasily. *Hmm. Rather presumptuous, aren't they? I don't know any of this bunch.*

Casimir puts on his best innocent expression. "I'm sorry, but I'm afraid I'm not sure what you mean."

With a scoffing sound, the man rakes his hand through his scruffy black hair. He drops his voice lower. "We know you three hit their temporary armory. We were right there—because *we* were planning on trashing the place as well as we could. You beat us to the punch."

The woman jerks her head toward a quieter corner of the square with a swish of her sandy-blond ponytail. "So can we have this conversation somewhere it's less likely to get us killed?"

Apprehension prickles over me, but the group hasn't made any aggressive moves, even though they've got us outnumbered. The cautious twitch of their gazes reminds me more of our own wariness than the cocky air most of the Order members and allies give off.

If there are other people in the city willing to strike out at the scourge sorcerers, shouldn't we find out what they can tell us? It's not as if Julita's said anything concerning about them—she won't have known most of the city commoners, I'd imagine.

Rheave keeps his protective pose, but Casimir seems to agree with me. "We'll come. But we want to stay somewhere we can easily leave if we feel the need to."

The woman laughs, making the scar across her cheek jump. "The sentiment is mutual. Come on."

The group tramps over to a side-street and then down it to

an open-ended road by a stable no one appears to be attending to at the moment.

The three who haven't spoken so far spread out as if to watch for unwelcome interruptions. The man dips his knobby chin to us. "Since you trusted us enough to come along, we can do the first introductions. I'm Emor, and this is Voleska. We've been trying to figure out a way to get these Order of the Wild pricks out of our city since they first showed up."

Voleska studies us. "You aren't from Pima. I'd have noticed you before."

I'm not ready to give her our names yet, but I'll acknowledge that point. "We were in the capital when the palace there was attacked. When we heard about the uprising in Eppun, we came to see what we could do to help before the situation gets even worse."

Emor hums and glances over his shoulder toward the smoke still wafting up toward the sky. "You've made a decent start of it, I'll give you that."

"What have you been doing?" Rheave asks. "You have gifts—can you use those?"

He nods to the obvious signs of their dedication sacrifices: Emor is missing a little finger and Voleska her left thumb.

It's not generally considered polite to prod people about their gifts, but I can't help being glad Rheave didn't know that—because I'd like the answer too.

Emor doesn't show any sign of being offended. He rubs the stump of his missing finger. "Unfortunately, mine isn't good for much other than ensuring our people have decent meals."

He glances at Voleska a little awkwardly, but she simply shrugs. "I didn't receive a gift, and fairly so. I was a lot more selfish at twelve than I've learned to be since."

*Yikes,* Julita murmurs.

Rheave's eyes widen. I don't know if he was aware that not every sacrifice is recognized by the godlen it's made to.

I suppress a shudder at the thought of losing a whole thumb

for nothing, but Voleska spoke without rancor. I guess a situation like that would make you rethink a lot of things about your life.

The daimon-man cocks his head. "So you want our help because we can do more than you can."

I give his arm a light swat to try to tell him to ease up on the attitude, but Casimir speaks before I can. "Our friend might not be the politest of gentlemen, but he does raise our main concern. Why did you approach us? It'll be easier for us to decide how to respond if we know where this conversation is going."

Voleska clicks her tongue. "Straight to the point. Fine. You *are* clearly working with some impressive gifts. But we have the local connections. We could accomplish a lot more if we combined forces and tackled these assholes together."

Julita lets out a skeptical sound. *I don't know. This bunch seems awfully… rough around the edges.*

I restrain a snort. The small apartment Hanie found for us to squat in didn't come with a mirror—my ghostly passenger has no concept of how scruffy I must look at this point.

Rough around the edges could be exactly what we need.

But we still have to be careful about it.

I raise an eyebrow. "We've gotten by all right without extra connections. What could yours tell us that we don't already know?"

Emor smirks. "I'm sure you've heard all the victory celebrations, but did you know that one of the king's magical advisors, a fellow named Lothar, has come with the latest troops to try to negotiate with the Order?"

Lothar—the royal advisor Stavros said specializes in potions… and hunting down riven sorcerers. The one who sacrificed an entire arm for whatever his gift is.

Has the king sent him to try to learn more about the scourge sorcerers' illicit magic?

A chill ripples down my spine. "I didn't know that, but how does it help us?"

"It shows how ineffective the royal army's been," Voleska says in a sneering tone. "Sending all these soldiers out here, and they either get cut down or have to retreat. At this rate, they'll negotiate the whole province away just to save the rest of the country. We have to do something big."

"That's right." Emor rubs his hands together. "And because we've lived here our whole lives, we also know the best ways to appeal to our neighbors. We just don't have the power to speak to them without getting dragged off and tossed in a ditch. We need to show the people of Pima that someone *can* get the upper hand over the Order of the Wild."

Voleska jumps back in with a triumphant smile. "*And* we know that the Order is planning some big meeting tomorrow morning. That'll give us the perfect opportunity to make a stir when there are fewer of their stooges looking to bash dissenters' heads in."

I hadn't known about the meeting either. A flare of hope lights inside me.

Casimir slips his hand around mine with a light squeeze as if to say he'll stand with me. The subtle smile he shoots me suggests he's ready to trust this bunch at least a little farther.

I've thought so many times about how difficult it'll be for us to take on the scourge sorcerers alone. How can we dismiss any advantage that presents itself?

I let my lips curl with a small smile of my own. "I like the sound of that. Let us check with our companions, but maybe we can meet up later tonight and form a real plan."

# Twenty-One

*Ivy*

I crouch on the ledge in the pre-dawn darkness, watching a devout cross the main temple room in the glow of the single, central lantern. He vanishes through the back doorway.

Like all towns and cities of decent size, Pima has one temple dedicated to the All-Giver and the nine lesser gods together. It's nowhere near as impressive as the Temple of the Crown in Florian, but the vaulted ceiling and the statues watching from the alcoves below me still set my nerves wobbling.

I'm about to steal Nikodi's greatest religious treasure from right under all the gods' noses. Or right over their noses, as the case may be.

Hopefully they'll feel the ends justify my means.

My ghostly passenger seems to be feeling similarly apprehensive.

Julita's presence shivers in the back of my head. *This is where I had my dedication ceremony and made my sacrifice to Creaden. I never thought I'd be back here just to pillage the place.*

I speak under my breath, so quietly no one other than the soul lodged in my head could possibly hear the words. "They'll get the artifact back afterward. I'd imagine Creaden would approve of you making sure your county isn't taken over by questionable leadership."

Julita makes a skeptical sound, but she doesn't argue as I creep along the narrow ledge toward the decorative shield mounted on the wall high above the floor. The aged wooden surface tells the story of its significance with its carvings.

Supposedly, many centuries ago, the neighboring country of Bryfeen tried to steal Nikodi and the other nearby counties away from Silana. As the legend goes, the locals weren't well-prepared enough to fight off the Bryfesh army on their own, and they were worried the royal forces wouldn't reach them in time.

So they prayed to the godlen of leadership and justice for help.

The current countess woke from a dream of Creaden to find she had a plan for securing Nikodi's freedom in her head—and this shield resting against her bedframe as a symbol of the godlen's support. She led her supporters to push back the Bryfesh soldiers and ensure the people of Nikodi got to choose who governed them.

From what Emor and Voleska told us and Julita confirmed, the people of Pima still avidly celebrate that long-ago triumph. They have a festival in honor of the countess every year, and people who feel oppressed by their circumstances come to the temple to pray both to the statue of Creaden and beneath the shield.

As a symbol to convince the citizens that they should resist the Order of the Wild's mutinous rule rather than bowing to them, you couldn't ask for much better. But it's a shame the artifact might end up damaged in the process.

The ledge takes me to just beneath the shield. Ever so carefully, I slide my fingers beneath the wooden surface and detach it from the hooks that hold it in place.

Thankfully, the leather arm strap must be periodically replaced or kept in good condition through magic. I slip it over my arm almost to my shoulder without any fear that it'll crumble.

Julita lets out a nervous giggle.

Keeping my own mouth clamped tight, I brace the shield against my back and slink along the railing to the main entrance. Then I pull out the canvas sack I brought and wrap it around the shield to hide my cargo.

With a deft leap, I land on the stone floor near the entrance with only a soft thud. I hurry out into the city without waiting to see if anyone will come to investigate the sound.

*Creaden forgive us*, Julita murmurs. I have the vague impression of her making the gesture of the divinities, as well as she can in her current state.

It's dark enough that I don't need to use my magic to conceal myself. Which I'm grateful for, since I'll need it later this morning. Sulla's warnings linger in the back of my mind.

I haven't felt any negative effects from the ways I've worked my power since leaving the Haven, but my attempts have been fairly minor. I'd like to keep it that way.

I dart through the streets to the café where I'm supposed to meet the others. The storefront is shuttered, but the door around back opens at my tug.

A small crowd is waiting for me in the room beyond. Stavros insisted on joining Casimir, Rheave, and me for this undertaking, since we're expecting to do at least a little fighting. I can't help being glad that Alek is off on his research trip so he won't be caught up in the violence too.

Near my men, Emor and Voleska stand in a cluster with a few of their associates. They turn to face me with eager expressions.

"You got it?" Voleska asks as she takes in the sack, her tone hushed.

I suspect the shield is pretty meaningful to her too, even if she's willing to use it for this gambit. When I nudge down the canvas fabric to reveal part of the wooden surface, she, Emor, and their companions go still with awe.

I nudge it toward them. "I don't know how long it'll be before the temple staff notice it's missing."

Emor hums dismissively, his attention still fixed on the shield with a reverent air. "To avoid creating a panic, they'll keep the disappearance quiet for at least the first few hours while they search. By then, we'll have already shown everyone why they *should* be panicking."

Finally, he tears his gaze away to consider me and my men. "We'll set up in the square at the ninth bell. Everyone's clear on what they're meant to be doing?"

We all nod. As far as the local rebels know, I have a gift for moving things with my mind, which covers both of the purposes they want from me. Once the expected chaos starts, the three men will join in, working on cutting down the scourge sorcerers' support.

If we can turn the tide here, maybe word will spread and more of the province's people will reject the Order of the Wild's claims.

Voleska pauses to peer at Rheave. "You'll help us identify these… daimon in conjured bodies? We don't want to hurt anyone who was simply duped by the traitors."

Her group took the news about what Rheave actually is—and how many others like him the scourge sorcerers are manipulating—with a certain amount of skepticism. But this is the perfect chance for us to free some of those captured daimon.

"I know them as soon as I see them," he assures her, and pats the quiver on his back. "I'll only shoot the captured daimon. I can guide the arrows well with the power I have. If my effort doesn't break their body, the arrows will show you which ones you should go after."

Emor raises his eyebrows. "What if you run out of arrows?"

It appears Rheave has already considered that possibility,

because he answers without hesitation. "I'll send my power on its own. I don't want to burn anything too badly when there'll be a lot of people around, but I can char their hair as a signal."

He sets his fingers against the wall with a spurt of crackling energy. When he lifts his hand, a small scorch mark remains.

The rebels stare at it for a moment, Emor's shoulders stiffening. This is the first time they've seen his daimon powers in action.

"It's a good thing we have Rheave on our side," I remind them. "Otherwise we'd have no idea who the Order conjured out of clay."

Emor gives a rough laugh. "True, true. Well, we'd better wrangle some breakfast before we wage our little war." He tugs one of his companion's sleeves. "Come on, you can help me whip up some of my famous scrambled eggs."

Most of the rebels duck into the next room, which I guess is the café's kitchen. Voleska remains, crouching down to study the shield where she's propped it against the wall.

I move to the window, peering out into the faint dawn glow that's just touching the streets. Casimir starts helping Stavros with the false hand he's made to help him blend in—a leather glove partly stuffed to fill out the fingers, that they're hoping to fit over his metal prosthetic in disguise.

Rheave ambles over to join me. He gazes out into the back alley for a few moments before saying, "I wish we could give them the choice."

I glance over at him. "Who?"

"The other daimon. I'm sure some of them simply want to be free. That's all I wanted at first. But they're not getting the chance to really own these bodies if they'd like to experience this kind of life for a while."

My stomach twists. I hadn't thought of the situation like that. "If there was a way we could simply snap them out of the scourge sorcerers' control…"

Rheave aims a quiet smile at me that suddenly makes him

look much older than his youthful looks suggest. "But there isn't. I know. And it's better for them to be free in their usual state than forced to do horrible things for the sorcerers. Once we've defeated the Order of the Wild, though, we should let the ones who are left decide what they'd prefer."

"Of course."

He lapses into an unusually pensive silence before turning his gaze more intently toward me. "You're sure this is a good plan, aren't you?"

"I wouldn't have agreed to it otherwise." I furrow my brow. "Why—do you think it isn't?"

The daimon-man shakes his head. "I don't know either way. It's only that… I realize that in the long time I was in this world before, I wasn't interacting with humans the same way I do now. I didn't fully understand what I saw happening between them. But there was an atmosphere around them sometimes… When they become angry, it's difficult to predict how they'll act. And anger seems to keep going and going until someone stops it."

*Hmm*, Julita says. *That's rather wise from a being who's only been semi-human for a few weeks.*

It is. I can't deny that he has a point.

Sometimes I forget that as young as Rheave can seem with his inexperience in the physical world, he really is much older than the rest of us. By human standards, I'd imagine his spirit self is nothing short of ancient.

"That's true," I say. "But sometimes you need to stir up that anger if you want to shake people out of complacency or fear. The important part is directing it at the right targets."

"People aren't that easy to direct when they're upset, are they?"

I grimace. "No. We'll do our best. We have to do *something*, and this seems like our best shot at making a significant difference quickly."

Rheave offers me a wider smile, with a gleam of affection in his eyes that makes my heart skip a beat. "Humans are always doing something. All that sense of purpose used to confuse me. Things didn't matter the same way to me before."

He hesitates and then pats my shoulder. "But now that I understand, I like it."

Something about his vocal appreciation makes my pulse wobble more—and a glow of hope light in my chest.

Yes, human beings are pretty amazing. They can create all kinds of horrors, but they can also fight with so much conviction to see those horrors overturned.

I don't ever want to forget that.

Emor's voice carries from the kitchen, calling us to breakfast. We eat standing along the counters, anticipation thrumming through the air. I barely taste the eggs, as good as I'm sure they are.

Casimir rubs my arm, pitching his voice so it's just for me. "Are you okay with everything you committed to?"

I let myself lean into his warmth briefly. "Yes. I really am getting a handle on things. It's… it's good to be able to help without constantly worrying about doing damage at the same time."

I glance down at the short sword he's wearing on his belt and then over at Stavros, who's drawn closer. "Are you two ready? It could be a mess."

Stavros smiles grimly. "All the better for us to get in there and thin the scourge sorcerers' numbers without being obvious about it. It's about time they realized they can't conquer Silana so easily."

Casimir touches the hilt of his sword. "I may not be anywhere near as experienced in combat as our general is, but I'll put what skills I do have to good use."

It makes my heart ache to think of this sweet man spilling blood for the cause, but I know there's no point in protesting. The scourge sorcerers set the tone with all the violence they've already carried out.

We all have to give this attempt everything we have. If it

goes well, most of the beings we cut down won't die, only fly free of the bodies that caged them.

If it doesn't… I can't afford to worry about that right now.

# Twenty-Two

*Ivy*

All too soon, the peal of the eighth bell rings through the café. We double-check our equipment and prepare to split up into our positions.

I pause for long enough to kiss Stavros and then Casimir. "I'll find you in the crowd after the important bit is over."

Stavros clasps me tightly to him. "Stay safe before anything else. You're taking your own risks, and we'll take ours."

Rheave watches us in his quietly intent way. I go over and give his hand a squeeze because it feels wrong to leave him completely out. "I'll see you soon."

He bobs his head. "I'll fulfill my part of the plan as well as possible. For you."

We part ways just outside the café, making our journey to the square where our demonstration is going to take place by separate routes. The streets are already starting to bustle with people on foot and horses pulling carts.

At the square, I slip around a shop Voleska pointed out to me and hurry up the back staircase. From the second-floor

window, I have an excellent view across the square—the most central and largest in Pima.

Dozens of people mill around across the cobblestones, going in and out of eateries and shops, stopping at the stalls set up here and there, lounging by the fountain. Water streams around the marble statue of Creaden in the center of the pool. The godlen peers down over the square from his high pedestal with an air of benevolent authority.

Finally, a nearby temple bell rings in nine brisk peals. I brace my hands against the window ledge, already picturing how I want to shape my magic.

Two figures leap across the fountain and scramble up the pedestal to the statue of Creaden. Bracing themselves on either side of the marble figure, Voleska drops the canvas from the shield as Emor pitches his voice to carry across the square.

His words resonate loudly enough that I hear them faintly through the window. "People of Nikodi, listen to us!"

That's my cue. I focus all my attention on the shield in Voleska's hands and loosen my hold on my power.

My magic ripples out of me and rushes toward the shield. As the force I'm propelling forward wraps around the wooden object, I picture a branch cracking on the old willow tree by the abandoned farm where we borrowed a wagon.

When I lift the shield into the air, the branch falls to the ground.

With the heft of my power, the shield floats above the statue's head where everyone in the square can see it. A flare of light conjured by one of the rebels' gifts washes over the civilians —and condenses on the shield to make it glow.

Every gaze in the square jerks toward the spectacle. Gasps and shouts rise up across the crowd.

Emor speaks quickly before the spectators can become overwhelmed with confusion. "My friends! We took Creaden's shield from the Temple of Divine Grace this morning—just before the Order of the Wild could ruin it. We heard them plotting to destroy this great symbol of our city because they don't like us having loyalty to anyone other than them."

A horrified hush sweeps through his audience. He jabs his hand in the air. "The Order says the king has a false claim on the throne, but they're trying to lay claim over us just like Bryfeen did all those ages ago. Why should we let them? They have no right. They're just as bad as the rulers they say they hate."

The murmurs that follow are fraught with tension. The crowd shifts, but no one seems to know quite what to do yet.

And then the moment Emor predicted arrives. One of the scourge sorcerers or a lackey pushes toward the fountain.

"You can't talk like that," he hollers. "We've freed you from a royal family that only wants to exploit you. Show some gratitude."

I wind my magic back into my body gradually, letting the shield sink toward Voleska.

As she raises her arms to catch it, Emor pivots toward the newcomer. "You expect gratitude when you want to exploit us just as much so *you* can be in charge? That sounds like an awful deal to me."

The instant Voleska grasps the shield, I yank back the rest of my magic and flick my gaze around the square. I can already spot a few more figures shoving their way toward the fountain from the edges of the crowd.

Julita lets out a soft chuckle. *Here they come.*

No doubt at least one conspirator has raced off to tattle to the head honchos at their meeting. Let them send as many of their forces as they like.

I don't think they're going to enjoy the outcome.

I whip my attention back to the fountain just as the first Order member reaches the base. He jumps up on the barrier around the water. "Come down from there and stop telling lies."

"Or you'll what?" Emor asks.

Voleska lowers the shield as if to defend the two of them—and I propel my magic in their direction once more.

This time I'm not aiming it at the shield. I fling the force into the conspirator, sending him lunging forward and wrenching up his hand as if he intends to strike out at them.

What he actually does is pound his fist against the shield hard enough for the sound of the impact to reverberate through the square.

Julita flinches inside me. I'm too caught up in the necessary concentration to apologize.

Off at that old farm, the backlash yanked the door off the dilapidated house at the same moment as I shoved the man on the fountain.

And the crowd erupts.

The angry shouts of the locals drown out anything else the Order member might have said. As he stumbles into the fountain water, the nearest civilians grab his arms and yank him away from the shield and the woman wielding it. He's swallowed into the churning crowd.

"Down with the Order of the Wild!" Emor yells from his perch on the statue. "Kick them out! Take back our city!"

More people stream into the square from the nearby streets and buildings. Many are locals coming to see what's happened, but others are clearly Order members.

I spot a man taking a swing at a couple of the conspirators, only for them to wrench his arms behind his back. A woman springs at them with a frying pan she bashes over the nearest conspirator's head.

As more fights break out in knots throughout the square, arrows start streaking down from the rooftop where Rheave hid himself. Shimmers of electric energy send them racing toward their targets.

Stavros and Casimir will be in the middle of the chaos along with Emor and Voleska's people, striking down every captured daimon Rheave identifies for them. And maybe a few of the fully human Order members as well, if they force the issue.

My main work is done. I can't leave them to the riskier battle alone.

I shove open the windowpane and clamber out. My gaze drops to the building fronts directly beneath me, and I freeze.

Hanie is standing just a few shops over from the one I'm staked out above, cringing against the wall with her arms folded tight around her middle. Her brass-brown hair has fallen across her face.

I bite back a curse.

*You told her not to come to the square this morning*, Julita mutters. *She's not a fighter—she shouldn't be here.*

I did warn Julita's old maidservant when I saw her briefly yesterday. I suggested she should stay clear of the central square all morning.

Apparently she was more curious than concerned.

She spins and darts away down one of the side streets. At least I don't have to worry about her getting trampled now.

I scramble to the edge of the roof. My gaze catches on Stavros's blood-red hair about halfway across the square, his head above the figures around him thanks to his massive frame. Casimir will have stuck near him.

Girding myself, I pick a section of clear ground and jump. As my feet hit the ground, I'm already braced to leap forward.

I weave through the rioting crowd, dodging jabbing elbows and grasping fingers. My gaze snags on a woman who's staggering with one of Rheave's arrows in her back, and I hurtle forward to slash my knife across her neck.

She collapses in a crash of shattering clay.

One fewer daimon the scourge sorcerers can send to attack us. Every one we set free is a victory.

A projectile sings through the air beside me, this one all daimon energy. It sizzles into the side of a man's head several paces off through the crowd.

The man flinches where he's trying to wrestle a thrashing woman to the ground. I push through the churning bodies toward him and stab my knife between his ribs straight into his heart.

Another mass of clay topples onto the cobblestones.

I whirl around, trying to regain my sense of where my allies are. At another glimpse of dark red hair, I hustle through the crowd.

When I get a clearer view of the two men, it takes me a moment to figure out what's going on. Casimir has drawn his sword, but he's mostly reaching out to people with his empty hand, guiding them past him.

Directing them to a nearby pub where they can escape the chaos if they want, I realize. Of course the courtesan would be more focused on making sure the innocents are safe than murdering the villains.

Stavros is just charging farther into the crowd to slam his sword through the torso of another man with a charred blotch where some of his hair should be. The conjured body collapses in a burst of clay shards.

I expect the former general to look my way so I can flash him a quick smile, but his stance abruptly stiffens. Without warning, he dashes off.

I try to follow, but a current of bodies pushes between us, jostling my scrawny form. Squeezing my way between the furious citizens, I hop up on my feet here and there to peer over their heads.

Over by one of the stores, a teenage boy cowers on the ground while a man kicks him and bashes at his head with the pommel of his dagger. If I had any question about which side they're each on, it'd be answered by the tattoo inked on the side of the man's neck: an inverted All-Giver sigil.

That's the symbol the scourge sorcerers use to try to call the Great God back to our realms.

Stavros lets out a roar of rage loud enough for me to hear it over the tumult of the crowd. He rams into the attacker and knocks the man off his feet.

In my next glimpse, their blades are clanging together. I grit my teeth and shove through the milling bodies with more force.

I stumble into the less-packed fringes of the crowd just in time to see Stavros dig his blade into the man's throat.

This body doesn't transform. It simply slumps, gushing blood.

And Stavros is so intent on finishing the man off, he hasn't noticed another attacker who crashes into *him* before I can even shout a warning.

My cry breaks from my lips, too late. Julita yelps like an echo of it.

I sprint over, my fingers tight around my knife. My heart hammers against my ribs.

My magic wrenches at me to unleash it, to let it fend off the attacker, but the impulse comes with a cold jab of fear. I didn't plan for that—I can't stop to concentrate on a counter-action—

The two men wrestle each other, blood splattering the cobblestones around them. I shove down my power and lunge forward with my blade raised.

Just before I can plunge my knife into the attacker's skull, Stavros heaves the man off him with a meaty rasp of his sword.

The man collapses, the short sword he was clutching clanging on the stones. Relief surges up inside me for just an instant before Stavros sags backward too.

Blood gushes from a cut on his side, drenching his tunic red.

My own blood freezes in my veins. A flood of terror and anguish sweeps every other thought from my mind.

"Stavros!" I cry, dropping down beside him.

No, gods, no. Not like this.

Not again.

What am I supposed to do to save him?

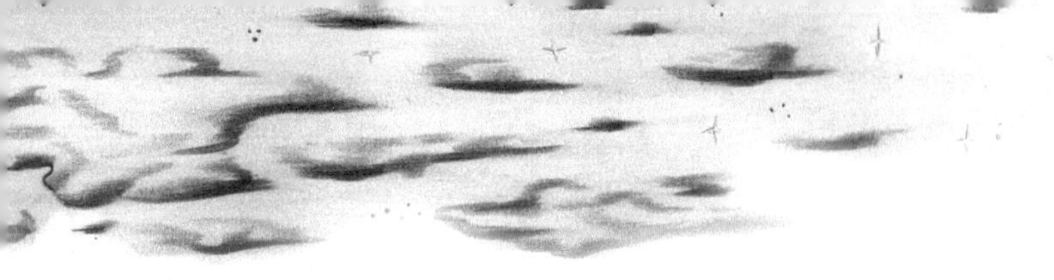

# Twenty-Three

*Stavros*

Even as pain burns through my abdomen and blurs my sight more than usual, I can't help jerking my gaze toward the boy. The boy whose shaggy blond hair and freckled face make memories of another teenager swim up from the depths of my mind.

*Michas*, some part of me calls out, but this isn't my old friend. It isn't the boy I watched a riven sorcerer rip apart.

Still, a pang of happiness resonates through the pain when I see this other boy getting to his feet with no obvious injuries other than a scrape on his forehead and a reddish blotch on his cheek that'll probably bruise.

The shouts and cries of the riot have blurred too, my sense of the rest of my surroundings going increasingly hazy. The press of frantic fingers around my arm brings me back.

Ivy is staring down at me. Her blue eyes have gone so wide I could lose myself in them, but the wax-pale shade of her face sends a jolt of panic through my veins.

Is she hurt? Did the bastards—

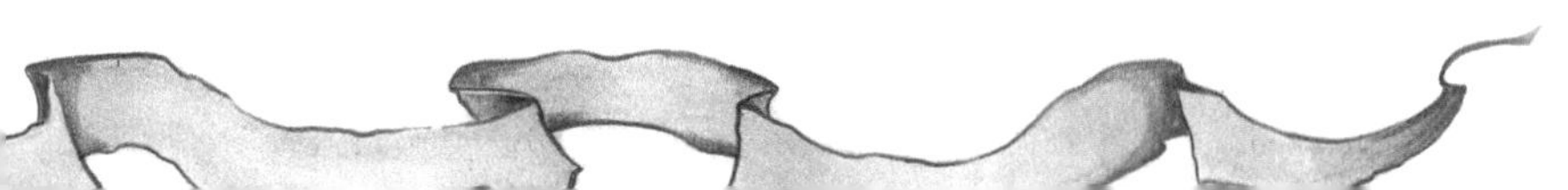

I try to ask, but the pain searing through my abdomen seems to have stretched to my throat. All I manage to do is croak, "Ivy."

"I'm here," she says, her voice quavering, and the pain in my side sharpens. Her other hand is pressing against the worst spot —*fuck*, it hurts. "Do you think you can walk at all? There are more Order members coming—we have to get you out of the way—"

A rotund figure appears at the edge of my vision, standing over us. His voice comes out in a rough baritone. "He protected my son. I'll protect him, as well as I can." He motions to the boy. "Sebias, here, we need to get this man inside."

More hands grasp my shoulders, my thighs. As they heft me into the air, the blaze of agony knocks the breath from my lungs.

That fucking asshole ramming into me from out of nowhere —I should have been watching my surroundings more—first fucking rule of combat—

My back jars against a tiled floor. Ivy is babbling thank yous to the man whose shop we've intruded on.

"It's the least we could do," he says, sketching the gesture of the divinities with a shaky hand. "Take whatever you need to stop the bleeding. I don't know how else to help. Sebias, let's clean that scrape of yours."

Their footsteps shuffle away. Ivy's still here, leaning over me.

The pain clenches around my lungs, stabbing deeper as I haul in a breath.

"Stavros," Ivy says, sounding choked, "you're bleeding so much. It's deep. I don't think I can stop it like this."

She's so upset. Terrified. I've seen that emotion in her before, but this time she isn't afraid *of* me but *for* me.

We've come that far. I could laugh at the wonder of it, but I can barely suck enough air into my chest to grunt.

Ivy strokes her hand over my hair and cheek. Her fingers are shaking. "What do you want me to do?"

Something clicks in my head through the hazing of my thoughts. She's afraid of herself too. Of what she could do.

She's asking me if she should pour that fathomless, mad magic of hers into me.

My muscles tense automatically as if trying to shut out the very idea. Flickers of Michas's blood-splattered voice, his screams, whirl through my head.

Riven magic always destroys in the end.

Great God help us, how bad must I look for her to even offer?

I part my lips and focus all my attention on forming my breath into words. "I—I'll be fine."

The last word breaks into a groan at a fresh wave of agony. A sob breaks from Ivy's throat.

We both know I'm lying. A chill is starting to seep through my limbs like nothing I've ever felt during any battlefield wound.

My own fear stirs.

I don't want to go like this. I'm not *done*.

Ivy bows her head close to mine, her voice falling to a raw whisper. "I promise I won't do anything you wouldn't want."

I stare up at her, her face hazing before my eyes. Sunlight gleams through the window behind her, glowing amber as it passes through her red-blond hair.

Like the golden halo artists give those god-blessed in their paintings and tapestries.

The glow seeps into me with a sudden, sharp clarity.

Ivy didn't destroy anything when she hid us in the forest or concealed Rheave to carry out our plans. No catastrophe rained down on us when she pulled off her tricks with the shield.

How did I not see it before? The power I'd normally revile passes through her… and she colors it with all her strength and compassion.

What she works isn't just riven magic. It's *hers*.

A strange sense of peace washes over me. Ivy has given me the choice, because that's who she is—the woman I believe in, the woman I love.

And I do believe in her, more than I hate the errant energies she can channel through the cracks in her soul. This woman can take the vilest power in the world and transform it into a force for good.

In the sudden calm, my voice detaches from the pain. I hold Ivy's gaze as well as I can and force out the hoarse words. "I want… to live. Don't want… to leave you. Don't want… to fail the… kingdom. I trust you. Anything… you do… will be right."

Ivy's breath hitches. She leans so close her lips brush my forehead in a ghost of a kiss. "Are you sure?"

I can only manage one more word, but it contains everything I need to say. "Yes."

The pain is swelling again, eating at the edges of my consciousness. But Ivy makes a resolved sound low in her throat and clamps her hand tighter against my side.

Warmth bursts through my torso. It swallows the pain and the creeping numbness; it melts the agony gripping my lungs.

I gulp one full, hungry breath—and my mind spirals away into darkness.

Alek's voice penetrates through my consciousness first, muffled as it passes through the wall. "Should we try to find a healer, just to look him over?"

Casimir answers in a softer voice I can't totally make out—something about not knowing who's with the Order.

I blink, my sense of my surroundings coming back to me. I'm sprawled on my back on one of the heaps of folded blankets that's served as a mattress in our temporary apartment. Another blanket is draped over me to my shoulders.

Memories of my last conscious moments rush in: the boy, the pain, Ivy's desperate questions…

Tentatively, I push myself into a sitting position. A faint twinge passes through my abdomen, but more like a bruise that's nearly finished healing than a fatal wound.

Ivy did that. Ivy poured her riven magic into me, and it fused the injured pieces back together.

No horror pierces me at the thought. Only bemusement at the irony that I've been fixed thanks to the part of her that's broken.

She wouldn't have done it if she wasn't sure she could control the consequences in a way I can accept.

She and the others must have carried me back to the apartment. And cleaned me up. My bloodied clothes are gone—I'm wearing my other woolen tunic and pair of trousers.

They left my harness on my left arm but removed the prosthetic, maybe so I didn't accidentally smack myself with the metal contraption in my sleep. It's lying on the floor within arm's reach, gleaming and untarnished as if they washed that up too.

The voices in the other room have fallen silent. Did my companions leave?

I'm about to get up and check when the door eases open. Ivy peeks inside.

Her face both brightens and tenses at the sight of me. "You're awake! How do you feel?"

"Impressively normal." I glance down at my side. "I'd almost think it was only a nightmare."

She lets out a rough laugh. "If only. Let me just—"

She slips away for a few seconds and returns with a steaming mug. When she hands it to me, a warm, meaty smell fills my nose—it's broth, both food and drink.

As I raise it to my lips and take a tentative sip, Ivy sits down next to me, leaving a small space between us as if she isn't sure how close I'd want her to get. She waits quietly while I fill my stomach with a few larger gulps.

"Are you sure you're okay?" she asks. "With… everything?"

From the wariness in her expression, it's obvious which part of everything she's specifically concerned about.

All at once, it hits me just how difficult that moment must have been for her too. Not just because of my past reactions to her magic, but because of how it would have reminded her of the one other time she brought someone she cared about back from the brink of death.

The only other time she's used her power to save a life, she lost an equally dear one… and the woman she saved turned on her for it.

An ache swells in my chest. I set down the mug and turn toward her, reaching to grasp her hand.

With the squeeze of my fingers, I hope I convey the truth of my next words. "I meant what I told you, Ivy. It doesn't matter what magic you used to heal me. What matters is you were the one doing it. I trust you."

She exhales a little raggedly. How long is it going to take before she fully believes that statement?

She twines her fingers with mine, but her head droops. "I keep thinking back to the moment when it happened. Maybe I could have reacted quickly enough to stop him from stabbing you in the first place, and then I wouldn't have needed to use any magic on you. But I hesitated—I didn't have time to think of where to aim the backlash— Even after the training and practice, I'm still scared."

I stroke my thumb over the back of her hand. "I think that's a good thing. The consequences of being cautious should be much less than the consequences of going too far. I'm glad you were there to save me from *my* carelessness."

I pause, but I know I need to ask this question. To find out who or what paid so that I could live. "What backlash came out of healing me?"

Ivy takes a deep breath. "I was going to focus on the tree I've been using on the abandoned farm. But then I glanced out the window and saw one of the daimon Rheave had marked with a burn. I figured it'd be safer using a target I could see, and something almost human, for an effect that big."

"It killed him?"

"He at least fainted from whatever injuries I passed on to him. I think one of Emor's people took care of the rest."

I let that knowledge settle. I can't even feel guilty about keeping my life at the expense of a conjured body that was more a prison than a living thing itself.

So Ivy shouldn't feel guilty either.

I pull her closer to me, hating the wariness I feel in her stance as she comes. As if there's still a small part, however deeply she managed to bury it, that's afraid I'll lash out at her for doing what was outright miraculous.

The ache deepens, wrapping around my heart.

I tuck her head against my shoulder and kiss her temple, enveloping her slim but strong frame in my arms. "Thank you. You found a way, just like I knew you would. Are *you* okay after using so much of your magic?"

Ivy nods against my shoulder. "I was pretty worn out after, but I got some rest too. You've been out for most of the day. Alek just got back from the temple."

The tension in her body gradually loosens as she nestles in my embrace. Every subtle sensation of her accepting the affection I'm only too happy to offer feels like a gift.

We haven't had many moments where we could just *be* with each other. Even more so with me than with the other two men who've claimed a spot in her life, because I had my head up my ass for too long while they saw her worth.

I tease my fingers under her chin to nudge it upward so I can brush my lips to hers. So I can show her that nothing at all has changed about any of the ways I adore her.

Ivy lets out a strained but hungry sound that sends a bolt of lust straight to my cock and kisses me back hard. She slings her arm across my shoulders and hugs me tightly.

When our mouths part, she keeps holding me close. "You were dying. When I saw all that blood… I don't know if I've ever been more scared."

Fear, horror, and relief at the ultimate outcome mingle in her voice.

A lump rises in my throat, but I manage to find the casual drawl that's served me in the past keeping spirits up in the midst of battle. "I'm sorry I worried you. I'll try my best not to let it happen again."

Another noise, half snort and half sob, escapes Ivy's mouth before she yanks me in for another kiss.

Gods above, I want her so much. Want to remind both of us of how alive I am thanks to her; want to celebrate that victory by worshipping the woman who made it possible.

As our mouths meld together again, I ease around to lay her on her back, bracing myself over her. When I stroke my fingers over her breast, Ivy hums eagerly.

I tear my mouth from hers to chart a path along her jaw and down the side of her neck. The feeling of having her beneath me, of her hands running down my chest over my tunic, sets off a throb of desire in my groin.

I nip her earlobe before murmuring into her ear. "I'm going to fulfill the promise I made. It's my turn to take you."

Ivy's shiver is all delight. "I guess you are feeling better."

"The only thing hurting me is that I'm not inside you already."

Her chuckle comes out breathless. "Then you'd better get on with it, hmm?"

She pries at my clothes as avidly as I tug off her dress. I toss the plain thing she deserves better than to the side and let her peel my tunic off me. But when my gaze returns to her, my hand stills on the hem of her chemise.

She's more wounded than I am. Fresh bruises mottle her

upper arms as well as one standing out against the pale skin over her collarbone. There's a scratch that looks just scabbed over at her elbow and another on her thigh.

Ivy halts too, peering down at herself and then glancing at me with a wry but tight smile. "I don't look much like your noble ladies, I know."

Does she assume that's what I'm thinking? That I'd even care?

With a dismissive growl, I pin her down on the blankets again. "You're beautiful just as you are," I say, working her chemise slowly up her chest.

Ivy arches an eyebrow. "You don't need to say that. You've already got me half-undressed."

"I'm not saying it because I need to." I yank the chemise the rest of the way over her head. Then I drop my hand to her hip so I can undo the straps of her thigh sheaths and strip off the pants she's wearing as an underdress.

I want to see every delicious part of her.

"There's no woman I'd rather look at. I love this strength." I drop a kiss to her bicep. "I love how hard you fight." I brush my lips across a bruise. "I love all the cleverness and compassion in this pretty head of yours." One more kiss to her forehead.

When I ease back, Ivy stares at me for a moment as if startled.

"I love *you*," I add, in case I need to emphasize that specific fact.

The smile that lights up her face is bright enough to make my heart skip a beat. She trails her fingers along my jaw.

Her voice comes out soft but steady. "I love you too."

It's the first time she's said it. For a second I can't breathe, I'm so overwhelmed by the rush of emotion.

Then I'm tipping over her, capturing her mouth while I wrench her drawers off her, groaning in approval when she unbuttons the top of my trousers.

We've come this far. She trusts *me* enough to give me a piece of her heart.

As I kick my pants aside, my gaze catches on the gleam of metal by the wall. A flicker of memory passes through my head of the rasp of desire that colored her voice the first time we came together, when she told me she liked that part of me.

I grasp my prosthetic and twist it into the harness, watching Ivy. The flush that darkens her cheeks that suggests my gamble is a good one.

With past lovers, I've never worn any prosthetic except the wooden hand-shaped one. My former fiancé recoiled from even that.

But Ivy, as she pointed out, isn't like any woman I've been with before. None of them were quite what I needed.

I shift my position to Ivy's right and stroke the curved metal loop down the middle of her chest. Ivy licks her lips.

I grin at her. "I seem to remember that you enjoy me making use of both 'hands.'"

Her flush deepens, but she answers without hesitation. "I do."

"Then I'd like to see just how much you can enjoy it."

As I graze the edge of the prosthetic over the peak of one breast and then the other, a whimper works its way out of Ivy's throat. Her nipples stiffen at the contact.

I tease them a little more, gliding the metal back and forth and then rotating it in a tantalizing circle. Ivy's breath has gone shaky. At every eager noise that escapes her, my erection strains against my drawers.

Her reaction fuels my confidence. Eyeing her even more closely, I slide the prosthetic down over her belly to her sex.

As the tip of the loop brushes her clit, Ivy's hips cant upward. "Fuck, Stavros."

"Fuck? I can do that."

A giddy sensation spreads through my own chest as I dip the prosthetic over her folds and let the upper section press against her clit again. Ivy emits a mewling sound of need that has me painfully hard in an instant.

The loop is only about as wide as two broad fingers together. I think I could…

I turn my wrist and adjust the angle so I can push the curved tip right inside her.

Ivy gasps, tipping her head back against the blankets as she clutches my other wrist. "Gods, that's… I've never felt anything like that."

I guide it a little farther. "Good?"

"Strange, but so good." Her gaze darts to me, her blush darkening to outright red. "How much deeper can you go?"

I'll take that challenge.

I bend over to claim another kiss while easing the prosthetic up into her body bit by bit. Ivy shudders beneath me with the most delicious whimper.

No one else will ever make her feel quite like this. Seeing her quake with the pleasure, I can't feel the slightest regret for the sacrifice I no longer benefit from—at least not in the typical way.

The metal loop only hooks a couple of inches around, hardly allowing for a full sense of penetration. But as I adjust it between Ivy's legs, I realize it's perfectly shaped for the outer edge to rock against her clit while I pulse the tip within her.

Ivy bucks with the movements, ducking her head under my chin, clutching me as if she's afraid she'll spin away completely. My cock throbs, but I love seeing her lose herself too much to stop this yet.

Pumping faster earns me another shudder and a guttural moan. Ivy's fingers dig into my arm deep enough to hurt, but it's the most blissful sort of pain.

I feel her come with a ripple that spreads through her whole body. A choked cry escapes her, and her head sags back toward the blankets.

Even through her ecstatic daze, she gropes at my drawers. "I need the rest of you."

Gods be sure I'm not in any state to deny her.

I practically tear my drawers off and kneel between her legs, encompassing her with my much larger form. Ivy simply beams up at me, caressing my chest, tilting her hips to urge me on.

Trusting me with her body every bit as much as I trusted her with mine this morning.

Knowing how wet she is from her arousal shining on my prosthetic, I don't hold back quite as much as the first time. But I still grasp her hip and study her face as I slide into her slick channel.

Her sex grips my cock as if we were made for each other. I can't restrain a groan at the pleasure that spikes through my nerves as I push even deeper.

"So good," Ivy murmurs. "So fucking good."

I want to make it even better for her. I pull back and plunge into her again, and again, and again, flicking my gaze to get a better read of when the most pleasure floods her expression, easing her ass a little higher off the blankets.

I drive home again. Ivy's lips part around a cry.

And a ghost of an image wavers in my vision—her hand reaching for my face.

My pulse hiccups. Her hands are still braced against my chest.

Except—now she's lifting one to stroke her fingertips over my cheek and jaw.

Even through the carnal bliss of the moment, a different sort of exhilaration races through my veins.

My gift. I glimpsed an act before it happened. Only a few seconds before, and I wasn't trying—but I know what my magic looks like.

I was focused so intently on anticipating Ivy's needs that my gift must have activated somehow despite my damaged vision. I never knew that was even possible.

I never tried to use it in a situation like this before.

Or maybe it's just because of her. Because of Ivy and this love that makes my heart soar like nothing I've ever felt.

I dip my head to kiss Ivy's hand and ram into her swaying body even faster. Ivy keens, her fingers rising higher to grip my hair and tug me to her.

As I bow over her, our sweat-damp bodies sliding closer together, she trembles and clamps around my cock. Her fingernails scrape over my shoulder as she hits her second climax—and the force of her release drags me with her into a rush of the headiest pleasure.

A hoarse sound escapes me as I spill myself inside her. Ivy gives a gasping sort of laugh and clutches me even tighter.

Careful of the ridges of scarring on her back, I enfold her in my arms and roll us onto our sides so I can meld her body to mine without worrying that I'll crush her. Ivy tips her head against my chest with the most contented sigh I've ever heard.

I can't lose this woman. I simply can't.

We cuddle like that for several cozy minutes, until the cool air seeping through the walls starts to chill our skin. Ivy squirms even closer for just a moment before reaching for her clothes. "We should probably confirm to the others that you're alive. Although I suspect the walls are thin enough that they've already figured that out."

At the meaningful clearing of a throat from the other room, my face heats, but only a faint warmth.

There's nothing really to be embarrassed about here. We all know where we stand—and how much Ivy means to us.

We should still discuss our next steps in regards to the Order of the Wild. I don't even know what the results of the riot were.

I yank on my clothes and walk with Ivy into the outer room. Rheave glances over from where he's standing by the window with a nod of acknowledgment, his gaze trained on Ivy rather than me.

Casimir smiles where he's standing by the table. "It's good to see you up."

Alek pushes aside the book he was paging through and considers me with a furrowed brow. "Are you sure—"

The slam of the door being flung open cuts off his question. Four men burst into the room, swords drawn.

The man in the lead points his blade at me. "You're all under arrest!"

# Twenty-Four

*Ivy*

At the sight of the blades flashing in the late-afternoon light, my body goes rigid. My men all whip around to face the intruders.

The burly guy at the front of the group said they were here to arrest us, but none of them wear any kind of uniform.

Rheave's expression twitches, and he points a finger at one of the men flanking the apparent leader.

I think he's saying that one's a daimon. These are Order of the Wild members, come to exert their ill-gotten authority over us.

How did they find us? How much do they know?

Stavros tucks his prosthetic slightly out of view, his posture drawing up with his full military authority. Every muscle in his massive frame is braced to spring into action.

In spite of the precarious situation we've found ourselves in, a pang of gratitude fills me at the sight of him so steady after his bloody collapse this morning.

I didn't know if I'd ever see him standing again.

"Arrested for what?" he demands.

My magic shudders through my chest in anticipation of their answer. I could tear straight through them all.

But how will I balance out those consequences? Uncertainty scatters my thoughts, which were already a bit dizzy from everything I pulled off this morning.

The lead Order member opens his mouth to speak, but he hesitates at the creak of the steps behind him. He and his colleagues ease to the side so two more intruders can push into the cramped room.

The first to enter is an even beefier man so vacant-eyed I'm expecting Rheave's gesture toward him before it happens. Then a tall figure strides in with a haughty, authoritarian air that has me tensing up before my eyes lock on his face.

Julita gasps, her presence flinching in the back of my skull. *It can't— Oh, gods help us. Ivy, that's Borys.*

My stance stiffens even more. Borys, her brother—the one who introduced my ghostly friend to scourge sorcery by making her the subject of his sadistic experiments as a child. The brother who vanished on his way to enter Sovereign College three years ago and who she'd hoped was dead.

As he considers us with his lips curling into a smirk, the resemblance jumps out at me. He has the same chestnut waves as the woman I first saw dying in an alley, just long enough to tuck behind his ears. The same porcelain complexion, though his features strike me as sharper than I think Julita's were.

"So," he says in an arch voice that's like a harder, masculine echo of Julita's typical sultry tone, "this is the company my little sister has been keeping lately, is it? It's a shame Julita couldn't be here herself."

If only he knew.

Julita chokes back what sounds like a wail, her presence twitching and trembling, rattling my thoughts even more. *Oh, no. Oh,* fuck. *We have to get out of here.*

I don't know how justified her terror is. She hasn't seen her brother in three years. It sounded as if he hadn't managed to harm her much once she came into her own gift three years before that and could force him to accept her refusals.

Is she simply in shock, or is he an even greater threat than I could anticipate?

My magic thrashes to be let out at him, but it's even harder to concentrate through my ghostly passenger's frantic babbling. I swallow hard and imagine a leafy vine wrapping densely around me to bolster my control.

Julita never told the men she allied with just how painfully Borys involved her in his dabbling, but they've heard enough. Anger flashes in Alek's eyes as he gets up from the table. Casimir's hands have clenched at his sides.

Stavros keeps his voice even, but a thread of menace winds through it. "What do you want?"

Borys draws the short sword at his hip and waggles it at the bunch of us. "I heard the little pipsqueak sent some people to nose around and interfere with our work. You sparked quite the riot this morning. You couldn't really think you'd get away with it."

Rheave, the least emotionally affected of us all, stares at him with a totally deadpan expression. "We don't know anything about that."

I might believe in his ignorance if I didn't know better. But it appears Borys knows better too.

Julita's brother lets out a dark chuckle. "Nice try. It really is too bad that Julita couldn't see this. Me, in charge of not just Nikodi but half the province as well. I've got too many more important matters to address to bother playing games with you lot."

He makes a brisk gesture toward his underlings. "Take them. Preferably alive, but dead will do too."

Julita yelps, the men lunge, and I latch my mind on to the image of that poor battered oak tree on the abandoned farm as tightly as I can.

I have to stop them. I *have* to.

My magic bursts out of me in a blasting force. It hurls the four closest men including Borys to either side, bashing their heads into the walls.

As the thump and crack of the impact resonates through the air, I have the sense of branches ripping off the distant tree. Nausea pools in my gut.

The men slump where they crash to the ground, a couple of them bleeding through their hair and so still they might be dead. Borys lets out a groan.

My mind whirls with a starker flash of panic. He's going to murder us all. He's going to stab his sword into me right now—

I sway with the wave of dizziness, my gaze catching on the sword in question. It's spun across the room away from Borys's hand.

Before I can pick apart my confusion, the other two Order members hurtle straight at me with their blades drawn.

As I start to grope for my focus and power, Rheave leaps into the way with a wordless snarl.

He slams his fist into the nearer man's belly with a sizzle of energy. A smoking hole sears deep into my attacker's guts.

As that man topples over with a bloody gurgle and shifts into a mass of clay, Stavros smacks his prosthetic against the final intruder's head.

The man reels toward Rheave, who doesn't so much as blink before wrenching the attacker's head around.

With a crack of the man's neck and a gristly hiss, the daimon tears the head right off the man's neck and flings it across the room.

Okay, then. I stare at Rheave and the blood splattered across his hands. The feral intensity in his stance sets off an unnervingly giddy shiver down the middle of me.

Then Stavros's urgent tug of my arm and another groan from Borys launch me into action.

Casimir snatches something from beyond the table. "Stav, your sword!"

The former general catches the thrown belt and sheath, and we rush out the door.

As we pound down the stairs to the ground level, Alek pulls at Rheave's cloak. "You did an incredible job protecting Ivy, but we can't have you seen like this. Wipe off your hands on the inside of your cloak and pull it close around you to hide your shirt."

Away from the battle, the daimon-man looks as disconcerted as I feel, but he follows Alek's orders. We barge out into the chilly air of the street.

I don't spot any other Order members close by, but a faint shout brings my head jerking around. I don't see any reason for concern farther down the street, though, and none of my men react.

"I think it's time we get some distance from Pima," Stavros says under his breath. "Let's grab the horses."

Sticking close together, we hustle along the street toward the public stable where Hanie arranged for us to keep our steeds. We veer sharply left at the first cross-road—and nearly bump into Julita's old maidservant herself.

Hanie jumps back where she was poised by the building on the corner. She gapes at us, her face blanching. "You're still—They didn't—"

My thoughts settle enough for one clear revelation to shine through the whirlwind. "She's the one who turned us in!"

We never told Emor and Voleska's group where we were staying. Hanie looked upset seeing the rioting start this morning, and she knew we were involved.

And she's clearly surprised that we haven't been arrested.

*What?* Julita cries. *Hanie gave us up?*

The maidservant backs up another step. "You're as dangerous as the Order of the Wild," she hisses, and raises her voice to a yell. "Help! Someone! There are traitors to the Order here!"

Stavros growls and moves to catch her arm, but Hanie bolts

in the opposite direction. She dives through the nearest shop doorway.

Footsteps drum against the cobblestones from around the corner.

Alek waves us on. "We've got bigger problems than her!"

I spot a narrow alley a few buildings down and race toward it with a jab of my hand to direct the others. We dash into it and sprint past several buildings, emerge onto an unfamiliar street, and duck down another alley.

Near a stinking waste bin behind a tenement building, I pause to regain my wind. No sounds of pursuit have followed us this far.

Rheave glances over his shoulder, his brow knit. "All those angry people in the square made her afraid." He pauses, and his voice drops lower with a sorrowful note. "And so did I. So she blamed us."

I reach out to squeeze his arm through his cloak. "It's not your fault. You didn't do anything to her. We were trying to *help* her and everyone else in this city."

Casimir peers farther down the alley. "Do you think it's safe to go for the horses? Hanie knew where they were too. If Julita's brother has even half his wits, he'll have cut off our easiest means of escape."

I suck in a breath. I hadn't thought that far ahead. "You're right. Curse it all."

Stavros frowns and squares his shoulders. "We should get within view of the stable and take stock. She might not have mentioned that part."

And if the Order of the Wild has confiscated our steeds, we could always steal others. Although I'm not sure how the former general would feel about that kind of criminal activity.

We continue through the city, taking alleys and the quietest roads we can, until we can spot the front of the stable building from a couple of blocks away.

Alek tenses beside me. "They have it staked out."

They do. The scourge sorcerers are trying to be subtle about it, but you wouldn't normally see three figures with swords in hand just hanging around outside a stable.

The men and woman stroll a little this way and that, pretending to have a casual conversation, but their gazes dart furtively over the street at regular intervals.

My jaw clenches. The conspirators have ousted us from our latest sort-of home, and they've stolen our horses too.

I guess you could say we stole the horses from the royal college in the first place, but Toast at least was mine as far as he and I were concerned. No one else wanted him back at the college anyway.

Here's hoping he's kicked several ribcages in for their trouble.

We draw back out of view of the stable, clutching our cloaks tight around us and scanning our surroundings. Even though the daylight is fading, barely any of the nearby shops and eateries have lit lanterns to welcome customers. The front window of the restaurant we're standing outside is dark and unwelcoming. Only a few pedestrians other than us are walking the streets, and those with a hurried stride.

Stavros's vision may be faulty, but he reads the atmosphere quickly enough. "The locals are holing up after the riot, bracing for what the Order might do in retaliation. They know the conflict isn't over yet."

The conflict we kicked off. For their benefit, but it still seems horrible to run off now.

What choice do we have, though?

"What should we do?" Rheave asks, his normally luminescent eyes shadowed with worry.

Alek adjusts his stance, and I realize he's still clasping the book he was reading under his arm. He never let go of it when we made our hasty dash out of the apartment.

"We should be able to find some other place to 'hole up' ourselves," he suggests. "At least for long enough to get a sense of—"

Casimir makes a gesture to silence him, his gaze fixed across the street. "Someone's coming to us. I think—that's one of Emor and Voleska's people, isn't it?"

I jerk around, but I do recognize the face of the woman approaching.

When she sees we've noticed her, she lopes the rest of the way across the street, her expression fraught. "We were told to keep watch for you. Voleska caught word that the Order of the Wild was hunting down people with your descriptions. If you come with me, we'll see what we can do to help."

As the men and I exchange glances, Alek tugs his cloak's hood farther forward with a twist of his mouth. He must have left his mask behind at the apartment. No one but us has seen his uncovered face and its scars before.

But the woman doesn't show any sign of horror. Her gaze latches on to his face for a beat longer than the rest of us and then flicks back to me.

I haven't seen any reason to doubt our newer allies' loyalty. If this woman wanted to get us caught, she could have avoided our notice completely after seeing us and simply roused the nearest Order members.

Rheave fixes his intense gaze on her. "No one there is planning to hurt Ivy?"

The woman blinks as if startled by the question. "Of course not. You've all helped *us* pull off more than we expected to so quickly."

Stavros sets his hand on my shoulder protectively but makes the decision for all of us. "We'll come."

The woman leads us on another winding path through the city. She's clearly more familiar with the back ways than I am, understandably.

We end up behind the Bright Bloom Café where we met with Emor and Voleska before. The woman hustles us inside to where the two leaders of the local resistance are consulting with a couple of their comrades in urgent tones.

Voleska's face brightens at the sight of us, a sharp contrast to the hostile reception we got from the other woman we thought was our friend. She and Emor move to join us.

She glances at Alek first, with an expression that's more sympathy than anything else. Her people didn't have the chance to meet the scholar before, but I mentioned he'd likely be masked if they did. I guess now she can see why.

She bobs her head in greeting. "You must be Alek. I'm glad Bessa was able to find all of you together."

Emor studies us. "You all look well enough. Did Bessa reach you before the Order of the Wild people did? I assume she told you they're out to 'arrest' you."

I grimace. "We ran into a few of them, but we managed to get away." It seems wisest not to mention exactly how.

"They've taken our horses too, though," Casimir puts in.

Emor sighs. "I'm not sure you'd have gotten away safely even on horseback. Whatever the Order found out about you, they're not happy. We've gotten more reports since Voleska first sent people out to warn you. I'm sorry if we dragged you into a bigger mess than you were prepared for."

Stavros tips his head. "We knew the risks."

"What exactly are you hearing?" Alek asks, his head still low beneath his hood.

Voleska pipes up in a strained tone. "From what we've gathered, a fairly large bunch of the people with the Order are heading out of the city as if they've got something important to do elsewhere. But just about everyone they're leaving in Pima is under orders to focus on tracking the group of you down. They've already sent patrols around the surrounding countryside to keep watch there too."

My heart sinks. Are they pursuing us this avidly because Borys is giving the orders, and he particularly wants to crush anyone associated with his sister?

Julita seems to think so. She recovers from her stunned silence to simply say, *That treacherous prick.*

I hug myself. "We thought maybe if we laid low here for a little while, it might blow over…"

Voleska is shaking her head before I'm even finished speaking. "They're busting into people's homes and businesses, searching everywhere. I don't want to promise we could hide you when I'm not sure you'd be safe."

Emor steps in again. "I don't know if you'd be in a position to accomplish much more anywhere in Eppun at this point. They've sent messengers out—the Order members in other cities and towns may be on the lookout too. Frankly, you'd face an awful struggle just making your way out of the province back to the rest of Silana."

Stavros raises his eyebrows. "Well, we have to either stay or leave. It can't be neither."

"We had another thought." Voleska nods toward one of the men she was speaking with when we arrived. "There's a trade caravan heading out tonight for Bryfeen. It's only a few hours journey across open countryside, with plenty of ways you could be concealed, and then you'd be out of their reach."

I stare at her. "You want us to leave Silana completely?"

She holds up her hands in a gesture of surrender. "I don't *want* you to. I'd rather you could stay and keep chipping away at these assholes. But it might be the only way we can ensure you don't end up dead within the next few days, and we owe you that much. Within a week or two, we might have been able to sway more people across the province against them, or the king's forces might have taken back control."

Emor offers us an apologetic smile. "If you stay near the border, you can monitor the situation and come back when the pricks have been driven out."

The bottom of my stomach drops out. Is this really the best option we have? We meant to stop the scourge sorcerers, and instead we end up fleeing the country?

But am I really going to insist on staying and seeing the men who've committed themselves to this cause—to *me*—slaughtered because of my stubbornness?

Voleska clears her throat. "There is one condition." She gestures toward Rheave. "The offer doesn't include the daimon. We're concerned that the Order may find a way to trace his movements, and the caravan runner is nervous about his powers."

My body balks automatically. "We can't leave him behind."

But before I can protest further, Rheave hangs his head and then turns to me. Anguish contorts his beautiful face. "It's all right, Little Vine. I understand why people are nervous. I want to be with you making sure you're safe… but if the best way for you to be safe is for me to stay back, I'll stay and do my best from here."

The despondence in his voice wrenches at me. He thought it was his fault that Hanie betrayed us, and this situation is only going to drive that idea home.

If Voleska and the others knew what *my* real powers were, they'd be far more frightened of me than they are of him. It doesn't make any sense to punish him.

He's still got blood on his clothes from protecting me, and I'm supposed to leave him to be recaptured by the horrifying masters he escaped?

What are my other options, though?

*I don't know what would be best anymore*, Julita murmurs, echoing my uncertainty.

As I rub my temple, Stavros touches my back as if to steady me. "I don't want to leave anyone behind," he says quietly. "But times like this call for awful decisions. I'm not going to argue for one outcome over another. You have the most at stake. It's possible I'll be more useful to the royal family by learning what I can along the border—certainly I'll accomplish more that way than if the Order of the Wild does manage to get the upper hand on us."

If even he's willing to give up… I glance at Casimir and then

Alek and find the courtesan and the scholar watching me, their faces set in similar expressions of supportive but pained resignation.

They'll go where I go, even if they don't like the idea any more than I do. Just like they have since King Konram first called for my execution.

The right thing to do would be to protect *them*, wouldn't it? To put their safety first, to slip away where the scourge sorcerers won't reach us.

And probably kiss our chances of getting a pardon goodbye, since we won't be instrumental in undermining the scourge sorcerers if we're not here. Will we really be able to return if we leave when the king is still calling us traitors?

That's what Stavros meant when he said I have the most at stake. Maybe they could reach an understanding with King Konram once all this is over, but there's not much short of stopping a civil war that would prove the riven sorcerer has the country's best interests at heart.

My magic squirms in my chest, wanting to defend me but not sure how.

I look down at myself, at the spot where Kosmel once branded me with a magical glow, at my hands that have directed more power in the past few weeks than I ever thought I'd allow myself to.

Though Emor and Voleska don't know what I'm really capable of, I do. An ordinary group of resisters might not be able to evade the Order of the Wild and continue weakening their attempted coup, but we aren't ordinary.

*I'm* not ordinary.

If I bring all my power to bear—carefully, thoughtfully—I can ensure the scourge sorcerers never touch so much as a hair on our heads. We can stand together—all of us, including the daimon who's fought just as hard—and finish the mission we came here for.

A twinge of anxiety shivers through my nerves, but not

potent enough to shake the sense of resolve that's welled up inside me.

"No," I say. "We're going to keep fighting. I'm not letting the scourge sorcerers get the better of us. We've still got a few tricks up our sleeves."

# Twenty-Five

*Ivy*

Even in the nook I've tucked myself into by the roof's looming dormer, the icy night wind tugs at my cloak and bites the skin I can't completely cover. I raise the fabric higher over my face to block out as much of the chill as possible.

*Things have been awfully quiet,* Julita remarks. *Maybe you should get some sleep.*

"We need to know where the scourge sorcerers are going and what they're up to," I whisper in reply. "I don't want to stay in Pima any longer than we have to—we're putting everyone else who's working to resist the Order of the Wild in danger."

Julita makes a noncommittal sound. She's been a little quieter than usual since our encounter with her brother this afternoon.

I peer down into the street where I've seen a lot of Order activity in the past—where I overheard the conspirators talking about sending arms ahead with manpower to follow.

No one's come by since I took up my post here an hour ago.

The windows around me are dark. But I'm not quite ready to give up yet.

A sound like a snicker wavers up from somewhere to my right. My head snaps around, but I can't make out the source of it.

A jolt of fear shoots through my chest. I need to be prepared —if they find me—

Gritting my teeth, I close my eyes against the momentary panic.

No one's nearby. *I'm* going to find *them.*

And I need to stay calm and alert to do that.

When I scan the street again, there's still no movement. Maybe the sound was just the wind moving across one of the buildings in a strange way.

I adjust my position to ease the stiffening of my muscles and speak in the barest whisper. "How are you doing? It was obviously a pretty big shock, seeing your brother like that."

Julita shivers. *Perhaps I should have guessed he was involved. I don't know how he ended up collaborating with actual scourge sorcerers—he must have met this group before he ever left for school and used the trip as a cover to join them completely. Either that or it was a very unhappy accident.*

Unhappy for us. I don't get the impression Borys would see it as anything other than delightful.

"I'm sure it stirred up some bad memories," I venture.

*Oh, I've had to deal with all kinds of awful recollections since I first crossed paths with Wendos back at the college. I'm sorry I fell apart a little when he first turned up—there was so much going on at once… Now that I'm prepared, I can keep a better handle on my feelings.*

I offer her a small smile. "And it means you can help us even more. You've got to know him pretty well, so you can help us prepare too." I pause. "I assume he made some kind of dedication sacrifice to get a gift."

He wouldn't have any power for his attempts at scourge sorcery to enhance otherwise.

Julita lets out a pained hum. *Yes. Not a large sacrifice, since he wanted other people to pay most of the price for his ambitions. He gave up both of his smallest toes. Walked funny for a few months before he totally got used to the small change in balance.*

"What's his gift?"

*He was secretive about that. Always gave vague answers if anyone asked—and my parents weren't the type to insist. Obviously they were entirely too permissive.*

She sighs. *I know he dedicated to Creaden like I did, so it probably has something to do with bossing people around. He did enjoy doing that even before he made his dedication.*

I frown. "He never used his magic on you?"

*Not that I was aware of. It could have been a subtle effect. It wouldn't be anything all that showy for a couple of little toes. And once I got my gift and could force him to accept a "No," we barely interacted regardless.*

As horrifying as the circumstances that prompted her choice of gift were, I'm glad she had some defense.

With extra power from the sacrificial accomplices, who knows what Borys might be capable of? We don't know what kind of magic we need to watch out for from him.

Of course, it couldn't be clearer that we need to watch out for that asshole in every possible way regardless.

"We'll stop him too," I say quietly. "We stopped Wendos and Torstem, and we'll keep getting in their way until their whole horrible conspiracy falls apart."

Julita gives a huff. *It shouldn't all be on you. If King Konram could get his head on straight and his army doing their job… I wouldn't have blamed you if you'd run for cover, you know.*

I grimace. "I'm not sure I'd really be safe anywhere I go. At least here I'm working toward getting a pardon. Is there anything else about—"

I cut off my whispered question at the scrape of footsteps beneath us.

Two cloaked figures have just stepped into view farther down the street. They murmur something to each other and push inside a nearby building.

After a moment, lantern light flickers in one of the windows.

Finally, I can take action.

I clamber down the side of the building I was perched on, using every stealthy trick I know, and peer across the street at the doorway the two arrivals vanished through. I'll have to step into plain view to reach the shop.

Unless I use the magic trick I've already performed once with Rheave.

My heart no longer thumps quite so uneasily as I concentrate on the purpose I want my magic to fulfill. I've managed several spells like this—and at least one so much larger—and everything is still okay.

It could always have been okay, right from the start, if I'd known how to handle the demands of my broken soul properly.

I compel my power to wrap around me, fading my body from sight, while projecting the image of it on the rooftop I just left to balance out the effect. Then I slip across the street and tuck myself close to the glowing window.

Muffled voices filter through the glass. "…place isn't worth the bother now anyway. We'll set them right when it's time."

"It shouldn't be long now. I'm taking the last bunch along the Coliz-ward road to join the march tomorrow."

It's a man and a woman, neither of them familiar. They drop into a lower tone that fades into a warble.

I dare to press my ear right against the glass, concentrating as hard as I can without losing my grip on my magic.

The words come back into focus. "…sure they can actually pull this off?"

"Great God willing. I've seen how well the magic works when the blessed ones contribute."

The "blessed ones"? What does she mean by that?

The man must already know, because he doesn't question the phrase. "I guess once we're past the front lines, it'll be smooth traveling most of the rest of the way. No one will be looking for us there."

The woman lets out a raspy chuckle. "Exactly. We're going to slip right past the king's forces and hit him where he's hiding before he has any clue we're coming."

My pulse lurches at her claim—and my control wavers ever so slightly. Enough that just for an instant, I lose my sense of where I'm aiming the consequences of my magic.

Some sort of image must appear in a less discreet spot, because a yelp of surprise sounds from a second floor farther down the street. The conspirators I'm spying on whirl around with a thump of their feet.

Shit. Ducking low, I dash past their building and on into the maze of alleys around this part of town.

As soon as I've left the open street behind, I yank all my magic back inside me. Sweat has broken out on the back of my neck.

Was that a cough right behind me? I dive around a corner and freeze there, listening.

No further sound reaches my ears. I swipe at my face, both chilled and flushed, and hustle onward.

The scourge sorcerers have come up with a plan even more awful than I could have guessed. And if we don't get a move on, we'll miss our chance to stop them.

It's a good thing I didn't opt to flee to Bryfeen, or there'd be no one to sound the alarm at all.

When I get closer to the Bright Bloom Café where we've been hiding since the early evening, I force myself to slow my pace so I don't look odd to any night owls who happen to glance out their windows. I rap on the door in the pattern Voleska told us and dart inside the second it opens.

My men are leaning along the wall. Stavros and Rheave both

sit up straighter at the sight of me, but Casimir and Alek drifted off with the late hour. At the tap of Voleska shutting the door behind me, Alek flinches and snaps back into wakefulness.

He's let his hood drift back, and he doesn't leap to retrieve it. In the past few hours, with their nonjudgmental reactions, he's adjusted to the idea of the rebels seeing his scars.

I'd be more glad to see him relaxed about it if I wasn't bearing such awful news.

Stavros takes in my expression with a brief twitch of his head. "You found out something."

Casimir stirs awake at his voice. I swallow hard, waiting until he looks fully conscious before I report on what I heard.

"We need to head out," I say quickly. "Now—I don't know how much ground we need to make up when they might all be on horseback." I turn to Voleska, too many worries colliding in my head. "You should try to pass on word to the king's forces however you can—someone on the royal family's side needs to know."

Rheave springs to his feet. "What happened?"

I drag in a breath. "I heard a couple of the Order members talking. They're gathering a 'march' somewhere down the Colizward road—the last bunch of conspirators from Pima are joining them tomorrow. Apparently they've got enough magic between them to get past the army unnoticed… and then they're going to strike straight at the king when he isn't expecting it."

Stavros curses under his breath.

Voleska's eyes have widened. She glances around at us. "Do you know where that is? The royal family left Florian after the attack there, didn't they?"

The former general grimaces. "I can make a fair guess, and I suppose we'll be able to confirm it once we see what direction this 'march' heads in. What's the most discreet route we can take to reach that road from here?"

As Voleska considers and offers a series of directions, Alek comes up beside me and takes my hand. "Are you all right? You look a little ill."

I rub my face. "I'm fine. I'd imagine we could all use a little more sleep, but there isn't time for that yet."

Voleska motions to the rest of us. "Wait just a minute. We put together a few bags of supplies when we thought we might be sending you off to Bryfeen… When you decided not to take that route, I thought I'd make one for Rheave too."

She aims a faintly apologetic smile at the daimon-man. "You'll all need more than the clothes on your backs if you're hiking across Silana."

She slips through the inner door and returns with five packs. "There's food and blankets and canteens—just the basics. It's not really enough for a trip like this."

"We'll figure the rest out as we go," Stavros says.

I grasp her arm. "Thank you. For everything. And please, pass on that warning if you can."

She nods. "If we can manage to pass on word quickly enough, maybe they won't even make it past the edge of the province."

I glance around at my men. A silent sense of conviction passes between us.

We know what we have to do, and we're going to make it happen together.

We shoulder our packs and rush out into the night.

By the time we've left Pima well behind us, my entire lower body is aching from hips to feet. My shoulders offer a periodic twinge under the pack's straps for good measure.

Nothing shows on the road ahead of us except darkness. The moon is a thin crescent casting the faintest of glows on our surroundings.

The lack of light means it only takes a tiny bit of magic for me to thicken the shadows around us enough that we shouldn't be spotted by sentries. We've already passed a couple of clusters of figures—most of them daimon, from what Rheave said—patrolling the lands just beyond the city.

Unfortunately, the extreme darkness also means that I'm only sure of where exactly the road *is* by noticing when I've suddenly stumbled off onto grass instead.

"Crossroads," Alek points out, tapping his fingers lightly against a sign post I can only make out when I step closer. "I can't read where the other route leads."

Julita speaks up in my head after a long quiet. *Given our course, that should be Lumya to the east and Dalo to the west.*

As I relay her information, Stavros studies our surroundings with a discontented air. "We only have another hour or two before it gets light enough that we'll need to seek better shelter. There hasn't been any sign of campfires or torches."

My gut twists, but I prod him forward. "Let's keep going just a little longer. If we haven't found the scourge sorcerers by daybreak, we'll wait and follow that last bunch from Pima when they go to join them."

Hopefully they won't be traveling too fast or too far from here to meet up with the others.

"You're going to need to rest soon, Ivy," Casimir says gently as we tramp onward.

I shake my head. "I can push through until we know what we're dealing with. I've missed nights before. This—"

I hesitate, taking in the faint tingle that's just drifted over my skin.

My men freeze around me.

"What is it?" Alek asks in a faint whisper.

"Magic," I murmur, and bring my finger to my lips to urge them silent.

They keep pace with me as I walk forward at a more cautious pace than before. The tingling sensation gradually thickens, as if I'm pressing into a fog of magical energy.

When the tingle starts to fade, I adjust direction, seeking out the most intense patches of it. My feet travel off the road and over the wilted winter grass.

Nothing around me looks as if it's been altered by magic, but I keep walking.

*Something* is going on here. If I can just—

I take one more step, and a totally new scene swims into reality before me. I have to clamp my lips shut against a gasp.

Tensing, Stavros flicks his hand down his front in the gesture of the divinities.

We're standing at the edge of what looks like a vast military camp. Starting just ten paces away, dozens of tents dot the field off to the side of the road. At least twenty supply wagons are parked in their midst. I glimpse equine bodies shifting restlessly near the far end of the camp area.

Guards stand around a few firepits, warming themselves while they watch for intruders. It's only thanks to my magical concealment that they haven't spotted us.

Rheave pitches his voice so low I can barely hear him even standing right in front of him. "There are a lot like me here. So many I don't even need to see them to feel it."

I swallow a slightly hysterical laugh. "The scourge sorcerers are sending an entire army to attack the royal family. And no one will have any clue unless they stumble right into their march."

The only chance of stopping them might be the five of us.

# Twenty-Six

*Ivy*

Alek paces back and forth in the small clearing where we've set up our barebones camp, more keyed up than I'm used to. The tense vibe he's giving off matches the ominous gray of the clouds that've congealed overhead in the dwindling twilight.

"You won't want to spend too much time near the scourge sorcerers," he says, glancing at me. "We don't know what other magic they might be using to ward off intruders."

"They didn't notice us this morning," I point out. "But of course we'll be careful."

None of us were in a state fit to challenge an entire army after a night's hiking with no rest. After we'd determined where the Order of the Wild people had camped out, we were able to grab some sleep for ourselves while they finished with their own slumber and waited for the final group from Pima to arrive.

They took up the march again in the mid-afternoon, and we followed at a distance. The sorcerers in their midst must be covering all signs of their passage with magic, because we passed no trampled ground or extinguished fire pits.

Little do they know, that works in my favor. I can pick up the traces of their lingering magic as a trail to follow them.

They stopped again not long after sunset. Now it's time to see what we can learn from their campfire conversations—and whether our small group can weaken this army before they slip past the king's forces at the provincial border.

The scholar lets out a terse hum. "What's the information it's most important we determine? We need to find out as soon as possible where they're planning to attack the royal family. Whether they're expecting more people and supplies from elsewhere in the province. Who's in charge—here, and if we can find out who the mastermind behind the entire Order of the Wild is, so much the better."

"How many of their people are actually people and how many are daimon," Casimir suggests from where he's sitting by our mostly buried fire. "So Rheave will need to go."

The daimon-man lifts his chin. "I'm not afraid. I want to see what they're doing."

Stavros looks up from where he's been constructing snares in the hope of adding fresh meat to tomorrow's breakfast. "We do know there's a huge contingent of Order members right here with ill intentions. If we could simply knock them all on their asses in one swoop, most of that won't even *matter.*"

I raise an eyebrow at him. "You figure you're going to charge in there with your sword and win the battle five hundred to one?"

I expect him to glower at me, but the former general's expression turns solemn instead. "Your magic could tackle five hundred at once if you let it, couldn't it?"

Julita speaks up tentatively. *I mean… I suppose you could.*

My stomach has given a sickening lurch.

It's true, there are stories of riven sorcerers destroying entire villages and tearing through armies with vast swells of their limitless magic. But the thought makes me recoil, even when it's an army of murderous psychopaths.

Regardless of the target, wouldn't that kind of carnage be a monstrous act? What would it do to *me* to hurl so much power from the crack in my soul all at once?

How could I ever imagine an appropriate counterbalance?

What looks like regret flickers across Stavros's face as he takes in my reaction. He pushes to his feet. "I only meant—if you thought you could handle it safely—you've accomplished a lot already. None of us would ask anything of you that you felt might be a mistake."

My voice comes out rougher than I like. "I know. I suspect that might be a bit too much of a leap from conjuring invisibility and levitating shields."

Alek has paused, inspiration sparking in his bright eyes behind a shadow of concern. "Rheave's magic hasn't had any negative backlash. If the scourge sorcerers can mingle their gifts with the accomplices they've pushed sacrifices on… I wonder if you two could work your magic together as well. Rheave could provide most of the power, and Ivy, you could simply propel it farther."

I have the impression of Julita clapping her hands in excitement. *Oh, that's perfect. Alek's always so clever.*

Stavros is nodding slowly, something like hope relaxing his expression. "That's an excellent idea."

Casimir grins at the daimon-man encouragingly, and I realize with a rush of warmth that we really are a united group now. All three of my lovers have accepted our new ally wholeheartedly.

Rheave has perked up at the suggestion. "I would give it a try. There do seem to be limits on how far I can send out the energy on its own. Without the arrows to guide it, I could only strike the daimon figures who were close to my spot in the square, and then not even hard enough to kill their bodies and free them."

I let the idea stew inside me for a few moments. It doesn't unnerve me as much as the possibility of slaughtering a whole horde of people directly by my own power, but it's still an unpredictable unknown.

"Let's see exactly what we're up against first." I tip my head toward Rheave. "We should go while they're still distracted by setting up camp."

Casimir pats Rheave's shoulder and aims his gorgeous smile at me next. "The rest of us will get dinner ready to welcome you back from your mission."

Stavros holds out his fist. "Go forward boldly and wisely."

Instinctively, I tap my knuckles to his. The other men step forward to follow suit.

"I can quickly start the fire before we leave," Rheave offers, and Alek moves to grab the kindling we gathered as we walked. Casimir opens a pack to take out some of our stash of food while Stavros begins heaping earth to cover the fire.

Watching them move together in comfortable harmony brings an odd lump into my throat.

Julita's voice comes out quiet. *We've made some strange kind of family here, haven't we? And as strange as it is… I never had anything like this while I was alive back home.*

Yes, that's what this feeling is—this mix of homesickness and happiness. I haven't felt like I could count on people like this since my riven magic burst out of me and ruined the family I had when I was just seven.

Rheave rejoins me after sparking the kindling with a measured flare of his daimon energy. He peers at my face. "Are you all right?"

I smile past the tightness in my throat. "Yes. More than I expected. Let's get moving."

The daimon-man and I slink through the woods carefully. I keep my senses alert for the first tingles of magic.

So far, the scourge sorcerers' strategy has worked in our favor. Their sentries remain inside the haze of magic they cast around them to avoid being seen by anyone outside—which means as long as we can't be seen from *their* camp, no one will stumble on ours. I don't have to expend magic concealing us once we're at rest.

As the trees thin, I do need to draw on my power. I've taken inspiration from the scourge sorcerers' strategy and combined it with my previous tactics.

Rather than picturing our individual bodies vanishing like I did with Rheave back in Pima, I imagine a current wrapping around the two of us together, whisking away all visible trace of our forms to anyone outside. I balance it out by having those forms appear back in the forest where we're actually not.

That way we can still see each other. And it only takes a whiff of my magic, one I can easily keep under control.

"We'll walk through the camp," I murmur to Rheave. "Keep quiet, avoid touching anything, and stay close to me. You can focus on identifying the daimon-people."

He nods, peering ahead toward the camp we can't yet see.

"Thank you," he says abruptly before we've quite left the forest.

I pause and glance at him. "For what?"

Rheave offers me a softer smile than usual. "You could have left and been out of danger. But you stayed, and that meant I could stay with you. As much as I want you to be safe… I'm not sure what I would have done on my own. I'm glad we're still together. The men too."

He adds the last bit like a fleeting afterthought, which makes my lips twitch with amusement. But the honest gratitude in his voice brings back the bittersweet ache I felt earlier.

I touch his arm. "I'm not sure you should thank me. I made the decision for a lot of reasons, and I'm probably going to get *you* into a lot of danger with what we're trying to pull off here. But it wouldn't have seemed fair to abandon you either way. I'm glad you've been with us on this journey, as awful as parts of it have been."

Rheave's tone brightens. "I'm glad too. And I'm not worried about the danger. I'd like to keep this body, but if I don't, I will still be me. The scourge sorcerers can't hurt me that much."

For his sake, I hope that's true. Gods help me, I wish I had the same confidence that I'll stay who *I* am even while I'm still breathing.

I nudge his elbow. "Come on then. Let's see how we can hurt them."

We walk cautiously across the open fields beyond the stretch of forest. The march veered farther from the road during the afternoon—I'm no longer sure I'd be able to see travelers journeying along it from this stopping point.

As expansive as their concealing effect is, now that I'm familiar with it I picked up a hint of the tingling sensation before we even left the forest. When the tingle wriggles right into my skin, I know we're passing through the outer barrier.

I tap Rheave's arm again to alert him. With a few more strides, the sprawling camp materializes in front of us.

As we expected, they're deep in the midst of preparing for the night. Several campfires burn at intervals, a few figures at each cooking tonight's dinner in pots over the flames.

The greasy meaty odor makes me think they've added some kind of waterfowl to their stew. My stomach gurgles in anticipation of our own dinner.

Other men and women are setting up the tents and cleaning equipment. Many sit in clusters, chattering with each other as they work.

I take the lead, weaving between the Order members and their supplies in silence, careful not to walk too close and risk someone accidentally bumping into me. My ears stay pricked to the conversations around me, my gaze roving over the objects caught by the flickering firelight.

Someone's left a shallow camp pot on a stone near one of the fires. I glance around to confirm no one's close enough to see the small item disappear and pluck it up to slip it under my arm. That'll make for easier meal prep.

Around the back of one of the supply wagons that no one is currently bothering with, I pilfer an apple for each of us to go with our dinner. With a twinge of longing, I consider a spare tent lying on the ground still folded, but I suspect that theft might be too noticeable.

Most of the would-be soldiers I pass are talking about immediate practical matters like their aching feet or who they'll share their tent with. But I pass one cluster made up of people who don't look much older than I am enthusing about getting to see more of the country for the first time, and another group that's all teens, chatting about their trek like it's a grand adventure.

"Just imagine it," one of the boys says with a swish of a dagger he clearly doesn't have much practice with. "We're going to be part of the battle to see a real king on the throne—we'll prove we deserve the gods' favor and show the All-Giver it's time to return! People will write songs about us."

The girl next to him grins. "Fuck yes, they will. And all those stuffy snobs in the capital will realize the outer provinces can get things done that they can't."

Julita's presence squirms in my head. *Gods smite me, I hope I was never quite that much of an idiot at that age. They really have no idea who they've actually thrown their lot in with, do they?*

I grimace in answer. It definitely seems not.

How could they? The scourge sorcerers must have been spreading the seeds of dissension out here for months if not years before they launched their full uprising. They've made it sound as if their quest is heroic.

I doubt most of these people even know enough about King Konram and what he and his family have done to evaluate his claim to the throne. And they probably have no idea how the scourge sorcerers are fueling the magic that's keeping this march hidden.

There must be sacrificial accomplices along for the trek,

adding power to that magic. Maybe that's what the Order member I overheard meant about "blessed ones."

They haven't revealed themselves any time I've been watching. I suspect they're being kept hidden away in the three large, covered wagons currently parked in the center of the camp, with several older men and women posted around them on guard detail.

Stavros talked about simply wiping all these people out, but I have no idea how many of the newer recruits are villains and how many simply misled.

All the more reason we need to get a clearer idea of who is in charge.

I slink closer to the central wagons and pass a smaller cart that's equally well guarded. Peeking through the slats, I make out several cloth bags and a pile of smaller leather pouches, their bulging sides lumpy in a way that's familiar from my days as the Hand of Kosmel.

Are the scourge sorcerers carrying a heap of money with them?

It certainly looks as if they have plenty to spare.

Avoiding the two guards standing by the end of the cart, I duck down by its side and use one of my knives to slit a small tear in one of the cloth sacks pressed up against the slats. With a little subtle prodding, I push several coins out into my waiting hand.

In the dim firelight, the round shapes shine gold before they disappear in my grasp. I stare at the cart for a second before pocketing the coins.

Usually no one but nobles would carry gold rather than silver. Is the whole cart full of gilts?

Where did the scourge sorcerers get all of it? Is it from Julita's estate and others like it?

And what exactly are they planning to use it for? I hate to think what they could buy or bribe with that kind of wealth.

I slip around the guards with Rheave keeping pace behind

me, and ease even closer to the central wagons. Two of the Order members standing there are talking with another man who's just come over.

"...and give them to Borys when you're done," he's saying when I get within hearing range. His companions salute him, and he saunters away.

Julita shudders. *It sounds like my brother is along for the march. If he really has gotten as much authority as he claimed, he might be leading it.*

I incline my head in acknowledgment, scanning the camp for any sign of where Borys might be right now. How much of a problem would it solve if I simply killed *him*?

My skin tightens at the question. I worked so hard not to take Ster. Torstem down through cold-blooded murder. I didn't want to become some kind of assassin.

But if it would help stop the march...

I wander farther through the camp, but I don't see any sign of Julita's brother so far. Maybe he isn't even here right now. I do catch a few conversations about other "Wildings" this bunch expects to catch up with tomorrow before they leave the province.

And who is giving Borys's orders? That's the most important question we still haven't answered.

A defiant whinny reaches my ears. I spin around to spot one of the conspirators struggling to hold on to the reins of a very familiar stallion at the edge of the camp.

"Fucking beast," the woman mutters as she tries to yank Toast's head around to lead him to the other grazing animals. He grunts at her and rears up, forcing her to dodge his hooves.

A man strides over carrying a whip. "If he won't settle with peaceful treatment, you'll have to beat him into obeying."

I wince, and a decision snaps into place in my head.

Firming my hold on the magic I'm sending around Rheave and me, I let another tendril dart free toward my horse and his soon-to-be tormenters.

The woman takes the whip—and one side of the reins breaks off the bridle. Somewhere in the field, a patch of grass I visualized melds together to offset the fracture.

The severed leather strand slips from the woman's grasp. Toast doesn't waste any time taking advantage of his sudden freedom. He wrenches away with an angry snort and gallops off across the field.

The man who brought the whip sighs. "Well, he wasn't doing much good for us anyway. Let him go then."

A sense of confidence fills me alongside the brief rush of triumph. I do know how to make a difference with my magic—my way, without resorting to the kind of butchery the scourge sorcerers enjoy.

I complete my circuit of the camp, taking note of the other supply wagons. Then I drift over to the edge of the magical border.

Rheave stops beside me and speaks in a cautiously low voice. "A lot of them are daimon. From what I sensed, about half."

After what we saw of the scourge sorcerers' forces in Pima, that doesn't surprise me.

I glance up at the clouds still smothering the night sky and lean toward Rheave to whisper right by his ear. "What do you say we see how well I can propel your magic right now?"

A sly glint comes into the daimon-man's eyes. "I'd like that. What should we hit?"

I hum to myself. "Let's start with a few lightning bolts charring their cargo. I don't think we should try for smaller targets until we're sure of our combined aim."

The daimon-man lets out an eager noise of agreement. "That makes sense. How do you think it will work?"

I bite my lip, pondering the possibilities. "I think if you throw a surge of your power upward, I should be able to catch it with my magic and throw it in whatever direction I want. It shouldn't be too different from moving a physical object. I just have to focus on something else that can move in the opposite direction without the scourge sorcerers noticing and realizing what's really going on."

And do all that while maintaining my focus on the magic keeping us invisible too. But I managed it when I cut Toast's reins. This won't be so much harder.

I picture a couple of gnarled trees I noticed in the woods about an hour before we came to our halt. Far enough away that no one at either camp should be disturbed if their branches start whipping around in unexpected ways.

A faint sheen of perspiration forms on my forehead, cooling immediately with the winter air, but the chill only sharpens my concentration.

I fix my eyes on a wagon full of bread, cheese, and dried meat that I want to scorch first. "I'm ready."

Rheave inhales slowly and then thrusts out his arms with enough force that the air ripples against me. Magic crackles toward the sky.

I toss my own magic after it. With a shove of my will, I hurl the sizzling bolt farther up toward the clouds and then down straight at the wagon.

The supposed lightning smashes into the canvas covering with a warble and a boom like thunder. Yelps ring out throughout the camp as those closest leap away and everyone else stops to stare.

I suck back a laugh at their frightened expressions. Do they really believe the gods approve of their goals? Maybe this will get them thinking things through a little harder.

"Again," I murmur to Rheave, picking out a second wagon that was carrying crates with unknown but presumably needed contents.

He obliges with another swing of his arms. I fling the second bolt upward and down at the next wagon, with the distant sense of one of the trees I picked out wrenching right out of the soil by its roots.

"What the fuck kind of storm is this?" someone shouts, staring up at the sky.

Another voice rings out, steadier but still nervous-sounding. "Keep low to the ground. It's striking taller targets."

I brace myself. "Again."

And at the same moment, a swell of uneasiness washes through me. Is it really enough to just lash out at the *things*? These people—they want to kill me and everyone I care about. How can I stand here and let them—

In the middle of my frantic clash of thoughts, Rheave hurls his power into the air. I catch it automatically and launch it upward, but I haven't picked a target.

My gaze darts through the now-chaotic camp and snags on a teenage boy scowling in the midst of the turmoil, his sword raised. Like he wants to run it right through me.

I pull at the power without thinking, just as the boy's expression falters with a flash of fear.

Gods, he really is just a kid. What the fuck am I doing?

With a hiss at the effort, I swing the bolt to the side at the last second. It crashes into the side of a tent just a few paces from where the boy is standing.

Rheave whips his arm around me and yanks me backward. The next thing I know, we're stumbling through the grass out of the area of concealment.

My pulse hitches, and I focus on the one thing I'm sure of—the images of us I'm projecting far off into the forest so that our bodies here can stay invisible.

Rheave tugs me farther away from the Order of the Wild camp, his arm still clamped around me even as he lets me turn in his grip.

"For a second, I felt the spell you put on us fading," he says under his breath. "I didn't want them to see us—I didn't hurt you, did I?"

My bicep feels a bit tender where his arm smacked into me, but nothing all that bad. Nothing I can blame him for.

Curse it all, what's wrong with me? I nearly burned up a guy who's nearly a kid, *and* I started to lose focus.

"It was a little too much," I mumble. "I tried to do more than I should have."

If that's all it took for my concentration to falter, then camp-wide destruction is definitely off the table.

We hustle back into the woods. As I pull the rest of my magic back into my chest, a sigh rushes out of me. But my stomach knots tighter with each step we take back to the others.

Sulla warned me that I hadn't practiced enough. What if I can't control my power even well enough to protect us now that I've insisted that we continue on this dangerous course?

When we reach our own little camp, the other three men are standing tensed around the faint glow of the fire, strips of dried meat heating on a makeshift rack of sticks. Alek looks more exhilarated than worried, though.

"Did you try it?" he asks. "Was that Rheave's magic we heard?"

I nod, managing a weary smile. "We threw a couple of 'lightning bolts' out of the sky at the march's supplies. They don't have quite as much food to keep them going as they did before. But I couldn't stay focused for long enough to do more."

Casimir pulls me into his arms. "You've been incredible this entire time, Kindness. There's nothing wrong with pacing yourself."

I sink into his embrace, not wanting to explain exactly how wrong things could have gone.

Alek grins and waves the book he brought back from the temple he visited—with the corners of several aged envelopes poking from between the pages. "You might not have to worry about stretching yourself thin for much longer. I think the answer we need is right here."

HISTORIA

# Twenty-Seven

*Alek*

It's hard to be careful with my little treasure while we're walking. The fragile paper crinkles as I ever so carefully unfold the pages of the letter.

But I can only study the faded ink by daylight, and whenever there's daylight, we need to be on the move to keep up with the scourge sorcerers' march.

I roll some of the stiffness out of my shoulders and study the scrawl of archaic Bryfesh that slants across the page. At least I'm not quite as tired as I was two days ago, thanks to the steeds we've added to our party since then.

Toast turned up in the middle of the night, snuffling at Ivy's hair where it poked out from under the layers of blankets we huddle under together to sleep. The following night, she stole another stallion the scourge sorcerers had let wander close to the nearby woods.

The plan is to keep picking off one here and there until we all have a mount. We suspected that taking four at once would alert the march to our presence.

The horses didn't come with saddles, so Ivy is riding Toast

bareback at the moment, frowning at the rolling grassy hills in front of us as she keeps us hidden behind a barrier of magic. When I glance up at her, the furrow on her brow sets off a jab of guilt in my abdomen.

If I could have pieced together the information I've been trying to decipher sooner, she wouldn't have needed to look like that at all. We might already have set the Order of the Wild's makeshift army into irreparable disarray.

Casimir is riding on the other stallion at the moment, having recently swapped off with Stavros. We each take our turns riding for an hour to rest our legs.

Ivy only swaps with Rheave, when she insists that she'll feel better if she stretches her legs for a while. For whatever reason, her irritable stallion won't tolerate anyone riding him except her and the daimon.

I suppose it makes a certain sort of sense. Daimon are spirit creatures in essence, which puts them on another level of existence from us. The "creature" part probably makes him seem more a kindred spirit to the horse than the average person does.

Or else Toast just enjoys being as divisive as possible. I could believe that too.

I tip the page to the sunlight and squint at the faintest patch of words. My comprehension of Bryfesh is far from perfect. I've spent much more time reading ancient sources in old Silanian, Veldunian, and Darium, which are the three most common languages in Silana's archives. Even my Woudish is stronger thanks to a set of journals I wanted to peruse years ago.

My head is starting to ache from contemplating the various meanings of the message I think I'm reading—and all the alternative possibilities if I've misidentified one or another bit of the messy handwriting.

Casimir gives his steed a gentle tap to bring it trotting up next to me—on the side that won't block my sun, because the courtesan is always considerate. "Any more luck with those letters?"

I shrug with a regretful twist of my mouth. "It's difficult to tell how much the writer is using metaphor and how much they mean literally. And some parts seem to contradict others. But this was a direct witness to the Great Retribution in Bryfeen, telling another cleric what they saw. Including how it affected the scourge sorcerers."

"I don't think we're in a position to set off a second Great Retribution," Stavros says dryly. "The point is to avoid one."

I shake my head. "I know. But if we understand *why* the specific methods the All-Giver and the godlen used devastated the practice of that kind of magic for so long, there might be something we could use on a smaller scale."

I shouldn't have these letters at all, really. I found them lost behind a stack of dusty books in the temple library, and a quick glance at one told me how relevant they were to my search. But I knew if I admitted my discovery to the cleric, they'd probably want to hold on to such a rare resource.

So I hid them inside a much less valuable book they were happy to let me borrow and kept my mouth shut.

Ivy glances over at me with a quizzical arch of her eyebrow. "I thought the Great Retribution 'devastated' the scourge sorcerers just by burning them all up. Pretty hard to keep practicing illicit magic when you're ashes."

"I mean, that does seem to be part of it." I turn the page to squint at the opposite side. "There was definitely quite a bit of fire involved. But the way the writer talks about it, it sounds like something about the situation made the sorcerers give up before that point. They faltered before the power of the gods so utterly…"

I fall silent and tap my fingers to brow, heart, and gut before spreading them over my sternum to honor all the divinities. Then I press my hand against the brand in the middle of my chest, sending up a prayer specifically to my patron godlen of wisdom for guidance.

Like the many times I've called on Estera before, no brilliant insight sparks to life in my head.

She clearly wants me to unravel this puzzle on my own. But time is running out, and our opportunities are dwindling.

At least another hundred more followers joined the Order of the Wild's march late yesterday. According to Stavros's observations, we must have left the Eppun border behind sometime this morning, without coming within sight of any soldiers we could signal a warning to.

Last night, Ivy broke a few of the wagons' wheels and sent rot creeping into some of their food, but she was shaky after just those efforts. And the scourge sorcerers fixed the wagons with their own magic and as far as we know simply ate less.

Can we pick away at them enough to stall their progress before they're within reach of the king—and without wearing Ivy down to her breaking point? How much can the five of us do against an army of several hundred?

We can't defeat them in might, so we need something clever. Something they couldn't be expecting.

Something *I* should be able to—

The wind whips past us so violently I need to clutch at the pages in my hand. My heart lurches in the panicked moment when I think I might lose them—and then skips another beat at a sudden flap that's appeared at one of the corners.

"Thanks be to Estera," I mumble, and then clearer, to the others, "Hold a moment."

The riders draw their mounts to a stop as I tuck most of the papers away in my pocket.

Stavros comes up beside me. "What is it?"

"There's another page there. They were stuck together, so perfectly aligned I couldn't tell. I thought the writer had just used different weights of paper, whatever they had on hand."

With careful fingers, I peel the two pages apart inch by inch. A laugh that's almost giddy tumbles out of me at the sight of the writing I'm revealing—a piece of the account I was missing up until now.

Gripping the papers in one hand, I tap the other down my chest in another gesture of the divinities, in case my verbal gratitude for whatever role Estera had in revealing this secret wasn't enough. Then I sweep my gaze greedily over the uncovered prose.

The once disjointed account melds together into a much more coherent stream of thought as I translate each missing line. A smile stretches across my lips alongside a growing surge of exhilaration.

My excitement must be obvious. Ivy leans over on Toast's back. "What does it say?"

I wet my lips. "The writer claims that when the flames rose up, the scourge sorcerers fell to their knees before the fire even reached them. They…" I frown at the next line with its awkward conjugation. "They pictured their death in the flames? 'And there's nothing the sorcerers who gain power through the dying of others fear more than their own mortality. They tried to set themselves among the immortal gods… and in seeing they'd failed… they lost spirit and gave up, letting the flames consume them.'"

Casimir's eyes have widened. "It wasn't just straightforward destruction, then. The fire defeated them before it touched them."

Rheave scratches the back of his neck. "Are they really afraid of fire? The scourge sorcerers who made this body used it all the time. I've never seen them frightened of flames."

Ivy nods. "They had big bonfires at their larger meetings near the college. They put it to their own purposes, burning up effigies and so on."

I consider the apparent contradiction. "I suppose it'd be impossible for anyone to survive a single winter in these realms if they couldn't stand to be around fire at all. I'd imagine it doesn't affect them the same way when they're in control. It would be when they feel it's coming for them rather than aimed at their own purposes that they recognize they can't escape death."

Stavros peers over my shoulder at the pages, though I don't imagine he can read a word of Bryfesh. The language component of military training is focused on Darium, since Dariu has been our only consistent opponent for ages. He might have picked up a little modern conversational vocabulary for encounters with our bordering countries, but that'd be the extent of it.

I'm the only one who could have uncovered this revelation.

Stavros hums softly. "When Ivy turned his followers against him, Ster. Torstem did give himself up to the fire. There could be something to this theory."

His approval stokes my confidence. "And why would they see fire as an ideal weapon against their own enemies if they didn't recognize just how powerful it can be?"

Toast huffs as if impatient with our stop and paws the ground restlessly. Ivy pets his neck. "They definitely saw it as a force to be reckoned with. How do you think we can use that fact to our advantage?"

An image has already been forming in my mind, but her direct question makes me hesitate. An uneasy ache resonates through my chest alongside the thrill of the discovery.

I found what might be the key to overcoming the scourge sorcerers… but Ivy's the one who'll have to put my theory into action. One more burden weighing down on her.

But if it's the last burden she'll have to shoulder, won't that be worth it? Isn't that exactly what I was searching for?

I lift my gaze to meet hers, watching for any sign of discomfort. "Tonight when the Order of the Wild is making camp, you could conjure a wall of fire that moves as if to consume them. If the actual scourge sorcerers among the 'Wildings' have the same mentality as those before, you won't need to take it any farther than that—you won't have to actually hurt anyone. They'll lose their resolve, and their dedication to their mission will fall apart."

"You could burn up some of the daimon to free them as well," Rheave suggests.

Ivy frowns, but it's more of a thoughtful expression than an unsettled one. "If I make a wall big enough to terrify them, I'm not sure I should try to stretch my control even farther. But just a big mass of flames moving in one direction shouldn't be that difficult. I'll have to freeze a lot of trees to balance things out." She lets out a short laugh.

"It seems overly simple," Stavros says. "And if the trick doesn't shatter their conviction, they'll know someone was working magic against them. They'll search us out."

Ivy shrugs. "If it comes to that, I can stop them from finding us. None of our smaller attempts have had a real impact—we need to do *something* big."

Another spark of inspiration lights in my head. "Perhaps you could shape the flames just a bit, make the impression of a face in the fire. Give them the sense that it's a warning from the gods rather than a magical attack."

Casimir smiles crookedly. "That might frighten anyone into giving up a quest, scourge sorcerer or not."

"Perfect." Ivy squares her shoulders, and just for an instant, I think I see her jaw flex with tension she quickly masters. The ache in my chest expands.

I could tell her to forget it. That we'll find another way that doesn't require her tapping into the magic she avoided for so long even more than she already has.

But I honestly can't imagine what that other way could be. This one move could be the end of our struggle. We leave the scourge sorcerers shaken and demoralized, and they'll either scatter back to their homes or be so much easier for us to finish picking them apart.

And we can return to King Konram not just victorious but with a proven strategy for snuffing out the rest of the conspiracy that threatens him and his family.

"We have plenty of time to think over the best approach

while we're still marching after them," I say. "We'd better keep going before they get too much of a lead."

Ivy makes a sound of scoffing amusement. "I can follow their trail anywhere."

By the time Ivy senses that the march has stopped, it's fully dark other than the moonlight that casts an eerie glow over the landscape. I suppose we should be glad even that's not swallowed up by clouds tonight.

To our benefit, the Order of the Wild seems to prefer to make their camps with a border of woodland around them, presumably to keep them even more hidden from afar if there's a brief faltering of their concealing magic. That makes it easy for us to find a sheltered spot nearby to set up our own camp.

Tonight, Stavros doesn't bother building a fire or unpacking the blankets. We find a clump of bushes with leaves the horses are happy to strip, and Ivy gulps down a quick meal of pilfered dried venison and bread to fortify herself.

My stomach has clenched too tightly for me to think about eating before we set my plan in motion. When she tugs her cloak closer around her and looks toward the Order camp as if ready to set off, I clear my throat. "I'm coming with you."

Ivy jerks around to stare at me. "What?"

I hate that she's so startled by the declaration. That it never even occurred to her I might stand by her in this.

I draw myself up to look as confident as possible. "It was my idea. You should have someone with you who can keep an eye on everything that's going on while you concentrate completely on your magic."

Rheave steps forward. "I can come too."

Stavros clears his throat. "If anyone's going to watch out for Ivy, I should—"

"Men." Casimir's soft voice is firm enough to cut through

Stavros's words. He aims one of his fond smiles at Ivy. "We all want to protect Ivy. But the more people go with her, the more she has to worry about keeping hidden. Let's not strain her with our desire to prove ourselves?"

Rheave deflates with a guilty expression. He looks at Ivy. "I don't want to make it harder for you."

Stavros sighs. "There should still be someone with her."

"And that should be Alek," Ivy says before he can go on, holding out her hand to me. "He has the best understanding of what we're trying to accomplish. The rest of you, be ready in case we need to retreat quickly."

As her fingers close around mine, there's no more argument from the others. Even through our gloves, the feel of her touch reminds me of the first time I removed my mask for her, the brush of her hand across my scarred cheek where the breeze grazes it now.

Out of all the people in the world, she's the only one I'm sure has never seen me as a lesser man for my flaws.

We walk to the edge of the Order camp in careful silence. Ivy gives my hand a light squeeze in warning that we're about to step through.

It's still a shock when the sprawl of tents and wagons appears out of nothing in front of us. I come to a stop next to Ivy with a hitch of breath.

I knew more people had gathered since the first time we stumbled on the camp, but I wasn't totally prepared to see the whole vast sprawl of it. All at once, I feel incredibly small.

Ivy releases my hand, her face already tensing with concentration. I can't imagine what it's like trying to hold everything she's doing in her mind all at once, wrangling the threads of her magic when it always wants her to give it free rein.

The Order of the Wild members don't appear to be worried about anything unusual befalling them. They're circulating around the camp, readying their dinner and prepping the tents.

The hum of conversation feels unnervingly companionable,

as if they think they're off on a leisurely jaunt across the country, not a mission to slaughter the royal family and throw our entire country into upheaval.

Next to me, Ivy inhales with a faint rasp. That's my only warning that she's about to begin.

With a warbling roar, a wave of fire some twenty paces wide and twice as tall as any man surges up at the edge of the camp. Even though she's conjured it at a safe distance from the two of us, the heat wafts through the air to where I'm standing.

The scars on my face tingle with the sudden warmth. I haven't worn a mask since I lost my usual one in our hasty flight from our apartment in Pima.

The conspirators scramble away from the flames with a chorus of gasps and shouts. I scan their faces, trying to make out which are the scourge sorcerers and which merely their dupes.

Is anyone cowering in terror of their mortality already?

Someone points at the wall of fire, and I flick my gaze toward it long enough to make out the shapes of eyes and a mouth curved into a sneer amid the flames.

Ivy's really pulling it off. This is worth a whole forest of frozen trees.

"Back to the other side of camp!" someone yells in an authoritative tone. "Pull whichever wagons you can reach."

Some of the figures simply race to the far end of the camp area, but just as many leap to the wagons and start hauling them. They're obviously scared, but no one seems to be falling apart the way I hoped.

I turn to Ivy to suggest she push the fire closer and show that it's coming for them. My voice snags in my throat.

Her face has turned wan, the whites of her eyes gleaming as if she's as worried as the people she's threatening.

All at once, the flames shoot higher and farther. They lash out, licking across the nearest tents.

Ivy's lips move with a hushed muttering I can't decipher, but there's no mistaking the urgency of her tone. Her hands twitch at her sides.

Another burst of flames smacks into the side of an abandoned wagon.

"Can't let him…" I think I hear her say before her words muddle again.

The face has vanished. The Order members are still retreating in the wake of the fiery destruction, but no one's cowering or pleading for forgiveness for their sins.

My gut plummets. It didn't work. And Ivy—

She trembles next to me. I reach for her but hesitate, not sure if distracting her would make things better or worse.

Before I can decide, she sucks in a breath, her stance going rigid. There's a whoosh as the entire wall of flame snuffs out as swiftly as it rose up.

She sways, and I catch her arm to restore her balance. Her gaze is fixed on the blackened swath of camp.

"I had to—I had to stop…" she mumbles.

A holler reverberates from the far side of the field. "Wildings, prepare a search! The traitors who want to prop up their false king are here!"

Great God smite me, one of them's already seen through our trick. They barely appear shaken, and Ivy—Ivy teeters as she spins around.

Guilt clamps around my innards from throat to belly. All I can do is throw my arm around her back to hold her steady as we race back to the others.

Is she in any condition to even keep us hidden much longer?

I thought I understood—I wanted to believe I'd found the answer so badly. Gods, how I've fucked up.

And my mistake could be the ruin of us all.

# Twenty-Eight

*Ivy*

I wake to faint early dawn light and a pine needle dropping against my cheek. The boughs Stavros hauled into the shape of a tent late last night block the worst of the wind, but it's still a pretty rough shelter.

The best we can do in our present situation.

With a heavy pang in my stomach, the memory of the panicked dash that brought us here fills my head.

We piled onto the horses two apiece with Stavros jogging alongside us. As well as I could tell in the midst of the turmoil, he led us in a wide circuit around the scourge sorcerers' camp before they'd had much of a chance to conduct their search and continued on to give us at least a few hours' lead on their typical marching pace.

Are we still in their path or safely out of reach? I'm not sure we'll know for certain unless they crash right into us.

A clinking sound and a rustle outside the shelter tells me at least a couple of the men are already up—and cooking some part of our breakfast. As I turn my head to look around, an arm tucks around my waist from behind.

Beneath the layers of blanket, Alek scoots a little closer so our bodies are aligned. His breath tickles through my hair to the back of my scalp. A quick glance shows it's just the two of us left in the shelter.

The scholar dips his head to press a kiss to the nape of my neck. His voice comes out low and rough. "I'm sorry about last night."

I twist in his embrace so I'm facing him. As I meet his anguished eyes, I rest one of my hands against his chin. "You didn't do anything wrong. We tried our best, and it didn't work out after all."

He swallows audibly. "I encouraged you to take on a bigger challenge with your magic—I know how much you hate grappling with it—"

"Hey." I caress Alek's unscarred jaw with my thumb, my throat closing up around the truth of what happened. "You didn't ask for too much. I did what I could handle, and I stopped when I needed to."

There really wasn't anything overwhelming about the effect he asked me to create. Fire balanced by ice is an easy equation.

The real problem was that while the flames I'd conjured wavered and roared, I thought I caught a glimpse of Borys in the disarray—and a sudden urge to blaze straight through the camp to destroy him blotted out everything else for a moment.

In that moment, I was so convinced that I *had* to make the fire bigger. That I needed to flood the whole camp with flames before… before the scourge sorcerers and their lackeys lashed out at us. Or something even more horrible happened.

It didn't totally make sense. I'm not even sure it *was* Borys I saw, the glimpse was so fleeting.

But the feeling just kept growing, and I lost my grip on my intentions. More magic leapt out of me than I'd meant to release.

Maybe if I'd let it, it would have scorched the entire camp

and everyone in it to embers: deceived civilians, sacrificial victims, horses, and all alongside the actual villains.

But I didn't let things go that badly. I felt my control slipping and I yanked it back, just as I always have. Everything is still okay.

If I repeat that to myself enough, maybe I'll totally believe it.

Alek's mouth twists. "I thought the strategy I suggested would accomplish *something*. I don't see how we made any progress at all. Instead, we've ended up with the scourge sorcerers actively on the lookout for us."

I caress his face again. "We gave them something to worry about. We distracted them. The blaze might have made some of the locals they drew in question what they've actually signed up for."

Alek sighs and hugs me tighter, his lips brushing my temple. "I'm still sorry it didn't work out better. And I think you need as much of a break as you can get from working more magic. It looked like it's starting to wear you out."

The uneasiness lingering in my gut won't let me argue. I'd already come to the same conclusion myself. "I think that should be manageable. But I guess we'd better get up so we can all figure out exactly where we're going from here."

He lets out a softly disgruntled sound and nuzzles my cheek before seeking out my lips.

I sink into the kiss, wishing I could give myself over to it completely. Wishing we didn't have so many threats looming over us.

"I love you," he murmurs after he's eased back. "Nothing else matters if you're not all right."

I stroke my fingers into his thick hair, a swell of emotion momentarily stealing my words. "I feel the exact same way about you. So don't push *yourself* too hard either."

The scholar snorts as if that's impossible, but he sits up and we clamber out of the shelter.

Casimir has the small pot I lifted from the Order camp

braced over an equally small fire. I spot several little white orbs bobbing in the bubbling water.

"I found some ground fowl eggs," Stavros says from where he's checking Toast's shoes. The stallion eyes him warily but seems to have accepted that the former general means no harm. "Only bird that lays in the winter. We should get going as quickly as possible, but we can eat them on the way."

Rheave emerges from between the trees, holding up one of our canteens. "I filled all these up at the stream! And I also saw…" His gaze latches on to me, and he gives me one of those smiles that's all daimon, eager and mischievous. "Ivy, come over here."

I gamely walk over to the spot he indicates several paces beyond the edge of our cramped clearing. He grasps the branch of a nearby tree and clambers up it, disappearing momentarily between the needled boughs.

"Hold out your hands," he calls down.

When I do, he shakes the branches above me. A deluge of glossy brown nuts almost the same shade as his hair rains down, some into my waiting hands, others pattering across the forest floor.

Rheave leaps down to collect the strays. "I know I've seen people eating these before—they seemed to like them."

I can't help laughing. Somehow our situation seems less dire when the daimon in our midst is all but conjuring a meal out of the sky.

Stavros considers our loot when we've carried them back to the camp. He claps Rheave on the back. "Nice find. Pry the tops off with your teeth, and you can get at the softer flesh inside the shell. They've got an almost toffee-like flavor, and they're quite filling too."

Rheave and I distribute the nuts between us. I stuff my own portion into a pocket and hurry to collect the rest of our supplies.

By the time Alek and I have folded the blankets for our

packs and pulled apart the shelter, Casimir has finished cooking and doused the fire with the pot water. Stavros kicks dirt over the spot to cover the most obvious signs of our stop here.

"Where are we going now?" I ask.

The former general glances toward the sun, shimmering through the trees just above the horizon. "At this point, I can tell where the scourge sorcerers' march is going. Since it doesn't look as if they've faltered in their ambitions, we should aim to get there first so we can alert the king and summon reinforcements."

My pulse stutters. "How can you be sure?"

The former general passes out the last of the dried plum Voleska included in our packs. "There are only a few cities with fortified palaces that the royal family would move to when facing a threat like this. The march has been heading southeast since we crossed the provincial border. There's only one option they could be heading to: Regica. And that's the one I'd have expected King Konram to choose given every other consideration."

Rheave offers his hands to me to boost me onto Toast's back, since there are no stirrups to help. I'd insist that he should ride first, but after how stubborn he's been in the past, that'd only waste time.

"Are you sure we can get to Regica quickly enough?" I ask as I swing onto the stallion's back. "The conspirators running the march must know they have to hurry too."

Stavros smiles grimly. "One of the benefits of having a small party." He boosts Casimir onto the other horse. "We have less to pack up and less to carry than they do. And I'd suggest we rest as much as we can while we have our turns on the horses. We can use the blankets to make a sort of sling. If we stay on the move for as much of the night as possible as well as the day, we should continue to pull ahead of them."

*Sleeping on horseback?* Julita mutters. *That's army men for you, I suppose.*

The thought of the tiring journey ahead of us makes me feel

about as dejected as she sounds, but I gather my spirits as well as I can. "How much farther do you think we have to go?"

"I'll have a better idea once we've gotten a look at a crossroads sign, but if we keep a good walking pace and limited time at camp, I think we can cover the distance in four or five days' time."

I drag in a breath. Okay. Less than a week, and we'll be done with the trek.

And facing the king who wants me executed again. So much to look forward to.

As we set off through the woods, I send out a little of my magic to flow around our group. By daylight, when we're not too near to the march, I've found the simplest effect for avoiding notice is to deflect attention rather than making us outright invisible. It's a perfect balance, the magic to nudge anyone's eyes away from us having the consequence of pulling their gaze toward something else.

If Stavros is right, the scourge sorcerers won't get close enough to have us in their sights anyway.

He takes the lead, guiding us through the forest and across a sprawling field until we reach a country road. "Now that we're setting our own course, we don't have to stay so far off the beaten path," he says. "We'll make better time on even ground."

By the second peal of a town bell, I think I can see the town it belongs to off in the distance to our right. Stavros turns his head that way as Casimir and Alek swap places so Alek can ride for a bit. When I look at Rheave to offer a similar exchange, he simply shakes his head with a defiant expression.

I tap his shoulder with the side of my foot. "Next time. Your body can't keep going without rest no matter how much you'd like it to."

Stavros glances back at us. "Actually, I think our daimon should take the horse now—but not to rest just yet. We don't know how well Voleska and the others were able to pass on the message about the scourge sorcerers' plans, and we weren't sure of where the march was going back then. Rheave, you're the only one of us not officially wanted for arrest. Ride over to that town as quickly as you can and warn them that the uprising has sent a concealed army this way and that they're only a few hours behind us."

My body balks at the idea of our party splitting up even briefly, but I force myself to slide off Toast's back so Rheave can take him. We have to get a warning to the royal troops as soon as possible.

I just have no idea what kind of reception he might get. We don't know what's been going on in the rest of the country while we were tangling with the scourge sorcerers in Nikodi.

"How's Rheave going to find us again while Ivy's keeping us hidden?" Alek asks.

The daimon-man pats Toast's neck from where he's hefted himself onto the stallion. "Her horse can find her without seeing. He already did before in the forest."

He lifts his hand in a casual salute and launches Toast into a gallop. As they race across the open ground toward the distant town, Stavros motions for the rest of us to tramp onward.

I loosen my cloak a little to let in a bit of warmth from the rising sun. Now that we've left the northernmost part of the country behind, the winter chill isn't quite as biting.

Casimir chuckles at me, the collar of his own cloak folded up to shield the lower part of his face. "You've all got stronger constitutions than me, I think. I like my warmth and comforts."

I bump my elbow against his. "And you should have them."

He hums, the sound faintly muffled by the fabric. "Eventually. For now, I'll appreciate the beauty of the wild countryside and the lovely flush that nippy breeze brings to your cheeks."

Even more of a flush creeps over my face at the compliment. I push myself to walk a little faster, thinking of the mass of angry scourge sorcerers and their allies behind us.

It isn't long at all before Alek alerts us with a noise of

concern. "I think that's Rheave on his way back now. He's coming at quite a clip. I don't see anyone pursuing him, though."

Stavros peers across the terrain from his lower vantage point. "He's probably simply hurrying to rejoin us." His forehead furrows all the same.

We don't slow our pace on the road, but I move to the side closest to Rheave in case that'll help Toast find his way to me. How much it's the daimon-man's senses and how much the horse's, I'm not sure, but they hurtle straight toward us without hesitation.

Rheave only pulls on the reins when they're so close I can hear Toast's huffs of breath. At that distance, maybe ten paces from the road, my magic wouldn't be enough to divert anyone's attention from the sight of us.

He urges the stallion into pace alongside our group. "I don't know if that went well."

"What happened?" Stavros demands.

The daimon-man glances back toward the town, frowning. "There were men at the gate—guards. I told them about the people from the uprising heading this way, planning to attack the king. Instead of seeming concerned, they asked me how I knew and something about frozen trees."

My stomach flips over. The counteraction to my fire magic. Did someone see it and realize it was caused by illicit magic of some kind?

Have I drawn the attention of even more enemies down on me and my men?

"I told them I didn't have time to do more than give the warning and headed right back," Rheave goes on. "But when I was turning around, I saw past the gate—on the other side, there were a couple of people in uniform nearby. Uniforms that looked like the royal army's. Why would they be here?"

Alek knits his brow. "We're only about a day's walk from the main front where the army's been fighting the Order of the

Wild. It wouldn't be very strange to have a few soldiers stationed in the area to monitor things, would it?"

He aims the question at Stavros, who rubs his jaw. "Not necessarily. But they should have been asking about numbers, how well armed, and matters like that, not acting as if they weren't sure they should even believe you."

Rheave deflates a little. "Maybe they didn't. I might not have explained it well enough."

"I'm sure you did as well as any of us could," I tell him.

Julita sighs. *I'm starting to think the king only employs idiots. Other than Stav, of course. And even he was pretty idiotic about you for a while.*

Alek stiffens on his horse. "Someone else is coming."

He has a better view than the rest of us. I peer across the terrain but can only make out the slightest hint of a shape that might be a person outside the distant walls of the town.

Stavros stares, twitches his head, stares again, and then lets his gaze slide over the rest of us as if to give his eyes a moment to recover. They rest on me for a beat longer than the others.

All at once, he exhales sharply. "Ivy, pull around your cloak —or the top of your dress—something. Everyone! Cover your mouth and nose as well as you can."

Even as he speaks, he's fumbling with his own cloak. He presses a flap of the thick fabric over his lower face.

With a lurch of my pulse, I follow suit even though I don't understand. As I push the scratchy woolen cloth against my nose, my breath condenses in the thin patch of air left behind it —and my feet stumble beneath me.

The ground feels suddenly, strangely uneven, as if it's bobbing and dipping like a raft on a river.

I try to concentrate, but my thoughts have started to float away from me. My head is full of clouds.

Julita whips around in the back of my skull. *Ivy, what's happening?*

Something Stavros caught on to, but maybe not in time. He staggers to the side before righting his balance.

Alek has tugged the neckline of his tunic all the way up over his nose, but he sways on the horse's back and has to snatch at its mane to stay on. He leans close to its neck the way Casimir rested before, his hands trembling. "Is that some kind of drug? How…?"

"It's a trick… the sorcerer-hunters use," Stavros rasps through his cloak. "Can't easily confront one of the riven head on. They carry sedatives on them, sometimes traveling with a companion who has a gift… that can carry it long distances through the air. There are a few enchanted tools around… that do the trick too."

Rheave wobbles on Toast and pulls the side of his cloak tighter against his face. Only Casimir seems relatively unaffected, but he already had his collar up before Stavros's warning.

He's adjusted his cloak so it's more tightly molded to his face. "How did you know?" he asks Stavros in a muffled voice.

The former general's laugh is dark. "It seems my gift hasn't completely abandoned me. I looked at Ivy and saw her faint, and I guessed that scenario was the only reason it would happen so quickly. We took precautions… before the full effect could take hold."

Alek turns his head where it's resting on the horse's neck and gives a soft yelp. "Soldiers coming."

When my head jerks around, sending a fresh wave of dizziness through my body, I spot the blue specks of their uniforms against the greenish-yellow of the grass. "Shit."

Our pace has slowed in our muddled state. Stavros manages to take command. "Ivy, get on Toast with Rheave. Alek, I'm joining you. Casimir's the only one in a state to walk at a decent pace on his own. The horses will have to forgive the extra weight one more time."

I don't see how we'll go *that* much faster, but before I can find the words to debate, Rheave has already jumped down. He wobbles but still manages to scoop me up and heave me onto Toast's back right by his withers.

The daimon-man hauls himself up behind me. The stallion grunts in protest but clops onward.

Toast might be able to speed up to a trot with the two of us, or even a canter if I really pushed him, but I'm not sure *we* could stay on. And there's definitely no way to bring Casimir on as well.

Stavros has managed to swing himself up behind Alek, his massive frame swaying, but their horse is only a little larger than Toast. It'll be having an even harder time carrying both of their weight for long.

The blue specks in the distance are growing larger, along with the brownish blotches beneath them. They're on horses too, I realize hazily. Riding much faster than we can.

Can they see us? Great God smite me, I've lost all my focus on my magic.

It's roiling in my chest, where I must have pulled it back inside instinctively. A chill breaks over my skin.

Even with Casimir jogging between us now, there's no way we can outrun the soldiers. If I could just…

Julita's voice pulls my thoughts into order. *You could make a mirage, Ivy! Send them off after a ghost.*

She laughs as if it's a joke, but I understand what she means. The natural consequence of the invisibility effect I've created before.

Yes. Yes, that might be exactly what we need.

I clench my jaw to try to steady my addled mind. I have to concentrate.

Have to direct the magic nagging at me so it does what I want and not all the other chaos it could create.

Rheave had his arms braced on either side of me, but now he wraps one around my waist. He must be able to feel the tension as I ready myself.

"Whatever you're doing," he says quietly, "I've got you. I won't let you fall."

As the heat of his body cocoons me, an unexpected sob rises in my throat.

I need every bit of support I can get.

I drag air into my lungs and hone my consciousness as sharply as I can onto the image of the five of us hustling along the road.

Erase that sight from where we actually are. Project it swerving around and rushing away in the opposite direction. Off the road. Beyond the next field and into the woods, where the soldiers can think they lost us.

Rheave grips me tightly, grounding me even though we're not touching the earth. I twist my head to watch the soldiers, and my cheek presses against his shoulder.

His warm, fresh scent fills my nose. I ignore the impulse to nestle even deeper into his embrace. Ignore the pang of affection and possibly more that I can't grapple with right now.

Maybe a hundred paces behind us, the two soldiers gallop across the road and on toward the woods. Or are there three?

I'd swear I do see three of the blue-uniformed figures careening away from us, but when I blink, they meld back into two. My gut lists with that floating sensation again.

When I yank my head around, my gaze snags on another blotch of blue back by the town. My heart leaps into my throat. "There's another…"

Stavros follows my gaze and then peers over at me. "I don't see anyone."

I squint and swipe at my eyes. It's all just yellow-green grass.

Dread pools in the pit of my stomach.

At my shiver, Rheave rests his cheek against the back of my head. His arm stays tight around me. "I've got you," he repeats.

He does. But how much do I have myself?

I thought if the worst effects of being riven hit me, it'd be in one big crash. I thought my unsteady moments over the past couple of weeks were only fatigue and nerves.

But what if this is how the madness comes: not a sudden slap of insanity but a slow, subtle creeping of it through the mind?

One you might not even notice until you're already lost.

# Twenty-Nine

*Ivy*

Stavros appears to cheer up at the sight of the first fortress. My skin crawls with apprehension even noting it from a distance, but I keep my qualms to myself.

"That'll be Fort Alnaw," he says with a weary smile. We're well into our fifth day of near-constant tramping and riding. "Regica, which holds the palace I expect the royal family has moved to, is about four hours' hard riding from here. We won't risk getting that close just yet."

Julita sounds as if she's as tired as the rest of us. *Yes, let us not walk right to the front doorstep of the ungrateful king who wants us killed for saving him.*

I stifle a yawn, propelling my feet onward one after the other. "Where are we going, then?"

The former general pauses in thought. "If we take the next crossroads, we'll reach the town of Iblin before nightfall. It'll give us an opportunity to reequip ourselves and possibly pass on another warning, but it's farther from the military outposts, so there's less chance we'll run into trouble."

Alek lets out a weak laugh where he's tramping beside me. "I approve of that plan."

Casimir had been dozing in the rough sling of blankets we've formed on the second horse's back, just as Rheave currently is on Toast. At our voices, the courtesan stirs and pushes himself more upright. "Iblin… There's a fairly large temple of Ardone near there. We're close to the border of the current Darium empire."

Stavros's expression darkens. "Yes. King Konram will be maximizing his military resources. A significant portion of the army is already posted in this province, but Dariu hasn't staged a major attack in over a year, and they rarely attempt even minor offenses during the winter months. He'll count on that threat being relatively low, but this way he's surrounded by his soldiers without needing to draw them away from their typical posts."

A shiver ripples down my spine. I've never actually seen a Darium soldier, but the stories passed around of their efforts to regain the western half of the continent could make one's blood curdle.

I once overheard a retired captain comment that the Darium emperor is like a jilted lover who'd rather see his former paramour savaged to death than in the arms of another.

I try to keep my tone light. "So we don't have to worry about an invasion on top of the uprising?"

"I shouldn't think so." Stavros shoots me a smile that's more wry. "In the extremely unlikely chance that the empire launches a larger offensive, it'll be easy enough to know who to avoid. They dress their soldiers in black uniforms painted with bones, as if they're walking skeletons."

Casimir grimaces in disgust. "That sounds awful—and awfully morbid."

"From what I gather, they want to horrify their opponents and remind us of the fate they expect us to meet."

*Here's to those horrors staying on the other side of the Seafell Channel, then,* Julita mutters, a sentiment I fully agree with.

We veer right at the crossroads, picking up our pace despite our fatigue at the thought of almost reaching our destination. All the names Stavros mentioned spin in my head.

I glance over at Alek. "Were there any former bug club members from this province?"

His bright eyes go distant as he considers. "Not that I recall. We do know one prominent figure from this region, though. Romild—her parents are the current provints."

Julita gives a faint groan that I can almost feel reverberating through my response. "Wonderful."

Romild is probably still off in Florian attending her leadership classes at the royal college, which is for the better. She never went out of her way to harass me like some of the other noble students, but she made it clear that she believed I'd nabbed my position as Stavros's assistant—a role she coveted—through unfair and unsavory means.

As the shadows stretch longer, the town Stavros mentioned comes into view up ahead: walled as you'd expect in territory that sees a lot of military conflict, red and brown rooftops poking up over top, and a gold spire in the middle that indicates the local temple of the All-Giver.

My pulse gives a tiny hitch, a mix of anxiety and longing. The latter sensation spreads up through my chest.

Gods above, I could use some guidance right now. More than any of my men would know how to supply.

I've already burdened them with enough troubles anyway.

"We're going into the town?" I ask.

Stavros shakes his head. "We'll find a sheltered place to set up a camp a safe distance away. We should be able to do a little business with merchants coming and going thanks to the bit of money you were able to lift from the scourge sorcerers. Passing through the gate will put us under too much scrutiny. Even Rheave's description may have been passed on after our last encounter with the patrols."

I pick my next words carefully, far too conscious of the shakiness of my thoughts that could be due to more than just exhaustion. "I could get in without needing to go through a gate. Find out if there's any talk around town about the uprising and their march—grab a few things we could use right away."

Stavros cocks his head. "'Grab'?"

I lift my chin. "I'll only borrow what can be spared from people who have more than enough already. They should be happy to support a good cause."

The former general snorts, but he knows I picked my targets fairly when I roved through the outskirts of Florian as the Hand of Kosmel.

Alek touches the back of my arm. "We've been surviving all right—and now we can get more of a rest. You shouldn't take the risk."

I shoot him a reassuring smile. "I'll be careful. I'll feel better if we can understand more of the big picture."

Casimir's expression has shadowed with concern too, but he doesn't argue with me. "I'd like to take a look at that temple of Ardone. My godlen's followers have certain policies that might be helpful to us."

Stavros hums to himself. "And I'd like to survey the area to decide on our best plan for passing on our warning. Let's pick a campsite in the woods over there. Alek and Rheave can set it up and do a little foraging, Ivy will sneak off to the town, and Casimir and I will take the horses. Assuming that beast will tolerate Casimir now." He motions toward Toast.

Casimir chuckles. "I've made better friends with him over the past few days. I think we'll get along all right for a short trek."

Another knot of anxiety forms in my stomach. "I don't know how to keep you concealed when I'm not with you. There's probably a way to work the magic, but keeping track of the consequences too when we're all in different places—"

Stavros steps closer to grasp my shoulder. "We can manage on our own for a few hours, Lady Thief. The patrols are looking for a group of four or five, not a solo rider. I won't get close enough for anyone to notice my prosthetic, and I'd imagine Casimir knows how much caution is needed around his fellow dedicats. We can always send out a signal through the lockets if we run into problems."

I force myself to relax. If I'm asking them to trust me to take care of myself, I have to extend the same trust in return. "Sounds like a plan, then."

Rheave finally rouses as Toast's gait shifts when we leave the road behind. It only takes a little arguing to convince him that I don't need him to attempt to shadow me on my stealthy mission into town.

We tap our fists together before we part ways as if reaffirming the bonds we've formed. I make sure that Toast isn't looking to buck Casimir off, remind the stallion to be good, and then set off for Iblin with only my own scrawny body to conceal.

It isn't hard to find a decent place to make my entry. I've got a lot fewer concerns about being caught when I'm effectively invisible.

I pick out a spot where the stone blocks that make up the wall are a little uneven, leap up to snag my fingers around one thin ridge, and scramble the rest of the way up and over just fifty paces from a guard standing watch.

I wasn't lying when I said I'd like to know what sort of talk is going around in town. As I weave through the streets, I keep my ears pricked for any mention of the Order of the Wild, Eppun province and its counties, or uprisings. But with every turn, I work my way closer to the main temple.

*You seem as if you know where you're going,* Julita remarks.

"There's someone I'd like to talk to, if he'll bother to talk back," I reply under my breath.

We come around another corner, and at the other end of the street, the white-washed walls of the grand temple shine in the setting sun.

Julita goes still. *Ah, I see.*

I hurry along the road toward the temple, dread warring

with hope in my chest. I haven't felt Kosmel's presence or heard his voice since the dream that led me to Sulla.

He told me he couldn't interfere quite as much anymore. Maybe he's angry that I was so quick to leave the sanctuary he directed me to.

Who can say what goes on in the mind of a godlen?

The square outside the temple is bustling with locals. No one looks or sounds at all concerned about an approaching army.

I dart between them and climb the steps to the arched doorway. The vast hallway beyond swallows me up.

It feels strange walking into the domed worship room, heading toward the statue of the Kosmel in his alcove. This rendition has the trickster godlen in his typical hooded cloak, his marble eyes peering keenly from beneath, with carved playing cards fanned in one hand and the other raised over his lips as if to encourage secrecy.

As usual, a few dice lie scattered around the marble base, but the question I have can't be reduced to a yes or no answer. I sink to my knees in front of the statue, feeling abruptly awkward.

Even when I prayed to Kosmel back in Florian, it was as much for show as out of any actual divine piety. For most of my twenty years of life, I never prayed to any of the lesser gods at all.

But he's helped me. He's kept me alive and directed my magic away from harm.

If anyone can help me through the mess I've found myself tangled in, it's him.

I bow my head and think the words I want to say. *Kosmel, please hear me and answer. I'm trying to use my magic to do good using the strategies the woman you sent me to offered. But I think it's become too much. I'm seeing and feeling things that don't totally make sense… I don't want to go mad. I don't want to fail the men who've been counting on me. I don't want to see the country upended because I faltered. Where do I go from here?*

A lump fills my throat as I wait. Faint voices drift from the other alcoves, but no divine words ring through my head.

I look up at the statue. As much as I'd like a real conversation, he's answered with simple signs before.

Nothing appears to shift on the statue's face. I peer into the shadows around the marble figure, the ache of dread expanding in my chest.

Is he totally ignoring me?

The shapes flicker with the lantern-light, and I have the impression of coins tossed as if at a betting table. When I blink, the cards seem to ruffle in Kosmel's hand as if he's adjusting them impatiently.

As if he's waiting for me to call or fold.

Is he telling me I have to make the decision for myself?

That does fit with our past conversations. He's always told me to figure out what I'm doing and then tell him what I need, not expect him to make my plans for me.

I guess I should be reassured that he thinks I can still figure my way onto a path that won't ruin everything I've worked toward.

I wait a few minutes longer, but no other impressions jump out at me. Grudgingly, I push to my feet and stride out of the temple.

Julita doesn't speak until I'm crossing the square. *I have no idea what went on between you and the trickster, but I get the sense you're not happy about the answer.*

"More like the lack of an answer," I mutter in return, and follow the scent of frying dough on the breeze. I want to come back to the men with *something* gained on this mission.

A bagful of dumplings would really hit the spot before the longest night's sleep we've had in days. My only decision right now is whether I'm going to pay for or pilfer them.

One of the streets off the square has rows of restaurants, culinary shops, and food stalls on both sides. I spot the stall the dumpling smell is wafting from down past a fishmonger and a fruit and vegetable stand. But I'm only halfway there before

Julita's voice breaks through my thoughts in a panicked tone. *Wait!*

I freeze in the middle of the street and dodge to the side to avoid a local who was strolling along behind my invisible form.

"What?" I murmur.

*I thought I heard… Look around, to your left. Farther behind you. Oh, maybe I was just imagining—*

Her words halt as I catch the voice she must have heard before too. A harshly arch masculine tone drifting from the butcher shop a few storefronts back, muffled enough that I only catch one phrase: "…long will it take?"

With my heart thumping twice as fast, I backtrack and ease closer to the butcher's entrance. Even though I can feel my magic wrapped around me, the sight within makes me want to shrink out of view—not least of all because of Julita's cringe in my head.

Her brother is standing at the butcher-shop counter, his hands on his hips in an arrogant pose. "I rode ahead of most of my party to ensure that my companions will have all the necessary supplies when they arrive. Are you saying you can't come up with the steers and fowl I asked for in time?"

The butcher glances around with a harried expression. "I suppose… If you pay in advance, you can have most of the next delivery I'm expecting. You said you need it for tomorrow evening?"

"That's right. And I trust my money is good enough." Borys slaps several gold coins down on the counter. "I can give you more if you'll meet the delivery escort outside one of the gates with the fee to save me some of my hassle coming and going."

The butcher mumbles instructions I don't catch, and Borys bustles off without another word—farther into the shop, where there must be a back door.

I scramble away and scan the street for alleys. Where is he going?

Should I try to ensure he never sees his companions again?

But the buildings along the street are densely packed. By the time I find a narrow passage around the backs toward the far end, Julita's brother is long gone.

I stand there in the dingy alley, another layer of dread settling into place.

*He's already here*, Julita says in a strained voice.

"He rode ahead to make preparations." I swallow thickly. "And the rest of the scourge sorcerer's march is only a day behind us."

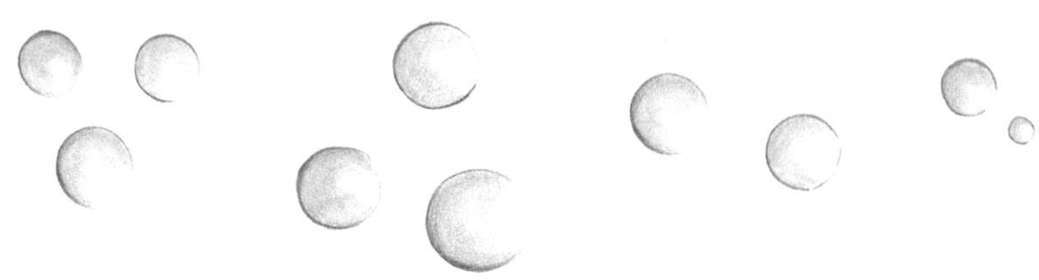

# Thirty

*Casimir*

The etching of Ardone carved into the pinkish stone wall smiles tenderly. All the same, a niggle runs through my nerves with her gaze on me.

I've served my godlen faithfully for as long as I knew how to. Surely I've earned the temple hospitality we're going to take advantage of tonight?

But I can't help wondering if I've strayed too far from the path I dedicated myself to. If some of the misfortunes we've faced reflect the gods' disapproval—of *me*.

My mother would certainly have said so.

Stavros peers warily at the small door I've led my companions to. "You're absolutely sure the cleric will harbor us unquestioningly?"

I shoot him a reassuring grin. "Ardone has a clear policy on those seeking shelter in her temples."

I step toward the door and press my hand to the print carved into the wooden surface with Ardone's sigil marked deeper on the palm. I bring my other hand to my chest.

It isn't hard to summon the deep-rooted pang of emotion

associated with the woman behind me. I swallow thickly and lift my voice. "I'm here out of love."

The truth of it resonates through my words, and something clicks over in the door. It swings open at my nudge.

With a rush of relief that I've been able to provide at least this much, I glance over my shoulder at the others and motion for them to follow me. "Come on in. These will be separate chambers from the rest of the temple. A building this size should have at least a few rooms that can be individually secured for privacy if there are other needy travelers in residence."

My four companions ease after me through the small doorway and down the short hall on the other side.

Three inner doors stand on either side. Checking them for signs of being claimed, I push open the second.

The room beyond is small and carefully organized, but still manages to give a sense of comfort. Ardone's devouts and clerics believe in providing all possible pleasures.

A thick rug covers the floor, with a mat near the door for us to leave our boots on. Walls in a warm shade of peach surround us. Shelves mounted on one side hold several rolled sleeping mats and blankets I can tell at a glance will be softer than the rough woolen ones we've been huddling in. Heat trickles into the room from a vent near the ceiling.

Ivy lets out a sigh that seems to contain a century of stress. I turn toward her with a bittersweet pang through my heart that's both anguish over the burdens she's had to carry and joy that I can help relieve her of them for just a little while.

"There's no need for you to use your powers here," I tell her. "The devouts won't invade our privacy unless they notice signs of trouble, and no one saw us arrive thanks to your magic. You can simply relax."

She looks as if she's suppressing a yawn. "And I need it."

The anguish I felt digs deeper into my chest. The strain of the past several days shows on her face and in her voice more than any of the rest of us, because it's taken so much more out of her.

And for reasons I don't totally understand, I think. I've caught a look on her face from time to time that has an almost panicked edge to it when there's been nothing immediate to fear.

Something we'll need to address as soon as we're in a state to.

At an emphatic gurgling sound, Alek clamps his hand over his belly. His face flushes. "Sorry. It's been a while since we last ate."

And a while since we ate anything you could call a full meal.

Ivy's fingers tighten around the small sack she brought back from town, but a different sort of longing crosses her face as she takes in the room. "I feel like I've got about ten layers of grime on me that I'd rather not add to my food. I don't suppose there's some kind of a bathing room here?"

I grin again, pleased that I can answer that request, and motion her over to a doorway covered with a curtain near the far corner. "I'd imagine they have some sort of accommodations for that…"

As I peer past the curtain, my smile widens. "We've got a latrine and a couple of shower stalls. Not as relaxing as a bath, but it'll get you clean enough. And the temple has provided soap, towels, and robes as well."

Ivy sets down her cargo and hurries over. "I call first dibs on one of the showers!"

Rheave cocks his head. "Shower? Like rain?"

I laugh. "Quite a bit. If the pipes are set up properly, often with the help of an enchantment, they can convey water to a spot near the ceiling where it sprays down over you. It's a fairly efficient way of getting washed."

Stavros undoes his cloak and tosses it over by our boots. "In the army, we frequently had to make do with buckets. I'd call this luxury enough." Already peeling off his shirt, he heads past the curtain to take the other stall.

When it's my turn in the shower, I want to linger in the

streaming, steamy water until it washes away all my doubts. But that isn't possible anyway.

I force myself to scrub the rosy-smelling soap over my body and through my hair as quickly as possible, grimacing at the streaks of dirt that swirl down the drain with the water.

I return to the main room to see Ivy swathed in one of the pinkish-beige bathrobes, which on her slight frame falls nearly to her ankles. She's holding up her one remaining dress.

She looks over at me with a grimace. "The thought of putting this thing back on makes my skin crawl. Maybe we can wash our clothes in the showers too?"

My body recoils at the thought of pulling on my own travel-soiled clothes. I adjust my robe around me, grateful for the clean fabric against my freshly scrubbed skin. "I don't see why not. And if we need something more presentable, a temple like this will have clothes available for the needy. There are always a few dedicats who are fashionably and also charitably inclined."

Ivy lets out a rough chuckle. "Now we're the needy."

"Hmm," Alek says, emerging from the bathing area rubbing his thick hair with a towel. "I think we've contributed enough to Silana's security to take a little charity in return without feeling guilty about it."

An avid gasp from beyond the curtain tells us Rheave has discovered how delightful a shower can be after days on the road. We all exchange an amused glance.

Ivy snatches up her sack. "Forget clothes. Let's eat."

A low wooden table with folding legs leans against the wall next to the rack of bedding. Stavros and I set it up on the floor, and we sit around it while Ivy lays out the spread she brought us. Rheave returns, his curls damp and his eyes gleaming eagerly, just as she's setting down the last of her scavenging and shopping.

"We found some frost berries in the woods," he announces. He draws a bundle of the dimpled purple fruit from his discarded cloak, sets them on the table with the rest, and peers at Stavros with a flicker of uncertainty. "You said you like those?"

Stavros blinks at him and then smiles crookedly. "I think everyone should like them. One of Prospira's few winter blessings. If you haven't tried them before, they're a treat."

Ivy plucks up one of the plump dumplings that form the center of her spread and aims a teasing grin at all of us. "I got these mostly for me, but I'm happy to share." She taps my knee with an extended foot. "I think the round ones have duck in them, so you should definitely try one of those."

My mouth is watering just at the word "duck." We haven't eaten any meat other than campfire-cooked rabbit and wild birds in over a week.

I haven't tasted my favorite fowl since we left the college.

I take one of the dumplings she indicated and nudge the cluster of roasted velvor nuts toward Alek. "And I see you were able to find our scholar's favorite snack." He practically swooned when we brought a bag of them back to the apartment in Pima.

Alek pops one into his mouth and closes his eyes with a blissful expression before rolling a sugared apricot toward Rheave. "And extra-sweetened fruit. Even the daimon will be happy."

"I'm glad just to have so much to fill my stomach with," Rheave says, but his eyes widen when he bites into the apricot. "Oh. That's very good."

Stavros pops a few frostberries into his mouth and grabs a dumpling for himself. Ivy takes out one of her knives, gleaming from its own washing, and starts slicing a hunk of cheese into equal pieces so we can all enjoy it.

For a few minutes, we're totally immersed in soothing our long-empty guts.

As I relish a third duck dumpling, the rich gravy flooding my mouth, my gaze drifts around the table. A warmth far deeper than the temple's heating system can offer rises up inside me.

We're in an unfamiliar room with few possessions to call our own other than the clothes we've worn ragged, but there's a glow of happiness in the air all the same. For what we do have. For making it this far.

And for having each other.

The stress of our journey could have put us at each other's throats, but instead we've only grown closer. I couldn't imagine men much more different from me than the three sharing this table, and yet I also can't imagine anyone I'd rather share this moment with.

Ivy hums contentedly as she nibbles at her portion of cheese and tips her head toward Stavros. "Did you find out anything at all useful from your scouting?"

He pauses to swallow a bite of dumpling. "I could see the troops here are sparse on the ground. I assume some were sent up to Eppun, but I'd still have expected more."

Alek frowns. "That's bad news if the scourge sorcerers are arriving tomorrow evening."

Rheave echoes his expression. "I *told* the men to warn the king."

Ivy reaches over to pat the daimon's arm reassuringly. "They must have passed on some kind of message. Just before I left the town, I overheard a couple of soldiers discussing the uprising. They mentioned the claim that the conspirators were sending an army this way… and laughed about it. It sounded as if they decided it must have been a lie to distract the patrols from hunting *us*."

"Naturally," Stavros mutters, and shakes his head. "I have a few ideas, but I don't think I'm in a good state to make a wise decision right now. Once I've slept on it, we can put some kind of plan into motion in the morning."

Even though he's talking about taking action soon, a shadow crosses Ivy's face. Something I see her gird herself against a moment later to put on an unflappable front with the rest of us.

What else is bothering her that she doesn't want us to see?

As we clean up the remains of our dinner, I consider the best approach. It may be difficult to encourage her to open up even with the three of us who've been with her from the start. I'm not sure how much she'll want to reveal to Rheave as well, especially given how extreme his reactions can be to anything that distresses her.

As Stavros and Ivy start laying out the sleeping mats, I turn to the daimon. "For extra security, I'm thinking we should have someone on watch just outside the door, to let us know if any other visitors arrive. Are you up to taking the first shift?"

Rheave draws his posture straighter with a flash of determination in his eyes. "Of course. No one will get past that door."

He hurries over without any further discussion. I certainly can't fault his dedication.

Alek watches him go. "Do you really think we have reason to worry? You said the temple should be secure."

"After what we've already been through, I don't think we should skimp on precautions," I say, and grab a couple of blankets from a shelf.

I lay mine out on the unrolled mat next to Ivy's and reach over to rub her shoulder. "How are you holding up, Kindness? You've had to stretch your talents more than any of the rest of us."

Ivy shrugs, but she leans into my touch with a muted sigh. Tension twines through her muscles even as my light massage starts to loosen a few of them. "I'm just glad to have the chance to rest."

"Did anything else come up during your trip to the city that worried you?"

She pauses for just long enough for me to believe there was and then gives a short laugh. "What is there that doesn't give us reason to worry these days? I'm getting by."

I brush some of her pale amber hair aside in a gentler caress. "I just want you to know that you can talk to us about anything, no matter what's on your mind. We're here for you in *every* way."

Her shoulders stiffen slightly, but then she glances at me through her eyelashes with an arch of one eyebrow that makes my heart skip a beat despite my intentions. "You know, it's been too long since I've gotten to enjoy you being here in one particular way."

She leans over to claim a kiss, her fingers tracing the line of my jaw.

Heat flows across my skin with the gesture. I can't help kissing her back.

I've missed our most physical intimacies too… but I can't shake the impression that she's dodging the question.

When our lips part, I keep my head bowed close to hers. "Ivy—"

Before I can do more than murmur her name, she glances toward Alek with a beckoning motion. Her gaze slides to Stavros in turn.

Both of the other men step closer and then hesitate. Ivy lets out a soft huff—and reaches for the tie of her robe.

She tugs it loose and lets the fabric slip from her slim form, leaving her sitting naked in a pool of linen. There's still a little self-consciousness in the way she holds her arms as if to partly cover her breasts, but I can't help smiling at the confidence she has gained since our earliest encounters.

"We've come this far," she says in a low voice. "It's about time you showed me that I really am your Signy."

A sharper heat rushes through me and condenses in my groin. This isn't how I intended our private moment to go, but —if I'm not meant for this kind of request, what *am* I good for?

With a slight flex of my jaw, I reach for my gift, fixing my attention on Ivy. Taking in the stream of images that follow, which should tell me what I can do that would really make her happiest right now.

The swell of sensation only heightens my desire, fed by what I can sense of her own. There really is nothing that would set her more at ease than tapping into my greatest talent.

Nothing *I* could do, anyway. But how can I refuse what I'm able to offer?

Alek is already in motion, sinking down next to Ivy with his arm tucking around her back beneath the worst of her scars. His voice comes out rough. "You're more than our Signy. You're our *Ivy*."

She beams at him in the instant before their mouths collide. Another niggling thought passes through my head—that he fits her better than I ever could, with their scars and the ways they've kept themselves hidden.

She still wants me too. And it's beautiful watching them together, feeling their way through the sort of intimacy I almost take for granted.

Ivy clearly isn't in the mood to draw things out. She breaks from the kiss only to swing her legs around so she can straddle Alek.

As she kisses him again, yanking at the tie on his robe, I scoot closer and dapple kisses over the peak of her shoulder and down her arm. My hand strokes her back in tender circles with the wish that I could smooth away all the remainders of her mother's abuse.

Then I glance past her toward the final member of our quartet. Stavros stands poised just a couple of paces away, his hands flexing at his sides, his gaze smoldering.

Oh, he wants to be a part of this interlude. The hunger is written all over him.

But I suppose the only practice he's had at navigating this kind of sharing is when he joined Ivy and me toward the end of our encounter at the Haven.

I catch his gaze and lift my eyebrows as if to say, *Well, are you getting over here or what?*

After a momentary and only half-hearted glower, he kneels at Ivy's other side. He rests his hand on her bare waist and tilts his head to kiss the side of her neck. I can tell he's being careful not to impose too much on her attention to Alek.

When Ivy trails her fingers down Alek's lean frame to grasp his cock, he groans. I slip my hand around her thigh to tease between her legs. The slickness I find there makes my own dick jump to sharper attention.

"Already so ready for us," I murmur. I give her earlobe an affectionate nip before gazing past her toward Alek. "Maybe you have some suggestions from that poetry book for how we can best please our woman together?"

A ruddy cast has formed beneath the scholar's rich brown skin. He wets his lips, his eyelids drooping as his hips rock with Ivy's attentions. "There is… It's sounded as if it can be quite satisfying for a woman to be entered from… ah, both directions. At the same time. I'm not sure how easy that is outside of poetics."

A smile stretches across my face. "Oh, we can definitely offer her that experience." I caress Ivy's cheek. "If you'd like to give it a try."

I'm not sure there's anything in the world as lovely as the blush that turns her paleness the perfect shade of rosy. "That sounds rather incredible."

I swirl my thumb over her clit with just enough pressure to earn me a whimper and withdraw. "Why don't you fill yourself with Alek as you'll both enjoy, and I'll get the necessary supplies?"

This is still a temple of the godlen of sensuality, after all. I spotted just the thing in a little basket at the back of the bathing area: a pot of lubricating gel.

I return with it to find Ivy has followed my instructions to great effect. She eases up and down over Alek in steady strokes, their bodies united, their shaky breaths carrying into the air like the most thrilling music. He's just ducking his head to brush his lips against her collarbone while she turns her head to share a kiss with Stavros.

As their mouths meld together, the military professor slides his hand down her back and squeezes her ass. Ivy bucks onto

Alek a little faster, both of their chests hitching with ragged exhalations.

They slow down the pace again when I lower myself next to them. Stavros lets the kiss linger a moment longer and then looks over at me.

Excitement wars with trepidation in his expression. "I think you'd better do the honors. I'd be a lot to take."

I've never seen the man naked, but considering the size of the rest of him, I find that easy to believe.

Ivy punctuates his suggestion with a breathless laugh. "We can work up to that."

Stavros stares at her as if startled that she'd even want to try, and I can't look away from her face either. I don't know what was weighing on her mind before, but no trace of turmoil remains there now.

This is the gift I can give her, the benefit of the arts I've studied. Gods forgive me for not being able to imagine offering it to anyone else while she's claimed so much of my heart.

I shrug off my robe and sink down behind her. With Alek kneeling beneath her, she's in the perfect position.

I dip my fingers into the gel and trace them into the cleft of her ass.

As they glide over her back opening, Ivy gasps. A little shiver passes through her body.

Leaning closer, I kiss her spine at the top of her back. "Good?"

"Mmm," she hums, still swaying over Alek. "I have the feeling it's going to get even better."

With a chuckle, I continue. The ring of muscle there loosens gradually with my massage. When I delve my fingers right inside her, my lover lets out a truly glorious series of needy sounds.

While I stretch her with two and then three fingers, she alternates between kissing Alek and Stavros. Stavros cups one of her breasts and rolls her nipple under his thumb. Alek slips his hand between them, provoking a moan when he must find her clit.

A curse tumbles from the scholar's lips at the sound. "I don't know how much longer I'm going to last," he admits.

Ivy gives a defiant little growl. "Stay with us. Not done yet."

His laugh is strained with building desire.

I kiss Ivy's shoulder blade and slick my fingers over my cock to prepare it. "Let's see how this goes, then. Stop me if you're feeling anything but amazing."

At her impatient noise, I line myself up with her opening. As she stills, I press inside her.

Her entrance is so tight, the heat of her enveloping my cock so intense, that suddenly I'm not sure how long *I'm* going to last. Arousal pulses through my shaft, my release already swelling at the base.

"Oh, gods," Ivy mumbles. She clutches at Alek with one hand and reaches back to clasp my braced arm with the other.

As I sink in as far as I can go, my head bows over her. Pleasure reverberates through my body, so heady it's dizzying. "Let's take this slow. We move together."

I pull back a fraction as Ivy eases up over both me and Alek. When she sinks down again, a guttural moan spills from her lips.

The scholar echoes it with a choked sound. I swallow a groan of my own, buoyed by the blissful haze.

But as we start to find our rhythm between the three of us, I can't help noticing that our fourth companion has sat back on his heels, simply watching.

Reaching around Ivy, I tap Alek's arm. "Do you have any inspired ideas for how we might bring Stav into the fun?"

Alek peers around, his bright eyes glazed with pleasure. He pauses for a second, and I think his flush deepens.

"Hands or mouth?" His gaze darts to Ivy. "Whatever you'd like most."

Ivy lets out a husky chuckle. "Maybe I could try both."

She waves Stavros closer and grasps the tie of his robe. As he sheds it, she tugs him higher on his knees.

Stavros watches her with the same air of disbelief I saw before, mingled with the passion flaring in his gaze. When she grips the base of his erection and dips her head to flick her tongue over the tip, his eyes roll back.

"Fuck," he rasps, tangling his fingers in her hair. "Ivy, you don't need to—"

She interrupts him with a dismissive noise. "I *want* to have all of you."

Then she takes the head of his cock right into her mouth, and he rocks to meet her with a groan. "Gods, you're a fucking miracle."

That she is.

All of us move together, we three thrusting up to meet Ivy as she descends over us. She swallows us up again and again by every means she has.

The quivers of pleasure that race through her body in answer to my own delight reassure me that she's enjoying this interlude just as much as I am.

We're like a wave, surging up over and over. Lifting her higher and higher while we spiral toward our own climaxes.

I dapple kisses across her shoulder blades between my panting breaths. "So lovely. Our Ivy. You're perfect."

The giddy heat builds in my groin. I push into her harder, faster, determined to bring her over the edge before I give in—

Ivy gasps around Stavros's cock. Her muscles clench around me, and I'm lost, spilling myself with my last several thrusts, clasping her tightly as she shudders against me. The ecstasy of the moment sears through me like a surge of the most delicious fire.

With Ivy's cry of release, Alek grunts and stiffens too. He buries his face against her neck.

Stavros shifts as if to withdraw, but Ivy's hand tightens around his shaft. She pumps him faster, her lips pursing around the head of his cock as if determined to haul him with the rest of us.

His hand twitches in her hair, and his breath hisses out through his teeth as he gives himself over to her demand.

Ivy slumps between us with a wordless but happy murmur. I wrap my arms around her and kiss the side of her neck, not willing to let go of the moment just yet.

I may not be serving my mother's ambitions for me or the godlen I dedicated myself as fully as I'm capable of… but I'm not sure I could regret what I've given to this woman. Even if this is the last chance I get before this quest proves my undoing.

# Thirty-One

*Ivy*

After so long riding Toast bareback, it feels strange to have a saddle beneath me again. Also strange to be wearing fine linen rather than coarse, dirty wool against my skin.

Both Stavros and I took a new outfit from the temple's offerings this morning. The former general particularly wanted to look more like his noble self for our current mission.

The tunic he's wearing beneath his cloak is embroidered with regular thread rather than gold or silver, and the fabric isn't quite as fine as he'd have worn at Sovereign College. But he looks more like his old self as he rides beside me.

I tug my own cloak closer around me against the chilly but not biting breeze and scan the countryside. We skirted the town about an hour ago and haven't passed any close settlements larger than a farm since. Regardless, I'm keeping concealing magic wrapped around us.

For this particular task, we can't be too careful.

As if picking up on my thoughts, Stavros glances over at me.

"Are you sure you want to take this risk? We'll be dealing with royal military security—and if we're caught—"

I make a dismissive sound. "Sneaking in and out of places is one of my specialties even without magic. It's not as if you could knock on the door and expect them to agree to your request."

"I can occasionally make a case with words rather than weapons," he replies in a wry tone, but his solemn expression doesn't shift.

"I suspect this would not be one of those times." For one thing, I doubt he's ever had to contend with a royal notice for his arrest before. "This is the best way I can help. It's not as if we have any better options."

My magic is the *only* way I have any hope of stopping the scourge sorcerers' current plans, as far as I can tell. I just need to be smart about it. If I don't use it any more than I absolutely need to, I can hope my mind stays reasonably steady.

I haven't had any strange impulses or glimpses of things that aren't there since we hid ourselves away in the temple last night. Maybe all I needed was a little break from constantly tapping into my power.

And a chance to indulge in my men's affections. The memory of our joint encounter sends a thrill of lingering heat through me—along with a twinge of guilt.

Casimir could obviously tell something's bothering me. I did want all of them; I did want to lose myself in pleasure for a little while. But I was also deflecting further questions I'm not totally sure how to answer.

*This is a rather daring exploit even for Stavros,* Julita remarks. *He'd better know what he's doing. It's been over a year since he left the army, hasn't it?*

Her uneasy rambling makes my nerves jitter.

"*You're* sure that the mirror will be there?" I ask the former general. "And he'll answer it quickly?"

Stavros nods. "I was stationed out here a couple of times during my former career. For each of the main royal residences outside of the capital, there's a means to communicate quickly with the royal family from the primary military fortress in the area. If fighting breaks out when they're in residence, they want a swift means to communicate with the local forces."

"So you're going to signal King Konram, and he'll think it must mean war has broken out."

Stavros offers me a crooked smile. "Isn't that essentially what we're dealing with?"

I guess he has a point. Imagining the battle we could be facing as soon as this evening makes my stomach clench up.

There has been unnervingly little military presence in sight during our ride. Stavros pointed out a couple of smaller forts that we passed at a distance, but I didn't see much sign of activity around them. Not many soldiers on hand to form a solid defense.

Definitely the strangest part of this experience: wishing there were *more* soldiers around rather than fewer.

At least for me. As our conversation has been a clear reminder of, Stavros is used to being surrounded by military figures.

I take in his assured poise and the resolve on his handsome face. A deeper pang forms in my chest.

This is the man I've fallen for: strong and confident, determined to do what's right. Looking to defend those who can't defend themselves.

I admire those qualities, but they could also be what separates us in the end.

"When we had that clash with the patrol on the way here," I venture, "you said your gift warned you. Has it shown you anything else since your injury?"

Stavros pauses. "Only once, also recently."

"It might be returning, then. Adapting to the new limitations on your sight. Would you see about getting your old position back if that's the case?"

I've done my best to keep my tone casual, but Stavros's gaze has turned penetrating when he looks at me. "Gift or not, I'm hardly in a position to lead masses of troops when I can't see clearly for more than a second at a time. And that's assuming Konram ever does pardon us."

I shrug. "I'd imagine your gift could still be useful in some sort of military role. It's bothered you, not being able to participate at all—being relegated to teaching."

He can't deny that fact when he's told me as much outright.

Stavros exhales in a rush, but he doesn't argue. "I don't think any of us can make decisions about what the future might hold beyond the next few days, Ivy. I'd rather focus on making sure all of us have a future."

His voice softens. "But whatever does happen, I wouldn't want to go back to exactly the way my life was before. I'm not leaving you behind."

My cheeks heat. "I wasn't saying—"

"I know." His smile has softened too. "I simply thought *I* should say that. My life has felt awfully empty for a lot of the past year—but it would also feel empty without you in it keeping me on my toes. I wouldn't mind being back at the royal college feeding you crescent rolls right now."

Even as I snort at the remark, my mouth waters at the memory of my favorite pastries.

Stavros cocks his head. "Honestly, it's hard to picture carrying on without Casimir and Alek in the mix somehow too. I think you're stuck with all of us permanently."

I roll my eyes and wish the affection in his words had eased more of the tension in my gut.

I can tell he means them in this moment. How much he will if so many more possibilities open themselves up to him, who can say?

I think I'd hate feeling I've held him back even more than I'd hate losing him.

Julita hums to herself. *I'd trust him on this one, Ivy. I may not have ever gotten all that close to Stav while we were working together, but I can see how much he's loosened up since he figured out he wants you. You've been good for him.*

Coming from the woman who was once jealous of the attention her former companions offered me, the sentiment does warm me a little.

We pass through a thin strip of forest. On the other side, a broad stone structure looms at the top of a low rise.

Stavros gestures for us to slow down. "That's our destination. I wasn't able to get this close yesterday. I'll need to determine the most direct route to the room we need…"

Movement by the side of the building makes my pulse stutter. "Someone's coming."

The former general stiffens. "They can't see us, can they?"

"No, but we should probably get off the road to be safe."

Even as we direct our steeds onto the overgrown grass along the throughway, I realize the figures I noticed aren't heading our way. Three men on horseback set off to the west. Two wear soldier's uniforms, but I catch a flash of purple robes beneath the cloak on the man in the middle.

And when he shifts his tall frame in his saddle, the sight of his lopsided body sends a shiver through my nerves.

"Lothar," Stavros says, identifying the king's secondary magic advisor at the same moment I did. "Obviously he's returned from the front. Perhaps he's consulting with the local forces on techniques for combating scourge sorcery in case the threat we warned about is real after all."

He speaks without much hope in his voice. I can't summon a great deal myself. "Well, at least he's leaving so we won't have to deal with his riven-hunting inclinations." And whatever immense gift he received for sacrificing his entire arm to his chosen godlen.

We come around the front of the fortress, giving the building a wide berth. No one's posted right at the door, but Stavros points out a few guards on watch in the towers at the corners. We definitely can't stroll right in.

Wetting my lips, I consider the magical strategies I'm most confident in. "How close to the front entrance is the room we need?"

Stavros pauses, his expression going distant as he must navigate the building in his memory. "One floor up, but the stairs are just past the main hall. It's only a couple of doors down from there. Locked, of course."

"That won't be a problem." I drag a breath into my lungs. "I think I can let us stroll right inside. We'll just have to be careful about it. And obviously the horses can't come with us."

Since I'm not yet confident in my ability to work magic multiple places simultaneously, we secure Toast and his unnamed companion in a sheltered spot amid the trees. Then we tramp back to the fort on foot.

As we approach, I concentrate on the door in front of me. I visualize how large a space I need to carve out for us to pass through without needing it unbarred.

The guards up top can't see the door from their positions, but I don't know about the other side.

"Would there normally be anyone stationed in the front hall?" I ask Stavros.

He shakes his head. "Not unless they were preparing to defend from an attack."

That'll have to do. I'll keep our entrance as discreet as possible just in case. "Walk right behind me, straight through the door."

"What—?"

Before he can even ask the question, I toss a surge of my magic toward the wooden surface. It removes a slab of the door —while another slab forms in the trees next to the horses where no one will notice the consequence—and fills in the space with a darkish brown haze as close as I could manage to the color of the wood.

I step straight through. Stavros follows with a brisk stride, but he's canny enough to set his boots quietly on the floor on the other side even if he's startled by my tactic.

With another push of my magic, I reform the wood in the door while disintegrating the stuff that conjured elsewhere.

My magic quivers eagerly as I yank the power back into my chest other than the strands keeping us invisible. My heart thuds amid the energy churning between my ribs.

Was that a yelp?

I barely hold back a flinch, my head jerking around, but Stavros doesn't react to any sound. He simply strides forward to where the staircase must be.

A chill ripples down my back. Another hallucination. My break didn't buy me much of a reprieve.

But I can't turn back now.

I keep pace with Stavros through the dim, stone-walled hallway, past a few soldiers who are heading into a room farther down on the first floor, and up the narrow staircase. Muffled voices waver from other parts of the fortress, but I'm no longer sure which are real and which my mind has made up.

We pad carefully over the thin carpet in the second-floor hallway to a door with the king's sigil etched on it.

At Stavros's gesture, I set my hand against the bronze knob. It's only sealed mechanically, no enchantments reinforcing the lock.

With a twist of my magic, I yank the deadbolt over in exchange for a few cracked twigs on one of the distant trees.

We wait for another soldier to amble by and then push into the room as soon as the coast is clear.

It's a small, windowless space, the air dank between the stone walls. There are no furnishings other than the lantern that flares on automatically at our entrance—and the gold-framed mirror hanging on the wall opposite the door.

I lean against the side wall where I hope I'll be out of view and release the magic that was concealing us. "He'll be able to see you now."

Stavros shrugs his cloak back from his arms and then hesitates. Just for a second, his jaw tightens with the emotions he's reining in.

I can't imagine what he's feeling right now. I never pledged myself to the man he's about to contact—the man who'd like to see us all sent to the gallows for our supposed betrayal.

The former general presses the notches in the mirror's frame in a pattern I don't follow and steps back. We wait in silence, hearing footsteps scrape by in the hall outside.

A niggling fear rises up in the back of my head. The soldiers could have realized their fortress has been breached—they could be gathering outside the door right now—

I give myself a mental shake and force myself to listen hard. There's no sound beyond the door at the moment.

Just my mind addling itself again.

As I resist the urge to hug myself against the realization, the mirror's surface shimmers. An image of King Konram appears on the glass as if he's reflected there.

His eyes widen, his stance going rigid. "Stavros."

Stavros drops to one knee in a supplicating pose. "Your Highness, I apologize for intruding this way. I have urgent news that affects the security of the entire country. Please, hear me out."

The king's mouth presses flat. He gives his former general a wounded look, as if *he's* the one who's spent the last several weeks being harassed all across the realm.

I'd like to stop the scourge sorcerers from murdering this man, but right now, I'd also like to punch his pompous face.

His voice comes out sharp but commanding. "General Leslam gave you access to this—?"

"No," Stavros breaks in. "He doesn't know I'm here. I couldn't risk— Any rumors you've heard that the mutinists from Eppun are marching on your current residence are true. They're using their scourge sorcery to conceal themselves. From what we understand, they expect to arrive in the vicinity of Iblin by this evening. There are several hundred of them, and they have their magic on their side—you'll need more troops—"

"Giving military advice is no longer your job," King Konram interrupts, but he sounds at least as disheartened as he does angry. "I've heard no reports confirming any significant force nearby. Surely even their illicit sorcery couldn't hide them completely."

Stavros gazes at him as if willing his king to believe him. "I've seen them with my own eyes—and seen how well their magic hides them and covers their tracks. There must be reinforcements you can summon. I expected to see more troops on hand already."

"Scouts have noted Darium gathering forces where the channel narrows. They may have heard of the uprising and—" Konram cuts himself off with a grimace, as if reminding himself that he shouldn't reveal anything to the man he considers a traitor. "It will take at least a couple of days to summon a significant additional force. But I have plenty of soldiers on hand as it is."

Stavros bows his head. "Please, Your Highness. You know I'm not one to beg. But I'm convinced that these menaces will do everything in their power to destroy your family. Take every measure you can to prepare and protect yourself. I'd suggest you move to a different residence if I wasn't afraid that you'll be even more vulnerable on the road."

The king considers him for a long moment. "You're truly worried."

I hear Stavros swallow. "We've done what we can to disrupt the uprising and stop the scourge sorcerers, but there are many more of them than us. And the power they can wield…"

Something shifts in Konram's expression. "'We.' I suppose that's how you accessed the mirror. Is your riven sorcerer there with you?"

Stavros's chin comes up. "Ivy has given more of herself than any of us to ensure your safety and—"

"I don't want to hear it," the other man snaps, and then seems to gather himself. "I'll take your report into consideration. Turn yourselves in, and I can withdraw those soldiers from their patrols."

"My king—"

"That's all I have left to say to you."

The mirror dims, and then it only reflects Stavros, his shoulders slumping.

Julita sniffs indignantly. *You'd think he's forgotten how well Stavros served him for all those years before. What a knobhead.*

I have to suppress a sharp guffaw at the crude insult in her noble tones.

Cautiously, I step toward Stavros and touch his arm as he stands. "Do you think he'll listen?"

Stavros sighs. "I can't tell. We've never had this kind of distrust between us before. At least he gave me the chance to say the most important parts."

I turn toward the door, my skin starting to creep in the cramped room. "There's nothing else to do here, then. Let's get out of this place."

I lean close to the door and hear nothing from the other side. Ignoring my trepidation, I extend my magic around us again to hide us from view. I ease the door open, step into the hall—

And wrench to the side with a heavy hand clamped on my shoulder and a blade tapping against my throat.

"Don't move an inch," the soldier who's grabbed me snarls as I'm already freezing in place. My magic shudders, the invisibility effect faltering when he's pressed right against my back.

He must have heard us through the door, managed to grab me through practiced instincts even when he couldn't see me.

Now it doesn't matter.

His blade digs into my neck with a faint sting. "All right. You're going to walk with me down to the dungeons, and then you'll explain to the general what the fuck you're doing here."

My lips part, but my entire body has gone deathly cold. I don't know what to say. Stavros won't intervene when my captor could slit my throat in an instant.

My power flares through my limbs, making my muscles ache, clambering for me to release it all. To blast through the prick who's threatened me.

And all the others. Raze the whole fucking fortress to the ground. Crack skulls and smash spines. Ensure there won't be a single one to give chase—

Gory images flood my mind, and I recoil inwardly.

No, no, that isn't want I want. We *need* these soldiers alive to stop the real villains.

I'd become the monster Stavros used to see me as.

But my magic keeps flailing at me. My mind whirls, and I can't hold on to a single steady thought.

The jolts of rage break through again and again, alongside Julita's frantic voice. *No, no, we can't get caught like this. It isn't* fair. *Oh, Ivy, no…*

Something clicks in my head. The soldier starts to drag me backward, and my voice spills hoarse from my throat. "Julita says no."

I pull my thoughts deep inside my skull, letting my vision fog and my mind haze, hoping she understands.

Nothing happens except the soldier sputtering, "What the fuck are you babbling about?"

Then the tingling presence at the back of my head leaps forward.

My lips move again, but not through my will. Julita's spirit grips my body and propels my voice—with the gift she gave up two ribs for years ago. "I will not go to the dungeon. You will not stop me from leaving by any means. You cannot prevent me from doing as I wish."

The soldier lets out a sound that starts as a snort and then seems to choke. His grasp on me loosens, his sword sinking.

Julita propels me out of his arms and then flings herself back into her usual place in my head, letting my consciousness hurtle to the fore again. I yank the strands of invisibility around me, glimpsing Stavros staring at me with a grayish tint to his light brown skin, and grab his hand. "Come on. I don't know how long Julita's gift will last."

The soldier is gaping at what must now look like only empty air again. But he doesn't snatch at me or raise any shout of alarm as we bolt past him.

We rush down the stairs and through the hall. I have just enough wherewithal to remove a chunk of the front door just in time for us to dash through it.

My magic batters me from the inside in a fury. My nerves jangle with the insistence that we should flatten the whole building and everyone in it to the ground.

They aren't going to leave me alone until I—

No, no, *no*. I pull the image of the protective vine tight around myself, but the power keeps wrenching at me.

Gods above, I wish I could use Julita's gift on myself.

Her buoyant laugh rings through my head. *It really worked. Thank the gods! I'm so glad I could do something real for once.*

"You were pretty amazing," I murmur to her. I don't want to think about what might have happened if I couldn't have turned to her, but my stomach churns with the horror anyway. "We're still a good team."

As the last words leave my mouth, a holler carries across the hill from the fortress behind us. Stavros and I exchange a frantic glance and run for our mounts as if the world depends on it.

Which, unfortunately, it very well might.

# Thirty-Two

*Rheave*

Ivy bites her lip as she paces the room. There's been an agitated energy to her ever since she and Stavros returned.

A tiny red mark mars the pale skin of her neck. A soldier held a sword to her throat there.

He wanted to hurt her.

My fingers curl around the urge to storm out of the temple's refuge rooms and across the countryside until I can tear that villain apart.

I should have been there to protect her. But I couldn't go, because it would have been more strain on her to conceal me too. Stavros was the one who knew what needed to be done at the fort.

I would have made things *harder* for her, not easier.

The knowledge sets me even more on edge.

I bare my teeth. "They're all idiots. They won't listen. Maybe they deserve to get blasted with scourge sorcery."

The horrified look that crosses Ivy's face makes me want to catch the words and stuff them back down my throat.

"We broke into their fortress," she says. "The soldier who

  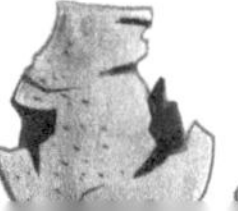 

caught me and the ones who came after us—they were only doing their jobs."

A growl creeps up my throat. "Not well."

Stavros gives a dark chuckle. "We should be glad they didn't perform better, or we might not have made it back here safely."

Casimir comes up behind Ivy and sets his hands on her shoulders. He squeezes them with gentle circles of his thumbs, and she partly relaxes into the massage.

I could have done *that*. It doesn't look very hard. Why didn't I think of it first?

There are so many things she needs, and I'm not sure I've been doing any of them lately.

The courtesan tilts his head toward the wall nearby. "I made decent use of the time while you were gone. Purchased a few items from passing merchants that could come in handy."

I can't stop myself from stroking my fingers over the feathered fletching on the arrows Casimir brought back, bundled in their quiver along with a simple bow. At least I'm ready if there's anyone around I need to shoot at.

He bought some sort of instrument too, like a long metal tube with a flared end, that he said could be used to sound a warning across long distances. And more food.

I turn back to Ivy with a spark of inspiration. "You should have something to eat. It's past lunchtime. Casimir got us stuffed buns and dumplings."

From the way Ivy's eyes light up, I can tell he made a good choice. He's known her longer than I have—he's gotten to see more of her at times when she got to pick what she actually wanted to eat rather than having to settle for what we could hunt or scavenge.

She sits down at the table we unfolded this morning, and Casimir grabs the box with his acquisitions. Alek glances up from where he was peering at his book of letters again and scoots over to pluck up a stuffed bun.

I'm not particularly hungry, but the mix of buttery pastry

and spiced meat in the buns is very enjoyable. It's amazing how many flavors the physical world can hold.

Before I found myself in this body, I could see and hear even if I didn't pay attention quite the same way. To some extent, I could feel the textures of the things I flitted past. But I had no sense of taste at all.

I lean over to take another one—and a different sensation sears through my body like a fishing line yanking at my spirit.

I lurch to the side with a yelp I can't contain. Magic shivers through every muscle in my body.

It's the scourge sorcerers. They're trying to call this body back to them again. I can't let them—I have to focus—

But even as I start to concentrate on the thin rug beneath my feet and the thump of my heart to remind myself that this body belongs to *me* now, my pulse hitches with the impression that it's not enough. Something's different this time.

The magic wrenches through me harder—but it isn't hauling me toward the doorway. It flings me around, whipping out my arms.

My hand has closed into a fist without my realizing. It smashes into Stavros's jaw where the big man has hurried to my side.

He jerks away with a grunt of shock, and the energy of my daimon spirit crackles through my nerves. My body turns frigid from the inside out.

I could burn them all up if the scourge sorcerers manage to make me.

A frantic cry bursts from my lips. I yank myself away from Stavros before any of my power can explode out, but my body wheels toward Ivy.

A flash of an image passes behind my eyes—her face charred, her lithe frame blackened.

*No.* Anything but that.

I heave myself away with a surge of desperation. My limbs flail out.

Energy sizzles across the wall, scorching black streaks in its wake.

I need to stop this. I need to stop *them*.

But the best I can seem to do is to make sure I destroy something other than my companions.

I crash into the shelves of bedding. Sleeping rolls and blankets tumble to the floor.

The magic propelling me whirls me around. I throw myself into the spin so it takes me farther—away from Ivy and the others.

My body slams into the door shoulder-first. More energy flares from my skin, and the wood hisses and cracks apart.

I burst into the hall in a shower of splinters.

The impact resonates through my bones. I hit the floor in the hall with another jolt.

Pressing my hands against the floorboards with bits of broken wood digging into my fingers, I close my eyes and heave the awful influence away with every bit of my strength.

The raging of magic inside me dwindles. I push the side of my head against the floor too, absorbing the feel of the solid surface.

This is my body now. *Mine*.

As a breath shudders out of my lungs, footsteps rush over. I cautiously peel myself off the messy floor to find all four of my companions around me.

"Are you all right?" Ivy asks, her face blanched.

Stavros looks grim. "It was the scourge sorcerers again, wasn't it?"

He has a red blotch on his jaw. I must have hit him hard.

Guilt winds through my gut. "I'm sorry. Instead of trying to call me to them, they were making me lash out. As soon as I realized, I did my best not to hurt any of you."

The big man rubs his jaw. "I've had worse."

Alek studies me, his expression tense. "They must have realized that dragging you away wasn't working, so they figured they could use you to do damage in other ways. Do you think—"

Before he can finish his question, the door at the end of the hall swings open. A woman in a cleric's robes, flanked by two devouts, bustles inside and stalls in her tracks at the sight of me crouched amid the remains of the door. "What in the realms are you doing to our temple?"

Casimir holds up his hands. "All our apologies, Your Holiness. Our friend was ill and had a fit. He's come out of it now."

I don't like the lie, but I've seen how people react to finding out the truth of what I am enough to keep my mouth shut for my companions' sake.

The cleric steps forward gingerly and peeks into the room. I wince at the thought of the mess I've made.

She sucks a breath through her teeth in a hiss. "This is unacceptable behavior for guests. We can't have anyone so disruptive staying here. You need to leave at once."

She tenses as if bracing for an uncomfortable argument, but Stavros lowers his head. He's keeping his prosthetic hand tucked behind him, I notice. "We'll gather our things and be out before the next bell."

"Here." Ivy steps forward with a flash of gold in her hand. She offers the coin to the cleric. "To cover the costs of the repairs."

The cleric takes the coin, staring at it and then the rest of us. It occurs to me that she must wonder why people carrying gold coins would need to shelter at a temple rather than paying for regular accommodations.

I may have caused even more harm than what I can see.

The compensation appears to mollify the woman at least for the moment, though. She dips her head and hurries away with her devouts in tow.

Stavros waves us toward the ruined room. "Let's get our

things quickly. She may decide to call for help if she gets any indication that we're hesitant to leave."

I shove myself to my feet and scramble into the room. My spirits sink lower at the sight of the scorch marks and the shelves I didn't realize I'd cracked when I smacked into them.

I snatch up my cloak, my new bow and arrows, and the older clothes still damp from this morning's washing.

It only takes a minute for us all to gather our meager supplies. We hustle out to the temple's adjoining stable, where Ivy and Stavros retrieve the horses they returned there less than an hour ago.

Ivy's stallion snorts as we head for the nearest stretch of forest, as if he's annoyed we interrupted his rest. I've even upended the animals' lives.

We finally had a warm, clean place to stay where Ivy didn't need to constantly work at hiding us, and I destroyed it all.

A gloom settles over me like nothing I've felt before. It feels as if a dark, suffocatingly thick cloud has descended to swallow me whole.

As we tramp between the trees, my head droops. An uncomfortable sense of resolve fills me.

I know what I should do. What maybe I should have done from the first moment I realized how the creators of this body could still affect me.

All this time, and I still can't fend them off properly. How can I say I deserve this body when I can't even prevent it from hurting the few people who've accepted me?

I'm not sure how much time passes before Stavros lifts his hand to stop us. "I think we've gotten enough distance from the temple. We don't want to stray too far from Iblin when we know the scourge sorcerers are using it for supplies. We can set up a camp and monitor the situation from here."

We're standing at the edge of a small glade ringed by leafless trees and a few that bristle with dark green needles. Casimir immediately moves to start arranging our possessions.

I set down my damp clothes and the bow but hold on to my quiver. An arrow tip would do better than a stick.

"I'm going to take a walk and make sure there are no threats nearby," I announce, and set off before anyone can question me.

I walk until I can't make out any hint of my companions through the trees and then keep going a little farther for good measure. The wind rattles the branches over my head, bringing a crisp, wild scent I try to commit to memory.

How well will I recall all the bodily experiences I've enjoyed once I no longer have a physical presence? Will my existence as a sort-of human fade as if it never happened?

I set my quiver against a tree and slide out one of the arrows. As I look at the afternoon sunlight glancing off the sharp metal tip, all my innards seem to clench up.

I turn the shaft between my fingers, in the grips of a silent debate.

I'd be leaving her behind. I promised to protect her.

But have I really managed to do that, or have I only put her in more danger, again and again?

There's so much more I hoped for. So much that my chest aches with it alongside the pangs of regret for what I *have* done.

At the snap of a twig, I jerk around.

Ivy stops several paces away, her worried gaze fixed on me.

She got this close without me hearing her approaching. I don't know whether to credit my distraction or her skills in stealth.

When I don't speak, she walks closer. "What are you doing, Rheave?"

It's difficult to concentrate on my intentions when she's looking at me like that.

I grope for the right words. "It's dangerous for me to be with you. I keep ruining things."

Somehow her face turns even sadder. "None of that was your fault. The scourge sorcerers were messing with you. When we've dealt with them, that won't happen anymore."

"But we don't know how long that'll take or what else they might do before then. What else they might make *me* do."

Ivy frowns. "So why did you come out here? Did you think you'd just walk away? You didn't take any food—you didn't even bring your bow..."

Her gaze slides from the quiver I set down to the arrow in my hand, and her stance goes rigid. "Rheave, you weren't going to— I thought you wanted to *keep* your body."

A sudden, unexpected heat wells up behind my eyes. I find myself blinking hard against the moisture that starts to collect there. "I do. It's been incredible—but giving it up is the easiest solution. If I don't have this body, if it's only chunks of broken clay, then they can't force me to do anything I don't want to do."

Ivy grasps my wrist by the hand holding the arrow. "I wouldn't ask you to give up this new part of your life just because you've struggled a little. None of us would. We'll figure something else out."

"But it keeps happening, no matter what I try. I can't even tell they're sending their magic at me until it's too late."

She pauses, studying me. "Do you *want* to go back to being just a daimon? So you can be free of all the trouble?"

"No!" The answer bursts out of me before I can contain it. "I still haven't—I haven't done anything that really matters."

Ivy knits her brow. "What do you mean?"

My frustration constricts my chest. "I never understood before... Humans exist for such a short time in the scheme of things. But you leave your mark on the world in so many ways that I never have in the entire time I wandered without caring... I want to make a difference. Change something for the better."

"I think you already have," Ivy says quietly. "But you *can* still do more."

A lump has clogged my throat. I have to swallow it to speak. "I want to matter. But that's selfish, isn't it? I should do what would make things better for the most people right now."

Ivy's hand tightens on my arm. "I don't think killing this

body would be the best thing. Because you do matter already. You matter to me."

I lift my gaze, searching her expression. She still looks sad and worried, and there's something else shimmering in her eyes that I can't decipher.

But it isn't quite what I'm looking for.

"Not like they do," I say, tilting my head in the direction she came from.

Ivy's mouth twists. "Rheave—"

"I want to *really* matter to you."

All at once, it feels immensely important that I make this much clear. That she understands what she means to me before I do… whatever I decide I have to do.

I let the arrow slip from my fingers as I step closer, bringing one hand to her cheek, the other to the fall of her hair by her neck. The softness of those waves against my fingers sends a tingle over my skin.

She is so loving and so strong, so willing to risk herself to save me no matter what danger I've put myself and her in. The most incredible part of this incredible world.

Ivy draws in a breath as if to speak, but I start first. "I want to be here for you the way they are. I want… I want to be able to make you smile and laugh like simply being near me brightens your life. I want to be able to touch you and know my presence makes you feel safe and happy. It's like a kind of magic, how they are with you—how you are with them— I don't know how to conjure that kind of joy, but if I did, I'd never leave."

My fingers have traced down her cheek to her jaw. A quiver passes through Ivy's body.

She lets out a strained little sound, and then she's bobbing up on her toes to brush her lips to mine.

Oh. This—*this* is what kissing is meant to be. The sensation of our mouths pressing together sparks a heat nothing like the careful overtures I offered to less intimate places before.

I cup her jaw and adjust my head, trying to find the angle

where our lips meld together most perfectly. The hint of a gasp that spills on her breath to mingle with mine sends another jolt of heat straight to the appendage between my legs.

By all the gods, there's so much more I want than I even fully recognized. Every inch of my body aches to align with hers, to soak up her warmth and the softness of her skin beneath her clothes.

My other hand falls to her waist, instinctively tugging her closer against me. But the gesture must startle Ivy.

She stumbles backward, a flush spreading up her neck to her cheeks. She presses her hand to her lips. "I—"

Then she seems to master herself, with all the fortitude I'm used to. Lifting her chin, she grabs the arrow I dropped and slings the quiver over her shoulder.

She fixes me with a firm gaze. "You matter a lot, Rheave. You—you remind me of how much joy a person *can* find in the world. Why it's worth going through all this awfulness to protect this country. It would hurt me a lot more to lose you than to help you deal with the assholes who made your body. Please, come back with me."

So many emotions are colliding inside me that I'm afraid to move. She came to me—but then she pulled away. I'm not sure if I can do the right thing when I *want* so much.

The idea of walking straight back to face the men she wouldn't hesitate to embrace only sets me even more off-kilter.

I wet my lips. "I'll come. But I need… a few minutes. By myself. To be sure I'm totally in control now."

I don't say exactly what I need to control. To my relief, Ivy doesn't ask.

She aims a determined finger at me. "I can give you that, but you have to promise me you're not going to hurt yourself. Or leave. You can take some time to think, but then you'll come back to the camp, and we'll keep doing things that matter."

I'd like to ask whether the things that matter could include more proper kissing, but I sense that isn't a wise direction of conversation at the moment. There's too much giddiness and light in the tangled sensations rippling through my veins for me to even consider going through with my former intentions until I've seen where this could lead. "I promise. I won't leave. I wouldn't do anything that would hurt you on purpose."

"Good. I'll go see what everyone else is thinking. But whatever plan we come up with, I'm sure it'll include you too."

She strides off between the trees, leaving me staring after her in a daze.

Has she pulled me back from the brink of a tragedy—or straight toward one?

# Thirty-Three

*Ivy*

Amusement rings through Julita's coy voice. *Well. The daimon too, hmm? He is rather something to look at, but I have to admit, I didn't see that coming.*

"Hush," I mutter, hefting Rheave's quiver higher on my shoulder and peering through the forest for a sign of our newly formed camp.

Heat is still coursing under my skin from that kiss—from the way the daimon-man's hands started to move over my body—

I shove the memories to the back of my head. Guilt has soured the first brief rush of exhilaration that came with the passion in his words.

I've already devoted myself to three other men. Three men who showed their devotion to *me* ever so vividly last night.

How could I give in to the impulse to kiss Rheave? I don't think I can blame my magic for that lapse of judgment.

This is insane, though, isn't it? He's an ageless spirit creature in a conjured body. I don't even know how to explain it.

Curse it all. How can I look them in the eyes now?

But I have to. For them and for Rheave.

I might not know what to make of all the feelings he's stirred up, but I'm completely sure that I never want to see him pushed to the desperate brink again. He needs to know that we all want him here.

When I reach the edge of the small clearing Stavros picked out, the three men all glance over from the shelter they've already started constructing out of branches under the former general's guidance.

Casimir's forehead furrows as he takes in the arrows I'm holding. "What happened to Rheave? Isn't he coming back?"

"He is," I say, setting down the quiver next to the bow. "He was just upset after the incident at the temple, feeling that he'd put us in a bad situation, and he was thinking of…" My throat constricts for a moment before I force the words out. "Of killing his body so the scourge sorcerers can't control it anymore."

Alek jerks to his feet with a flash of distress crossing his dark face. "He shouldn't do that. He's got as much right to the life he has now as any of us do."

His immediate support warms me despite the churning of my stomach. "I told him that as well as I could. I think he was already struggling with the decision—he didn't really want to go through with it. He's taking a little more time to gather himself, but I made him promise that he'd return in one piece."

Casimir's gaze glides over me, his deep blue eyes turned darker with worry. "And when he does, we'll do everything we can to assure him that we all value his company. I'm glad you were able to talk him down, but that must have been difficult to witness. I'm sorry you had to handle it alone. I could go find him now and start the rest of the conversation."

My skin itches with self-consciousness. Great God filet and fry me, I can't let Casimir apologize to *me* when I'm the one who fucked up.

"I think we should give him some space," I say. "He asked for a little time alone."

Stavros frowns. "Are you sure he won't do anything drastic now?"

"I believe his promise."

The way he looked at me when he said he'd never hurt me on purpose. The memory of his brilliant eyes sears through me.

I sink onto a fallen log at the edge of the glade. The only honorable thing I can do is spit out the truth.

"There's something else. When I was talking with him, he got so emotional, and I just wanted to show him how much everything he's done means to me—I don't know…"

Stavros turns to fully face me, his frown deepening. "What is it, Ivy?"

I look down at my hands. "I kissed him. I'm sorry. It was just supposed to be a quick peck—not that even that would necessarily be all right—but he kissed me back and it ended up going on a little longer. And then I realized I was being an idiot and pulled away, but… what's done is done."

There's a moment of silence. It's broken by a soft laugh that tumbles over Casimir's lips.

My gaze flicks upward with a jolt of surprise.

The courtesan shakes his head at me, nothing but fondness in his expression. "I was wondering when it'd come to that."

"You thought— But I'm with the three of you—"

"I don't think any of us could quite match the daimon's level of dedication," Casimir says lightly. "He's proven his devotion to you dozens of times over. And he's proven himself an essential part of this group as time's gone on, I think. He's brought a different sort of light. I'm not surprised you were drawn to him."

It's easy for him to see things so casually when he's had dozens, maybe hundreds of past partners. Sharing never gave him the slightest hesitation.

"I still shouldn't have acted on what I was feeling like that." I glance at Alek and Stavros. "I don't want him *instead* of you. I don't even know how much I actually want *him*. Nothing else needs to happen. I've been so happy with what we have… I don't want to ruin it."

Alek hesitates and then speaks in a careful tone. "How exactly do you feel about him?"

I run my fingers back into my hair, which is tangled from this morning's riding. "I don't really know that either. I haven't let myself pay that much attention—I've had plenty of other things to worry about. There've been moments when I felt attracted to him. I appreciate how much he's helped us. There's something special about the way he looks at the world. But—gods help me, he's not even human."

"In some ways he is, now," the scholar says. "He's become more than a daimon. And Casimir is right—he's also become part of… whatever we are, working together like this. I trust him. I respect his judgment, even if sometimes it's odd."

I stare at him. "Where are you going with this?"

Alek offers me a sheepish smile. "You've been able to handle three of us. If you decide you could have something real with Rheave too, I'd understand it. I wouldn't be angry. It seems wrong to shut him out of that one aspect of what we have together, if that's what you both end up wanting."

I have no doubt about whether Rheave would want it. At least, the physical side. What do daimon know about actual relationships, romance, any of that?

But his expression when he talked about how much he wanted to matter to me, how much I mattered to him… It was the emotion in his face and in those words that drew me in.

He's always been beautiful, but I had no idea anything that intense was going on in his head.

Argh. This is so ridiculous. I have so many more important problems to sort out.

I press the heel of my hand to my temple. "If no one's pissed off at me, I think it'd be easier if we just pretended this never happened and never let it happen again."

"But it did happen."

All of our gazes dart to Stavros. The former general looks only at me, unwaveringly.

I can't read his expression, but my heart starts to sink.

He's been the most hesitant about Rheave's presence in our lives. He had the most trouble accepting his own feelings for me. I don't think any of us has a clue how he'll react to this situation.

Without another word, he crosses the short distance between us and cups my face between his hands, flesh and metal. The next thing I know, his mouth has captured mine.

He kisses me deeply, lingering in the moment until I can barely remember there's anyone else in the world, let alone anyone else I'd want to kiss as well. When he eases back, his hands drop to my shoulders.

One corner of his mouth crooks upward. "Obviously you figured I didn't have enough competition for your affections. You're so set on making me work for it, hmm, Lady Thief?"

A blush flares in my cheeks. "I didn't purposefully—"

He chuckles and brushes another kiss to my forehead. "I know. And I told you I wanted you to be selfish more often, didn't I? Maybe I haven't reminded you of that fact often enough. I'm not going to start caging you now if there's more happiness you could find."

My heart is suddenly thumping twice as hard. "You're really saying…"

When I can't find the rest of my words, he answers the implicit question. "You're not sure. That's fine. We'll see how it goes. But you're more than worthy of four paramours. As Casimir would probably say, you should have all the joy you can get in your life while it's there for the taking."

Something about his tone and that last sentence sets off an ache in my belly. None of us know how much more life we're going to get, and mine has always been especially precarious.

Is that the only reason he's giving his approval? Because he thinks I need to stuff as many experiences as I can into the little time I might have left?

I have the sense of Julita beaming in my head. *I knew I'd chosen well. Other than the matter of Benny. Three out of four excellent men is still quite a success.*

I swallow the sputter of a laugh that tickles up my throat.

Before I can figure out what to say next, a shout and a crash in the underbrush bring me leaping to my feet.

"Rheave?" Casimir calls as we all rush in the direction of the sound.

The continuing noises of a struggle make it easy to find the daimon-man, just beyond a shaking bush some fifty paces away. When we reach him, Rheave is pinning the hands of the man he's tackled to the ground.

"He's like me," he says, his voice a little ragged from the exertion. "Daimon in a conjured body. He must be from the march."

My pulse hiccups. We draw in around the fallen man, who stares up at us defiantly.

"What are you doing here?" Stavros demands.

The man's flat tone sounds a lot like Rheave's did when I first met him at the college. "I don't answer to you."

Rheave scowls at him. "You don't have to answer to the ones who made that body. Your spirit is still your own. You can claim the body and shake them off. I did."

His captive blinks at him. "No. You must—" A more urgent tone breaks through the refusal. "They told me to scout ahead and report back. I—" His voice flattens all over again. "Let me go. You have no reason to detain me."

Alek lets out a faint snort. "Oh, I'd say we have plenty of reason."

I kneel by the new daimon's head. "How close is the march? Which direction from here?"

Whatever bit of freedom the daimon managed to regain, he's lost it again. His mouth stays clamped shut.

Rheave glances around and lifts his chin in one direction.

"He was coming from that way. They can't be *very* far if he was able to scout over here on foot, can they?"

"I wouldn't think so," Stavros says darkly. He peers down at the man. "If you'll let us help you, we'll do our best. But we can't do anything as long as you're working with them."

The man jerks against Rheave's hold. "I don't need your help."

Casimir rests his hand against my hair. "What are we going to do with him? We can't let him go running back to the march."

But we're not in any position to keep prisoners. My stomach knots as I grope for an answer—

Rheave bows his head. "I will release you from the bonds they've forced on you."

As the last word leaves his lips, a surge of energy crackles out of him. It blackens the man beneath him for just an instant before that body stiffens into the clay it was made from.

A brief glimmer that could have been just a quiver of sunlight flits away from my view. I guess that is the other way the daimon can get free.

Rheave sits back on his heels. Just for a second, he looks weary.

I know he thinks his brethren are better off back in their natural state than under the scourge sorcerers' control. Still, destroying their chances of enjoying their new bodies the way he has mustn't feel good.

"I'm sorry," I say.

He glances up at me, and the flicker of a smile that crosses his face brings back his adoring words and the eager press of his body against mine. "It had to be done. I'm glad I could deal with him on my own."

He stands abruptly and tucks his arms around me in a tight embrace. "I came back like I promised."

My heart skips a beat with his warmth and woodsy scent

wrapped around me. There's a soft chuckle behind me that I think is Casimir.

I'm still too jumbled up inside to know where I'd want to take the affection the daimon-man insists on offering me, if anywhere at all. But I am relieved that he kept his promise.

Even if nothing more intimate ever passes between us, I don't want to lose him, especially not out of some misguided sense of martyrdom.

So I tip my head against his shoulder just for a second, my hands resting on his sides and then easing him back from me. I make myself meet his unearthly blue-green gaze. "Thank you. I don't want you ever doing that again. It'll only make things worse, not better. None of us wants you gone."

"That's right," Stavros says in his commanding military tone. "We're our own kind of squadron now, and you've contributed just as much as the rest of us. We're stronger together."

Casimir steps forward to grasp Rheave's shoulder. "One thing you should know about humans is we all make mistakes. No one goes through life without causing any damage at all, accidentally or otherwise. We won't judge you for it."

Rheave's eyes widen. His gaze slides to Alek, who nods with a small but warm smile. "I can't imagine us going forward without you."

The daimon-man's mouth forms a hesitant smile of his own in return. "I've been so glad to live alongside you all. I'd very much like to keep doing so."

I resist the urge to hug him all over again. "Then let's all go see what the scourge sorcerers are up to."

We veer back toward our fledgling campsite so Rheave can grab his bow and arrows. Inhaling deeply, I focus my mind on the now-familiar pattern of whisking our images away from sight while presenting them some other place where no one's likely to notice.

Feeling the magic seeping out of me to do my work makes me tense up, but I push away those worries.

It's just a little power expended. I've been doing this much for days on end without getting all that addled.

And we can hardly stroll up to the Order of the Wild's march fully visible and expect a warm welcome.

We emerge from the woods and venture across the field beyond. A carriage rattles by along the road to our left, but otherwise there's no sign of human presence.

Which of course doesn't mean anything as far as the scourge sorcerers are concerned.

Just as the town bell peals for the fifth hour of the afternoon, the first tingle of nearby magic grazes my skin. I halt, absorbing the sensation, and adjust my course.

The men follow close behind me. I veer a little more to the right and then to the left again, judging where the sensation intensifies and fades by tiny increments. After a minute or two, I'm sure we're heading straight toward its source.

As we tramp across the yellowed winter grass and through another thicket of trees, the aura of magic thickens. A few paces beyond the thicket in a sprawling clearing, the tingle penetrates right into my bones.

I stop again and make a gesture to warn the others that we're almost on them. Then I push forward, one careful step at a time.

It takes five more, and with the last of those, the camp materializes before my eyes.

An Order member is standing guard so close at my right that I could touch him if I leaned over. With a hitch of my pulse, I scoot in the other direction to give us some breathing room.

Throughout the rest of the camp, men and women are bustling around. It looks as if they've just arrived. No tents have gone up yet, and the horses are all still saddled, standing amid their potential riders. Only a couple of campfires are burning toward the middle of the area, near the three covered wagons that I suspect hold the sacrificial accomplices.

As I take in the activity, my heart sinks. Have even more scourge sorcerers and unwitting dupes joined the march since we last saw them several days ago? There must be over a thousand figures hurrying this way and that.

Maybe not much compared to the entire royal army, but most of that army isn't *here*. And none of it is truly prepared to contend with the power of scourge sorcery.

Fuck.

Alek comes up beside me. He nudges my arm and points to a cluster around one of the carts.

The people there are all grabbing objects out of the cart… and suiting up in a mix of padded vests, chain mail, and wooden or metal helms.

My lungs constrict. When my gaze darts across the terrain more intently, I notice a woman pointing out features on a map to a small group of on-lookers.

"They're already preparing for battle," I murmur.

Stavros frowns. "It certainly appears that way."

If we had any doubt left, Borys's voice rings out through the camp from somewhere at the far end, beyond my view. "Let's get on with it! The faster we can make the final march, the less prepared King Konram will be."

Julita's presence winces in the back of my head.

I stiffen with a lurch of my gut. "They're going to attack tonight. There's no way any reinforcements could have arrived already."

Stavros's face has grayed. "We need to sound a warning. There are troops in the area—local guards—it wouldn't take long for them to ride here. Most of these people aren't even armed yet. If we can strike *them* when they're not prepared… We can at least stall them."

"And it'll be clear the threat is real," Casimir adds. "But how are we going to bring anyone here to help us when they won't even see an army gathered?"

My heart thuds even faster, a nauseating but firm sense of resolve rising in my chest. "Casimir, you brought your new horn, didn't you?"

"Yes, but it won't do any good if anyone it summons can't see the problem."

"Let me worry about that." I turn to Stavros. "Get one of the horses and ride to town or whatever the nearest fortress is. Alert whoever you can and send them this way. When they're in sight, I'll take care of the rest."

Stavros gives me an anguished look. "Are you sure?"

Ignoring the dread pooling in my belly, I give him a shove. "Yes. Get going, before it's too late to do anything at all."

The former general raises his fist, and I tap it automatically alongside the other men. As he lopes back toward our camp, I extend my magic along his path.

When he's well out of view, I yank the stream of power back to me. The other men gather closer around.

I touch Rheave's arm. "We're not going to do anything to call attention to ourselves until we have back-up. But when I give the word, you can start shooting anyone you can tell is a daimon. And anyone at all you see giving orders."

He shrugs his bow off his shoulder and retrieves an arrow, his beautiful face set with total determination. "I'll take down as many as I can."

I reach to Alek and Casimir next. "You two will also need to be ready with your weapons. If you stay close, I think I can keep us concealed while I'm working more magic—the invisibility effect doesn't take that much concentration anymore—but they might realize where my power is coming from. I won't be able to focus on defending myself."

Despite his past hesitations, Alek draws his knife immediately. Casimir unsheathes his dagger as well.

All my men are in this with me. I just have to make sure I don't let *them* down.

But we have to wait until we have reinforcements of one sort or another. We can't take on a thousand would-be soldiers all on our own.

Or, maybe I could, but I can already feel a shudder running

through my thoughts just preparing for what I'm about to do. Even if I wanted to slaughter all these people indiscriminately… I'm pretty sure I'd lose myself in the process.

And that might be even worse for the kingdom than letting the scourge sorcerers attack.

The sun sinks to the tops of the trees. The Order of the Wild members pass around a hasty dinner. Sweat beads on my back beneath my cloak.

And off behind us, a holler carries alongside the pounding of dozens of hooves. "This way!"

I drag a breath into my clenched lungs. "Now!"

Then I hurl out a wave of my power—not at the people in the camp, but at the haze of magic surrounding it.

# Thirty-Four

*Ivy*

The power I've heaved out of me passes through the scourge sorcerers' concealment spell like a horse bolting through fog. That's not what I need.

I rein my magic in and will it to collide with the haze. Eat away at the opposing magic that's hiding the Order of the Wild's army. Reveal them to the world.

I don't know what consequences my power would create when left to its own devices, so I turn to my usual technique, just in reverse.

When I make us invisible, I let an echo of our forms appear somewhere else.

When I'm taking *away* the cloud of invisibility around the march, I'll send that invisibility someplace else.

As I push my magic against the thick barrier around us, I concentrate on the span of forest beyond the far edge of the camp as well. Quivers of sensation race through my soul as the haze starts to disintegrate—and at the same time, the trees at the edge of the forest fade from view.

I'm vaguely aware of the men moving around me. Rheave

fires one arrow after another into the milling bodies; Alek and Casimir brace themselves in front of me.

I batter the concealing spell again, holding my focus tight against the shouts of alarm that are going up throughout the scourge sorcerers' camp. Against the flickering images at the edge of my vision that send jolts through my nerves, as if someone is lunging at me.

No one's there. If they were, my men would be fending them off.

I can't fall for my mind's tricks now.

The trees at the edge of the forest vanish completely. I can't tell how much of the fog I've worn away while I'm standing inside it.

How close are Stavros and the soldiers he called in?

At least one of our enemies must realize what's happening, because all at once, the haze of magic shoves back. It hits at me so suddenly I rock on my heels at the impact, unprepared.

The trees swim back into view. My magic contracts and writhes.

"Ivy?" Casimir asks, worry wound through his tone.

I gasp a breath. "I'm okay. Just—they're fighting back with their sorcery. I haven't been able to completely sweep away their magic yet."

Clenching my hands at my sides, I whip my own power forward with more force.

An invisible pressure jabs at me from multiple angles. I have the sense of someone at the other end of that magic lashing out, not knowing where their opponent is but tracing my assault on their spell back to me.

I can do this. I have to be able to do this.

Scourge sorcery is limited by the sacrifices of their supporters. Riven sorcery can do anything.

As long as the person using it pays the price.

My teeth set on edge. A growl seeps through them as I push my will forward.

Tear down the magic that's cloaking this field. Wash it away as if in a vast torrent.

I won't be shaken. I won't be stopped.

Julita's voice quavers through my thoughts. *Ivy, are you sure this isn't too much? There's so many of them working against you…*

I tune her out too, narrowing my concentration even farther.

The concealing fog seems to lurch against my onslaught. It shifts and weaves, strands darting free from my attempt to dissolve it.

Alek stirs in front of me and belts out a name. "Ster. Torstem Dymasek of Florian—a scourge sorcerer, dead." Another. "Wendos Hubarek of Nikodi—a scourge sorcerer, dead. How many of you are going to join them today?"

Whatever strategy he's attempting, it might be worthwhile. A tremor passes through the magic pressing in on me, loosening its impact.

With a renewed surge of determination, I thrash the concealing fog with my own power.

Alek keeps hollering names—other people he suspects from his research were scourge sorcerers who've also died? The shouts around me merge into a warbling roar.

Just a little more. Strip away their defenses. Stop them. *Stop* them—

A new swell of magic crashes over us.

The thicker force punches me in the gut. I hiss and stumble, and my control slips.

The wave of magic I was casting out of me sweeps across the whole camp, toppling men and women, smashing wagon wheels, snapping horses' leads, sending the animals running.

And there are more enemies—more coming. Voices everywhere, flashing swords. I have to crush them all before they—

My magic flings to the side before I've fully processed those thoughts. It slams into a cluster of blue-uniformed figures on horseback who're racing down the road.

Bodies fly from their steeds. Someone cries out at the stomp of a misplaced hoof.

Yes, destroy them all. Destroy everyone who—

I clap my hand to the side of my head.

No. Those were the soldiers we wanted to fight the traitors *with* us, not more attackers.

My power leaps at them again, sending one of the horses staggering to its knees. I hurl myself backward, my mind reeling, my mouth gone ashy dry.

*I* have to stop. I have to stop… before I can't.

The world has morphed into a chaotic whirl of color and shape. I wrench myself around and somehow end up on my hands and knees.

Fabric tears. Wood crunches. Someone screams.

How do I stop?

My hand swims into view, pale against the trampled soil and patchy grass.

I'm here. Not out there. Not ravaging all those people.

An urge grips me, and I follow it. I snatch the knife from my boot and stab it into the back of my hand.

I keep good enough aim that the blade passes between the bones, severing muscle and sinew with an explosion of pain. Pain that reminds me of exactly where and what I am.

"Ivy!" someone cries out.

I haul at my raging magic, and it hurtles back into me. I can't prevent it from flinging the knife out of my flesh and sealing the wound, but the thought of who else might be bleeding in my place comes with a smack of horror that grounds me even more.

I clamp down tight on my power, picturing ivy coiling tight around me, sealing every gap. Caging the magic inside my body yet again.

Arms wrap around my middle. "I've got her!" Rheave says, and then, softer by my ear, "I've got you. They won't hurt you anymore."

Doesn't he see that I'm the one who hurt me?

My thoughts are still too scrambled for me to figure out how to speak.

The daimon-man hefts me against him and runs. As my head settles beneath his chin, I recognize the rustle of branches we race past, crackles of twigs underfoot.

We're back in the forest.

Am I still keeping my men hidden? I yanked *all* my magic back to me. I have to…

I try to extend just a tendril, and the frantic surge that jerks at my innards has me shutting down again.

Fuck. I don't know how to do this anymore.

"Here!" someone hollers. A large equine body pushes in front of us, and Rheave is lifting me onto Toast's back before hauling himself up behind me.

There are other horses around us. We careen on through the underbrush, dusk falling in our wake.

My thoughts float in spirals and gradually settle into some kind of order.

Rheave thought he was ruining everything, but I really just did. I could have torn even the men I love apart, and I'd hardly even have noticed.

Tears prick at the backs of my eyes. I squeeze the lids shut.

Sulla was right. It's too much. I don't know enough.

Maybe I never will. She's stayed on that mountainside her whole life to avoid a catastrophe like I almost unleashed.

"This way," a voice says, one I now recognize as Stavros's.

When I force myself to lift my head, I make out the former general on the other stallion just ahead of us. Alek and Casimir are sharing another horse, cantering along a few paces away through the trees.

They must have stolen it from the camp in the chaos.

Well, now we can all ride, as long as the horses are capable of carrying two. One small gain.

A hysterical giggle bubbles in my throat. I clench my jaw against it.

Stavros draws to a stop and dismounts. As Rheave helps me down off the horse, I make out a stone wall mostly swallowed up by moss and vines.

The former general waves us inside. "It's an old outpost, abandoned since well before my time. But at least it'll keep us completely out of sight for the time being."

We lead the horses inside, past clumps of rubble from the partly collapsed ceiling. A pungent earthy scent fills my nose.

I rest my hand against one of the gritty walls. A pang shoots through my palm where the place I stabbed it has sealed over.

Rheave touches my back more carefully than usual. "Ivy? Are you injured anywhere else?"

I turn to face him. The worry on his face breaks my heart.

My voice comes out hoarse. "No. You got me away before anyone could hurt me. You see? It's a good thing you were there."

He beams at me so brightly that an answering rush of affection wells up in my chest. "It was." He tips his head toward the other men. "Casimir stabbed someone who tried to lunge at you. And Alek grabbed another horse so we could get away quickly."

Giving them credit too. When I look around at the others, I'm met with smiles so tender I can't doubt they're genuine.

They really do accept our daimon-man. He's become a vital part of our group so gradually I didn't totally recognize it.

And maybe I can accept that this man who isn't totally a man fits into a piece of my heart I didn't know was still empty. But that's hardly my biggest concern right now.

How many people did *I* injure in the past hour? How horrible a fate did I consign my lovers to?

My legs wobble. I drop to a crouch, and Casimir is there, wrapping his arm around me from the other side.

"It'll be all right, Kindness," he says.

The gentleness of his voice that I don't deserve cracks through the dam inside me. I sob, and tears flood my eyes.

"Ivy!" Alek drops to his knees in front of me. Rheave makes an anguished sound and tightens his own grip on my body.

All I can do is gasp and press my hands against my face in a futile attempt to stem the deluge of tears.

Have they ever seen me cry before? I can't remember the last time I did—really wept, like this—since even before I met them.

My chest hitches, and more tears gush out.

Julita squirms in the back of my skull. *Oh, Ivy. Whatever's gone wrong, I'm sure we'll work out a new plan. We'll still stop the scourge sorcerers. They haven't won yet.*

They haven't, no. But I've already lost.

I gulp a few breaths and manage to get a hold of myself. Stavros looms over us, peering down at me, his mouth twisted at an agonized angle.

"Tell us what you need, Ivy," he demands. "Tell me whose blood I need to spill for what happened to you back there."

Gods smite me. They all still think I was the one in trouble when the truth is, I was the cause of it.

I push my hands against my closed eyes as if I can force back the next wave of tears that way. When I'm sure they're not going to burst out of me just yet, I lower my arms and gaze blankly at my knees, encircled by the men I've failed.

The words fall dully from my lips. "Mine. I needed to spill mine. But I didn't do it soon enough."

I can hear Rheave's frown in his voice. "What do you mean?"

"It was me." My voice breaks.

I close my eyes again, and shadows waver past my eyelids. Distant voices no one else can hear screech in fury.

I gird myself and make myself keep going. "I thought I could do something good with my magic. I thought as long as I balanced everything out, no one had to get hurt, and it would all work out. But… I'm going mad. I'm seeing things, hearing things. It was small enough that I thought I could push through until we'd dealt with the scourge sorcerers; I *had* to. Except I can't. It almost took me over tonight."

Casimir and Rheave press closer in their combined embrace. Alek's hand comes to rest on my cheek.

The scholar's voice turns rough. "That's why you stabbed your hand."

Rheave lets out a growl at the reminder.

My head dips lower. "The pain brought me back, just barely. I'm the one who bowled over the soldiers Stavros brought. That wasn't the scourge sorcerers. When the magic gets right into my head, I start thinking I have to lash out at everyone…"

I choke up for a second before I drag my gaze upward to meet Stavros's dark eyes. "Part of me wanted to tear apart every soldier in the fortress this morning after the one put his knife to my throat. Like the riven sorcerer slaughtered your best friend. That's why I let Julita step in."

*Oh, Ivy*, Julita murmurs, sounding choked up herself.

"And why you stabbed yourself tonight." Stavros inhales sharply. "Curse it all, Ivy, I knew you'd fall on your knife before you let yourself go too far, but I never wanted it to actually happen."

Casimir strokes my hair. "You're clearly not insane now. You came out of it."

I let out a strained guffaw. "Not really. Just the worst parts. I'm still… not quite right. I don't even know if I ever will be again or if I've wrecked my mind permanently."

Alek touches his forehead to mine. "You'll rest, and you'll get better again. It isn't your fault. You never wanted this magic. You were only trying to help."

The hopeless sensation that's been building inside me since we rode away rises up so swiftly I could drown in it. "I didn't even take down the scourge sorcerers, not really, did I? They're still going to attack."

Stavros shifts his weight. "Not right away. Quite a few of them were injured, and their horses scattered. I didn't see what happened to the soldiers I led that way, but even if the Order of the Wild fell on them, the scourge sorcerers will want to move and regroup in case others are going to investigate."

"But they'll find another place to hide and get organized. And they won't wait long. Tomorrow or the next day, they'll go to slaughter the entire royal family."

I swallow thickly. "And I won't be able to help at all, because I can't risk using my magic again."

HISTORIA

# Thirty-Five

*Alek*

The flat, mottled yellow-and-orange tops of the mushrooms catch my eye in the early morning light. With a smile prompted by a flicker of happiness, however brief, I hustle over to the base of the tree where they've sprouted.

I may not have conceived of any brilliant battle strategies, but I did manage to pick up a little useful information from my reading. If one of the books I perused while in Pima is correct, these should be edible and decent-tasting if baked.

The country may be doomed, but at least we'll have breakfast.

I break the tops off the mushrooms' stems, gathering the whole cluster on my arm cradled against my chest. The snap of a twig brings my head up with a hitch of my pulse, but all I see is a sparrow taking off through the branches overhead.

Stavros and Rheave went out to patrol the area around the abandoned outpost, to watch for any members of the Order of the Wild venturing in this area… and to deal with them if they do find any, I suppose.

That job is definitely not one I could handle.

I walk back to the mossy stone walls as quickly as I can while being reasonably quiet. Casimir spots me from the uneven doorway and dips his head in acknowledgment.

"I'm going to check the snares Stavros set up last night," he murmurs when I reach him. "I don't think Ivy should be left alone right now."

I nod in return, my gut twisting.

When I step past him into the partly roofed room beyond, I find Ivy crouched by our fire, which is smoldering beneath a heap of collected rubble and a layer of dirt to diminish the smoke. Her face, a sallower shade of pale than I'm used to, looks as weary as if she didn't sleep at all.

She glances up at my entrance, and I offer her a small smile. "Hey. I found something for us to eat—they just need a little baking."

Without a word, Ivy takes a stick and pries out one of the larger chunks of rock at the edge of the pile. Last night, we used that spot to roast a ground hen Rheave managed to shoot.

I nudge the mushrooms into the hot space one by one. A delicate, rather pleasant herbal scent starts to waft into the air.

The despondence in Ivy's expression hasn't shifted. I hesitate and then sit down next to her, not sure if the physical closeness will comfort her, not knowing if there's anything else I can do for her.

"We'll find other ways," I say. "We got an awful lot done without you needing to use your powers before."

Ivy lets out a faint scoffing sound. "Even when I was mostly suppressing my magic, the most important things I pulled off relied on it. Stopping Wendos. Proving myself against Benedikt. Turning the tables on Ster. Torstem. Saving King Konram's life."

"You got us out of Florian under lockdown using nothing but your cunning and connections," I point out. "You've done plenty of fighting with just your knives."

"Not enough to go up against an army of scourge sorcerers."

I don't know how to argue against that statement. All I can say is, "There's the rest of us too. You're not in this alone."

For the first time, Ivy turns her head to meet my gaze. Her normally bright blue eyes look dulled, like the midday sky on an overcast day. "Do you really think the five of us can stop the march without me calling on my magic? Even with the cleverest plan you can imagine?"

I open my mouth and close it again. She's jabbed at the guilty uncertainty that's been coiled in the middle of my chest ever since my trick with the fire failed—ever since I first fumbled in Stavros's weapons training, really.

"I don't know," I admit. "But we didn't know when we first set off from the Haven either, did we? We simply knew we had to try."

My attempt at striking a hopeful note obviously falls flat. Ivy pulls her legs up in front of her, her head drooping until her chin rests on her knees.

She trails her finger idly through the grit that coats the worn stone floor. "You started shouting out names at the march yesterday while I was trying to tear down their magic. Scourge sorcerers who died. What was that about?"

I recall that impulse with a twinge of unfulfilled pride. "I was thinking about what the old letter said about the scourge sorcerers fearing death. It occurred to me that they might struggle more if I reminded them of those among them who have already died. I'm not sure it had much effect."

"It did throw them off a little," Ivy says. "They were pushing back, and their magic faltered right then. But I still wasn't strong enough."

My heart squeezes at the pain in her voice.

I loop my arm right around her. "It had nothing to do with strength. I've never met anyone stronger than you in my entire life."

Ivy doesn't answer, only stares down at her hands and the random lines she's sketched in the dirt.

What else can I tell her? It's not as if I know what *I* can do to stop the scourge sorcerers at this point either.

How can I encourage her when my own hopes have deflated?

What does any of this mission matter if the woman I love falls apart in the middle of it?

I take her nearer hand in mine. "How are you feeling after you've gotten some rest and half a day without needing to use any magic?"

"Am I still mad, you mean?"

I grimace. "I don't think you're outright insane. And I know the effects of your magic aren't going to vanish immediately. But have you noticed any change? Or whether anything other than using your magic makes you feel better or worse?"

She gives a soft chuckle. "Always the scholar. You can write a book about me—the first treatise on what it's really like living as a riven sorcerer."

At my wince, Ivy leans her head toward me, sinking into my embrace. "I'm sorry. That was meant to be a joke, not a criticism. I know you're trying to help."

I stroke my thumb over her knuckles. "Don't worry about me. If there *is* anything I can do to make your healing easier, I'd want to know—that's all."

Ivy exhales in a long, shaky stream. "It's hard to tell whether specific things scatter my mind more or just set off the madness that's already taken hold. I mostly notice the effects when I'm keyed up, aware of danger around me…"

"What kind of effects, exactly?"

"My thoughts get… jumpier. Like they're leaping straight to more extreme conclusions, assuming I'm in grave danger from everyone around me. And I think I see or hear things—things that scare me. Attackers approaching, weapons aimed at us, threatening voices."

My throat constricts. "That must be awfully disturbing."

I suppose it's no wonder most riven end up becoming as

destructive as they do if this is the main consequence of using their magic.

I can picture the sequence so easily. They discover their power and start using it to enhance their lives. The more things they want and get, the more addictive the power becomes.

But at the same time, it's eating away at their mind, convincing them that people mean them harm and that enemies lurk around every corner…

Without the self-control and awareness that Ivy's cultivated her whole life, how long would it take before a person with a riven soul found themselves drawing away into isolation, comforting themselves with luxuries without caring what damage their magic did in exchange? Lashing out at anyone who got close, imagining they were a threat?

Seeing the things they're most afraid of everywhere they turn…

Something clicks in my head with a jolt of inspiration. I hug Ivy tighter, but my mind is already racing with the thought that's struck me.

After pressing a kiss to her forehead, I ease back a little so I can rifle through my cloak's pockets. I still have the stolen letters I've kept tucked away in the temple's book.

Did I misconstrue the phrasing in my initial translation? Bryfesh is a complicated language with odd nuances.

"What?" Ivy asks as I unfold the letters.

"I'm not sure yet."

I scan the brittle page to the spot that prompted my idea to send fire at the scourge sorcerers. The devastation of the Great Retribution—making them fear the death they could imagine meeting from the flames...

Staring at the words again, a startled laugh slips out of me. The phrasing *could* be read that way, if I assume the writer was talking in metaphors. But most literally, they mean that the scourge sorcerers of old literally saw pictures of death projected in the flames.

Images of themselves succumbing to wounds? Or of their already-dead corpses?

The letter writer isn't specific about it. They might not have known the details. But I could have gone about our initial attempt in too vague a way.

If simply hearing the names of the dead could make the scourge sorcerers falter, then what would happen if they saw the actual deaths—or their own—right in front of them?

My expression must give away the exhilaration that's swept through me, because Ivy twists toward me. "You've figured something out."

As I look up at her, my excitement wavers.

I let her down before. I sent her to carry out a strategy that wore her down without accomplishing anything significant in our favor.

I can't be certain that my new interpretation is any more correct than the last one. Or that even if it is, it'll make all that much difference with the current group of scourge sorcerers.

My entire body balks. I should keep the idea to myself until I find some way to be sure.

But even as I make that decision, I see how the light that's come into Ivy's eyes is dwindling quickly in my silence.

For just a second, seeing me uncover reason to hope helped her find her own.

She shakes her head with a twist of her mouth, obviously taking my lack of answer as a refusal. "It's all right. Probably better not to put more ideas in my head."

My rejection of her remark wrenches through me with more force than my initial reluctance. "It's not that. I just—I don't want—"

What can I say that would make anything better?

Gods help me, how can I ask her to believe she can recover from the trouble she's found herself in if I won't push past my own mistakes? If she can come back from riven madness, don't I need to give myself another chance to do something right too?

I square my shoulders and look down at the letter again. "I think I might have misunderstood what the writer was saying when I read this before. The fire didn't frighten the scourge sorcerers into giving up because they were worried it'd burn them to death, but because the gods showed them images of their deaths like pictures on the flames."

Ivy's eyebrows leap up. "We definitely didn't try that the last time. And it did unsettle them just having you talk about the dead…"

She pauses, the glow that'd lit in her face snuffing out again. "But we can't paint pictures on fire with a brush and palette. The only way we could use the same tactic is with magic."

And she's the only one of us with a "gift" that could accomplish anything close.

I slide the letters back into their hiding spot and brush my fingers over her cheek. "Perhaps we'll find another way to use the concept. It's always better to know more so we have more possibilities to draw on."

"Spoken like a true Estera dedicate," she says with fond amusement, and leans in to kiss me. But the despondent air hasn't left her.

I've given her something, but what can I really say about her magic? I have none at all of my own, chaotic or not.

At the tread of footsteps beyond the doorway, we both tense, but it's Rheave who appears at the entrance a moment later.

"We didn't come across anyone nearby," he says to both of us. "Stavros is taking one of the horses to see what the royal soldiers might be doing now."

The daimon fixes his gaze directly on Ivy. "He thought you might come out with me again in the direction we think the march went. You'd be able to sense when their magic is nearby without using your own, wouldn't you?"

Ivy pushes to her feet but then stalls there. "I would. But…"

Seeing her so uncertain sends a stabbing sensation through my chest.

I get up beside her, touching her arm. "You should go. It'll do you some good to have a task to carry out. Here, you can bring some of the mushrooms to eat on the way."

As I remove them from the fire, Ivy still hesitates. "If we run into any Order members… I'm not sure it'd be safe for me to even conceal us…"

"You know how to be stealthy," I say, putting all the confidence I have in her into my voice. "And Rheave can protect you both better than anyone if it comes to that."

The daimon grins at my compliment and flicks his fingers together with a brief spark.

A different sort of confidence fills my chest.

I did what I could for Ivy, but she needs Rheave too. He can talk to her from a perspective none of the rest of us have—as a being dealing with unpredictable magic that's sometimes worked in ways he'd rather it didn't.

Our woman is something extraordinary. She could use someone who's more than human in her life, now and in the future as well.

"See what you can find," I say, giving her a handful of roasted mushrooms and a nudge, and this time she goes. The smile that crosses her face as she joins Rheave tells me I was right to insist.

May she find her way back to the woman she's meant to be before the looming war finds us all.

# Thirty-Six

*Ivy*

Rheave moves through the forest like a wolf, weaving between the trees, his eyes alert and his stance wary.

He makes a particularly stunning wolf, but anyone who misjudges him as an easy target for his beauty would be in for an immense surprise.

Despite all my practice at stealth, right now I feel like an oaf next to him. My body goes through the motions, but as if I'm slogging through water rather than air.

The weight of everything that happened yesterday is still pressing down on me.

My magic doesn't clamor against my rejection of all the ways it'd like to "help" me. It simmers in my chest as if biding its time.

And all the while, somewhere nearby, the scourge sorcerers are rallying their troops for their assault on the royal family.

*If you can just get a whiff of their magic…* Julita murmurs, but she doesn't sound all that much more hopeful than I feel.

Rheave mostly scans the forest around us, watching for any approaching threats, but here and there he shoots glances my

way. He lets me walk in silence for several minutes before he breaks it, in a low tone to avoid his voice carrying.

"Stavros looked at the area where the march stopped last night. They cleared most signs of their presence, but he saw a little evidence that they headed southeast."

Based on the angle of the rising sun, that's the direction we're going in now. I force myself to speak. "How far did you two travel without stumbling on them?"

He considers. "Three or four times farther than you and I have at this point. But we might have passed them without realizing it. We knew it wouldn't be safe to leave the shelter of the forest."

I hum in agreement. He and Stavros wouldn't have had any way to see where the march moved to unless they got lucky enough to stumble on another scout the Order of the Wild sent beyond the concealment spell.

I should have gone with them from the start, but I was still sleeping when they left. I guess they assumed I needed it—that I had more recovering to do after yesterday.

Even while unconscious, I let them down.

The daimon-man looks at me again, with a small furrow in his brow. "Are you upset that we kissed?"

As Julita lets out a soft snort, my gaze jerks to him. "What?"

"I thought I should check," he says. "You didn't want to before, and then you left quickly afterward. With everything else that's happened, I can't tell if the way you act with me has changed."

*I suppose it's a reasonable question,* Julita says.

Is it? It seems so absurd that it takes me a moment to pull my words together. "*I* kissed *you.* It'd be pretty ridiculous for me to have a problem with it."

Rheave lifts his shoulders in a slight shrug. "In my observations, limited as they were, humans frequently get upset about things they did themselves. Sometimes they're happy and then upset about the exact same thing in very quick succession."

He looks down at his chest as if peering through it to his heart. "I'm only starting to understand how that could be."

Julita outright laughs. *And that's a very reasonable point. The daimon has gotten quite wise.*

I think he's been wise all along, just in ways the rest of us weren't used to.

I shake my head to answer his initial question. "I'm upset, but it's nothing to do with you or anything I did with you. My head is pretty full with all my worries about my magic."

Rheave knits his brow. "If you don't use it anymore, then you should be fine, shouldn't you?"

"We don't really know that yet. And… it's not that simple." I make a face. "When I was refusing to use it before, it started eating away at me. Sulla said that if I'd kept suppressing it, my magic would have killed me. I'm supposed to find a balance… Just little things now and then. But I don't know if I've already gone too far for that to work."

He lets out a dismissive sound. "You're still all right now. A little shaken up, but you sound like yourself."

"That might not last if I keep tapping into my magic. Especially if I can't keep a tight rein on it when I do. It's like… It's probably like the hold the scourge sorcerers have on you. You don't totally control the magic that made you, so you never know when it might fuck things up."

*Oh, Ivy.* Julita stirs at the back of my skull, her tone full of compassion. *I'm sure you can still find a balance. The gods have to see how hard you've been working to set things right.*

I'm not convinced that the gods have much say in my sanity. Kosmel hasn't offered any solutions other than sending me to Sulla.

Rheave is quiet for a moment, absorbing the comparison I made. His voice drops even lower. "That is an awful thing. I wish we could break you free from your worries the way we'll hopefully destroy the sorcerer who can affect me."

I let out a rough chuckle. "No chance of that. This power is all in me. I can't get rid of it, but I want… I want to be more than my magic."

Those words reverberate through my body. The truth of them hits me like it hadn't quite before I said them aloud.

That's all I've ever wanted, isn't it?

But even when I roamed through Florian, dipping in and out of people's lives as the Hand of Kosmel, the power I was refusing to use seemed to taint everything. Knowing I had to keep it secret. Knowing my entire life was forfeit the second anyone found out that one detail about me.

Rheave grabs my hand and squeezes it tight. "You are more. If you asked me all the things I admire about you, I wouldn't even consider your magic. Do you think mostly about the scourge sorcerers when you look at me?"

After all this time, I barely associate him with the fiends who made him.

I grip his hand in return. "No. They didn't have anything to do with the parts of you that matter."

"And your magic is the same."

I can't quite accept his statement that easily, but hearing him say it so firmly takes a little edge off the ache inside me. I drag the cool winter air into my lungs, and they don't clench up against the breath.

Rheave doesn't push for my full agreement. He simply walks on with me, his thumb trailing across the back of my hand in a gentle, continuous caress. Showing he's here with me without expecting anything of me.

He was once a spirit creature with hardly any understanding at all of what went on between humans, let alone their darkest fears. And after that, he acted like a pedantic jerk in the grips of the scourge sorcerers' control.

Somehow he managed to grow so far beyond his origins that it's hard for me to imagine him being anyone other than the fierce and caring man beside me.

As the sun rises higher and the air warms from chilly to

merely cool, not the faintest tingle of outside magic grazes my skin. I keep my senses alert for any hint of it despite my inner turmoil.

*Hmm,* Julita mutters as we prowl onward. *Where did the fiends run off to so they could lick their wounds?*

Nowhere near here. We pass a spot Rheave identifies as the point where he and Stavros turned back and continue on.

With each step beyond, my spirits start to sink.

The march may have moved beyond my ability to track them—at least, to find them in any kind of reasonable time.

Maybe this is pointless. If we were back with the others, at least we could be strategizing.

The one thing we do know is where the scourge sorcerers' army will attack, even if we aren't sure when.

Rheave halts where the ground falls away into a narrow gully. I peer down at a stream even thinner than the one where we filled our canteens and washed up this morning.

It's not quite narrow enough to jump across, but the gully only descends about twice my height. Not too bad a scramble.

What are the chances we'll find anything if we keep going, though? Maybe we should take this as our sign to head back.

I open my mouth to say that, but Rheave speaks first. "A butterfly!"

Gripping the saplings sprouting from the side of the gully, he scrambles down to the stream bed. A pale blue butterfly is indeed fluttering around near the shrubs down there.

The insect darts toward him and then away. I spot another one, with wings a deep yellow that's almost gold, farther down the stream.

Julita makes a sound of appreciation. *Would you look at that. They're beautiful.*

Rheave cocks his head and follows the butterflies, and I can't see anything to do but go after him. I skid down to the bottom of the gully and pick my way across the stones along the stream.

At least we won't be visible to anyone up in the forest while we're walking down here.

"I haven't seen any butterflies since we went north," Rheave says in a hush. "Alek said they don't like the cold very much."

"I guess these are particularly resilient ones." I raise an eyebrow at him. "Are you looking to make friends?"

He seemed bewildered by the injured insect that landed on him weeks ago back at the college. But he cared enough to carry it to safety anyway.

Rheave appears to consider my question intently. "They feel… like they're already friends. I don't know why."

I study his avid expression as we hurry on along the stream bed. It was a little odd that the injured butterfly was drawn to him. Unless…

"Daimon are supposed to be creatures of all the godlen," I comment, "but in your natural state, it seems like Inganne would be the most approving of how you act, exploring everything and playing pranks. Butterflies are one of her animals. Maybe you and they can sense you're kindred spirits."

The daimon-man cocks his head, a little smile curving his lips. "Even when my creators still had a grip on me, I knew I should help that one."

Up ahead, the butterflies look as if they fly right into the wall of the gully. Strange. I pick up my pace—and come to a stop at the mouth of a sort of alcove veering off into the gully's side.

The small recess can't be more than five paces deep and the same across, but there's something grand about it all the same. The sapling at its far end is already budding. Delicate white flowers sprout between the pebbles strewn across the earth, heedless of the season.

And several more butterflies swoop between those flowers in a spiraling dance.

A startled laugh tumbles out of me alongside Julita's gasp. "I think Inganne must have blessed this place."

I venture forward and graze my fingertips over a few of the flowers. Their petals slide against my skin soft as silk.

*The godlen do work in mysterious ways*, my ghostly passenger remarks.

A butterfly flaps over to me and lands on my hand, its feet tickling my knuckles. Then it takes off again, as if it was simply coming by to say hello.

An unexpectedly carefree air comes over me, as if nothing could be all that wrong when places like this exist. As if the godlen of creativity and play herself has reached down and blown the worries from my head like seeds in the wind.

I turn, expecting to see Rheave gaping at our surroundings in awe… but he's looking at me.

There's something like awe shining in his eyes all the same.

He steps closer to me and touches my jaw, his gaze fixed on mine. "Ivy… I want to kiss you again."

Julita giggles. *All right, I can tell I'd better take my leave.*

As her presence dwindles in the back of my head, I wet my lips. The warmth that motion provokes spreads through the rest of me.

But one of us has to be at least a little sensible about this situation, don't we?

"You know," I say, doing my best to keep my tone even, "there are a lot of things that usually come with kissing. At least, when you aren't just scratching an itch and figuring you'll never see each other again."

Rheave eases slightly nearer. "Like what?"

It's harder to think the more his beautiful face fills my vision. "Well, you've seen how I am with the other men. We have a relationship. We support each other. We're committed to tackling problems together and spending time together and, um…"

The daimon-man's expression has become increasingly puzzled. "Don't you and I do those things too?"

"It's not exactly the same. We've never talked about or decided where this is going."

"That's easy." He traces his fingers along my jaw to my chin and then back to the crook. "I want to be here with you and see how it can be. I want to experience everything we could have. I've got nowhere else I need to be—I'm happy to stay with you wherever you go."

He offers himself up so easily, my heart squeezes in response. "I shouldn't be your whole *world*. There are other things you like."

Rheave makes a dismissive sound. "Those are all things I can enjoy while I'm with you. I've had the whole world, Little Vine. I had it for more years than I know how to count. Nothing I found in it ever made me as happy as you do. That's why I want so much to be able to make you happy too."

A rush of emotion chokes me up before I can speak. Memories of all the moments turned brighter by his presence flicker through my mind. "You do make me happy."

The daimon-man smiles brilliantly and must decide that's answer enough to his earlier suggestion. He dips his head and captures my mouth.

The kiss is just as sweet as the first one, sending a giddy shiver straight through the core of me. Warmth floods me from head to toe, flaring into a more thrilling heat when Rheave nudges me right against the gully wall.

I give in to the impulse to tease my fingers into his soft curls, and a rough sound works from his throat. He kisses me harder. One hand stays cupped against my jaw while the other trails up and down my side until I gasp.

"We need to stay quiet," I mumble against his lips.

"Hmm. Then I should keep doing this."

He claims my mouth again, his confidence growing. His hand travels across my torso, lingering on my breast when the skim of his palm earns him a whimper I try to swallow.

His hips rock against mine. There's no missing the bulge

between his legs that grazes my sex, setting off sharper pulses of desire.

A thread of fear creeps through my haze of arousal. Am I really doing this? Making out with a man who's not even exactly a man—and wherever else this will go if I let it?

Do *I* really know what I'm getting into?

My body tenses, and Rheave notices immediately. He draws back just far enough to meet my gaze, his dark curls falling across his forehead. "Is this all right?"

He looks so unsettled by the thought that it might not be that my stomach twists. I can suddenly see how it might go if I push him away again, put up my walls out of that fear.

I've already run off on him once. If it happens again, he'll never trust that I really do want him enough.

I'll ruin whatever odd relationship we've started to build here.

And the thought of losing this—him, everything we could be—frightens me more than the uncertainty of where we'll end up.

I want him. I do. This strange man who makes the strangeness in me seem a little more okay.

I trail my hand down to his cheek, holding his unearthly gaze that shines with longing and devotion. "It's wonderful."

Rheave's brilliant smile comes back. "I think so too." He nuzzles the side of my face and drops his head to nibble the side of my neck. "I feel… so much. I don't even understand everything my body wants."

When would he ever have experienced sexual desire before? I don't want to push him into anything *he's* not ready for.

"Just… do what feels good," I suggest. "What feels right. If it feels right to all of you, not just your body."

He makes an urgent sound and presses his groin against mine. "I feel like I should sink right into you. Like we're too far apart. But you're right here."

Okay, I guess I won't be the one pushing us along quickly.

I swallow hard, my own growing sense of urgency thrumming through my veins. "That's normal. It would be easier —usually you take off your clothes—but we can't really do that here."

Rheave lets out a low growl. "I'd like to touch all of your skin. But I— Do *you* want to wait?"

Another pump of his bulge against my sex propels an honest answer out of me on a surge of need. "No."

The daimon-man tilts my head back so our mouths can crash together. His kiss is demanding but without a hint of cruelty, as if he's only asking me to offer up what he knows I'll joyfully give.

His other hand sweeps over my chest, pausing to massage one breast until I moan into our kiss, then slipping down to my waist. He skims the curve of my ass before gripping it and pulling me against him even more tightly.

This time, it's me absorbing his groan into my mouth. My whimper echoes it as he grinds against me.

"Not quite enough," he mutters. "Not quite—"

He yanks the skirt of my linen dress up to my waist and fumbles along my trouser underskirt until he finds the ties. As he leans into another kiss, he flattens his hand against my bare belly beneath the fabric and then slides it downward, beneath my drawers as well.

The brush of his fingers over my clit sets off a flare of pleasure. I stifle a needy mewling sound as well as I can.

Rheave delves farther, devouring my mouth as he plunders the slickness between my legs. He strokes over my folds and lets out a shaky breath.

One finger slips right inside me. He muffles his next groan against my hair.

"This. This is where I fit."

All I can do is nod, my hips swaying with his teasing caresses. He strokes me several more times, both our breaths getting more ragged by the moment, and then withdraws his hand to lift it to his face.

His fingers gleam with the evidence of my arousal. Watching me, he sniffs them and then flicks his tongue over the collected slickness.

The sight sends a pang of hunger through me as if he licked me right on the spot those fingers were fondling earlier.

"Mine," he murmurs. "All for me."

A giddy laugh tickles up my throat. "And what do you have for me, my daimon-man?"

Another growl escapes him. "I need…"

He wrenches at his own clothes. As soon as it's clear he's sure about this, I help him yank his trousers down.

When he tugs his straining cock free from his drawers, I can't resist gripping it and stroking it up and down.

Rheave lets out a hiss that's pure heat. "That… That is very good just as it is. But I want more."

He yanks at my thigh sheaths so he can drag my pants and drawers down to my ankles. Then he hefts me up against the side of the gully. Only my cloak protects my bared ass from the cool earth.

My cloak and his hands, clamping around me as he presses toward me, angling my hips up to meet him.

As his shaft slides between my folds, we sigh in unison. Pleasure crackles over my skin as if he's let loose his supernatural energy on me in the most delightful possible way.

Rheave pushes into me until we couldn't be closer, his cock stretching my channel with a perfect heady burn. He stops there, his head bowed next to mine.

His voice comes out achingly tender. "This is where I belong. With you. No matter where your magic takes you, I'll follow. You can always reach for me."

Sudden tears prick at my eyes. But then the daimon-man eases back to thrust into me again, and the rush of bittersweet emotion is carried away by a sensation that's all bliss.

I clutch at his shoulder, my other hand digging into his curly hair. Every buck of his hips sends a deeper swell of pleasure through my body.

"I'm not letting you go either," I promise him between fractured breaths. "I'm not letting them take you away."

He makes a strangled sound and plunges into me faster. His fingers dig into my ass. "Cling to me, my little vine. Like we'll be twined together always."

My arms tighten around him. He adjusts our position with his next thrust and manages to hit the sweetest spot inside me.

That's all it takes. The surges of bliss expand with just a few more strokes until they crash right over the edge.

I sob and shudder, holding on to Rheave for all I'm worth.

"Oh," he mutters. "*Oh.*"

He shudders in turn, the movement of his hips turning jerky as he finds his own release inside me.

He hauls me right up against him and buries his face in the crook of my neck. His breath sears across my throat.

"I've got you," he says, like he did when he held me through the worst of my magic's torment.

In that moment, I believe him. The only question is who's going to save the rest of the kingdom.

# Thirty-Seven

*Ivy*

Rheave lowers me carefully to the ground, stealing a few more kisses along the way.

When he draws back, his pale cheeks are flushed, his eyes sparkling with glee. "That was fantastic. I don't know why humans aren't doing it all the time."

A laugh tumbles out of me. "I guess we wouldn't be able to get a whole lot else done."

"Hmm. Another area where there must be balance."

Even though my legs are still wobbly from the force of my orgasm, the ground feels more solid beneath my boots. As I wriggle my trousers back up to my waist and re-strap my thigh sheaths, a renewed sense of conviction fills my chest.

"Speaking of which, as amazing as this diversion was, we do still have an army of scourge sorcerers to find."

Rheave glances toward the top of the gully with a frown. "Which way do you think we should go from here?"

That is the question, isn't it?

I inhale slowly, considering our options, and my gaze settles

on one of the butterflies gliding through the eerie subterranean glade.

Kosmel has guided me before. All of the godlen offer signs to those who pray to them when they feel the need.

What has Rheave ever asked of the divinities before despite everything he's given of himself to protect the realm? I think they owe him a favor or two.

I motion toward the butterflies. "Ask Inganne for help. Ask the butterflies if any of them have noticed a place around here where there's a lot of magic. You said they feel like friends… Friends help each other."

Rheave blinks, and a grin flashes across his face. He secures his own trousers and turns toward the butterflies.

When he speaks, I don't know how much it's to them and how much to the godlen who might be watching over this place.

"Thank you for giving us a joyful spot where we could make more joy. There's something very important we need to do, and we could use your help. Have you noticed anywhere near the forest where a lot of magic is being cast? We need to stop those people before they cause a lot of pain, but we have to find them first. I would be grateful for your guidance."

He dips his head as if in supplication.

At first, I don't think the appeal did anything. Then the golden butterfly I noticed earlier flaps up toward the top of the gully as if to leave.

Rheave glances at me wide-eyed. We both clamber up the earthen wall after it.

The butterfly glides this way and that, the farthest thing from a straight line. But as we pad through the underbrush after it, moving between the trees as silently as we can, I can see that it's leading us steadily if slowly onward.

The sunlight glints off its wings as it soars over a log. It skirts a thicket and swings back and forth around a grove of saplings.

I'm starting to think it's simply enjoying a romp through the woods after all when a tiny tingle grazes my face.

I freeze, concentrating on the sensation. With my breath held, I scan the woods around us for any sign of the Order of the Wild.

We're still so deep in the forest that I can't tell how close the edge might be. The march has always camped on open ground before, so they can easily monitor the area beyond the borders of their camp without leaving the boundaries of their concealing magic.

If I can't see beyond the trees, they shouldn't be able to see this far within the woods.

Rheave has gone still at my side. I hold up a hand in a signal for caution and walk onward with even more care and all my senses on the alert.

The hint of magic intensifies in the direction the butterfly has flown. When I'm sure of what direction it's in, I draw back to where it's only a faint tingle and weave back and forth to chart the edges of it.

The scourge sorcerers are to the west of this patch of forest. The faintest hum of their magic stretches far enough that I can sense it along a course of a hundred and twenty-three paces through the brush.

I want to get a closer look. But I can't risk using my own magic to conceal myself.

I stare toward the camp I know must be there, and something flips over in my head. I could smack myself for my obliviousness.

How many years have I been sneaking around without any magical help at all? I've gotten so used to relying on it over the past few weeks that what used to be automatic didn't even occur to me.

I touch Rheave's arm and lean close to whisper to him. "I'm going to creep a little closer. It'll be easier on my own. Wait here and keep watch."

He nods and ducks his head to press a swift kiss to my cheek.

Crouching low, I ease forward within the cover of the underbrush. Most of the shrubs have lost their leaves, but their spindly branches will still hide me from anyone peering into the forest's shadows.

I slink from bush to tree trunk to clump of wilted ferns, straining my sight. The magic in the air thickens with every step.

Julita's presence expands at the back of my skull as she returns to share my full awareness. *I see we've made some progress. I take it the march is camped that way?*

I dip my head in a subtle nod.

*I knew we'd find them.* She pauses while I ease forward with a few more furtive movements, and a giggle escapes her. *You know, I think this is more fun than simply whipping some magic around you. Where's the challenge in that?*

I restrain a snort and scuttle onward.

When I've left Rheave some twenty paces behind me, I finally make out a less dense area beyond the nearest trees. I can't get a clear view of the camp when it's cloaked in magic, but it's got to be right over there.

Great. Now what? I can't spy on people I can't see.

To breach their concealing spell, I'd have to walk right into the field. Even the Hand of Kosmel can't hide behind blades of grass.

I squint at the more open area beyond the dense forest for any sign of movement. There might be some kind of clue about their plans that I could pick up if I got closer—but I don't know where their sentries are. The farther I emerge into the fringes of the forest, the more chance there is I'll be seen.

After several minutes, I draw back about half of the distance I covered before, to where I'm confident I won't be visible from the camp. I still stay low and silent as I move from tree to tree, listening and watching for anything at all that might help.

A bird calls in the distance. Twigs rattle against each other in a gust of wind.

I pull my cloak tighter around me and rub my hand over my

face, hating the idea of leaving without knowing more, aware that I might be more useful back with the others.

Julita harumphs. *They've got to slip up one way or another. Then we'll have them.*

But are they going to slip up while I'm here to witness it?

Then a crunch of dried leaves reaches my ears from the direction of the camp.

Every muscle in my body tenses. I peer between the branches of the bush I'm crouched behind.

A woman is striding away from the camp into the forest a short distance to my left. She holds herself stiffly erect, determined but a little nervous, her hand resting on the knife sheathed on her belt.

*Ah ha,* Julita crows.

This must be a scout. If we could take her prisoner, question her—

But how exactly are Rheave and I going to do that? I can't force answers out of her without using my magic. I doubt even Rheave could drag her away without her raising enough of a ruckus that someone at the camp would notice.

And do I really want to bring this woman back to the others in the hopes that, what, Stavros can torture information out of her?

My stomach lists queasily.

No, that's not who I am. I'm not a monster.

*You can't let her simply walk away,* Julita says. *You took on Ster. Torstem's whole club of scourge sorcerers—you've got to be able to handle one.*

Her words light a spark of inspiration in my head.

I'm not a monster—I'm a thief.

I'm the woman who convinced the entire royal college that I was a minor noblewoman rather than a street rat.

A grin curves my lips with a flicker of exhilaration.

I don't need to bully this woman. I simply need to steal her trust.

Gathering myself, I pull away from the bush and straighten up behind a tree. Then I walk forward quickly so I can pass near the scout as if I'm just returning to the place she left.

At the soft crinkle of my footsteps, her gaze snaps to me.

I pretend that I've only just noticed her as well and raise my hand in greeting. "Hey, there. Heading out to do the rounds? All's quiet where I've been so far."

The vast majority of the Order of the Wild members have never gotten a clear look at me. With hundreds of them in camp and newcomers joining here and there, I'm gambling that this woman won't find it totally strange that she might not recognize me as a colleague at a glance.

She slows, uncertainty flickering across her face through her hesitant smile. "That's good to hear. When did you go out?"

"Oh, the sun wasn't even up yet," I say easily, as if it'd never occur to me that she might not believe me. "Most were still sleeping. But we need the rest if we're going to see our purpose through, especially after that mess last night. Any changes to the new plan?"

The Order member still looks puzzled, but my chatty tone has lulled her enough that she answers automatically. "Not that I've heard. There can't be a better strategy than hitting the castle right before dawn, while *they're* mostly sleeping." She pauses, staring at me more closely. "How long have you been marching with us?"

My pulse hiccups, but I keep my easygoing smile plastered on my face. "I guess it's been a few days now? We were a late bunch, had to catch up but glad we did."

I give her another wave, this one intended to send her off. "May you discover no trouble."

I move as if to amble on by, knowing I can't walk too fast or I'll be seen from the camp. The woman takes a step but stops, twisting back around. "Wait."

I turn with a hitch of my heart and lift my eyebrows. "Is something wrong?"

She stares at me for a few seconds.

There must be something about my demeanor or my clothes that only an Order member would realize is off. I can see the shift in her from uncertainty to hostility in an instant.

She draws her knife. "You're not—"

Her mouth opens to gulp the air and holler a warning back to the camp. I snatch at one of the knives at my hips—

And Rheave is there first, leaping from the underbrush with his hands outstretched.

He tackles her, power bursting from his hands. The lightning bolt of energy sears through the woman's body with a soft sizzle, so quickly that she's disintegrating into cinders before her body can thump against the ground.

Her charred remains patter across the forest floor. All that's left is a sickening smell like burnt meat that washes away with the next gust of breeze.

Rheave stares down at the scattered chunks of ash and blackened bone. He looks a bit queasy himself.

As I hurry to join him, he lifts his head to meet my eyes.

"I didn't like doing it," he says quietly. "But either she died, or she'd have called the rest of them to kill you and me and our friends too."

I know that twisted feeling, sure that you did the right thing but wishing you hadn't needed to. Like when I had to stab Esmae before she could do the same to me.

The daimon-man didn't save me only from the attackers the scout would have called our way but also from having one more heap of guilt on my conscience, if I'd been the one to kill her.

I grasp his hand. "There wasn't really any choice. She'd already made hers. But I know it's an awful feeling anyway. Here, I'd better spread around the ashes so it's less obvious what happened."

Grimacing, I shove at the ashen remains with my boots, mixing them with leaves and dirt. Rheave follows suit until the spot where the woman fell could just be a darker streak of soil amid the rest.

As we hustle away from both her and the camp, the daimon-man smiles. "You tricked her at first. You got her to tell you things."

The joy of that small victory returns. I find myself smiling back at my new lover.

"I did. Without using a single scrap of magic. Now we'd better get back to the others so we can figure out how to stop their new plan once and for all."

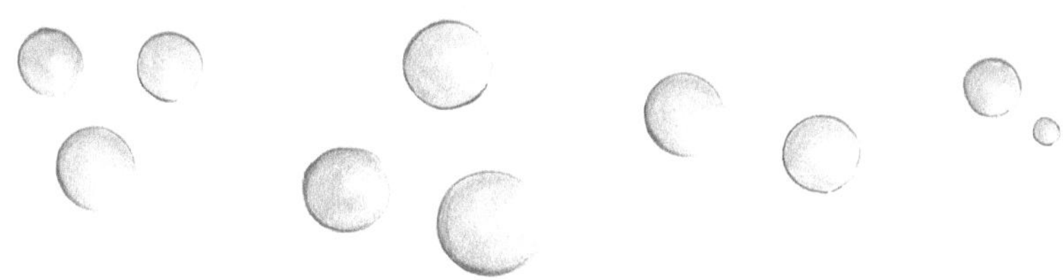

# Thirty-Eight

*Casimir*

Ivy lets out a little hiss and raises her hand from the stick she's holding. A drop of blood wells up on the tip of one finger. "I scratched myself."

Rheave leans over from where he's sitting next to her, his eyes widening with concern. "Are you all right?"

"It's just a tiny prick. But these are fiddly."

"Stavros said it might be easier if we slide the bits of fletching only part way down until they're all in, and then push them the rest of the way."

Ivy studies the arrow she's been making under Rheave's guidance after Stavros instructed him last night. The daimon lost all his previous projectiles in yesterday's chaotic assault on the march.

"I could see that helping," she says. "I'll try it with the next one."

As she tugs the last piece of the leaves they're using for fletching into place and sets the new arrow on the small pile they've been building, Rheave tips his head to brush his lips against her hair.

I've seen our newest companion show physical affection to Ivy in the past. There's nothing about the gesture that's inherently more intimate than before.

But the ardent gleam in his eyes when he eases away and the hint of a blush that colors Ivy's cheeks tell me something more passed between them during their foray this morning. They shift their bodies next to each other with a newfound sense of coordination I've normally only seen between lovers.

Good. She needed something ecstatic amid all the anguish she's been dealing with.

I haven't been sure how to offer that kind of release myself, not in a way she'll accept.

For now, I walk across the messy floor of the abandoned outpost and sit at her other side. "Show me, so I can pitch in too? I don't think we can have too many arrows if we're going to be on the front lines of tomorrow's battle."

A small shiver passes through Ivy's slim frame, but she smiles at me and hands over one of the sticks she and Rheave have carved into a straight rod from a small branch. "We've already put the notches in them. You just need to fit in the fletching and one of these pieces for the head."

She motions to the pile of triangular chips of wood she's honed to a sharp point with a few swift strokes of her knife.

"Like this." Rheave demonstrates how they've been wiggling the bits into the notches at either end of the arrow, tight enough that they don't need further tying.

I've never engaged in weapon construction before, but I've put my fingers to enough other nimble uses to be sure I can handle this. With a nod, I get to work.

As we add to the pile, a tense silence falls over the three of us. The sun has just dipped below the hole in the ceiling, evening creeping ever closer.

Alek is out foraging so we'll have some kind of dinner to ward off the weakness of hunger. Stavros hasn't returned yet from his survey of the nearby royal forces.

The question of what we're going to do about the scourge sorcerers' next planned attack has been hanging in the air since Ivy and Rheave returned with their news. I haven't come up with any answers.

The best we can do is make sure we're prepared for war.

When there are only a few of the base rods left, Rheave hums and gets to his feet. "I'll go collect more sticks we can use. I want to make sure no one from the march has come over this way too."

He gazes down at Ivy with a stalwart protective air, obviously hesitant to leave her even for that purpose, and then flashes a smile at me before striding out.

Ivy exhales in a huff of air and sets down her most recent creation. "I guess I should be glad I'm better at making arrows than launching them."

I nudge at the head of my arrow until I'm sure it's firmly lodged. "No person can be a master at every skill. I'm glad there's some way I can be of a little use myself."

She elbows me gently. "You've contributed much more than 'a little.'"

A short chuckle escapes me. "Perhaps, but this isn't how I was supposed to be making my mark on the world."

As the words leave my lips, Ivy's face falls.

She tries to recover with a brisk laugh of her own, but I wince inwardly. I've inadvertently stung her with my clumsy remark.

"You must be missing the college a lot right now," she says with forced lightness.

I swallow thickly and slip my hand around her arm. "I didn't mean it like that, Kindness. I haven't for one second regretted standing by you on this journey. I've only worried that… the debts I'm failing to honor may have brought bad luck our way."

Ivy's forehead furrows. "What debts? Why would they matter out here?"

I open my mouth and close it again, the shame of my

history congealing in my chest. But I probably should explain it to her so she understands the responsibilities I carry—and how deviating from my course could have lost us my godlen's favor.

"I told you that my mother was a courtesan as well," I say.

Ivy nods, picking up another rod but glancing over at me again.

I run my fingers over the leaves I've fletched my arrow with. "She was a very admired and prominent courtesan. Some say no one of her generation served Ardone's will quite so well. But her pregnancy with me and the birth were difficult—both took their toll on her. It strained her nerves in some way that she lost much of her former grace of movement; she developed tics that made it difficult for her to even hold a smile."

"And the royal medics couldn't heal the damage?"

I shake my head. "From what I understand, it was too extensive and deeply set. Apparently her situation would have been even worse without their intervention. As it was, the effects were mainly superficial… but appearances matter a lot in our line of work."

"Of course." Ivy frowns. "But what does that have to do with you having debts?"

Surely it's obvious?

The weight of the knowledge makes my shrug sluggish. "It was my fault. If she hadn't birthed me, she'd have been able to carry out her calling for who knows how many decades to come. So I've done my best to spread as much joy and pleasure in the world as she would have."

Ivy blinks at me. She puts down the arrow she only just started fletching and turns toward me. "Casimir, you don't *really* think you're obligated to do the same work just because she couldn't, do you? It wasn't your idea to be born. She made that choice—she must have known there were risks."

My mouth tastes ashy. "She couldn't have known she'd sacrifice anywhere near so much. I wouldn't be alive without her sacrifice. She always said I was the gift she was giving to the world in exchange. Ardone deserves a champion just as worthy as the one that was lost, after all."

"That's ridiculous! That's… that's as bad as the scourge sorcerers conning twelve-year-olds into carving themselves up for their purposes."

A flinch ripples through my body at the comparison.

I manage another chuckle. "I don't think creating beauty and pleasure is anything like their awful cause."

Ivy grimaces. "Okay, maybe it's a slight exaggeration—but my point still stands. Nobody's supposed to be able to demand that other people give up their lives in service."

"It's my calling. I chose it; I enjoy it. No one gets to decide how every part of their life turns out."

It's Ivy's turn to wince, though I wasn't even thinking of her situation when I made my last remark.

She sets her hand on my shoulder. "You have options. You can make your life about whatever you want it to be. If Ardone would punish you—or all of us—because you haven't been fulfilling your mother's legacy for a few months or some bullshit like that, then she isn't a godlen worth serving."

"Ivy—"

"No," she says. "You've fought and spied and scavenged and so many other things so we could make it this far toward saving the kingdom from the worst villains it's faced in five hundred years. All of that counts, even if it doesn't fit with being a courtesan." She kicks at a stray pebble on the floor. "Be glad that you can pitch in by all those means."

I don't need to ask to understand what she means. "You've offered more than your magic, Ivy."

"Sure. A little." Her head droops. "For just a moment this morning, I felt hopeful. But all I did was find out more information we don't know how to react to. I've been wracking my brain for hours, and I haven't come up with a single way I could block the scourge sorcerers' attack for more than a second or two without using my power."

"It isn't all on you. We'll figure something out together."

"But I'm the only one who *could* do it—who could wipe them all out in a matter of minutes, just by wanting to."

The laugh that tumbles out of her next is so dark it scares me. "If I truly care about the people they'll hurt, maybe that's what I should do. What the gods would want from me. Why Kosmel set me on this course to begin with. Forget about my sanity, forget about the innocent people in the mix who've been duped—blast them all away and have Stavros ready to put me down before I can harm anyone else."

The horror that rushes through me at her suggestion drowns out every other sensation.

I wrap my arms around her and hug her close, an anguished burn coming into the back of my eyes. "Don't say that, Ivy. Don't ever even think that. *You* are not a sacrifice."

Ivy tips her head against my shoulder. She sounds choked up herself. "How is it any different from you giving up your life to replace your mother? I'd be saving the whole kingdom."

Gods help me, have I pushed her toward thinking this way?

I tighten my embrace, grappling with the torrent of emotions coursing through my body.

Is what she said now how it sounds to her when I talk about fulfilling my mother's legacy? But that damage was already done by my arrival on this earth—

I suppose Ivy could say the same thing about the damage she's inadvertently caused in the past.

"No," I murmur. "I don't believe it that far. We both deserve to *live*. We deserve to have some part of our lives that belong to us. We can find our own ways to serve our gods without giving up everything that matters to us. I wouldn't be here if I didn't believe that."

But believing it and *feeling* it in every moment aren't always the same thing.

Ivy lets out a shaky breath. "I want a life of my own too. I just— I don't know if I'd want to live in a realm taken over by scourge sorcerers anyway. What if I'm the only chance Silana has? The king's hands are tied trying to protect the country against the Darium threat as well. And he thinks *we're* the enemy."

A snort escapes her that sounds more like her usual self. "Everyone's against us, even the people we're trying to save."

I rub my hand up and down her back. "We'll prove him wrong. And we may find support in places we're not expecting it. Look at Rheave. He started out as the scourge sorcerers' tool, but then he became our ally… and now he's even more than that to you."

Ivy stiffens just slightly. "I—"

"It's okay," I tell her before she has a chance to think I'm accusing her rather than simply acknowledging. "I love seeing that you've found even more happiness. But who would have thought it'd come from such an unexpected place?"

"True." Ivy hugs me back and then leans into my embrace with a sigh. "It doesn't seem as if any of the other captured daimon have been able to shake off the scourge sorcerers' control. And nothing we've done has rattled their supporters in the march enough for them to question whether the Order of the Wild really has good intentions. I don't see who…"

She pauses for long enough that I pull back to check her expression. Her eyes have lit with a feverish sort of glint.

Ivy straightens up. She stays silent for several more seconds, wetting her lips, before meeting my eyes. "Casimir, if I had an idea that sounded insane but didn't involve *me* going insane… would you trust me enough to try it?"

It's a simple, straightforward question, no pleading or cajoling. But I can see in the strain on her face how much she needs me to stand by her right now.

And I know down to the core of me that I'd follow this woman right over the edge of the world if she asked me to.

"Yes," I say. "Whatever it is. Just tell me what you need."

Before she can answer, footsteps rustle outside. Stavros

appears in the doorway, his hair rumpled from his ride, his expression unreadable.

A flicker of hope rises in my chest—that maybe he's seen thousands of royal soldiers already arriving to defend the king or evidence of some other response that'll make whatever danger Ivy's planning to hurl herself into unnecessary.

"Any news?" I ask.

The twist of his mouth makes my heart sink again before he even speaks. "The local forces are clearly more on the alert, but with the numbers currently stationed here, I'm not sure how much of a defense they'll provide. From what I overheard, there are reinforcements on their way, but they're more than a day out."

"Too far," Ivy murmurs, and focuses on him. "The scourge sorcerers are attacking before dawn tomorrow. But Casimir was just reminding me that sometimes enemies can become allies. I think we can set a trap that could mean the end of the Order of the Wild—or at least, of any chance of them harming the royal family tomorrow."

Stavros lifts his eyebrows. "What's that?"

Ivy's gaze slides to me. She takes my hand. "I'm going to need all your skills for putting people at ease, Cas. We'll have to win a little trust from both the scourge sorcerers and a bunch of Darium soldiers."

A different sort of glow forms in my chest. I have no idea where she's going with this, but my answer remains the same. "Any talent I have is yours as well. What's this trap we're going to lay?"

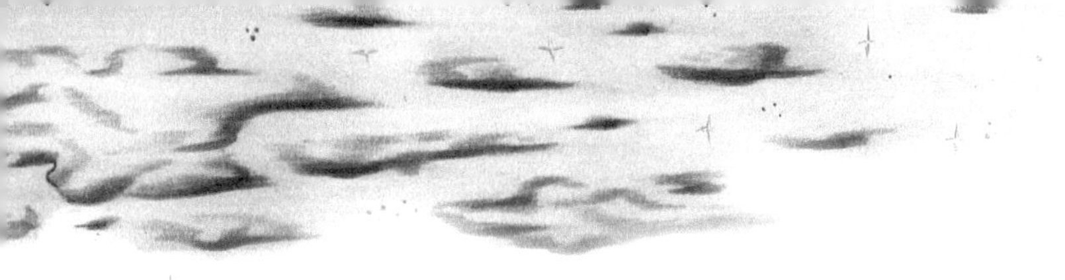

# Thirty-Nine

*Stavros*

The sight of the Darium words marching across the paper makes my skin tighten up even though I know it was a friend and not one of the enemy who wrote them.

I fought the pricks who want to take our country for themselves for years—trying to think as if I'm one of them is nauseating.

But right now, they could be the key to destroying a much more immediate threat.

With his scholarly knowledge of the language, Alek was the obvious choice to write the false letter. I coached him through the content with my understanding of the Darium forces and their interest in Silana, while Casimir guided the subtler aspects of our phrasing.

We need the letter to sound convincing but also not overly pointed. Anything too blatant might raise suspicions of it being a fake.

*We accept your appeal in exchange for the stake we're owed in Silana. If the flag on your fort a mile west of where the three pines*

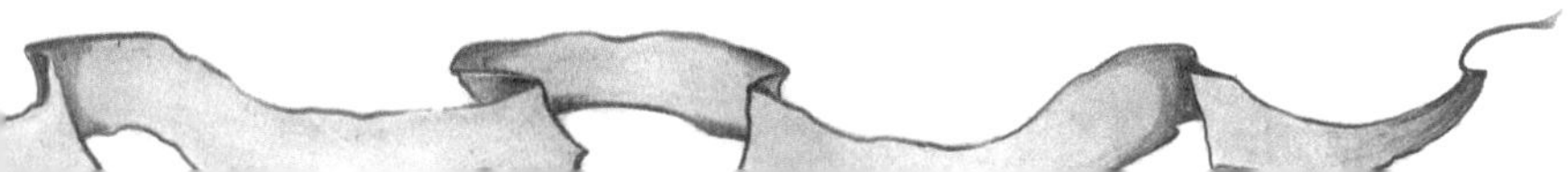

*stand at the Seafell's bank is burnt by the second bell of the morning, we'll cross to the pines and convey the item by the means you requested. Any deviation from your promise, and the deal will be forfeit.*

*Emperor Tarquin looks forward to reestablishing a partnership that benefits us both. In this alliance, you do the continent proud, King Konram.*

Ivy paces at the other end of the abandoned outpost's main room. "Julita knows that at least Borys can read Darium, so the Order of the Wild will figure out what it says. Would their army definitely write to our king in that language?"

I nod. "I don't know if any of the Order members are familiar enough with our former conquerors to be aware of this fact, but the empire has always presented their own language as superior to all others. They wouldn't want to deal with King Konram unless he was willing to engage with them on their own terms."

Casimir pokes his head through the doorway. "The horses are saddled. Are you happy with the letter?"

Happy isn't the word for it.

"I think it should be convincing in combination with the show you and Alek will put on," I say, and hand it over to him. "Make sure you're careful about how you drop it—it *has* to look completely accidental."

Casimir grins. "Ivy may be our expert at stealth, but I can pull off a little slight of hand. It's unfortunate how a bit of wind can snag on a piece of paper that's jostled from a pocket with hard riding."

Ivy rubs her hands together. "All right. You'd better go so we have as much time as possible to catch a scout."

She glances at Rheave, who's been watching the proceedings with quiet curiosity. "And *you* have to make sure they don't see you fire the arrow."

He hefts his bow eagerly. "I'll climb so high up a tree it'll soar right over the tops."

Alek tugs at the hood of his cloak. He's got it draped particularly far forward so it'll hide the scarred side of his face, but I can tell he's nervous. "We've worked out all the details. It should be simple enough."

I hold out my fist for the others to knock theirs to it. It's a simple ritual, but the resolve in the air firms as our knuckles tap together.

"Off we go, then." Casimir gives Ivy and me a playful salute and heads for the horses with the scholar and the daimon at his heels.

The moment we hear their steeds clomp off through the woods, Ivy resumes her pacing. "Between the dropped letter and the conversation we'll arrange for the scout to overhear, the Order will *have* to believe it, won't they? That Darium soldiers are coming to give King Konram a means to escape the uprising? If they don't go to confront the soldiers..."

"It should work," I reassure her. "And if it doesn't, we can send the Darium forces after the march. There are multiple ways to play the scheme. But you have your own role too. Let's go over those lines in Darium again."

Ivy grimaces at me. We're lucky she knows enough spoken Darium to be able to understand basic questioning and know how to respond. Not what you'd expect from a street rat thief, but I suppose nothing less would be fitting for the Hand of Kosmel.

All I needed to help her with was some minor adjustments to her accent and a few more specialized words of vocabulary. Boating isn't one of her regular pastimes.

I toss out the questions a regular patrol might ask her, and Ivy volleys back her answers with a casual air. I don't know if her Darium would be convincing in an extended conversation, but I can't criticize anything in the few sentences that are all she should need to speak.

When we're done, I rest my elbow on the makeshift desk we've formed out of chunks of rubble and a larger slab of stone.

"Good. I already know you can keep cool under pressure. As long as you act as if you have every right to be there, you shouldn't have any trouble."

"With that part, anyway," Ivy says dryly. She sits down by the wall and tips her head back with a sigh. "I guess you have your own letter to write."

I suspect she's more concerned about the plan as a whole than her own part in it, which plays to her strengths. The entire idea was hers. Crazy but brilliant, really.

If it saves her from the insanity of her magic while also saving the kingdom I've sworn to defend, I'll go with crazy. Even if the thought of this final letter makes my stomach clench around a fresh twinge of queasiness.

I retrieve the paper and the ink we acquired for our purpose. "Yes. King Konram will need to be informed of what's going on and why so he doesn't make any rash moves."

"He isn't going to be happy about this tactic."

"Most likely not," I admit. "But as long as he's pleased with the ultimate outcome, that's what matters."

And that has to be all that matters to me as well. Never mind that carrying out this plan is the closest I've actually come to real treason.

I stare at the paper for a long moment, grappling with the fact that I'm going to have to inform my king of that treason. But if he doesn't understand what we've set in motion, it could be disastrous for all of us.

I simply have to hope that he eventually sees that everything I've done, including this, has been for him and Silana.

Struggling my way through writing the letter at least gives me something to distract myself with while we wait for the others to return. Ivy gnaws on our last apple and goes out to stretch her legs with a stroll around the building.

I'm sure she'd have wanted to be right there with the other men if discretion weren't so important.

I hear the distant bells ring for one hour and then the next before I sign my name at the bottom of my missive. I fold it firmly and tuck it into the inner pocket of my cloak.

If everything goes according to plan, I'll be setting it on its course late tonight.

As I get up from the makeshift desk, Ivy reappears. She takes one look at my face, and hers falls. "I'm sorry. You must hate this."

My heart stutters. She and I are going to have to be apart for more of this scheme than I like. If something goes wrong, we may not make it back to each other, as much as I loathe to think about that.

The last thing I want is for us to part ways with her imagining that I resent what she's asked of me.

"Ivy." I walk up to her, holding her bright blue gaze. "This is a fantastic plan. I doubt I could have come up with anything more likely to work if I'd had weeks to consider it. And you're the one who put all the pieces together. I'm grateful to get another chance at destroying the scourge sorcerers."

"By turning your worst enemies into sort of allies?"

I make a dismissive sound. "They'll face their own dire end. What's a little more treason after everything I've already been accused of?"

Before she can do more than wince, I draw her into my arms, my voice dropping low. "The real treason is that King Konram hasn't yet seen how inspiring you are."

Ivy manages to form an incredulous sort of huff. "I guess even Signy faced plenty of doubt before she proved herself."

"And as far as I'm concerned, you've proven yourself a hundred times over already."

I dip my head to catch her mouth with mine.

Ivy sinks into my embrace, one hand gripping the front of my shirt, the other rising to trail along my neck. Her fingertips ignite sparks that shoot straight to my groin.

Gods help me, if we didn't need to be ready to ride out at a moment's notice, I'd remind her of just how much I enjoy being with her in the most concrete way possible.

I end the kiss but keep my head bowed over hers, our foreheads brushing. "I need you to know that no matter what happens tonight, it's been my honor fighting these pricks alongside you. No matter how hard the journey became, there was never anywhere I'd have rather been than next to you."

Ivy swallows audibly. "I don't know where we'll go from here, but I really want the chance to find out. I couldn't do this without you."

Not just me. It's all five of us and the strange sort of family we've become.

Somehow our joint relationship feels more fulfilling than when I had a woman I was meant to marry all to myself.

A sustained rustling in the forest outside puts me on the alert. Giving Ivy's shoulder one more squeeze, I step past her to peer out the ruined building's doorway.

It's Rheave, making his way toward us on Toast, who we didn't trust to carry Alek or Casimir appropriately through their charade. The stallion looks typically disgruntled but gives a soft snort at the sight of Ivy stepping out next to me.

The daimon dismounts with a smile. "I saw someone coming from the camp site and signaled Alek and Casimir. The scout didn't see. I rode back as soon as he was out of view, but the others shouldn't be far behind."

"Good." His report only offers a fragment of relief.

I motion to Ivy. "You should get on your horse. Every minute makes a difference."

The sun has already dropped lower than I like, though the dusk will make traveling unnoticed easier when we can't rely on Ivy's sorcery.

As she clambers onto the obstinate stallion, Rheave collects the bundle of additional arrows he constructed. The blankets and camp gear we leave on the floor.

We're not bringing much other than ourselves on this mission.

Another set of hoofbeats approaches soon after, announcing Alek's approach. He slides down from his mount, a little breathless. "We went through the conversation as soon as we saw the man coming through the forest. Obviously I couldn't look right at him or he'd know we'd noticed him, but he stopped and seemed to be listening to the whole thing."

He's only just finished speaking when Casimir appears as well, grinning widely from the other stallion's back. "And that blasted letter just happened to slip from my pocket without my noticing it. The scout will have plenty to tell his associates."

He hops down and nudges his steed toward me.

I take the stallion's reins. "You two keep an eye on the camp site and confirm that the march leaves at the right time. There should be some small indication of their passage when they pass through the forest, if you're watching closely. Meet up with us while keeping your distance from them, or sound whatever warning you can through the temple and the town if it appears they're sticking to their original intent."

Both of my comrades nod, tense but determined.

"Be careful," Ivy tells them as I prod my horse to pull ahead of hers.

I set off at a trot. "Let's ride."

By the time the Seafell Channel has come into view up ahead, the sun has completely set, only a faint glow lingering on the horizon. We approach the water at a cautious distance from the nearby fort that's my next destination. A hint of brakish salt laces the air.

It only takes a few minutes to find a suitable boat with its oars. The fishermen who don't live right on the waterfront have favorite places to stash them that I came to know in the time I was stationed near here.

We already carved Ivy a simple if suitable rod, and I find an old net that would only need a little quick mending for good measure.

"The Darium fortress is almost directly across from here," I tell her in a low voice. "It shouldn't be difficult to spot—there aren't any other buildings nearby. Just make sure no one spots *you* at an inopportune time."

"I have lots of practice at sneaking around," Ivy reminds me, but her expression tightens as she looks across the water. "I'd better get going. The sooner the message is delivered, the more likely they'll act on it."

She turns to me to claim a hasty kiss and then shoves the boat off the bank, hopping into it at the last moment. In the thickening darkness, it takes less than a minute for the small craft to blend into the shadows wavering across the water.

Rheave has been waiting back with the horses in the stand of trees where we'll leave Toast for Ivy to collect him. As I approach, he peers past me as if he was hoping Ivy might have returned with me after all.

"Are you sure it wouldn't have been safer for one of us to go with her?" he asks.

I'm never going to fault the daimon for his dedication to keeping our woman in one piece.

I give him a gentle clap on the shoulder in an attempt at reassurance, even though my own worries are knotting my stomach. "More people look like more of a threat. Especially when one of them is a large, fit man. She can handle herself."

Rheave makes a rough sound. "It just doesn't seem fair that she should have to go alone when the rest of us don't." But he draws his posture straighter with an air of resolve I also have to admire. "Now we go to our fort?"

"Now we go to our fort." As much as we can call it 'ours' when we're about to take it over like an enemy force.

There's one Silanian fortress watching over the channel in this area, a couple of hours ride from the larger palace in Regica where Konram and his family are currently residing. Unless policies have changed, they'll have regular patrols along the bank starting not long after dark.

Patrols that could ruin our plan before it's even really gotten started.

So we simply have to delay them for a while. Ensure both they and our scheme stay safe. It benefits them as much as us.

But as much as I tell myself that, my gut sinks with each stride my stallion takes toward the looming stone walls.

Perhaps my trepidation shows on my face, or perhaps the daimon has simply paid enough attention to past conversations to put the pieces together on his own. After a while, he glances over at me and ventures, "The people at this fort—they used to be your colleagues."

I nod. "In a way. We were all part of the royal army together. I was never stationed at Fort Cyprian specifically, and I don't know if any of the soldiers currently posted there ever served under me."

"But it must be hard. Even though what we're doing will keep them away from the danger. I wouldn't like it if I had to do something that would make you—or Alek or Casimir or Ivy—angry, even if it would be good in the end."

His acknowledgment lifts a fragment of the weight bearing down on me.

I find I can smile at him. "It is hard. But military life is all about making the best of many difficult choices. In a way, I'm using my training even more now than when I was officially a general."

Rheave smiles back at me. "I'm glad to act as your soldier, then."

I wouldn't have thought I could say this when he first stumbled into our midst weeks ago, but I can feel how true it is now. "So am I."

We leave the horses again in the patch of woods nearest Fort Cyprian and make our final approach on foot. As his gaze darts around us watchfully, Rheave walks with a spring in his step, clearly eager to leap into action.

What will the books of history have to say about the former General Stavros when this night is done? What we do here could be seen as a major triumph… or an even greater tragedy of my career than the battle that ended my work in the field.

I push down the gnawing uneasiness and stride onward. *I* know that I'm doing whatever I can to protect my king and my country. Would I rather stand back and let the scourge sorcerers ruin it all, just to avoid any risk that my name could be tarnished by those who don't understand?

No. So those doubts should sit down and shut up like new recruits who haven't yet seen what warfare really means.

Lanterns glow in the big stone building beyond the thick wall that surrounds it. I spot a few soldiers standing atop the wall, but they're watching for larger threats than a couple of men on foot.

They don't notice us until we step into the meager light that extends only a few paces beyond the fort.

"Who's that there?" someone calls down as we approach the door—wood fortified with steel, and presumably still locked with a heavy bar on the inside.

I motion Rheave over to the door and lift my voice. "I'm sorry about this, but it's necessary to ensure the security of the country. No one is to leave this fortress before the morning."

"What?" the first soldier says in a bewildered tone.

And then another sucks in a sharp breath. "Is that General Stavros?"

She must have spotted my prosthetic. My stomach contorts into a ball of nausea.

Some of the men and women inside *could* have served under me while I was still a general. There are so many soldiers who trusted me, counted on me…

I set my jaw. I'm not letting them down tonight. I'm leading them better than I did during my last battle, whether they'll see it that way or not.

I put on my best commander's smile and raise the metal hook of a hand to my forehead in a quick salute. "Please stay calm and remain inside these walls until we open the door. As soon as your assistance is needed, we'll let you know."

"As soon as *you* open the door?" someone else mutters, just as I nod to Rheave.

The daimon sets his hands against the door's edge. His supernatural energy crackles over the surface like tiny streaks of lightning.

The steel border melts into the stone of the frame. He'll be pushing his power straight through to fuse the crossbar in place as well.

A faint smoky smell laces the air. Rheave yanks his hands back before the wood is outright charred.

A yelp carries from the other side. "What the fuck are they doing?"

A strained chuckle catches in my throat.

Saving Silana is what—with this crazy, last-ditch plan that will hopefully look more like heroics than betrayal by the time we're through.

# Forty

*Ivy*

I've never thought of myself as sheltered, but I had no idea rivers so much wider than the Starsil that passes through Florian existed. Although I guess the Seafell Channel is called a channel rather than a river because it's on an entirely different level.

Generally, I'd be glad there's so much water between us and the eastern half of the continent, where the Darium empire still rules. Tonight, I wouldn't mind our enemies lurking just a *little* closer at hand.

I dip the paddles carefully into the darkened water so they won't make more sound than the warbling wind that tugs at my cloak's hood. On the opposite bank ahead of me, the few scattered lights there look so tiny they could almost be stars.

At this distance, I can't make out any structures in the thickening dusk. Only the thin crescent of the rising moon keeps me heading in the direction Stavros indicated.

To my left and right, there's no light at all. The channel just stretches endlessly away.

Is this anything close to what it feels like being on the ocean? I've never experienced that supposedly vast body of water either, only seen it in paintings and tapestries.

I peer toward my destination again and restrain a grimace. Stavros said it could take more than an hour to cross while I'm trading some speed for stealth. I've only covered maybe a quarter of the distance so far.

*At least we don't have to worry about anyone seeing you for a while yet,* Julita remarks as if picking up on my impatience. *I don't imagine the channel hosts many pleasure cruises with the current state of political affairs.*

I let out a soft snort. "I just hope the Darium sentries find it plausible that a local fisherwoman might be out plying her trade."

*I suppose people always have to make a living, regardless of who's trying to invade who.* She sighs. *As bizarre as this plan might be, Ivy, I truly believe you're going to pull it off. It all fits together. Let our enemies destroy each other—brilliant, really.*

"As long as it works." I dig the paddles into the rippling water again, keeping my voice low just in case. "I don't know if stopping the march will be the end of the uprising, though. They did leave some people back in Eppun. We still don't know who's at the top of the Order of the Wild, giving the orders."

I get the impression of a shrug. *It'll eliminate a significant portion of their might, including the people most willing to fight. And we can hope that those who were duped into joining under false pretenses will flee and spread the word that the Order means death rather than freedom.*

"That would be nice. And there have been people standing up to them already. Emor and Voleska might have made more progress."

*We're heading in the right direction, both literally and metaphorically. That's what matters most.* Julita pauses. *And if Borys finally meets his end by Darium hands, I won't be the least bit sorry about it. Good riddance.*

She's putting on that nonchalant tone she does when she's trying to pretend she isn't affected. A pang of sympathy forms in my gut. "He'll get what he deserves, one way or another. If the Darium soldiers don't finish him, the king isn't going to forgive one of the uprising's main figures."

*I'd just like to know it's taken care of. Who can say how much longer I'll keep clinging to what's left of my life to be able to see it?*

My hands hesitate for a second before I stroke the oars through the water again. "Have you felt as if staying is getting harder?" I haven't noticed any change in her presence in my head.

*I'm not sure. It seems like something that would happen so gradually I wouldn't perceive the difference. But I clearly can't haunt you forever, Ivy. I'm starting to think it might be nice to let go and meet my godlen. Once I know the worst of this catastrophe is dealt with and that you'll be all right, that is.*

The pang rises to the base of my throat. "I meant what I said before, you know. About how we could travel around after there's peace again, see and do things you missed out on."

I sense a smile in Julita's voice. *Oh, I appreciate that. And perhaps I'll change my mind when the conflict is over.*

I hesitate, thinking of Rheave's bright eyes. Of the life that animates the body he wasn't born with.

"You know… There might be a way you could get more of a life back without needing to keep haunting me. If it's possible to put a daimon in a clay body and bring it—"

*No!* Julita's shudder resonates through my skull. Her horror rings through her refusal. *What happened to Rheave—that was already done. I want no part in any of the ways the scourge sorcerers are twisting life with their horrible power.*

After her past experiences with scourge sorcery, maybe I should have expected that answer.

I wince inwardly. "I didn't mean to offend you."

*I know. I know you meant well.* Julita sighs, but it's a serene sound rather than fraught. *If it sets your conscience at ease,* you *should know that lately I've been feeling that what I've gotten already is enough. My life might not have gone quite the way I expected, but I accomplished important things before and after my death. Possibly more than I would have if I'd stayed alive. I'm genuinely happy with how things turned out.*

She sounds as if she means it. Any words I could have said in response stick in my throat.

How can she be happy with her existence cut so short, with only getting to act through me for the past few months? She had even less time than I've lived, and I'd still give anything to go back to the childhood dreams I had before my riven power awoke and—

The thought stalls in my head.

Would I, though? Would I rather have been helping Da run the print shop right now, never having met Casimir or Alek or Stavros or Rheave?

Never even knowing the scourge sorcerer conspiracy was happening other than hearing of the uprising—until what? The Order of the Wild swept across the country and slaughtered every noble who stood against them, including the royal family?

If I wasn't what I am, King Konram might very well have died the day the captured daimon stormed the palace in Florian. I wouldn't have spent all those years on the streets or all these weeks on the run, but I also wouldn't have gotten to experience the incredible love that glows in my chest, sustaining my strength through every hardship I've faced.

I can't imagine giving it all up for a simpler life. And could I really gamble the security of the entire realm to recover my sister's life?

What kind of life would either of us have had once the Order of the Wild took over?

It's possible I'm exactly where I need to be.

For the first time, I can't say I regret the journey here.

"I'm glad you feel that way," I say finally. "You should be happy."

*And you should too.* Julita stirs in the back of my skull. *The only other thing I worry about is Nikodi. Once Borys is gone, there'll be no one left to inherit the county. If I'm not around by the time that matter comes up, I'd appreciate it if you'd make sure the next count or countess is a good one.*

As last requests go, it's a reasonable one. But it makes me choke up a little thinking of the entreaty that way.

"I'll do my best," I say. "Maybe you should stick around at least that long, to make sure we choose well."

Julita gives a light laugh. *We'll have to see what the gods have in store for us next, won't we?*

"I guess we will." I glance up toward the sky as if I might catch a glimpse of a crow or some other sign that Kosmel is still watching over me, but all I see is indigo darkening to black with a scattering of stars.

The lights on the shore are gradually getting larger. Julita and I lapse into silence as I pull closer to the opposite side.

The actual country of Dariu lies much farther to the east, but the realm of Cotea lies within their empire, under their control, so it amounts to the same thing. It'll be Darium soldiers monitoring the channel.

Which is exactly what I want.

As I draw closer, I make out the tall, blocky walls of the Darium fort that's my final destination. Rather than heading straight toward it. I veer around in an arc until I'm gliding closer to shore on a subtle diagonal. To anyone watching, my approach might not even be intentional.

All the same, my magic wriggles between my ribs, tugging at me to let it loose like I have so often in recent days. It could conceal me completely, ensure no one sees me at all.

I ignore its nagging and the pang of hopes lost. For a little while, I thought the cost of my power wasn't so high after all. I thought I could be riven and sane and help the realms with my magic.

But that's proven to be a lie. The price I'd be paying is simply different.

I'm several minutes distant from the fort and some twenty paces from the shoreline when a voice hollers over to me in the Darium tongue. "*Hey there, woman in the boat! What's your business here?*"

My magic flares with a sharper wrenching, but it's exactly the sort of question I practiced answering with Stavros. I clamp down on my power with the rigid hold I perfected during my days on the streets of Florian's outer wards and the imagery of ivy winding around my chest.

As my heart thumps faster, I pull the foreign words to my lips, reminding myself of the specific inflexion I need to sound reasonably native. "*Doing some night fishing. The silverbreem fetch a good price. Is it a problem?*"

I've stopped rowing so the patrolling soldier can study me. All he'll see is a young woman in a simple dress, alone.

I've propped the fishing rod against the side of the boat within view to help sell my story, and I have the old net I can claim I haven't finished mending near my feet too.

But the soldier must decide I don't look like I could be a threat to any of his colleagues. He waves me on without even bothering to speak.

As I dip the oars back into the water, Julita chuckles. *Nicely done. They don't have the slightest idea how much destruction you could actually deal out.*

My stomach twists. They don't, and *I* don't know how much I could cause before I'd destroy my sanity as well.

I'd prefer to keep it that way.

Stealth and subterfuge are my specialties. If there's anything I should be able to do without relying on supernatural gifts, this is it.

Most of the shoreline here is pebbled beach or sharply sloping stones, but a few minutes farther along, I spot a clump of reeds that reach nearly to the trees beyond the water. A careful glance over my shoulder confirms that the soldier who called to me is no longer visible in the darkness.

I push my craft between the reeds. They hiss against the wooden sides.

The nose of the boat nudges up against the rocky bank hidden by the plants.

After testing several of the reeds, I find one I trust enough to tie the boat to it. Then I ease out onto the rocks.

The fort's few lanterns shine off to my left, too far away to illuminate my crouched form. I dart from the reeds into the even thicker darkness between the trees.

The looming oaks and maples aren't growing densely enough to really be considered a forest. Only a few shrubs have sprouted between them. It feels more like the lightly treed area of a park. But they provide enough cover for me to sneak closer to the fort.

For the last short stretch, I have to dash from tree to tree with gaps of several paces in between. The last of them still leaves me a good sprint from the fortress's stone walls.

But not far enough to be beyond the reach of my throwing arm.

I slip my hand through the slit in my dress's skirt to palm the smallest of the knives in my possession. Then I retrieve the other letter my men and I composed together from my pocket.

A dark symbol marks the outer fold—a sigil drawn in blood while swearing to the gods that everything written on the page is true. If the fort has at least a devout on staff, they'll be able to confirm it's valid.

I wish I could confirm my loyalty to the kingdom by the same process, but the sigil's confirmation only works if invoked completely freely rather than under duress. Honesty prompted by a fear of impending punishment isn't pure enough.

With Casimir's help, we ensured every word in the letter *is* true, though we intend the recipients to draw different conclusions about our meaning. Starting from our introduction as *the ones the king sees as traitors* to our assurance that *most of the royal troops are stationed elsewhere, and we'll ensure the nearby squadron is trapped and unable to attack when you arrive* and on to our conclusion that *we believe that working together is our best chance at putting Silana on the right course*, the letter has been crafted to fit our situation while sounding like it should mean it's from the members of the uprising.

Gods above and below, please let this missive be enough to convince them. Let the supposed offer of an alliance with King Konram's enemies tempt the soldiers stationed here to make the crossing.

And let my crazy plan get us closer to truly freeing our country rather than amplifying the disaster.

I wrap the letter tightly around the hilt of the knife and secure it with a few bits of warmed wax. Tuning out my power's renewed urging to bring it to bear, I study the terrain between me and the fort's door.

There's a certain trick I picked up from a prankster in Crow's Close who was happy to teach me a thing or two in exchange for stealing a trinket she coveted. If you flick your arm in a specific way with the right twist of your wrist, you can fling an object in an arc rather than a straight line, just like the trajectory I took my boat on.

I brace myself, wind up, and throw with all my strength.

My pulse thunders in my ears as the knife whips through the air. It swings around, and a brief gust of breeze brushes my face.

But even as my nerves hitch with panic, the blade flies true.

It thuds into the wood of the door just a tad off-center, gleaming in the lantern-light from above.

Julita lets out a victorious cheer. A surge of mingled exhilaration and fear rushes through my veins.

I did it. I'm really *doing* this, despite all the shit and smitings it might bring down on our heads.

As the first shout rises up within the fort, I bolt toward the shoreline. It'll take the soldiers a moment to scan for threats closer to the door and then to open it to retrieve the knife.

By the time any of them set foot outside to investigate further, I'll be long gone… until I see them again armed and armored, storming the bank on *my* side of the channel.

# Forty-One

*Ivy*

I appreciated the darkness when I needed it to hide me. I'm less fond of it right now when I want to be able to track our enemies' approach.

Stavros gives the back of my cloak a gentle tug. "Lean forward any farther and you'll topple right out, Lady Thief."

He, Rheave, and I are perched at the top of a lookout tower about half a mile back from the channel. It's also halfway between the fort he and the daimon-man sealed up and the three pine trees we've used as a landmark.

We want to be within viewing distance of the battle but out of the line of fire. I would prefer to continue keeping my head attached to my body long enough for the king to pardon both parts.

The wooden tower, the platform of which stands at the level of the nearby treetops, is only large enough to comfortably hold the three of us. Alek and Casimir, who found their way back to us before we left Fort Cyprian, are watching from its foot.

We've set everything up as planned. In the lantern light of the fort, the Silanian flag waving there has been burnt to tatters

by Rheave's magic—the signal to both the Darium soldiers and the Order of the Wild's march that everything is proceeding as they expect.

The Darium forces themselves arrived on several large watercraft not long ago. I can barely make out their forms over by the pines. They've drawn themselves into a rigid formation that could be a massive hedge for all my eyes can tell.

I think there are at least a few hundred of them. Not a huge crowd, since there wouldn't have been many soldiers stationed along this part of the channel within easy call, but enough to pose a significant threat to the Order when pitting trained military professionals against townspeople and inexperienced nobles.

And I'm still hoping that anyone in the march who's more misguided than malicious flees rather than getting caught up in the fighting.

Of course, that requires that the scourge sorcerers and their dupes show up at all.

No matter how I squint in the opposite direction, I can't make out any sign of the march's approach.

My hands tighten around the railing. A warble like a distant shout reaches my ears, sparking a jolt of nerves, but even as I turn toward it, I recognize that no one else has heard the sound.

It's only in my head. A reminder of why I can't set loose the magic that's been churning in my chest all night.

Rheave glances over at me and bumps his shoulder gently against mine. "The scourge sorcerers will be hiding themselves like they usually do, won't they?"

"Most likely." But that fact doesn't temper my impatience.

"We know they left at the right time to intercept the royal family's supposed escape to Darium," Alek says from below. "When we saw traces of them passing by the thicket where we were hiding, they appeared to be heading in the right direction, although obviously they could have diverted since then."

He and Casimir were only able to arrive ahead of the march

thanks to a wagon leaving Iblin that they hitched a ride on, traveling to one of the farms that scatter the lands just west of here. That could have put them as much as an hour ahead of the march that has most of its members on foot.

*Borys will come*, Julita says in a taut but confident voice. *He'll hate the idea that the king might have pulled one over on him and be slipping from his grasp. And you made it sound as if the royal family already traveled out here to prepare for the meeting without him realizing. It wouldn't make sense for them to attack the palace in Regica if they believe the people they want to murder aren't there.*

*If* they believe it being the operative phrase. Did Casimir and Alek's staged conversation on the road and the dropped letter prove convincing enough?

Even as that thought passes through my head, a tingle of magic grazes my skin.

I stiffen, braced to realize that it's only another trick of my currently questionable sanity. But the sensation only grows, spreading steadily into my flesh until my bones start to quiver.

It can only mean one thing.

The words fall from my lips in an urgent whisper. "I can feel their magic. They're here."

Here and coming closer with every passing second.

As far as I can tell, the Darium troops near the channel haven't stirred yet. *They* can't tell the march is approaching.

They don't even know that these people will see them as the enemy.

All at once, the flaw in my plan hits me with a jolt of panic. I was counting on the skeletal forms painted on the Darium uniforms unsettling the scourge sorcerers enough to diminish their magic. But I can barely see the soldiers themselves, let alone any imagery on their clothing.

The Order of the Wild members won't be able to see them either. The skeleton designs won't have any effect on their resolve if they launch their attack without catching so much of a glimpse.

Shit.

"We need light over there," I spit out. "By the Darium soldiers—quickly."

I glance around, groping for an answer that doesn't require my unpredictable magic, and my gaze lands on Rheave's bow. "Rheave, do you think you can propel an arrow far enough with your power to set one of those pine trees on fire?"

Without hesitation, Rheave snatches an arrow from the quiver he set at his feet. "I'll try my best."

He braces himself, his beautiful face set with concentration, the bow stretched as far as it'll go. With a twang and a crackle, he launches the arrow into the air.

It gleams as it arcs against the night sky. Anyone below might mistake it for a shooting star.

Then it plummets amid the branches in the cluster of three pines just beyond the Darium formation, and the needles flare with flames.

A few of the Darium soldiers I can now see more clearly whirl around at the apparent attack. Most of them are so disciplined they barely flinch.

The fire darts along the branches until all three trees blaze with flickering light.

At first the uniforms on the distant figures look like little more than white stripes on black. But then the troops stride forward to meet the source of the attack, and the soldiers drop the visors on their helms to cover their faces.

A chill ripples through my veins even though I was expecting the sight.

They have images like skulls painted onto their black helmets —gaping mouths and eye sockets so vacant they're obvious even across all the terrain between us.

I don't know how much it's because of the newly visible soldiers and how much because they need to focus their energy on attacking now, but the concealment spell hiding the Order members wavers. The horde of them, still several hundred strong, charges toward the Darium troops as if emerging from a haze.

The roar of their furious cries reverberates across the landscape loudly enough that it reaches my ears. I shiver, clutching the railing again, watching the collision in the eerie illumination.

More light flashes—magic, I think, bursting here and smashing into a cluster of soldiers there.

Stavros tenses, tapping his forehead, heart, gut, and sternum in the gesture of the divinities.

The Darium soldiers won't have any idea what's going on. They thought they were coming to ally with the traitors against Silana's rulers.

Maybe they figure their attackers are the king's people who got here first. Maybe they'll assume the traitors turned on them too.

It doesn't really matter. They're already pressing back with flashes of blades, hails of arrows, and a few flares of their own, regular magic.

I spot bodies crumpling on both sides—some among the Order cracking into chunks of clay when they hit the ground.

As the two groups crash into each other, the flares of magic falter. The tingling that touched my skin fades away.

It's working. The scourge sorcerers' will must be shaken, their concentration broken by their rattled nerves.

It unnerves even *me* seeing the Darium force from this distance. I can't imagine what the visual is like up close.

But the Order's greater numbers ensure they're not at a complete disadvantage. I see black-uniformed figures toppling throughout the fray.

The Darium troops will have no choice but to retreat even if they win the battle. They aren't going to try to take on the rest of the king's army on their own.

And the Order of the Wild's march will be cut down before they can do any more damage to our country.

As I watch, my spirits lifting, the Darium soldiers press their opponents farther back. More and more of the Order members bolt away from their comrades into the night—first a few, then several, then dozens abandoning their cause.

Rheave readies his bow with another arrow, guarding our little group from any deserters who head this way. I retrieve my favorite knife from my boot.

Victory won't feel worth it if any of my men gets hurt in the process.

Stavros scans the battle with an intensity that hums off him, flicking his gaze every couple of seconds to refocus his damaged vision. Alek and Casimir adjust their positions below us, unable to see much from their lower vantage point.

"How does it look?" Casimir asks in a hushed voice just loud enough to reach us.

I smile. "The Darium soldiers are carving their way through the march, but the Order members are taking down quite a few of them in the process. The scourge sorcerers don't seem to be able to—"

Before I can finish that sentence, a sudden wave of energy slams into the Darium soldiers.

As my pulse hitches, the front lines of the Darium troops topple into each other. Blood splatters red across the white-painted patterns on their uniforms.

More magic thrums through the air. I swallow thickly, a cold sweat breaking over my skin. "The scourge sorcerers have rallied. I don't know how."

Stavros's body goes totally rigid. "Rheave, take out that man, the one in green off to the side of the battleground!" He jerks his arm forward to point.

Rheave's arrow springs from his bow in the same instant. With the sizzle of his energy, it flies true.

The arrow strikes a figure in a green cloak in the side of the head, and he slumps into a heap at the edge of the fray.

Stavros's knuckles have whitened where he's gripping the

wooden railing alongside me. "I saw—my gift—that sorcerer was going to unleash a blast of power that'd have killed dozens of the soldiers."

Even as he speaks, more magic streaks through the battle. There are other sorcerers still ramping up their attacks.

The former general pushes away from the railing. "They're turning the tide. The Darium soldiers haven't felled enough of the Order members to ensure the march won't still attack the king. We need to finish them while they're distracted."

My stomach flips over. "What are you going to do?"

"Rally reinforcements." He motions to Rheave with his prosthetic as he grasps the ladder with his other hand. "Come with me. We need to open the fort and get the support of our own soldiers. Casimir, you ride with us too—maybe you can use your knack for diplomacy to convince them not to slaughter *us* for trapping them first."

He's already clambered down the ladder before he's finished speaking. The three men dash into the woods to grab the horses and set off at a gallop.

Uneasiness creeps over my skin. I glance down at Alek. "Do you have any idea how many soldiers would be in that fort?"

He shakes his head. What I can make out of his expression in the darkness looks sickly. "Less than a hundred, I'd imagine."

"Not necessarily enough to turn the tide if the Darium soldiers can't."

"No."

Julita shudders in my head. *I suppose Stavros feels he needs to take every possible chance to destroy the threat here. He's alerted the king—there could be more royal troops on their way.*

Maybe. But will even that be enough against the scourge sorcerers at their full power?

What shook them out of their demoralized state? I couldn't see anything from up here that explained it…

As I peer at the continuing battle, the currents of magic shift against my skin. My gaze veers to the west.

I could swear a significant waft of that energy is coming not from the battlefield but from farther afield.

Is someone helping them from a distance?

I didn't notice that current of power before. Has a new arrival come to rally their colleagues?

Squinting through the night, I can't distinguish any figures or even definite structures on the low hills in that direction. But as I stare, a crow circles beneath the stars and then flies to the southwest with a faint caw.

Julita lets out a ragged laugh. *I think your godlen is summoning you.*

Whether Kosmel is or not, I have to act. Someone's supporting the scourge sorcerers from over there, where the sight of death in the form of the Darium soldiers isn't affecting them.

And my sensitivity to their magic is the only means we have of hunting them down.

I waver for a second, but a glance at the carnage on the battlefield has me scrambling down the ladder.

I grasp Alek's arm. "I think there's another scourge sorcerer boosting their companions' power from the farmlands to the west. I'm going to follow the trail of their magic. It might be nothing. I'll signal you all with my locket if I need backup. If I don't, focus on the battle here."

"Ivy—" Alek starts, his eyes wild.

With a pang of regret, I squeeze his arm and let go. "I have to hurry. I'll see you when this is over."

Then I take off at a run in the direction the crow flew, hoping I didn't just tell the scholar my last lie.

# Forty-Two

*Ivy*

As exhausting as our weeks traveling across the country have been, they've hardened my muscles beyond any of my previous conditioning. I was never a weakling, but loping across the grassy terrain now comes much easier than it would have when I'd only just left Florian.

As I jog to the southwest, I keep my strides long and swift without pushing myself so hard that I'll get too winded to maintain the pace.

The tingle of magic gradually thickens. There's a whole torrent of it flowing toward the skirmish rather than seeping off the battlefield.

Someone's definitely bolstering the scourge sorcerers' strength.

If I can stop them before the Darium troops are completely overpowered, the two sides might still wipe each other out. Hopefully before any of the men I've given my heart to charge into the fray.

I catch one more flicker of dark wings against the stars up ahead, but I don't need the crow to guide me. I simply move

toward the deeper thrum of the magic, shifting course slightly when I sense it diminishing.

"Kosmel," I murmur, tapping my hand down my front like I saw Stavros do not long ago. The gesture of the divinities feels awkward.

I've rarely used it, rarely trusted on the gods to have my best interests at heart. But I need every bit of assistance I might get.

I lift my voice just slightly. "If you can hear me, please watch over me now. Help me see how to defeat this foe without losing myself."

I don't expect to hear the overwhelming divine voice resonating through my head. The godlen of trickery told me himself that he had to stay more distant. But I think I feel a subtle tug on my hair as if affectionately teasing.

Maybe it's only my mind playing tricks and not Kosmel, but he came through for me before. While I don't know what rules the gods have to play by, I actually believe he'll guide me if he can.

The trouble is, I don't know yet whether his guidance will be enough.

*We've gotten through plenty of tight spots without his assistance,* Julita remarks. *You came up with this whole plan without any divine intervention. Whatever's up ahead, we can handle it ourselves.*

She speaks in the archly confident tone I'm most used to from her, but I know her well enough by now to realize that it's usually a front. She's got to be nervous too.

"I have two knives," I say, taking stock for her benefit as well as my own. The third I was still carrying I had to leave on the other side of the channel. "Whoever's over there won't expect anyone to trace their magic, so I'll have the element of surprise. I just have to be smart about it."

*And I've no doubt you can manage that.*

The corner of my mouth crooks upward in half a smile at my

ghostly passenger's validation, but I lapse into silence—both for the sake of stealth and to avoid losing any more of my breath.

As I trace the reverberating energy through the chilly night breeze, the ground beneath my feet slants upward. I slow, peering up the slope.

A dark shape looms at the top. The faintest glow hazes one of the second-floor windows facing the battlefield, so slight I couldn't have made it out from even fifty paces further away.

Our enemy is up there.

I prowl through the overgrown grass to the plateau around the building.

Closer up, I can tell it's a farmhouse, but one that must have been abandoned. The weeds grow high along its walls, and the front steps have caved in. The glass in the windows is cracked.

In one of the first-story windows, the pane is missing completely.

I steal up to the side of the house and pluck a couple of lingering shards out of the frame. Gripping the base, I swing my leg inside and set my foot down ever so carefully on the floor.

It turns out I'm in a kitchen—next to a dusty stove that looks as if it hasn't been lit in years, with cupboards along the walls beyond.

Drawing out one of my knives, I creep out into the hall beyond, searching for the stairs.

A muffled murmuring filters through the floor from above, followed by a retort that sounds sneering. The hairs on the back of my neck rise at the tone.

As carefully as I'm setting my feet, a warped floorboard creaks at my next slow step. I freeze, my heart skipping a beat, straining my ears for any sign that those above have noticed.

There's no sound from the second floor except a whimper that filters through the ceiling. I suppress a shudder.

After a moment, the sneering voice mutters something else. When I don't pick up any indication that the people above are coming to investigate, I creep forward even more cautiously than before.

Down the hall, I spot the shadowy staircase. I flatten myself against the wall where the boards should be most stable and ease up one careful step at a time.

The dust that my movements sends whirling into the air tickles my nose. I rub it to restrain a sneeze.

When my head is level with the floor of the hallway above, I spot movement in one of the doorways. The door is slightly ajar, and a large form stands just beyond it, only his shoulder showing in the dim lantern light.

At least, I assume it's a man from his size.

The sneering voice speaks again from farther inside the room. "Come on, come on. You can give a little more. We've got to keep those idiots full of confidence, or they'll fall down on the job again."

Julita's presence twitches at the back of my skull. *Borys.*

I'd thought the tone sounded familiar before. I just hadn't wanted to believe it.

But then, it fits everything I know about Julita's brother that he'd choose to contribute to the battle by extending power from afar rather than risking his neck directly.

If I have anything to say about it, that neck is going to have a very large gash in it by the time we're through.

My fingers itch around my knife, but I don't dare throw it from here. I don't have a clear view of any vital part of the man guarding the doorway, and I don't know how many others are with him and Borys.

I reach into my pocket and flick open the locket to press its inner surface. It's quite possible I won't be able to tackle this problem all by myself.

But I have to do whatever I can manage on my own, because the battle might be lost and Borys moving on to join his comrades before any of my men reach me.

A sound like liquid pattering onto the floor carries through the doorway.

Julita outright flinches. *Oh, gods. He still does it. The blood...*

My stomach flips over at the thought of all the times he carved into her skin in the hopes that offering her blood would gain him additional power. Just like he's apparently doing up there right now.

Breathing shallowly, I slink up the last few steps and along the hall toward the room. Through the thunder of my pulse, my focus narrows down to the little details I've learned how to judge during my days of thefts and cons.

The light streaks in only one angle across the floor, which means there's a single lantern. Two shadows cross the floor by the threshold, so there's another figure standing guard just inside, beyond the door. I can judge their position by the patches of darkness in the wan glow.

Crouching low and inching even nearer, I peek around the closer man's leg.

Borys is squatting across from one of the scourge sorcerers' sacrificial accomplices, her shroud discarded, her eyeless, noseless face as haunting as all those I've seen before.

As I watch, he drags the knife he's holding through the flesh of her jaw just below where her ear should be. Blood springs up, nauseatingly scarlet against her sallow skin.

To amplify his own gift, he's making her sacrifice even more than she already has.

Their combined magic wafts through the air, vibrating through my bones. I tense against a cringe at the sensation.

I've got to stop him—fast.

I double-check the shadows to confirm my sense of where the second guard is standing. Then I retrieve my second knife from its sheath, brace myself, and lunge.

As I spring forward, I'm already flinging my first knife. It plunges into the first guard's throat.

He gurgles and staggers, blood spilling across the floor while I whirl around the door.

The second man standing guard is just starting to step forward when I toss the other knife to my dominant hand and stab it home into his chest. It must puncture his heart, because before he's even sagged to his knees, his form hardens to clay.

I clutch the hilt to wrench the blade free—and a body rams into me from the side.

*No!* Julita cries out.

An elbow digs into my ribs, and a fist clocks me in the jaw. I reel around with a swipe of my retrieved knife, driven by years of honed fighting instinct.

It should have been enough, even with the element of surprise my attacker had. But as Borys slashes at me with his own dagger, my magic roars up inside me, bellowing to tear him apart.

My mind spins, and Borys's image distorts into two, three men in front of me. I swing out half-blindly, shaking my head trying to clear it, wrenching back the power that's addled my awareness.

Borys's blade rakes against my side like a vicious burn. His arm smacks my hand hard enough to break my grip on my knife.

As the blade falls, he rams his knee into my gut and heaves me backward.

I lurch over the threshold and slam into the banister overlooking the stairs with a burst of pain through my scars. The wood creaks against my back.

Borys hurls himself after me, lashing out with his dagger with obvious experience but middling skill. He'd stab it right through my temple if I didn't yank my leg up in time to kick him hard in the chest.

With a grunt, Julita's brother stumbles back to the doorway. He pauses there for a second, his dark eyes glinting, brandishing his blood-streaked blade.

It's not just his accomplice's blood on that dagger now. Mine is seeping into my dress where he carved open my side.

I don't think he gouged deep enough to puncture any organs, but the throbbing ache sears through my torso.

Both of my weapons are in the room behind him. And I don't think I've managed to do more than bruise my opponent.

He's got the upper hand, as he can no doubt see too.

Julita's rambling takes on a panicked quaver. *Oh, fuck. Ivy, you have to get through this. You're better than him. You can find a way.*

Her brother lets out a dry chuckle. "It's Julita's friend again. She did pick a persistent one. And just like her, you don't appreciate what I'm trying to accomplish."

A snort tumbles out of me despite my desperate situation. "What's that—bringing on a second Great Retribution? Have you all forgotten that the gods wiped scourge sorcery out the first time around?"

Borys's chuckle expands into a low laugh. "This isn't scourge sorcery. Those imbeciles *wasted* potential. Snuffing out lives like that." He snaps his fingers. "We're finding out how much power we're all capable of together."

Is that what they're telling themselves?

*Gods help us,* Julita mumbles. *They're the insane ones.*

At least while I've got him talking, he's not stabbing me again. "The All-Giver abandoned us over magic like this. Even if it's not quite the same, are you really willing to take the chance?"

Borys scoffs. "We're going *back* to what the gods meant this world to be. Energy and action and wildness. The scourge sorcerers five hundred years ago wanted to bend everyone to their will, make up more rules, control the realms—but the All-Giver wanted us to be free."

*For fuck's sake.* Julita's voice starts to firm with a sharper edge. *As if he knows the slightest thing about freedom.*

"So instead you'll send us into total chaos," I retort.

"That's how the world began. That's what the All-Giver

thrives on. The Great God truly wants us to have it *all*. You'll see."

Is that what the gods would honestly prefer? For me to release my magic with all the madness that'll come with it?

What if that is why Kosmel led me so far and then left me to fend for myself?

I swallow against the dryness of my throat. I don't know what's right anymore—but I can't make any decisions about it either way if I'm too unhinged to even care.

*Don't listen to him,* Julita says, more forcefully than before. *All* he *ever wanted is to get whatever he can for himself.*

"Or rather, you won't see," Borys says, adjusting his grip on his dagger. "Because I need to get back to my work, and I can't have you interfering again."

As he shifts his stance to strike, my mind flashes back to Wendos in the All-Giver's tower. Wendos, turning his back on me rather than closing in for the kill.

Borys is obviously the smarter one.

And how ridiculous that back then my magic saved me, and now it'll only doom me.

Borys leaps at me. As I shove myself to the side to avoid his strike, Julita squirms in the back of my skull. *We need him off-balance. My gift won't help—he hasn't told us to do anything. But there has to be a way…*

Abruptly, her presence seems to stiffen. *I can—we can do this, Ivy. I won't let him cut you too. Be ready.*

With those words, she throws herself forward in my head.

My instinct is to resist the wave of dizziness that sweeps over me. I recognize what it means. I've felt her uninvited attempts to take control before.

But she knows the man in front of me far better than I could. She's got more of a plan than I do.

I let go, and Julita's presence floods to the front of my mind. With her in control, my body scrambles backward down the hall.

Borys whirls on us, and Julita hurls out my voice in a tone that's all her. "You haven't grown at all since you were twelve, making me bleed with Wendos, have you, big brother?"

Borys goes rigid in mid stride. He stares at me.

Before he can decide it's all a trick, Julita hurtles onward. "Oh, yes, it's really me. And I haven't forgotten a second of those midnight trips out to the woods—the time you used a sharpened stick instead of a proper blade, the time you scraped my skin raw with the rough edge of a rock."

In my hazy state at the back of my mind, I wince in sympathy. My ghostly passenger has always avoided going into detail about the torment she suffered at the hands of her brother and his friend.

What I imagined was horrible. It's worse hearing her describe it out loud.

Borys's jaw drops for a second before he reels it in.

"Julita?" he says, his voice ragged with disbelief.

She makes a disparaging sound. "Wendos tried to murder me back in Florian, but neither of you understood how strong I am. I managed to hang on with the help of my friend. And I've been helping *her* pick away at your idiotic, psychotic uprising bit by bit."

I'm not sure what she's aiming for here. Maybe she's simply letting out all her bottled-up anger.

But she told me to be ready. She must be going somewhere with this.

I have to watch for an opening.

Borys hasn't quite let his guard down. He still holds his dagger in a fighting stance.

His eyes narrow. "This is some stupid trick. Or magic. Julita can't really be here."

"I'm sure you'd like to think so," Julita says. "But I know how you pissed yourself that time Dad's stallion kicked you in the thigh when you were six. I know the town boys beat you up on your ninth birthday when you tried to boss a bunch of them around like you were already a count. I know that when you were ten, you ate slugs on a dare with Wendos and then vomited all over Mother's favorite tablecloth."

"Shut up!" Borys's eyes flash with fury. He steps closer, his jaw flexing. "You were never good for anything other than filling in when we had nothing better to practice on. I'll just have to finish what Wendos started."

"*You* have always been a spineless, pathetic bully who was too scared of taking responsibility to do anything worth respecting," Julita spits back at him. "This woman is the best friend I've ever had, and you're not taking her down with you."

Borys lunges—and the tickle of Julita's presence by my forehead heaves forward. My awareness jolts back into place in its wake just in time to see her brother clawing at his face as if there's something in his eyes.

I don't have time to figure out what's happened. He isn't looking at me—his knife hand is flailing aimlessly.

I spring forward, snatch his wrist, and wrench his arm around.

With a sickening sound, his own blade drives into the flesh at the base of his throat.

Borys's body spasms in front of me. I dodge backward as he crumples over, spewing blood from his neck and lips.

He sputters something as if he's trying to speak, but not with any words I can decipher. His hands fumble across the floor and drift to a halt.

His body sags, his head lolling to the side. The one eye I can see stares blankly at the wall.

Blood courses across the dusty floor in a steady current.

I got my gash, just like I wanted.

I suck in a shaky breath. "Julita? We did it. He's dead."

No one answers. And all at once, I realize I can't feel her—not the familiar prickle at the back of my skull, not the faint trace of a tingle that lingers even when she pulls herself as deep as her presence can go.

She must have flung herself right out of me to smack Borys in the face with whatever presence she did have left.

*She's* what he was clawing at, what distracted him enough that I could attack.

And now she's gone.

# Forty-Three

*Ivy*

I wake up to a cool breeze tugging at my hair and a warm hand on my cheek. When I blink, Casimir's gorgeous face comes into focus in the pale light, framed by looming trees.

A smile curves his lips. "There's our woman." He strokes my hair back from my temple. "How are you doing, Kindness?"

"I—" The first word comes out as a croak. I clear my throat and try again. "What happened? Where are we?"

The last thing I remember is the hall in the farmhouse, Borys bleeding across the floor, my head unnervingly vacant for the first time in—

My body tenses beneath the blanket that's been laid over me. My skull is *still* vacant.

I can't find any tingle of Julita's presence no matter how hard I strain my senses.

"We followed the locket's signal and found you in the farmhouse," Casimir is saying. "You must have passed out."

Stavros's voice carries from somewhere beyond my view. "Exhaustion and blood loss will do that."

Blood loss. I adjust my position on the ground—padded by another blanket—and an ache ripples through my side from the spot where Borys cut me.

No wry comment from Julita. No cheer that her sadistic brother is finally, definitely dead.

I pry at my mind as if I can summon her voice through sheer will, but nothing comes.

Casimir's brow knits at the emotion that must show on my face. "We patched you up thoroughly. Most of the blood wasn't yours."

Alek appears beside him, holding one of our canteens. "You should be all right, but it'd be good for you to drink something."

I stare at them, a much deeper ache spreading through my chest. It twines around my lungs, making it hard to speak.

"Julita—she helped me distract her brother—she… she *flung* herself right out of my head at him so I could get his dagger—"

A sob breaks through my words.

Rheave hustles into view in an instant, his stance poised for battle. "What did he do to you?" he snarls.

"He's already dead," the courtesan reminds him in a mild tone, and helps me sit up with his arm around me. "Have a drink, and then you can tell us the whole story."

As Alek hands me the canteen, Stavros steps closer as well, the four of them forming a semi-circle around me. I gulp the cool water that has an herbal tang to it, suggesting one of them has added a little supplement that's supposed to help me heal.

It takes a few slow breaths before I think I can get through the whole explanation. "I took down the two daimon Borys had guarding him, but he came at me too quickly, and I lost my knives. He would have killed me if Julita hadn't intervened. I let her take over so she could put him off balance, and like I said, she jumped out of my head at him. I think her spirit had enough energy to smack him in the face."

I lower my head and rub my face. "But I guess she couldn't come back. She's gone."

The ache of loss creeps up my throat, choking me.

She was already dead too, in most of the ways that count. She told me she was ready to move on.

I can't imagine any way she'd rather have gone than by ensuring her brother never caused any more harm.

But I didn't even get to say thank you. I didn't get to say *good-bye.*

Casimir hugs me closer, and Alek grasps my hand with a comforting squeeze.

"We'll have a proper funeral for her," Stavros says, sounding a little awkward. "As soon as we can. She deserves at least that much. I'm not sure what exactly we'll tell people, but they should know she's a hero."

I swallow thickly. "Yes. Yes, they should."

His remarks cut through my grief enough to remind me of the other heroics we were attempting tonight.

My pulse stutters. "The battle—the Darium soldiers and the scourge sorcerers—is the royal family safe?"

Stavros crouches down so we're eye to eye. "It must have been as soon as you engaged with Borys—the Order of the Wild army faltered again. The remaining Darium soldiers managed to cut down a lot more of them before they retreated to their side of the channel, and the soldiers from our fort mopped up the few stragglers who hadn't fled."

"And they didn't arrest you?"

Rheave lets out a disgruntled sound. "Arrest us for fixing their problems?"

Stavros casts him an amused sideways glance. "I think they wanted to, but we were able to evade capture. They were somewhat distracted by dealing with the sacrificial accomplice we pointed them to in the farmhouse, after we'd gotten you out."

"And we got our hands on a couple more horses, since the march didn't need them anymore," Alek pipes up. "So we can all ride. And we'd better soon, before the soldiers decide to get more serious about hunting us again."

Stavros's expression turns solemn. "I don't know where we stand after tonight's victory or where it'd make the most sense to go."

Casimir offers him a soft smile. "Farther from the fort does seem like a good initial idea, in any case."

They help me to my feet. As Stavros gathers the blankets, Rheave wraps his arms around me, keeping his embrace gentle. "You shouldn't have gone without us, Little Vine."

"You were busy doing something just as important," I remind him.

He gives a dismissive huff and ducks his head to claim a kiss.

My heart skips a beat with the knowledge that this is the first time my other men will have seen such an open display of our new intimacy. But when the daimon-man eases back, the three of them are simply smiling.

Casimir has led Toast over. The stallion nickers as if expressing his own concern about my injuries.

Stavros moves to my side. "I'd better help you mount."

Before I've positioned myself next to the saddle, a brisk female voice blares through the woods with an unnatural resonance. "Stavros Teodorek of Florian—on behalf of King Konram, I need to speak with you and your companions."

I flinch and then wince at the pain that sears from my bandaged wound.

Stavros's forehead furrows. "Whoever that is, she's using a magical amplifier to spread her call. I don't think she's that close."

We venture in the direction of the voice, coming to the edge of the patch of woods where the men brought me for shelter.

Across the nearby fields, a robed woman sits on horseback, flanked by two soldiers.

She holds her body with a stately air. A patch covers the eye she sacrificed.

I stare. "Is that... Hessild Korinya? The king's chief sorcerer?"

"I believe it is," Casimir murmurs. "And according to her, he sent her to us."

Stavros scans the terrain around the royal magic advisor and her small escort. The nearby fields are open enough that any additional threat should be obvious.

"Konram knew from my message approximately where I'd be," he says. "We should see what she wants—but with the horses, and keeping a safe distance so we can ride off if the conversation turns sour."

Hessild makes her amplified appeal again as we clamber onto our steeds. When we emerge from the woods, she turns toward us but stays where she is, maybe recognizing that we'll want to stay cautious.

Rheave keeps his bow at hand, his quiver over his shoulder. I scan the landscape all around us, but I don't see any sign of a trap.

We stop right at the edge of where we can comfortably yell and be heard. "I'm here," Stavros says, pitching his voice to carry. "What do you have to say?"

Hessild smiles. "It's good to discover that you haven't lost your knack for strategy, Stavros. You and your colleagues did the royal family a great service last night."

Stavros gestures toward me. "The main part of the strategy came from Ivy. She risked her life to see that King Konram's wouldn't be threatened."

The royal advisor inclines her head. "He recognizes that and regrets that he judged all of you so hastily. If you would come to Regica with me, he would like to discuss the conditions of a full pardon."

For a second, I lose my breath. This is the outcome we hoped for all along.

Can it really be happening? King Konram is willing to let me live with my riven magic?

"Do we have official confirmation of his intentions?" Stavros asks.

Hessild retrieves a paper with a blob of wax at its bottom from her pocket and holds it out. "He has sworn it with his seal."

"I'll get it." Rheave prods his horse forward and canters over.

I brace myself, but Hessild lets him take the proclamation without the slightest suspicious move. The daimon-man rides back and hands the paper to Stavros.

The former general scans it carefully. He keeps his voice even when he fills us in, but a warm glint comes into his eyes. "It looks authentic. The seal is his personal one that no one else has access to. He apologizes—says he can't help but honor our efforts on his behalf. He couldn't risk coming himself, but he sent Hessild as a gesture of trust."

He pauses. "I'd imagine he also wants her to evaluate Ivy, but I suppose it is true that as far as they're concerned, Hessild is putting herself at *our* mercy."

Alek shifts nervously on his horse. "Do you think we can trust him?"

Stavros nods slowly. "If we don't trust this, then we might as well commit to being outlaws forever."

He glances at me. "But I can't make the decision for all of us."

My gut twists. I'm the one in the most danger if we go to the king. But how can I give up the opportunity to get at least part of the absolution I've spent most of my life dreaming of?

If Julita were here, she'd be saying it was about time the king saw the truth. Applauding me for showing my worth.

The ache of loss expands in my gut.

We'll never be able to honor *her* if we spend our whole lives running away.

I draw myself up straighter. "Let's go see the king."

Stavros turns back to Hessild and her escort. "We'll come."

"Excellent." She guides her horse around and sets off toward the road without expecting us to quite join her. That consideration seems promising too.

We ride at a brisk walk that doesn't jostle my healing cut like a trot would, the five of us keeping a few horse-lengths back from Hessild out of additional caution. But with each minute that passes in peaceful travel along the road, my nerves settle more.

"How far is it to Regica from here?" I ask Stavros quietly.

"About an hour at this point and at this pace." He eyes me pensively. "Is your wound hurting you?"

"Only a little. I'll be fine."

"We'll get a medic to heal it properly once we—"

His voice cuts off as Hessild shudders in her saddle ahead of us. She lets out a strangled sound and slumps over, sliding right off her horse.

The soldiers on either side of her jerk around, only to get caught up in spasms of their own.

As they collapse from their mounts, Stavros reins in his stallion and leaps down. "What the fuck?"

The other men scramble after him. As they race to Hessild's crumpled form, I shift my weight to follow suit, but a sudden swell of magic rushes over me.

My own body seizes up, but not to go limp. My spine stiffens, and my hands tighten around the reins.

My heels tap Toast's sides of their own accord.

The horse gives a puzzled snort but moves the way I'm directing him, off the road. I wrench at my limbs with all the strength I have in me, but it's as if I've become a puppet on a set of strings.

Not like when Julita took over. Then I could tell I'd been pushed to the background, the world around me gone vaguer.

Now, I'm looking out of my eyes, hearing with my ears with full clarity, and yet locked inside a body that's taken on a mind of its own.

Panic jolts through my nerves. I reach instinctively toward my own magic…

But I can't grasp hold of it either. My chest remains clamped around the power, barely a wriggle of it passing through my senses.

Gods help me, what in the realms—

Alek glances up and notices my new course. He spins around. "Ivy, what are you—"

A strange laugh like nothing I've ever emitted before propels from my lungs. "I got what I needed, and now we're done. Did you really think I cared about you? You're ridiculous, all of you."

A silent wail rises up inside me through the next bark of a laugh that lurches out of me. Then my body is wheeling Toast around and jamming my heels against his sides so he breaks into a full-out gallop.

No, no, I can't let this happen.

I put all my will into yanking on the reins, but my arms refuse to budge other than a slight adjustment to Toast's course that wasn't my idea.

We hurtle across the countryside, my side throbbing with each thump of the stallion's hooves. I think I feel blood trickling from beneath the bandage.

I try to close my eyes as if that might do some good, but apparently my puppet master controls even my eyelids. They blink but spring open again.

Toast veers a little to the left and then farther. We crash through a stretch of forest, forced to ease up but still pushing onward as fast as the horse will go.

The second we're free of the underbrush, my legs kick Toast back to a gallop.

I don't hear any sounds of pursuit behind me. Is there other magic covering my tracks?

Will my men even want to come to my rescue when I made it sound as if I launched the attack on Hessild and her escort? When I insulted them and laughed in their faces?

Tears burn behind my eyes and start to trickle down my cheeks.

We cross uncultivated fields and skirt another clump of trees. The wind cools the streaks of moisture on my face.

Finally my hands pull the reins, slowing Toast to a trot.

But not through my doing. I still can't exert the slightest bit of control over any part of my body.

The magic thrums around me like a drone in my ears. We approach a derelict cabin at the edge of a larger forest, and I halt Toast completely.

Several figures step out of the cabin to meet me.

Most of them I don't recognize, at least not as individuals. There are two men and a woman in the blue uniforms of the royal army, which would make me think King Konram is behind my kidnapping if it weren't for the two pale shrouded figures with them who I immediately know are sacrificial accomplices.

A man and a woman in regular clothes flank one accomplice together. Another woman stands next to the second, her expression taut and sweat beaded on her forehead despite the cool air.

The man who emerges last, I do know. The sight of his tall, lopsided frame sends even more fear coursing through my veins.

Lothar Riosemek, the secondary magical advisor to the king and destroyer of riven sorcerers, is staring up at me with pale brown eyes and a hard-edged smirk.

"Look at her," he says conversationally in his thick baritone. "She can't move a muscle unless you allow it, Zaneta. How strong you've become after all those daimon spirits you've been directing."

The sweating woman dips her head in a hint of a nod. Her voice echoes the strain etched across her face and in her posture. "Yes, Master Lothar. It isn't quite the same when we didn't build the body. But I can hold her."

"Good." Lothar's smirk grows, seeming to crawl across his face.

My voice stays locked in my throat, as much as I want to cry out.

*This* man is behind the scourge sorcerer uprising?

Alek found out the clay purchaser had used a royal seal to keep the shipments concealed. We never suspected it could have come from someone quite so close to the king.

Gods above, what else has he done? What does he mean to do next?

What's he going to do with *me*?

Lothar takes a step closer, making my spirit want to recoil inside my puppet of a body. "Ivy of wherever you're actually from, you destroyed my army. I'm taking you and your wild magic in return. Not such a bad exchange, really."

He flicks his fingers, and his followers move toward a cluster of horses tied within the shadows of the trees. At a tug of magic, I nudge Toast to follow them, all the while screaming inside my head.

My body doesn't respond. This psychopath has me well and truly trapped.

And for the first time since I stumbled into this conspiracy, I'm utterly alone.

# The Gods of the Abandoned Realms

**THE ALL-GIVER** (the Great God, the One) - overseer of all existence, creator of the godlen

**THE GODLEN OF THE SKY**

**Estera** - wisdom, knowledge, and education

**Inganne** - creativity, play, childhood, and dreams

**Kosmel** - luck, trickery, and rebellion

## THE GODLEN OF THE EARTH

**Creaden** - royalty, leadership, justice, and construction

**Prospira** - fertility, wealth, harvest, and parenthood

**Sabrelle** - warfare, sports, and hunting

## THE GODLEN OF THE SEA

**Ardone** - love, beauty, and bodily pleasures

**Elox** - health, medicine, and peace

**Jurnus** - communication, travel, and weather

# About the Author

Eva Chase lives in Canada with her family. She loves stories both swoony and supernatural, and strong women and the men who appreciate them.

Along with the Rites of Possession series, she is the author of the Shadowblood Souls series, the Heart of a Monster series, the Gang of Ghouls series, the Bound to the Fae series, the Flirting with Monsters series, the Cursed Studies trilogy, the Royals of Villain Academy series, the Moriarty's Men series, the Looking Glass Curse trilogy, the Their Dark Valkyrie series, the Witch's Consorts series, the Dragon Shifter's Mates series, the Demons of Fame series, and the Legends Reborn trilogy.

*Connect with Eva online:*
www.evachase.com
eva@evachase.com

www.ingramcontent.com/pod-product-compliance
Lightning Source LLC
Chambersburg PA
CBHW030602310726
48979CB00003B/546

* 9 7 8 1 9 9 8 7 5 2 7 3 7 *